Books by Isla Dennes

Single Titles

Sex, Spoons & Salsa

Sex, Spoons & Salsa

ISBN # 978-1-78686-136-8

©Copyright Isla Dennes 2017

Cover Art by Posh Gosh ©Copyright 2017

Interior text design by Claire Siemaszkiewicz

Totally Bound Publishing

Published in 2017 by Totally Bound Publishing, Newland House, The Point, Weaver Road, Lincoln, LN6 3QN, United Kingdom.

SEX, SPOONS & SALSA

ISLA DENNES

Dedication

For Iain xx

Chapter One

"I have nothing. No husband. No friends. No life. *Nothing*. I might as well be dead!"

Through a veil of tears, I stared at the wilting rubber plant in the corner and tried to pretend I was anywhere but there. I don't think I could have been any more mortified. I sounded like a hack Shakespearean actor.

Crossing her arms over her matronly bosom, Margarita pushed a fresh box of tissues toward me before settling back in her chair. She didn't appear the least bit put out by my hysterics and I wondered what it would take to get some kind of reaction from her. *Talk about detached.* Fifty minutes into our first session and she hadn't even opened her mouth to impart any words of life-altering wisdom? For all I knew, she could be compiling her week's menus and their subsequent shopping list in her head. Was it possible my father had stumbled across the only deaf-mute therapist in the country?

"Therapy. I still can't believe I'm here," I mumbled tearfully. Had I not been so totally consumed by my own misery, I would have been burning up with shame. "Who goes to therapy, anyway?" I cried, ignoring the frown appearing on Margarita's face. "I'll tell you who — celebrities, bored middle-aged housewives, people who've taken to curling up in corners and sucking their thumbs. Total nutters, that's who! Not me."

This had to be a mistake. I didn't belong there. I didn't *want* to belong there. I wanted to have my life back. But the very act of coming to therapy was in itself an admission I had failed at being a grown-up and was in need of rescuing.

On the drive there, I'd made a promise to myself not to get all caught up in that whole touchy-feely crap. Sure, I might have been led dazed and blinking from the dark recesses of my room—and my mind for that matter—clutching a ratty old stuffed rabbit, my normally well-behaved shoulder-length mousy-brown hair long gone wild and my usually striking blue eyes dulled and barely recognizable. But make no mistake, I was there for one reason and one reason only, and that was to get Dad off my back and, in the process, prove to him what a complete waste of everyone's time and money this was. Alas, once I'd settled into that arse-numbing chair—no sign of a comfy leather couch, much to my disappointment—the silence, combined with the sympathy emanating from every pore of Margarita's round face, had triggered something in my brain—the blabbing switch. Before I could stop it, my runaway mouth had embarked on a journey of its own, climaxing in my recent outburst, still hovering in the air between us like a bad smell no one wants to acknowledge.

God, what have I done? Unfortunately, I couldn't take it all back now. I looked expectantly across to the Beige Linen Oracle—as she was from that moment christened—for any sign she'd come up with the magical solution for my ruined life. I'd done my bit. Surely it was up to her now to sort out this mess? But no, she merely stared back expectantly.

Waiting for exactly what, I wondered? A complete mental breakdown? By this time, I was little alarmed. *Am I a lost cause?* Maybe I really *was* losing my mind. *Great, this is all I need.* If it wasn't bad enough to be a twenty-six-year-old recently discarded wife, on top of that I was doomed to suffer the additional humiliation of losing the plot, going la-la, floundering in the emotional cesspool of life without a float.

Plummeting headlong into Loser Hell without a safety net.

"I wasn't always like this, you know. Once upon a time, I had a future to look forward to." I sniffed, trying to reclaim a little of my lost dignity. "I had a husband, friends and a social life." Yes, all very well and good to point that out now, but the truth remained through no fault of my own, I found myself once again living at home with my parents in the same room I'd occupied throughout my rather tumultuous teenage years, complete with posters of Robbie Williams, Justin Timberlake and Ricky Martin. Ah, the nights I'd spent dreaming of marrying Ricky Martin—who knew?

Resentment had bubbled up inside me, heralding an ill-timed return of teenage angst, directed, not surprisingly, toward those near and dear to me. In all fairness to my long-suffering parents, I have to confess their decision to seek outside help for their loopy firstborn hadn't been something they'd taken lightly. You might even say I'd driven them to it after they'd suffered through six hellish weeks of my rabid mood swings. This, I must point out, had come hard on the heels of the discovery that my moods were not the only things out there swinging.

Why is the wife always the last one to know?

Had it not been for the onset of a particularly nasty little rash on my privates, closely followed by the utterance of three little letters, STD—alas not the telecommunication kind—I might never have found out about my husband's affair. God, the shame of it when my doctor, who, I might add, was old enough to have been practicing medicine before the discovery of penicillin, had turned a deep shade of crimson before quizzing me about my supposedly promiscuous past.

If I have one, it's news to me!

Even while I continued crying buckets of shame in front of Margarita, I still found it difficult to comprehend how I could have been so blind not to see what had apparently been going on underneath my nose. Formerly known as 'Amanda, the five-thirty-step-class-bimbo,' from that day on I could only think of her as 'husband-stealing-silicone-enhanced-Botox-junkie-slut-with-the-clap', *or* 'that fucking bitch' for short.

Not that I'm bitter or anything.

Naturally, I'd done what anyone in my situation would have done and scuttled crying back to Mum and Dad, who, I must say, had been more than a little surprised to have had their dinner interrupted by their wailing daughter. Dad had gone totally mental, even threatening to shoot the Two-timing Lying Bastard dead if he came within sight of the house, therefore saving me the trouble of obtaining a divorce. Don't get me wrong, the thought of playing the part of the grieving widow had lifted my spirits momentarily, but having my shame plastered all over the newspapers — *Venereal Disease Scandal Triggers Family Tragedy* — wasn't something I'd felt I could comfortably have lived with.

Six weeks later and my father had again been mumbling about inflicting grievous bodily harm on 'the bastard'. But this time, I'd suspected that rather than a punishment for breaking my heart, it had been more out of retaliation for having inflicted a psychotic daughter on them in what should have been the peaceful twilight years of their lives.

In the end, out of pure desperation, Dad had decided to call in reinforcements, otherwise known as Rachel, Kim and Janine.

The four of us had been best friends since high school, since the time we'd found ourselves lumped together in the C grade team in the local netball competition. It wasn't as though we'd been fat, unfit or socially awkward, but, looking back on it now, it might have been because I haven't got a competitive bone in my body, Janine simply couldn't give a stuff and Rachel and Kim are incredibly violent and, to this day, consider netball a blood sport.

Back then, I was a shy, awkward thirteen-year-old and they were the cool girls, with the short skirts and permanent sneers on their heavily made-up faces. They had attitude. They had respect. They had class. To say I was impressed would be putting it mildly. Me, well, I was the girl no one saw, or if they did, only to pick on or hurl insults at. They were my saviors — the answer to my prayers. Of course, even then I knew their friendship equaled more a case of pity than any real connection between us—*and* the fact I was willing to run to the canteen for them every lunchtime and act as lookout while they smoked in the school toilets. Yes, I was their lackey, their stooge, their social groupie, but at least I'd made the In Crowd, and for that reason, I was forever indebted to them for taking me under their wing that fateful day on the netball court.

The savagely bitchy atmosphere that prevailed throughout our formative high school years further strengthened our sisterly bond. By Year Nine, we were indisputably top of the teenage-girl food chain and ruled the Block A girls' toilets with a ruthlessness that would have had seen Saddam Hussein crossing his legs and holding it in rather than risk running the gantlet of the smoky cubicles. Yes, we had finally found our foothold in the vicious world that constituted senior high school.

"It's not my fault, you see," I sobbed, grabbing another handful of tissues. "If I hadn't been bullied into going out with the girls, to that stupid RSL club, I wouldn't even be here. Jeez, it's not like we're still at school. But, no, my Dad had to get me out of the house, even if it meant going straight to Loser Hell, thanks to that bloody retro disco."

Not that I would be gyrating my wobbly bits on the dance floor. My role as passive observer and handbag minder had been firmly established years before with my girlfriends' decree that my 'unique style of dance-floor expression' was scaring off any potential action of the male variety. It wasn't all bad news, though. In recognition of my noble sacrifice I'd be kept supplied in alcohol as payoff to ensure my ongoing cooperation. Thus continued my role as protector of the sacred table.

After all, as Rachel was quick to point out, where you sit in these social occasions is a direct reflection of your status within the hierarchy of the nightclub. Sit too close to the bar, you're labeled an alcoholic. Too close to the toilets, you must be a lesbian. Too close to the door and everyone spills their drinks on you, and the only people who sit right next to the dance floor are, of course, losers.

Our table therefore was strategically the most sought after in the nightclub and jealously guarded. Not only did it give us a clear vantage point from which to spot any hunks as they walked through the door, but it was close enough to the toilets—but not too close to be considered creepy—in the event one of us might have mixed our Kahlua and milks with one too many bourbons, white wines or worse still, Tequila Slammers, and a toilet bowl and a moment of solitude were desperately required.

Walking into the foyer of the RSL that night, I experienced a mixture of disappointment, excitement and apprehension after my six-week self-imposed exile.

Excitement at finally, after three years, being able to fit into my favorite black leather miniskirt again—a broken heart is infinitely more effective than a Jenny Craig diet. Apprehension at the remote possibility of running into the Two-timing Lying Bastard as I made my triumphant return to society. And, to my disappointment, the Club foyer was still hideously furbished in the same bold purple, red and brown décor that once enjoyed a very brief period of being fashionable—May 1977 to January 1978, to be precise—before the rest of the civilized world moved onto the shag-pile and orange Formica era.

I'm not sure what I was expecting. Maybe a brass band to welcome me back into the fold. But realizing that everyone else's lives had carried on in my absence, callously unaware of my recent lifestyle changes, began to put things in perspective for me.

That was until I went to sign in.

Then I experienced a stab of uncertainty. After all, for the first time since the breakup I'd been faced with the question of whether I'd be resorting to my maiden name, or simply tack a Ms. to the prefix of *his* devil-scorned surname. A difficult decision to make, seeing as the Two-timing Lying Bastard's surname was the only decent thing I got out of the marriage.

For two years, five months and four days I had proudly gone by the name of Mrs. Fiona Maxwell, grateful at last to finally leave behind forever Miss Fiona McCrutchen, a name that had caused me endless grief since the moment of my conception, peaking to excruciating torment during my school years.

For months prior to my ill-fated marriage I had proudly practiced writing Mrs. Fiona Maxwell, Mrs. F. Maxwell and even Mr. and Mrs. T. Maxwell over and over for hours on end, until even the girls had begun hinting that maybe I was just marrying him for his nice, normal-sounding surname. In hindsight, they might have been right. After all, using marriage as an excuse to lose a last name that had plagued me since birth might not have been a solid enough reason to vow before God and eighty invited guests, to love, honor and cherish until death do us part—and in the process nearly bankrupt my parents with the cost of the wedding.

Well, decision time. I halted my hand at *M* and considered my options. Reverting back to McCrutchen would surely reopen the trauma of a childhood spent trying to ignore the chants of horrid little boys yelling "McCrusty, McCrusty", but, on the other hand, remaining normal, sane Fiona Maxwell was almost akin to saying I still hungered after his body. *Ummm, somehow, I don't think so!*

And with that last thought, Ms. Fiona McCrutchen was officially welcomed back into the Merryland's Returned Servicemen's League.

Chapter Two

"Come on, Fi, we'd better go in and grab our table before those skanks from last week try to steal it," suggested Kim, plucking a packet of cigarettes from the machine in the foyer, oblivious to my recent epiphany.

Apparently, the previous Friday night, while I'd had my head stuck in a box of tissues at home watching *Bridget Jones's Diary*, the skanks in question had attempted a hostile takeover of the sacred table. Now, they might well have been three years younger than us, twenty pounds lighter — all bulimic, of course — and desperate to usurp our superior social position, but they hadn't reckoned on the level of viciousness Rachel, Janine and especially Kim were prepared to stoop to.

What a stroke of luck, therefore, that the bouncer on the door last Friday night happened to have been Jason. For months, it had been common knowledge he'd had a massive crush on Rachel and, despite countless knock-backs, he was still living in hope that one Friday night she might oblige him in his weekly requests to take her back to his place.

Ironically, *his place* is a granny flat situated behind his granny's house.

Fortunately for us, Rachel possessed the good sense to ruthlessly string him along without actually putting out, in the hope that one day she might take advantage of his adoration. From all accounts, last week her abstinence had paid off big-time when what had started out as a battle of words between the girls and the skanks had rapidly deteriorated into a gangland-style war that, in the end, had seen Kim maniacally wielding a broken wineglass to drive them off and regain control of our table once more. I suspect though, in reality, it'd been over before anyone on the dance floor had been aware of the scrimmage at the back of the room, comprising nothing more than a few Fs and Cs screamed across the table and finally a frenzied slap fight to finish off.

Fortunately for the girls, instead of ringing the police, love-struck Jason had called in reinforcements and one by one the club's bouncers had removed the skanks, screaming threats of retaliation, from the premises.

Hence our early arrival at the club.

In the public lounge, old ladies sporting identical blue hairdos, glued together with enough hair spray to single-handedly rip open the ozone layer, poured out of the bistro after stuffing themselves full of the five-dollar roast of the day. Glancing across at our rather suggestive attire, they made tut-tutting noises of disapproval as they migrated to the gaming room fresh from feeding their stomachs and now ready to feed their pensions into the ever-ravenous poker machines.

It was barely eight-thirty and no self-respecting clubber would normally be seen in the vicinity until at least ten, but tonight the girls were prepared to risk a social gaffe just to be a step ahead of the skanks. That is, of course, if they were brave enough to show their faces here again, *or* had recovered from the injuries inflicted on them during last week's fracas.

I must say, apart from a few yellowing bruises and a couple of lingering scratches, the girls had come away relatively unscathed and were still reliving the ugly tale of what had by now had reached almost epic proportions.

As luck would have it, Jason was working the door again that night. Apparently it was his night off, but he'd swapped shifts to be back in, working again with Dangerous Dave – a revolting excuse for a man, who, in an attempt to appear menacing, went around in army fatigues, and if the rumors were to be believed, fake tattoos. Jason clearly considered that after his heroics last week, tonight *had* to be his lucky night with Rachel. Surely!

Unfortunately for Rachel, she also knew she had to pay the piper at last. One can only cock tease for so long. But, as she said, enduring a minute and a half of what she was certain would amount to nothing more than two grunts and a sigh was a small price to pay for retaining the sacred table.

"Hi, Rach!" Jason called out eagerly from the door. "You girls are early tonight."

"Well, I was *supposed* to meet this bloke at the bar..." Rachel lied, delighting in the disappointment reflected in Jason's eyes. "But seeing as he's late, I suppose you could get us drinks instead," she added with a sadistic gleam in *her* eye.

Like watching a hungry lion play with a cute furry little animal before devouring it—all Jason needed to complete the picture was a bunny tail and ears. He headed off to the bar to buy us all drinks, returning shortly with what looked like four very expensive cocktails.

"God, Rachel, why do you have to be such a bitch?" I hissed before Jason reached us.

She laughed. "Why? Because I can!" she responded triumphantly, flicking her perfectly straightened blonde hair back from her bare sun-tan shoulder.

Looking up at Jason, Rachel turned on a dazzling smile, guaranteed to make any red-blooded male weak at the knees, and graciously accepted one of the exotic-looking cocktails that must have set him back an entire night's pay.

"It *is* low-fat, isn't it?" she queried, her face a mask of innocence.

"Um, yes?" was all Jason could manage.

By his confused expression, he was wondering if they made low-fat Screaming Orgasms—and if they were cheaper without the extra calories.

I didn't have it in me to stand blithely by and watch Rachel torture poor Jason's heart. After downing my cocktail in one large gulp, I decided to take myself off to the ladies' on the pretense of touching up my makeup.

Rachel, I should point out, was undeniably the glamorous one in our gang of four, with a figure even Miranda Kerr would kill for, an angelic, heart-shaped face and long, naturally blonde hair that never seemed to go frizzy in the rain. Secretly, I couldn't help but envy her remarkable ability to attract a crowd of male admirers wherever she went. Me, well, I would have been thrilled to be the recipient of the odd wolf-whistle echoing out from any number of building sites, accompanied by shouts of, "Show us your tits, luv!"

Politically correct it wasn't, but a boost to the ego it definitely was.

Considering her ever-increasing band of dedicated male fans, Rachel was rarely without a boyfriend, a good thing in view of the fact she plowed through them at an astonishing rate, the only exception being the time she'd dated Wayne Jackson for six months, two of which he'd spent in jail.

At the time, she'd considered being the girlfriend of a convicted criminal—she still insists joy riding is a serious offense—to be totally street-chic and couldn't wait to experience the excitement of her first conjugal visit. It was only after an embarrassing phone call to the superintendent of the Junee Correctional Center to check on visiting times had she learned that conjugal visits had been abolished fifteen years previously after a serious outbreak of genital herpes among the prisoners.

Poor misguided Wayne Jackson had been dumped faster than a stolen purple Hyundai Excel with no petrol, and for Rachel, life had gone on.

Fighting my way through a solid wall of old ladies powdering their noses in the toilets proved more treacherous than I first imagined. Actually, seeing as all of them were under five foot one, maybe a solid hedge of old ladies would have been a more accurate description. After a short scuffle, I managed to secure a place at the mirror and began to apply the all-important one last layer of makeup to see me through the night — I hoped. Over the course of the years and a few stabbed eyes I've discovered that the only safe use for an eyeliner pen after a couple of hours drinking is to scribble down phone numbers, even if they're always wrong.

Finally, I felt ready to rejoin the rest of civilization looking absolutely stunning, and *not* a 'done-up strumpet'. Old ladies are incredibly bitchy. In my defense, I will add that whoever came up with the 'less is more' makeup concept was obviously a nineteen-year-old supermodel with freakishly flawless skin and unnaturally red lips.

Back in the club, the girls were busy guzzling their way through a large carafe of wine and firmly entrenched in conversation.

"So, Fi! What do you think?" asked Rachel as I plonked my butt down on the nearest stool, hooking my bag securely under my thigh.

"About what?"

"Jason, of course!"

"Jeez, Rach, don't ask me." In light of my recent relationship fiasco, I felt compelled to add, "After all, I'm hardly an expert unless you're after a complete bastard, in which case I'm perfectly qualified to give advice! Why don't you ask Janine?"

"No way," said Janine, leaning across for her drink. "'Don't you dare drag me into it. I reckon I'm ready to give up on men altogether. I haven't met a bloke who wasn't a complete wanker for ages. I'm better off just playing it safe for now. Good luck with Jason, but you're on your own with this one. I don't want any part of it."

"Okay. Your loss. Just don't bother coming back to me later on tonight asking me to hook you up with one of his dishy mates," replied Rachel, turning her back on Janine.

Unperturbed, Janine shrugged and helped herself to another glass of wine.

Knowing Janine wasn't about to be hauled back into the debate, Rachel again swung her attention to me.

"But tell me, do you think he's cute?" she pressed.

"Jason's a total babe, Rachel. Everyone but you knows that," I sighed, already tiring of a conversation which had been going on since high school.

Just like *The Bold and the Beautiful*, only with different leading men.

And he was—a babe, that is. Six foot one. Short blond hair. A smile that would turn any girl's heart to mush. A body just beefy enough without overdoing it. Generally speaking, he was considered to be an exceptionally good catch. Every girl in the place had been perving on him for years and privately hoping to be noticed. Except for Rachel, of course, who considered him to be too 'wholesome' for her cultured taste in men. In other words, he wasn't an unemployed wanker with an expensive drug habit and a string of convictions under his belt.

It was universally acknowledged that Rachel was in it for the chase, together with the thrill of the ride. Once she'd made the final kill, her interest in the subject tended to wane. Little wonder she didn't see Jason as much of a challenge. He would have gladly rolled over and played dead if he thought it might get her to notice him. A shame, really. Although she couldn't see it, Jason was really a nice bloke. Too good for Rachel, if we're going to be honest. She might be one of my closest friends, but I hated the idea of standing idly by and watching her stomp all over his lovesick heart.

To my eternal shame, I will admit in the past Rachel's love-them-and-leave-them attitude toward guys in general had impressed me to no end. I could only dream of possessing that sort of power and sexual magnetism over the opposite sex. Me, well, I used to take what I could get— usually her heartbroken cast-offs. But as I've discovered, it's not much fun being on the receiving end of someone's callous disregard for your feelings. For this reason, Rachel's calculating, cold-hearted attitude toward Jason in particular had begun to really grate on my nerves.

An hour and a half later, I found myself sitting alone at the sacred table, completely surrounded by empty glasses, some sad bag lady with a multitude of handbags dangling off my arms. The heat in the room rose steadily, along with the aura of excitement emanating from those lucky enough to have paired off on the dance floor.

A tiny suspicion lurked in the back of my mind I might be just a teeny weenie little bit loaded. Normally I'd be yawning by now and beckoning to the girls to come back and reclaim their bags so I could call a cab and sneak off home to *him* in search of a screw. But seeing as the reality of another lonely night on my own, listening to Dad snoring in the room next door, hung over me, I decided to risk just *one* more drink…

It might have been the great music or the luscious feel of leather against my thighs or the sight of all those good-looking available blokes strutting their stuff on the dance floor, but before I knew it, I swayed in perfect harmony to the beat, for once in my life feeling reckless. If it hadn't been for Robert Palmer's *Addicted to Love* I would have still been sitting harmlessly in my glass castle, rocking away. My arse remained glued to the chair, of course, but the top half of me really moved to the groove. Sadly, the next thing I knew, I'd shot out onto the dance floor and was dancing like I'd never done before. *Oh, my God. A bloody miracle!* I may well have lost a husband, but after twenty-six years of suffering from two left feet syndrome, I had finally found rhythm. Praise the Lord!

The music seemed to swallow me, caressing my body and bringing with it a sense of deep personal awareness. I'd been transported to another realm—or to *Saturday Night Fever*, but with better music. I took possession of that dance floor, to the utter amazement of all those around me, who stood back, stunned by my transformation from uncoordinated klutz to dazzling diva. This was undoubtedly my finest hour, my triumph, the moment I would treasure for the rest of my life, and I lapped every sweet-tasting moment of it like a starving woman let off a Weight Watchers' diet for Christmas.

My time had come. Finally, I could release all those painful memories of a life of uncoordinated shame, in a world that had no place for a dance floor pariah. Sure, the funky gene had taken its own sweet time to kick in, and I had only my parents to blame for that, but better late than never. Now it had arrived. I was blossoming at last.

All around me, above the sound of the music, I could hear my name being chanted, carrying me higher and higher on the crest of my dance floor victory. I had wings, *actual wings*. I flew, soaring in fact, and in that moment of clarity I knew for certain life really was worth living after all, husband or no husband.

But like every dream, it had to come to an end sooner or later and as the song finished I slowly emerged from my fantasy only to realize the wings that had carried me through the previous four and a half minutes of melodic magic were actually…handbags.

"Fi! Fucking stop, will you!" screamed Kim, almost hysterical with rage.

And I did, but not before something white, looking strangely like a tampon, flew past my nose. Finally, the room stopped spinning and my eyes regained focus. "Jesus, what happened?" I asked breathlessly.

Seconds later, some sadistic bastard turned on the Ugly Lights, leaving everyone blinking painfully as our eyes adjusted to the stark fluorescence.

Oh, the moment dreaded by all. Yep, it was always a wise move to make good one's escape before the lights revealed the less than glamorous, warts-and-all sight of oneself, and all pretensions of chic sophistication were proven to be nothing but an illusion created by alcohol and dim lighting.

There I was, marooned on the dance floor. Held hostage by the savage glare. Too stunned and too disorientated to flee. Only then did I finally take in the scene of sheer mayhem and destruction surrounding me. The place rang with crying and moaning. There must have been a small explosion in the disco and I missed it — or maybe an earthquake? All around me, people were either stumbling off the dance floor or sitting there clutching their faces. Some were even bleeding!

Just then I became aware of an ominous curdling sensation in the vicinity of my stomach and knew that for me, the dream had, sadly, well and truly ended. My departure from the dance floor loomed imminently. I began frantically looking around for the girls. Just then, I spotted Rachel advancing toward me. She didn't look happy at all. Taking in the dangerous expression on her face, I felt sorry for the poor bastard unlucky enough to have stirred the homicidal rage for which she was renowned.

Unfortunately, it wasn't until the moment when she swung back her fist it finally twigged *I* was in fact the poor bastard about to be smashed.

Suddenly my stomach exploded, leaping upward to meet my throat when my entire body convulsed violently. Oh, God, it was horrible. Rachel's enraged screams echoed around the room as the first wave of vomit hit her square between her tits, plastering her brand-new silver halter top with a lumpy cocktail of pure evil. An encore forced its way past my lips a second later, to secure a second direct hit before she had time to recover her wits — or cover her tits.

A shocked hush descended over the room.

Suddenly, the place erupted afresh once I doubled up and began retching again. It couldn't have taken more than a few seconds, but in that brief space of time my entire life — social life, that is — flashed before my eyes until it reached the present and I saw the wreckage surrounding me for what it really was.

Not only had the contents of the girls' bags been scattered to the four corners of the room, but in the process, it had turned out I had swung those bags with a ferocity rivalling Bruce Lee with a pair of nunchakus, causing quite a few facial cuts and abrasions to those unlucky enough to have been within striking distance. As for me, after being forced to surrender my membership card, I was officially advised by the club officials *never* to return. Oh, the shame.

* * * *

A fortnight later, and perhaps not surprisingly, I hadn't seen hide or hair of my girlfriends, and consequently, I felt totally ostracized from society in general. Yes, I had been well and truly sent to Coventry.

Throughout the uproar that followed, I continued moping-crying-yelling-sulking—not necessarily in that order—in my parents' lounge as I attempted to shut out the outside world with a nonstop television orgy of Jerry Springer.

In the absence of alcohol, my parents having since become Puritan teetotalers to discourage my alcoholic tendencies, the only thing stopping me from sticking my head in the oven and ending it all, apart from the fact that we have an electric stove, was good old Jerry and the seemingly inexhaustible queue of total nut cases lining up to air their dirty laundry in front of millions of likewise sick viewers, including me. Was I destined to die old and alone on Mum and Dad's couch, caught up in a bizarre half world of incestuous Southern marriages, warring hookers and big scary black women with a punch like Mike Tyson's? No, not if my parents had anything to do with it. Hence, my current sojourn into therapy.

* * * *

"And that's my life in a nutshell. No husband, no friends, no future and a family who are considering emigrating to Afghanistan just to get away from me."

I glanced across at the Beige Oracle. Her face now blurred by my tears, she resembled a warped Picasso painting.

"What now?" I blurted out. "Are the men in white coats waiting outside to carry me off to the lunatic asylum?"

Margarita pursed her lips disapprovingly. I suppose

I was being a bit melodramatic. But, in my defense, I felt numb and exhausted, my head drained of emotion, and five minutes remained before I could finally crawl out to where Dad waited outside, praying for a miracle.

"Well, Fiona."

Shit, she actually spoke!

"I can see you've had a difficult time of late…"

Difficult! Did she say *difficult*? I couldn't *believe* she'd just said that. Hadn't she been listening to a single word I'd said? *It's been an absolute nightmare, I tell you!*

"But, Fiona, I think it might be time for you to put the events of the past into some kind of perspective and start to take back control of your life."

All I could do was stare at her in disbelief with my mouth gaping like some dying guppy's. If I had any control over my life, would I be sitting there right then, listening to this crap?

No!

Well, Dad had certainly backed a winner on this one and I couldn't wait to get out to the car and gloat.

"Tell me, have you ever considered taking up a new interest? Maybe some kind of sport or hobby?"

"Excuse me?" I blurted out, instantly experiencing a nightmarish flashback to the dark days of my brief-but-life-altering netball career.

"A sport or hobby like…let me see, pottery or tennis, or even dance lessons. Maybe at night or on the weekends?" she suggested.

I stared back blankly and Margarita sighed impatiently.

"From what you've told me today, it's obvious the recent betrayal of not only your husband, but also your friends, has severely undermined your self-confidence and feelings of self-worth. The unfortunate incident at the nightclub only reinforces my view. Can you perhaps see a parallel between the anger you are holding inside you and the fact you were lashing out violently at total strangers with handbags?"

"Well, I suppose you could have a point there," I mumbled.

I still had no idea what this had to do with me taking up dancing or pottery, for that matter.

"It is only a suggestion, but I really think developing a new interest in your life at this point may help you not only express yourself in a more appropriate manner, but it would undoubtedly allow you to regain some confidence and direction in your life."

"But I'm hopeless at sport. Anyone who knows me will tell you that!"

The one thing the entire netball fiasco had proven without question was the sad truth that I had absolutely no hand-eye coordination. Or for that matter, hand-foot, foot-eye or brain-mouth coordination. Actually, while we're on the subject, after the whole dance floor disaster, it was painfully clear I haven't a micron of brain-body coordination in me at all.

"Fiona, think about it. The reason people take lessons is to learn and further develop their skills. No one is born accomplished at anything. They have to work at these things. I suspect you are allowing the opinions of those around you to limit you. Maybe some people are better than others in certain areas, but while you allow these so-called *friends* of yours to dictate what you can or can't do, you'll never reach your full potential as a person."

Suddenly what she was saying started to make sense.

Maybe she isn't a nuttier nut case than me, after all.

Chapter Three

"She said *what*?"

"She suggested I find a new interest, maybe take dance lessons," I repeated to my poor shocked dad as he came within a whisper of wiping out a passing motorcyclist.

"Are yer tell'n me I've just forked out eighty-five hard-earned bloody dollars for you ta see a professional, an' all she can come up with is bloody *dance lessons*?" he blustered, his Scottish brogue wound up to max along with his outrage.

Dad is not one for what he calls 'namby-pamby psychobabble'. When he decided the time had come for me to seek professional advice, it was out of sheer desperation, brought on by the very real fear he and mum might be stuck with me under their roof for the rest of their days. Quite a shock, therefore, when the day before, he had simply walked up to me, handed me an appointment card and said, "Fiona, yer mother and I love you very much, but we canna take this carry-on any longer. I'm sending you ta see a shrink, an' yer going tomorrow!"

Finito. Discussion over. Dad had then hastily made his escape, marking the end of our father-daughter chat. I couldn't believe it. I was in shock. And when the shock wore off, oh, the mortification that my own family thought me a basket case. And, believe me, they must have, to have resorted to this.

MARGARITA SHULTZ B.Sc., MA Psychol.
Registered Psychologist
Specializing in phobias, depression, grief and marriage counselling.

It wasn't until I read those little letters after her name that it sank in Dad was actually serious. I was being forced to go to counseling.

I felt sick with shame.

My dad, being middle-aged and Scottish, had graduated from the old school of Emotional Denial, where men are men and if you have a problem you hold it in and let it fester until such time as you either suffer a stroke or go demented. I can't blame him really. Men of my father's era are not big fans of expressing their feelings and having the occasional cathartic cry.

That's how I knew they were desperate.

Of course, let's not forget the whole money issue. Dad's tight with money, sorry, *careful*—did I mention he's Scottish? I can still remember when I was thirteen and the dentist told Mum I needed braces. We all thought Dad would expire right there on the spot when he learned it would set him back nearly fifteen hundred dollars.

For the next few days, Dad went around hinting crooked teeth just added character and individuality to a person's appearance. Then, out of desperation, he finally sat me down and told me gently that although I would always be beautiful in his eyes, I was never going to be a supermodel anyway, so what was the point of spending all that money?

Wonderful! Just what a teenage girl, already insecure about her looks, needed to hear. If I could have instantly developed an eating disorder, believe me, I would have, just out of spite. Unfortunately, bulimia was out of the question seeing as I'm not a big fan of throwing up and I like my food too much to ever become successfully anorexic. But that's my dad for you. Mr. Sensitivity.

It never came to that, though. Mum put her foot down and pulled out the big guns, threatening to sell off his precious spoon collection if he didn't sign the check.

Ah, and there we have it. Dad's spoon collection. The curse of the McCrutchens. The bane of my existence—no wonder I'd gone into therapy.

It had taken him almost twenty years of constantly harassing anyone who so much as spoke about going on holiday into bringing him back a spoon from their trips to amass the thousands of carefully polished little souvenirs displayed proudly on our lounge wall at home.

No one was safe.

Dad ambushed friends, relatives, neighbors and sometimes even complete strangers as they walked unsuspectingly out of travel agencies and pressed them into contributing to his spoon addiction.

Yes, Dad was, and unfortunately still is, known as the Mr. Big in the Western Sydney illicit spoon trade, much to both my and my brother's acute embarrassment.

Well, I would have gladly gone around with crooked teeth for the rest of my life if it meant seeing the end of those bloody spoons, but with Mum's threats still ringing in his ears, within three weeks, I was imprisoned behind a metal mouth guard and remained that way for the next eighteen months.

So, once again it comes down to the ugly subject of money.

I don't know what Dad expected from my first therapy session. Well, actually that's not quite true. He was banking on them putting me on medication. Instant happiness in a pill. It's ironic, really. All throughout my teenage years, anytime I was tired or hungry, or happy for that matter, I'd have to sit through the McCrutchen drug inquisition after *60 Minutes* ran a program on the escalating drug epidemic among our nation's youth.

Now, I suspect, he would be quite willing to track down the nearest dealer and score a party-mix bag full of any drugs available to ply me with in order to get me out of the house — even if it was straight into rehab.

"An' exactly wha' kind of dancing did yer shrink suggest? Because I can tell yer right now, yer wa' too big fer ballet!" said Dad sarcastically, his patience together with his sympathy at an all-time low.

"She didn't say."

"Well, fer eighty-five bloody dollars an hour she should be giving you the damn lessons herself in her office, and fer nothin'!"

We passed the rest of the drive home in tense silence.

Mum was waiting for us out the front of the house, praying for a miracle, when we pulled up in the driveway.

"How did it go, darl'n?" she asked me quietly, before noticing the dark look on Dad's face. "Oh, dear."

"Well," Dad began, slamming the car door behind him, "wa' could ha' saved ourselves eighty-five bloody dollars if we'd made her go to Highland dancing when she wa' ten, like I suggested. But did ye listen to me then, woman? *No!*"

Jesus, things were about to get ugly. About as ugly as the time Dad had it in his head he would not be doing his parental as well as patriotic—Scottish that is—duty if I didn't learn Highland dancing when I was ten. God knows if going around with a name like McCrutchen wasn't bad enough, he wanted me to put on a kilt and jump over swords, while waving my arms about and whooping. Then I really would have needed therapy, with all the drugs they could lay their hands on thrown in as well.

Ignoring him, I turned to Mum. "I think I might look into salsa lessons. What do you think?" I asked tentatively, not daring to sneak a glance over to where Dad still stood, all but smoldering with barely contained rage.

"'Darl'n, I think it sounds a lovely idea," Mum replied and gave me a reassuring hug.

What can I say? Dad exploded. Lost it. Went totally mental. The strain of paying out what he considered to be an outrageous amount of money to a psychologist, only to have her put the idea of dancing lessons in my head, had been just too much for him and his wallet to cope with.

"*Salsa!* Jesus Christ, Fiona!" yelled Dad.

"Alistair! Language!" admonished Mum angrily, as she tried to herd us all into the house and out of earshot of our incredibly nosy neighbors.

"Sorry, Mary! But bloody hell, Fiona, salsa! That's foreign, isn't it? Are yer trying ta kill me or something? Wha' the hell's wrong with something normal, like Highland dancing?"

That was it. I'd heard enough talk of Highland dancing to last me five lifetimes and I saw red.

"Dad, you're the only one who thinks Highland dancing is normal," I screamed back at him. "Look at me. I'm twenty-six years old. A grown woman. So will you get it into your head once and for all, I am not, I repeat *not* going to learn *bloody Highland dance!*"

If the neighbors had been hoping to hear something to gossip about, they certainly weren't disappointed. Curtains were flapping furiously all the way up the street, like a Mexican wave at a football game, as our neighbors strained to listen in on the McCrutchens at number twelve going for it out on the front lawn, for all to see.

An hour later, some serenity had returned to the street and I was digging the local paper out of the recycling bin in search of salsa classes. God only knows why I'd blurted out salsa, but after all the fuss Dad had made, I sure as hell wasn't going to back down on the idea now.

To be honest, I didn't really know what salsa dancing was exactly, only it sounded exotic and not Scottish. While I looked through newspapers with Mum, Dad stormed off into the lounge armed with an economy-sized bottle of Brasso and started polishing his spoons, accompanied by the sounds of his favorite Scottish band music belting out at full volume.

So, in the end, it was with the melodious thumping of *Scotland the Brave* ringing in our ears that we finally located a small ad in the community pages, inviting anyone interested in learning Latin dancing to come along to the local community center on Tuesday and Friday nights at seven-thirty.

For the first time since I'd moved back in with my parents, I didn't cry myself to sleep.

In the morning, to my mother's immense relief, I decided

I was maybe ready to return to work come Monday.

Back at Wanker Brothers & Co, otherwise known as my workplace, not a lot had changed in my absence, apart from with the new season's three-quarter flares that'd been all the rage just before I left. After having enjoyed a brief stint of popularity, they'd now been completely overshadowed by the new velveteen-look micro-mini. Sitting in a crumpled heap under the clearance rack, scorned by even the most ruthless bargain hunters, the aforementioned flares could now easily be mistaken for radioactive fallout, after only two months at the top of the fashion stakes.

I strongly suspected that Joan Clements, the floor manager and fellow divorcée, had gathered everyone for an emergency staff meeting following my phone call letting her know I'd be returning to work, because everyone seemed to walking on eggshells around me and talking about anything but the 'separation'. A relief, really. Despite the fact I'd returned to work, happy to at least have something to take my mind off my problems, I wasn't ready to face any prying questions from curious coworkers. Or even worse still, marital advice.

My only other concern was running into Rachel and Kim. Not that I actually worked *with* them, but we three do share one thing in common. We work in the same multi-level shopping complex. You see, Rachel is the sales manager of a cheap teenage fashion boutique there called Chick, selling clothes only anorexic, pre-pubescent supermodels could fit into, and Kim is a hairdresser and also works in the center, at Lucky Locks, as a specialist color technician and advisor, as we are *constantly* being reminded.

Janine, I might add, works as a boner at the local abattoir. Yes, the most hideous job imaginable, but she earns more money cutting up dead cows with a chainsaw than the three of us put together.

And there you have it. For the past five years, the three of us have faithfully met up outside the donner kebab store in the center's food court every lunchtime, but considering recent happenings, I couldn't face having to confront the girls again. So, eager to avoid yet more unpleasantness, I chose instead to remain in the store and eat my cheese sandwich in the relative seclusion of the staff room.

The only downside to sharing a lunch room with twenty-eight serial gossips was overhearing things that I would rather not be privy to.

By the end of my forty-five-minute lunch break, I'd learned that the skanks, otherwise known as Samantha, Sharon and Kate, had finally succeed in their quest to take over the sacred table, aided no doubt by all the confusion following the unmentionable incident on the dance floor. I might add I was the *only* person in a ten-mile radius *not* mentioning it. From what I gathered, it had been a hot topic in the lunchroom for a solid fortnight now, not that anyone said anything about it directly to my face, but honestly, I do have ears that work.

The other big news? The white-hot romance that'd sprung up unexpectedly between the tart who'd gotten thrown up on and the dishy blond bouncer at the club. Well, what do you know!

All afternoon, I kept telling myself I didn't care. But the truth remained, that for the first time since that all-important netball competition when I'd been thirteen, I felt like a complete social leper. Lost and left out. A pariah. By now my future looked bleaker than ever. Sure, they might not have been the most supportive of friends at times, but Kim, Rachel and Janine were the closest ones I had.

For the next hour or so, I tried to reassure myself our sisterly allegiance had hit a few rocky patches before now and as we had always managed to work through it, surely there was no need to panic.

Ever since I'd spoken to the psychologist, I'd been going over a few issues in my head and most of those things were to do with the way my life had been guided by the whims and fancies of my friends.

Right there and then, I reached a decision. As a grown

woman now, not the scared teenager I'd used to be, just as the Oracle had said, it *was* time to take back control of my life. So, on the pretense of heading off for a loo break, I decided my days of hiding from my problems were officially over, and I made the difficult journey up to Chick to apologize to Rachel for throwing up all over her new silver halter top. To be completely honest with myself, it was also absolutely killing me not knowing what had gone on with her and Jason...

Five minutes later I spotted Rachel standing in the front display window, resplendent in a lime-green off-the-shoulder top and black faux-leather micro-miniskirt — the very latest fashion on the scene. Caught up as she was, struggling to get a green and purple boob tube to stay up on the androgynous mannequin, she failed to notice me standing there. Every few seconds, though, the narrow band of fabric would work its way south, revealing a plastic nippled boob, much to the growing delight of a small group of ten-year-old boys gathered outside the window, giggling and pointing.

I had to admit, she appeared to be taking her recent humiliation in her stride. She hadn't lost her spark. At the same time, she sent those pervy little ten-year-olds scattering with one venomous glare. Ignoring the snarling, bitchy expression on her face as she snatched pins off the poor terrified trainee, it was obvious just from looking at her she was in love.

It could have been the glow in her cheeks, or the way she danced in the window in perfect harmony with the music playing inside, but I suppose what ultimately gave it away was the cluster of livid purple love bites covering her neck. She looked as if she'd been mauled by a rabid dog. Just then, I experienced a glimmer of hope that love might have softened the rage inside her, prompting her to finally forgive me.

Alas, at that precise moment she spotted me standing outside the shop window. Instantly my hopes plummeted.

Now I am the first one to admit I'm not a competent lip reader, but I was fairly certain, even through the double-glazed shop front, Rachel told me to fuck off. Well what did I expect after having been the one responsible for her walk of shame off the dance floor? Still, I had come this far, so I felt I may as well soldier on.

Overlooking her poisonous expression, I took a deep fortifying breath, gathered my courage around me and walked bravely into the store. Perhaps the hardest thing I had ever done, and I had to remind myself of what was at stake. Our friendship.

"Rachel, please talk to me!" I pleaded, watching her retreating back as she stomped past me to the sanctuary of the sales desk.

"I did talk to you, and in case you didn't hear me, I believe I told you to fuck off!"

· I sighed, walking up to her slowly. "I know you have every right to be angry with me, but I just wanted to come in and say how sorry I am about that night."

You could have heard a pin drop in the shop, even above Selena Gomez belting out her latest hit on the stereo. I thought I'd better try a different tactic. "I heard you and Jason got together at last."

"Well, at least you didn't screw that one up for me," she snarled, before going all dreamy and gooey-eyed. Strange—only the other week she'd described the prospect of sleeping with Jason as a 'pity fuck'.

"I'm really pleased for you," I added despondently, knowing this was going to be even tougher than I'd first imagined.

"And I suppose you've also heard, because of your disgusting display the other night, those skanks got our bloody table? Not that you'd give a shit, would you? Jason told us you'd been kicked out of the club!"

God, talk about one's ears burning. Mine should have been singed right off my bloody head with all the gossip and scandal attached to me in the last few weeks.

Me, the anti-celebrity.

Famous, but for all the worst reasons.

"Okay, Rach, I'd better be getting back to work, then. Maybe I'll see you around at lunch one day," I added, not wanting to push my luck.

At least I knew when to walk away. Besides that, I sort of feared for my personal safety when I noticed her reaching for the staple gun, her knuckles white with tension.

"Yeah, right, in your dreams!" she muttered, loud enough for the entire shop to hear.

Walking out of Chick, I could almost feel the daggers of hostility embedding themselves in my back, but strangely I didn't really care. At least it was better than being mowed down in a shower of staples.

Suddenly, I felt a weight lift off my shoulders. The ball was in her court now. I'd taken that all-important first step and apologized. I could do no more.

Chapter Four

Sitting alone in the car across the road from the community center, I experienced a brief moment of gut-twisting panic. On various occasions in the past I'd encountered this same sensation and it's nearly always an omen of impending disaster—my body's way of telling me to flee for my life before it's too late.

God, what the hell am I doing here?

As I attempted to pull myself together, I watched with interest as the yoga for beginners class filed out, all clutching foam mats under their arms. Some were yawning and bleary-eyed after nodding off during meditation, or alternatively hobbling in agony from their overly ambitious attempts to twist their stiffened limbs into unnatural positions.

I'd arrived early, but the woman who'd taken my application at the center the previous day had suggested I arrive twenty minutes early for the first lesson to meet my dance instructor. Anyway, too late to change my mind now. Not only had I already paid for the first ten lessons—Dad's wallet had since gone into cardiac arrest when he understood I'd be back to the Oracle next week—but if I showed my face at home before the appointed hour and a half had ended, Dad would never let me live it down. Yes, he was *still* ranting on about the whole therapy and dancing thing and, as a result, he'd joined the rapidly growing list of people not talking to me.

Also, I wasn't too keen to go home early because the entire house positively reeked of Brasso fumes, the result of Dad's three-day-long manic polishing binge. Thankfully, it doesn't happen too often, but when it does, we know he is seriously upset. Actually, I haven't seen Dad this distressed since Scotland failed to qualify for the 2010 soccer, sorry, *football* world cup. That last, sad image of Dad surrounded by mountains of different sized and textured polishing cloths finally propelled me out of the car and across the road into the community center.

Inside the lobby, a little handwritten sign guided me toward a large multipurpose room between the basketball, volleyball, badminton, kiddy-gym room, and another smaller room used by an assortment of community-minded groups.

Mesmerized by the dozens of fliers all fighting for prominence and haphazardly tacked to the door with push pins, I was stunned by the diversity of people making use of this humble-looking room. There must certainly have been something for everyone. Ranging from the Single Gay Parents' Support Group to the Parents of Single Gay Offspring, and not forgetting the various Mothers' Groups, Senior Citizens for Equal Rights, Claustrophobics Support Group, Cat Lovers' groups, Reading Groups, The Orchid Growers' Society as well as countless environmental and left-wing extremist organizations.

I had no idea the area possessed such a diverse social subculture.

It didn't take long for the seductive strains of Latin music to lure me into the adjoining room, though. I noticed with some trepidation I was the first to arrive, except for a fellow standing in the far corner sorting through CDs. Well, now or never. I took a deep fortifying breath and made my way over to meet the dance instructor.

Anyway, how bad could it be? I had two legs that worked. If Paul Mercurio could teach that weird chick to dance in that movie *Strictly Ballroom*, why not me?

Then, just as I'd begun to relax a little, he turned around and smiled.

Oh… My… God…!

Before me stood Antonio Banderas. In the flesh!

Well, not really, but if Antonio Banderas had a long-lost twin brother hidden away in the back blocks of suburbia, this was him. He was gorgeous with a capital *G*, and I instantly knew I'd landed in serious trouble.

Shit, this is all I need.

I suppose any other heterosexual single female under the age of ninety would have been thrilled by the prospect of having this living, breathing Latin god of a man teaching them sexy salsa moves. Anyone but me, that is.

Why? Because raw, undiluted, masculine gods like the one currently before me tended to draw out the normally dormant moronic facet in my nature. History has proven again and again, unfortunately, that the moment I'm confronted with divine maleness in the flesh, I immediately dissolve into a complete babbling idiot unable to articulate the simplest sentence.

So, then, why should today be any different?

"Welcome. I'm Antonio, your dance instructor," spoke the Latin god.

"*No!* Seriously?" I spluttered.

"Well, I think I am," he laughed, exposing perfectly straight white teeth that lit his face up while throwing my heart as well as my nether regions into wild palpitations.

Shit, shit, shit! I've done it again.

I knew I had to say something witty to camouflage my idiocy, but my brain had developed its own personal black hole, sucked out any rational thoughts and spewed them out to other side of the cosmos.

"What's your name?" he asked glancing down at a list of students beside the CD player.

"Melanie!" I blurted. "No! Sorry, it's Fiona, Fiona McCrutchen."

Oh, God help me.

As I stood there like a prize idiot in my long black leggings and oversize T-shirt with *I Partied Hard at Hamilton Island* splattered across the front, his smile softened with understanding and I could tell he didn't know if I was merely intellectually challenged or on day release from the local mental asylum.

"Is this your first time, then?" he inquired gently.

My heart practically stopped dead. What *was* he asking? Yes, I'll admit I looked a little ragged about the edges, but seriously, did I look that bad he'd automatically thought I'd never been touched by a man? *How rude!* I instantly regretted not making more of an effort. Maybe a little makeup wouldn't have hurt.

A puzzled expression spread across his face as I continued to stare back in horror.

Then it dawned on me.

"Ohhh, you mean, *dancing*?"

I saw him trying to smother a smile.

What the hell was wrong with me?

Holy shit! Someone help me before I ask him to ravish me right there on the floor.

"Yes, dancing! Have you had any dancing experience?" he purred, his seductive Latin accent making me lightheaded.

I giggled nervously. "No, I'm afraid I am a complete novice. Actually, a beginner novice on L-plates might be more accurate. Really, I can't dance at all unless I've had at least eight bourbon and colas, and even then it's all in my head, but my therapist thought it would be good for my low self-esteem."

Why, why, why did I say that? In the space of less than three minutes I've gone from suffering mental constipation to verbal diarrhea!

"Well, there's no need to be nervous, Fiona. I'm sure a pretty girl like you will have no problems mastering the art of salsa."

He *really* had no idea what he was up against.

The atmosphere in the room had thickened by this time to a state of almost uncontrollable lust and all of it generating from me. I couldn't tear my eyes off him. And the worst part? Being horribly aware of the fact I was making a complete and utter arse of myself and there was not a damn thing

I could do about it. I had to think of something urgently to take my mind off Antonio before I did something truly unforgivable.

Dad's spoons.

Vomiting on Rachel's tits.

Two-timing Lying Bastard.

Well, that worked!

God must have been glancing in my direction for once, because just at that point the other students started filing into the room in small groups for the class. Suddenly, I heard someone call out my name. I turned around hesitantly, fully expecting to look stupid while another woman called Fiona was greeted warmly.

"Fiona, it *is* you. You're the last person I ever expected to see here!"

"Hi, Jason," I answered flatly, not quite able to summon up the required cheerfulness necessary to mask my horror at being discovered and my humiliation being complete.

The question was, what on Earth was *he* doing there? Racking my brains, I couldn't see there would be much call for a bouncer in a Latin dancing class.

"I suppose you're here to protect the innocent from being maimed by me," I joked pathetically. Then a horrible thought came to mind. What if my reputation had preceded me all the way to the community center and he had been hired as Antonio's personal bodyguard to save him from being molested by sex-starved, psychopathic, motion-challenged morons like myself?

"Is this your first time, then?" asked Jason, in an attempt to break the awkward silence that had sprung up between us.

"Yes, I thought it might be fun," I replied.

Why the hell couldn't I have said that when Antonio asked me not five minutes ago, instead of automatically thinking of sex?

A great big lie, of course. I didn't think it was going to be fun at all. I'd known full well it was going to be sheer torture and now I'd proven myself right.

"Anyway, what exactly are *you* doing here?" I asked, desperate to steer the conversation away from me.

"I suppose there's no point trying to pretend I accidentally stumbled in here looking for the Kung Fu classes." He laughed, shifting uncomfortably from one foot to the other. "Fiona, promise you won't tell anyone, but I've been learning Latin dancing for a couple of years now. At first, I thought it might teach me…you know, a few moves on the dance floor, but now I'm really into it."

By the flush of embarrassment climbing his face, anyone would have thought he'd just confessed to possessing a serious heroin habit or being a cross-dresser in an all-male revue.

Immediately a mental picture formed of Rachel gliding smoothly around the dance floor in a frothy red Spanish dress and a rose clenched between her teeth before allowing herself to be dipped elegantly by her tuxedo-clad partner.

Nope! I knew there was more chance of her becoming a Bride of Christ than the bride of a ballroom dancer, making Jason's chances of hooking Rachel almost nonexistent if she were to discover his secret double life as a Latin dancer.

I instantly understood his uneasiness.

"Does Rachel know?" the bitch in me asked.

Jason immediately went an even deeper shade of red and I had my answer.

A sudden wave of guilt washed over me then and I decided to take pity on him.

"Don't worry. I won't say anything if you don't. She's not speaking to me, anyway, so your secret is safe with me," I added glumly.

"I wouldn't lose any sleep over it, Fi. Rachel will get over it eventually. The whole thing was really funny, actually — but maybe not if you're the one wearing the vomit top, I suppose," he said, trying to smother a smile.

It was the first kind thing anyone had said to me since that horrible night and suddenly I could make out a tiny pinprick of light at the end of my tunnel of misery.

Looking up into his smiling face, all I could think was that Rachel didn't deserve his devotion. Sadly, though, everyone but Jason knew in another few weeks he'd be nothing but another notch on her handbag when she discarded him with little more thought than for an empty can of hairspray, leaving him heartbroken and wondering what he'd done wrong, like all the others preceding him.

Right then, Antonio called for everyone's attention and instructed us to find a partner. For those brief moments chatting to Jason, I'd almost forgotten I still had to face my fears — and Antonio. Hearing his sexy drawl brought back my feelings of dread and I knew if Antonio swept me into his arms, there'd be no predicting what my reaction would be.

The potential for further humiliation was immense.

What am I doing here?

Jason, sensing my rising panic, offered to be my partner, this being my first lesson and all. Sure, I was nervous, but for a completely different reason.

Thank God Jason didn't inspire any such carnal impulses in me. I followed him to the middle of the room to begin my initiation into the mysteries, or should that be *miseries*, of dancing.

* * * *

Driving home later that night, I felt slightly euphoric, not to mention amazed, to realize I'd actually enjoyed myself for the first time in months.

I still couldn't dance for shit.

I couldn't so much as sway in time to the music.

I couldn't look at Antonio yet without wanting to have his baby.

But I'd had fun, a miracle in itself.

I had to admit, though, my disaster-free initiation to Latin dancing had been entirely thanks to Jason, who'd done his best to make me feel like Cinderella on the dance floor, despite me flapping about the place with the grace of Daffy Duck. Unfortunately for Jason, his patience had been rather ungratefully rewarded with two suspected fractured toes, courtesy of my terminal clumsiness.

That night, as I lay in my lonely narrow bed, Brasso fumes seeping under my door like a toxic fog, I finally drifted off to sleep with the melodic rhythm of Enrique Iglesias playing in my head, accompanied by *Scotland the Brave* coming from the lounge.

Chapter Five

Thankfully, by Thursday, my coworkers had regressed back to their usual tactless, bitchy selves. I say thankfully because the entire dynamic of our work environment relied heavily on a finely balanced tightrope of allegiances, gossip and speculation, and without the distraction of the various ongoing staff-orientated soap operas, I doubt any of us would make it through a single day without suffering a complete mental breakdown.

So, taking all that into consideration, our love-hate attitude toward bitching — we love bitching about other people but hate to be on the receiving end — is in fact therapeutic, our unique way of keeping the wheels of industry turning. The other advantage to turning up for work, apart from the money of course, is whenever one of us has a few days off unexpectedly, the slander and innuendo mills instantly roll into action. Honestly, a person's reputation can easily be chipped, mulched and spread out for manure in less time than it takes them to get over a mild case of the sniffles.

As you might well imagine, my reputation by now was positively ripe and steaming.

Confused? Well, this is how it generally works. While some poor unsuspecting bugger is at home with their head stuck in a jar of Vicks feeling like shit, instead of sending them a Get Well card, his or her loyal colleagues are generally placing bets on whether they have run off with the neighbor—my personal favorite— or are dying as they have been looking a bit pale lately, or pregnant — a good bet with the young single girls on the cosmetics counter — have been arrested for pilfering CDs from the Music Bar, *or* have slunk away to get a boob job.

The boob job bet always proves to be a guaranteed money loser. But unperturbed, the guys in management continue to throw their hard-earned dough in that direction, praying to their goddesses Pamela Anderson and Angelina Jolie that one day they'll be rewarded for their continuing devotion and one of us girls will turn up for work with a bust that would topple even Dolly Parton.

Honestly, they must have all been bottle-fed as babies.

The illicit betting ring upstairs might well have remained a carefully guarded male secret had us girls not begun noticing an alarming pattern of behavior developing among the senior male staff, or the 'stupid suits upstairs', as we mere mortals on the ground floor call them. It didn't take long to put two and two together, and we soon cottoned on to the fact that whenever one of us happened to have a few days off—apart from Mrs. Clements, that is—nearly every male employee in the store would be staring at our tits until lunchtime, longer in winter, until they came to a unanimous decision on whether or not we had been surgically enhanced.

A few months back there had almost been a riot in the top office when Tina Williams turned up on a Monday morning wearing a push-up bra after enjoying a week of leisure on the Gold Coast. The stupid suits upstairs got all excited and eventually money changed hands. The following morning though, much to their combined horror, Tina arrived accompanied by her modest B-cup breasts. Within fifteen minutes, a brawl had ensued when the losing punters angrily demanded their money back.

In all the commotion and confusion that followed, poor Tina very nearly got fired before sanity returned and a union official intervened, stating, "an employee cannot have their employment terminated for wearing a push-up bra to work," which he backed up by threatening to pull us all out on strike.

So compared with the *Twilight Zone* of compassion I had

been surrounded by for the past week, it was almost a relief when on Thursday afternoon the floodgates of pent-up malice finally burst open and Craig from the loading bay — an arrogant prat at the best of times — turned to me and said, "So, I hear your hubby's been screwing that chick from the gym with the huge hooters."

Well not only did that break the ice, but I swear every glacier on the planet must have shattered simultaneously. At that moment, with all the stress I'd been suppressing of late, something inside my head likewise shattered.

"What's the matter, Craig? You look disappointed," I began screaming, heedless of the spectacle I was making of myself and strangely enjoying the feeling of losing control. "Don't worry — if you wait a few weeks I'm sure my ex will get around to fucking you, as well. He's a very *busy man*, I hear!"

And with that I dropped on his foot the box of imported bath bombs I was hefting and stormed off, unshed tears searing the back of my eyes, leaving Craig hopping on one foot, encased in a cloud of powdery blue soap.

Within ten minutes, the entire store buzzed with excitement.

By the time the gossip mill finished with it, though, not only had Craig confessed to a clandestine homosexual love affair with my ex-husband, but I'd given him a verbal thrashing of biblical proportions and belted the shit out of him with a volley of bath bombs.

The entire store came to a screeching halt. Everyone, all the way up to the stupid suits upstairs, were agog that not only had someone finally faced up to Craig, but of all people it'd been quiet, conscientious Fiona McCrutchen who had done the unthinkable and put him in his place once and for all. Craig, you see, had the unique honor of being universally despised throughout the entire center, generally regarded as being a slacker and wanker all rolled into one, making him on the whole a very unattractive man.

Sipping a cup of coffee alone in the staff room, I was trying not to shake. Impotent rage at Craig's nastiness, combined with the knowledge Two-timing Lying Bastard was still shagging that bitch, had thankfully given me the burst of adrenaline I desperately needed to deal with Craig at the time. But now, in the wake of my outburst, I felt physically exhausted as well as emotionally spent.

Little did I know at the time the consequences of my little outburst in the loading bay.

Before I had even had the opportunity to finish my cuppa, it seemed someone must have announced over the store PA system, "Let the bitch-fest begin!"

Following that, it was on for young and old. Coworker against coworker. Husbands against wives. Management against lowly floor worker. Every grievance that had been carefully suppressed over the past week, as well as a few newly discovered ones, were dragged from the cupboard and thrashed out.

Not only was it a battle of the sexes, but, as it turned out, genders as well, when Ruth the lesbian from Sporting viciously set upon Morris, the store's token gay man from Men's Apparel. Poor Morris got the crap beaten out of him for allegedly wearing a groin cup to last month's Gay Mardi Gras, armoring himself against would-be gay bashers.

As it turned out, he had *borrowed* the offending groin guard from Sporting Goods then simply returned it to the shelf come Monday morning, thinking no one would be any the wiser. Normally, no one would have, but for a rumor that had begun to circulate among the gay social circles and eventually been overheard by Ruth concerning Morris's phenomenal ability to maintain a rock-hard bulge in his pink fairy tights for the entire parade, elevating him to almost legendary status.

So when Ruth went to do a routine stock take and found a lone protector stuffed at the very back of the shelf with *Handle with care. NOT!* written across it in indelible red ink, the game was unfortunately up for Morris.

All in all, a very interesting afternoon.

Because time tends to fly when the shit hits the fan, it was five-thirty before we knew it, and apart from a few snarls and black looks hurled across the staff room floor, everyone managed to leave the premises without any more blood being spilled.

As it happened, I was one of the last to leave, thinking it wiser and safer to wait until the staff car park cleared a little before risking the short walk over to the bus stop.

"Fiona! Fiona! Wait!"

I turned around to find Rachel and Kim running toward me and for a split second I wondered if I should make a bolt for it now or risk having to stand and fight. After all that had happened in the last couple of hours, why should I have been surprised Rachel and Kim wanted in on the action as well?

"Fiona, please wait up!"

Despite serious misgivings, I decided it was time to confront my fears.

"Oh, Fiona. We've only just heard what that arsehole Craig said to you. Are you all right?" said Rachel.

"I'll live," I replied stiffly.

"Is he really in a coma, Fi?" chipped in Kim, always eager to hear of someone else's misfortune.

"I wish!"

Kim and Rachel's sympathetic looks proved to be my undoing. Suddenly, all the strength I had gathered started to crumble and I burst into tears.

"Oh, Fi, don't cry, honey. Craig's a total wanker, everyone knows that, and he's not worth one of your tears," comforted Kim.

"I know that, really. It's just I never thought Two-timing Lying Bastard and that bitch would still be together and it came as a bit of a shock. I feel like everyone is laughing at me and the two of them are laughing at me right now and even you girls are laughing at me for being such an idiot."

I hadn't meant to actually voice that last bit, but now I had, I felt even more pathetic. Like I was begging for their sympathy or something. The only thing I had left was my pride and now even that had been thrown on the scrap heap of my life.

"Oh, Fi, we're so sorry!" they cried together as they rushed up for a group hug.

So once again, our friendship was mended, glued together and joined with sticky tape. Maybe not as shiny and pretty as before, but at least we were all on speaking terms again.

It's ironic, I know, but I really have to thank Craig for bringing us girls back together. You see, it's one thing for us girls to hurl insults at each other, reveal long-guarded secrets and generally behave like we hate one another's guts. But let a man step over the line of common decency and the gates of Hades are flung wide open, and even mortal enemies are reunited in the fight against the common foe.

It was also a case of Kim hating Craig with a passion after she'd unfortunately woken up in his bed after an unofficial work Christmas party had gone horribly wrong a couple of years back. Years later, we're still trying to unravel the sad sequence of events which on that fateful night resulted in the conception of three babies—two of which were twins, making it necessary for every bloke there to undergo a DNA test—one divorce, three fights and two arrests for malicious damage.

As previously mentioned, it had also been the Christmas party Kim had ended up in the sack with Craig. Oh, poor Kim's horror when her drink googles had fallen off and she'd finally sobered up to realize just who she'd been bonking. For three days after, she'd thrown up nonstop. Just when she'd thought she could stomach the sight of food again, she'd heard a rumor circulating that Craig was boasting to anyone who would listen that Kim gave the best blow jobs in town — *and swallowed.*

Four more days of constant vomiting followed, until they'd been almost forced to admit her into hospital suffering from dehydration. For Kim, it had been a long, painful road back to recovery and she'd vowed never to go near Guinness or Craig ever again.

Kim, Rachel, Janine and I made our peace over two pizzas and a carafe and a half of house white at Mario's Pizza Inn later that night. For the first time since the 'dance incident', as it was delicately referred to now, the four of us, the Fab Four, got together for a good old-fashioned gab about work, sex, getting pissed, men, sex, clothes, sex, sex and sex. Then Rachel finally shut up and let someone else talk.

Well, what an eye opener. I, for one, never thought I would live to see the day when Rachel, who prided herself on being totally mercenary when it came to men, fell head over heels in love with Jason.

And she had fallen. Big-time!

As it happened, on the night of the incident, Jason had offered to drive Rachel home after she'd scraped the worst of the vomit off herself in the ladies'. Feeling sorry for herself, Rachel had desperately needed some reassurance she wasn't the sad loser she'd appeared to be as she'd made her way back through the foyer of the club. So, no sooner had Jason closed the car door behind him did Rachel jump him. To her way of thinking, if he *really* loved her, he wouldn't be put off by her Odor de Puke fragrance. A trial by vomit, as opposed to a trial by fire.

Well, it seems Jason had passed with flying colors and Rachel had almost passed out as her screams of pleasure reverberated across the RSL car park, and in the process, had scared the shit out of a couple of late-leaving pensioners. When Jason had finally managed to disentangle Rachel from his body and start the car, they'd ended up at his flat, doing the horizontal tango all night long.

Though from what Rachel told us of their night of passion, they'd done it every which way but horizontally.

Well, eventually our night of a thousand sorrys came to an end and we departed with hugs and kisses, just like old times. Except there was still a slight, almost indiscernible, rift in our friendship which had yet to be addressed, and it involved our customary Friday night out.

As everyone from Queanbeyan to the Queensland border knows by now, I am no longer permitted to step within a mile and a half radius of the RSL, and I quote, "not to sully the premises with my unwanted presence ever again." So, no surprise I was not about to be welcomed back to the Friday night disco anytime this century. This little complication was not going to deter Kim, Rachel and Janine from returning to the scene of the crime, though.

Which sort of left me at a loose end.

Suddenly I remembered. Salsa lessons! They were not only on Tuesday but also Friday nights. *Perfect.*

Despite our recent reconciliation, I didn't feel entirely comfortable confiding in my friends about my new interest, knowing full well they would collapse laughing at the mere notion of me taking dance lessons. It would also be akin to advertising what a sad mess my life had turned into. Not that they didn't already know that, but after the series of disappointments I had been subjected to lately, I felt the desperate need to keep some part of my life safely tucked away from their jokes and judgments. Jason, of course, knew about the classes, but he was hardly in a position to blab, as it would also mean coming clean to Rachel about his own secret passion.

Apart from Friday night Latin dancing, there was someone else I had to visit after work. The Oracle!

I couldn't believe an entire week had passed since I'd rather embarrassingly blubbered my way through an hour's session with Margarita, chewing a sizeable hole through Dad's wallet in the process. So, after I finished up at work on Friday afternoon, rather than join the three of them for a spot of late-night shopping, I lied and told them I had to visit Granny in the nursing home for her birthday.

Nothing more needed to be said.

Knowing they would endure a bikini line wax, or for that matter an appendectomy without anesthetic, rather than spend half an hour listening to Granny's constant ravings about sadistic nurses, kleptomaniac Alzheimer's patients and her bowel movements, it was safe to assume no one would be volunteering to come with me.

This week, I decided it would be wiser to make my own way to the therapist's, leaving Dad at home crying tears of blood all over his checkbook. Honestly, the way he'd been behaving the past week, I half thought to book him in to see the Oracle, as well.

A father-daughter therapy session.

Two loonies for the price of one.

But then a horrible thought popped into my head. What if Dad got all enthusiastic about it and embarked on some kind of self-improvement crusade? God help me, he might even decide to follow me to dance lessons. Or, worse still, drag Mum and Alex into it as well. Family therapy, he'd call it. I began to hyperventilate at the mere notion. A horrible thought and more than enough to persuade me that his sulking and strange spoon fetishes weren't too hard to live with, after all.

"Fiona, how have you been feeling this week?" the Oracle asked cheerfully after finally maneuvering herself onto her new ergonomic chair which at first glance resembled a custom-made perch for some kind of enormous exotic bird. Not that I'm one to talk, but with the Beige Oracle being neither slim nor waif-like, I felt it was only a matter of time before her new, and probably staggeringly expensive, executive toy ended up in the Dumpster, mangled and wrecked.

"I'm feeling a lot better, actually. I went back to work and decided to take your advice about getting a new hobby and joined a Latin dancing class."

"Wonderful news, Fiona, just wonderful. Tell me, what made you decide on Latin dancing, exactly?"

Before I knew it, I was relating the entire Dad, temper-tantrum, Highland dancing and spoon-polishing episode and could have kicked myself by the time I'd finished. It was one thing to live with Dad's peculiar hobbies but quite another to witness the look of benign interest on her face morph into an expression of concerned understanding.

Instantly, I regretted dragging him into it and launched a salvage mission worthy of the Green Berets in order to rescue Dad's reputation, telling her how much we'd learned of world events and geography because of his unique interest. Somehow, I don't think she was convinced, though.

"Tell me, Fiona, how long has your father been collecting spoons?"

She said it fake-lightly, almost dismissively, and I got the impression she was frantically trying to work out some kind of a connection between my recent neuroses and Dad's prized spoon collection. Laughable, really, and I was tempted to make up some horrendous story about Dad punishing us by dipping his spoons into scalding hot cups of tea before sadistically pressing them against our bare flesh, inflicting all sorts of pain on our innocent little persons.

But this was hardly the time or the place for making jokes. Besides, the mere suggestion Dad might actually use one of his precious spoons to stir his tea was not only ludicrous but completely beyond the realms of possibility.

"Oh, jeez, I must have been about eight or nine, I suppose. Yes, it would have been about the same time he wanted me to learn to play the bagpipes, just before the Highland dancing thing."

As soon as the words were out of my mouth, I cringed. I'd done it again. This time, she didn't even bother to disguise her concern and launched into a whole lot of garbage about if I felt culturally isolated by my father's inability to fully integrate into Australian society.

Instantly, I felt ashamed of myself. I felt such a traitor. Alex and I could constantly take the piss out of Dad's dorky hobbies and embarrassing idiosyncrasies behind his back, but strange or not, he was still my father and I was very fond of him.

Sensing my growing defensiveness, the Oracle thankfully

decided to drop the subject of my father, steering our conversation back to my dancing classes.

"Standing up to your father concerning the dancing lessons is a positive sign, Fiona. It indicates to me you are beginning to take control of your life. I think the next step is to address the subject of your estranged husband. Your anger toward him is completely normal, you understand, completely normal, *but* have you put any thought into confronting him in a calm and rational manner about the pain he's caused you?"

Sure, I'd thought about confronting him, but those thoughts were usually accompanied by other, darker thoughts of inflicting severe bodily injury on his severely adulterous body. The harsh reality was that the thought of seeing him again made me feel physically ill. My shock at his betrayal, together with the whole humiliation aspect, remained within me like an open sore, festering and raw with hurt. Every stray thought of him made my wounded heart bleed afresh.

"I really don't think I'm ready to deal with him just yet," I answered quietly, fighting off an unexpected rush of tears.

And it was true. After wavering at the edge of an emotional abyss for weeks, I had only just stepped back from the edge, but the urge to make a running, jumping leap into the deep black hole of a complete mental breakdown hadn't entirely left me just yet.

"It's too soon."

"But surely you've spoken to him since your split. What about your finances and your house?"

"We rented and he cleared our joint bank account of its pitiful contents the day after I walked out. We don't have any children, not even a dog. What possible reason is there for me to contact him?"

"Well, Fiona, there is the matter of closure."

The Oracle's persistent emotional probing finally ruptured the last reserves of my patience and control, and my temper suddenly erupted.

"Closure! He doesn't deserve my closure," I yelled. "I'm sure he'd like nothing more than to relieve himself of guilt by thinking I was getting on with my life. But I'm not. I'm only just holding myself together and doing a terrible job of pretending to forget him. What I would really like to do is wake up tomorrow and realize it was all a bad dream that would be nothing but a faint memory by lunchtime."

Suddenly I was angry. Very angry.

Angry at the Oracle for bringing up the subject.

Angry at Two-timing Lying Bastard for reducing me to the state I'm in just for the sake of a quick fuck with that blonde bimbo.

And, above all, I was angry with myself for allowing him to still affect me like this, even after all he'd put me through.

Up until this point in my life, I had never experienced this kind of sharp, violent emotion. Not only was it alien to my normally placid temperament, it was physically painful, a stabbing pain deep in my chest, viciously sucking the breath from my body. All my initial hurt, rage and shock at his betrayal returned in a fresh wave of pain and the pressure of hot tears built at the backs of my eyes, ready to burst forth at any moment.

The Oracle, no doubt sensing another emotional outburst, pushed a fresh box of tissues across to me.

Suddenly, the horrible truth dawned on me. For the last few weeks, I had been kidding myself. As much as I tried to convey an attitude of cold, sneering contempt whenever anyone spoke of him, it was a sham, a guise to fend off the pity of all those who saw me as a helpless victim. As much as I hated myself for it, I realized then that I still fanned a tiny flicker of love for him in my heart.

Don't get me wrong, I also despised him with a passion that hovered dangerously close to psychotic, but I suppose, having read too many Mills and Boons over the years, I harbored the faint hope he would come crawling back to me on his belly, tearfully begging my forgiveness and pleading for my return.

Bitter pill to swallow, therefore, to realize he was not racked with guilt and remorse, sobbing into his pillow each night, but out shagging anything with tits with the abandoned glee not seen since Caligula's orgy-heavy heydays.

"It is perfectly all right to cry, Fiona. Within these walls, you don't have to pretend to be strong. Anger is in truth very therapeutic when directed constructively. If you have the urge to hit something, I can help you, dear."

Shit, what's she suggesting? Maybe she's sicker than me and gets her kicks from being abused by her patients!

The shocked look on my face abruptly changed to confusion, though, when she reached behind her and passed me a big round cushion.

I stared at it, completely at a loss.

What am I expected to do with it? Sit on it? Use it as lumbar support?

"This is known as an anger release bag," she offered, as if reading my mind. "It is perfectly safe within this environment to strike out at it and vent some of the rage inside you."

No! I wasn't fooled for a minute.

She might well refer to it as an anger release bag, but it was glaringly obviously a homemade cushion and there I was, a total nutter sitting holding it tightly while trying my best to conjure up the face of my ex onto it. The thought of punching the beige chenille fabric in the company of this throwback from the bra-burning, hallucinogenic-taking, free-loving sixties filled me with mortification. I've heard of being outside my comfort zone, but at that moment I was well into another solar system.

"Thank you for the offer, but I don't really think I need to hit something right now."

And having said that, I quickly pushed it back across the desk to her, desperate to put some distance between me and the freaky abuse cushion.

God, what time is it? I glanced quickly around and noticed for the first time the lack of clocks on the walls or on her desk, for that matter. What a day to forget my watch.

Sitting there in Margarita's office, I prayed hard my hour was almost up and I could finally escape from her presence. Kind of funny in a sad way. When I was away from here, back in my own little world, I felt somewhat normal, but opposite the Beige Oracle, with her aura of smug self-assurance weighing down on me, I felt like an extra on the set of *One Flew Over the Cuckoo's Nest*. All I needed to complete the picture was a straitjacket, padded cell and drool running down my chin.

Walking out to the car a short time later, I felt wildly relieved to have escaped before I got committed. But, at the same time, I was totally disgusted with myself. Sure, I'd avoided the asylum for now, but ever conscious of Margarita's deep concern for my mental well-being, I'd buckled under the pressure and booked another appointment for the following week.

I couldn't help thinking I was merely on week release from the funny farm — but only until my return to Bedlam next week.

Chapter Six

Just as I'd suspected, the Friday night class was a lot smaller. Bordering on intimate, really, and my stomach did a little nervous flip-flop as I walked through the heavy glass doors of the community center and noticed the small group of ladies waiting outside the room.

As expected, Jason wasn't there—he was hardly about to pass up a Friday night at the club with Rachel to have his toes smashed again by me on the dance floor. On Tuesday night, in between my pathetic attempts at the cha-cha and rumba, he'd told me Pete was manning the door with Dangerous Dave again this week, leaving him free to spend the night with Rachel. By the slight color that rose on his face, I'm sure he didn't just mean at the disco, either.

Despite my initial reservations, I was happy for him. The poor guy had been bidding for a share in the Rachel love corporation for years and had always been pipped at the post by the more aggressive punters. Now that he was the successful candidate, I only hoped he knew what he was getting himself into.

I knew only too well that life with Rachel carried inherent dangers.

As I walked through the foyer of the community center, one of the middle-aged ladies recognized me from Tuesday's class and waved me over to join them.

There were only nine of us tonight, including one lone male. Obviously, a long-suffering spouse of one of the chatting women. The poor man tried desperately to look invisible as Helen relayed for the benefit of the other ladies a blow-by-blow description of her radical hysterectomy, together with all the ghoulish aftereffects she'd apparently suffered until such time as they got her rebellious hormones back on track.

By the look on Barry's face, I reckon he was seriously considering escaping out of the nearest fire door, especially when they all started sympathizing with poor Helen over her vaginal dryness and hot flushes. I might add at that particularly low point in the conversation I'd considered following him, Latin god or no Latin god.

By this time, it was approaching seven-thirty and still no sign of my him The panic I'd experienced the other night hadn't really left me and I dreaded the idea of finding myself alone with him again. I knew there remained a grave danger of me regressing back to the babbling idiot of old and I couldn't face the thought of making a fool of myself. Again.

So, with that in mind, I think part of me hoped he wouldn't show, leaving me free to skip out of class with a clear conscience and my dignity intact to face another day.

My wishful thinking accomplished nothing. Apparently, Antonio was always a little late on Friday nights as he joined the mass exodus of people leaving the city for the weekend.

"Oh, lives in the city, does he?" I inquired politely, desperate of course to find out anything at all about him but reluctant to appear a nosy bitch, or worse still a smitten girl hankering after a desperately gorgeous man totally out of her league.

"I'm not sure, but I know he owns an antique store in the city. He did mention once he grew up not far from here, and I think his mother still lives around here somewhere," offered Lorraine, with a dreamy look on her face.

I wasn't sure if her look of longing was for Antonio or the antiques, but either way, it was comforting to see he affected all the women here in one way or another, not just me.

This realization alone made me feel a lot better about the

volatile state of my own hormones and I finally lost the hair-trigger urge to make up some totally lame excuse and do a runner.

"Ladies, and of course, not forgetting you, Barry, I'm sorry for being late," announced Antonio, rushing through the main doors. "The traffic on the way out of the city tonight was a nightmare as usual. Can you believe it, road works, and right in the middle of rush hour? It's absolutely ridiculous. Honestly, I think I would have been quicker to walk," he said as he began searching through his backpack for the keys to the room.

It's my guess Antonio would have been instantly forgiven had he announced his lateness was due to stopping off to gun down a couple of old grannies in their beds.

So, predictably, even after waiting for over twenty minutes, they all smiled sweetly and one of them said, "Oh, don't you worry, dear. We hardly even noticed the time. We were all enjoying a lovely chat together!"

Speak for yourself, I thought. My womb still clenched in horror as a result of their so-called lovely chat. Jesus, if Stephen King ever runs out of material, all he'd have to do is chat to this mob and he'd be back in business in no time.

By the look on Barry's face as he stood over by the community notice board, I wasn't the only one thinking along those lines. Glancing pointedly at his watch, he made it clear he wasn't taken in by Antonio's charm like the women currently following him into the room, and I shot him a look of sympathy.

Within a few minutes, the melodious sounds of Latin music filled the room and Antonio glided over toward us, swiveling his hips and waving his arms around in perfect time to the music like a matador fending off a bull.

"Fiona, it's wonderful to see you here again. It's a shame Jason couldn't be with us tonight. You both looked as though you were getting on well together. Anyway, I had better get things moving. Are you ready to dance, then?"

I managed to nod dumbly in response.

"Wonderful."

Oh, God, he was gorgeous.

Sex on legs!

Fearing I'd begun to drool, I discreetly wiped my mouth with the back of my hand — *better safe than sorry,* I figured.

"Ladies and gentleman, if you would like to partner up, tonight we will begin with the rumba. Just remember, nice and slow to start off with until everyone gets into the rhythm of it. We don't want anyone to strain a muscle, do we?"

Everyone was seemingly magnetically charged. Instantly, they gravitated toward each other without a word needing to be said and in a matter of seconds were paired up, leaving me standing in the middle of the dance floor, alone and lonely.

"Oh, well, I'll just watch for a bit, then," I stammered to no one in particular, embarrassed to be the only one without a partner.

Obviously, they hadn't forgotten Jason's stifled groans of pain echoing throughout the room the other night and valued their toes enough not to willfully inflict my clumsiness on their unsuspecting feet. Not that I could blame them, really. As nice as they seemed to be, they weren't masochists, after all.

Suddenly, I looked across and my heart plummeted even further. Antonio, at that moment, made a beeline toward me, gesticulating wildly in a manner only hot-blooded European men can do and get away with it.

"No, no, Fiona. You won't learn anything by standing in the shadows being shy. You need to *feel* the music in your body. Let it run through your veins, firing up the *passion* in your soul. So, tonight, you will be my partner and let me see if I can bring out the *passion* in you."

Shit!

Now I really wanted to run. But being truly, deeply a coward at heart, I couldn't summon up to courage to flee, but rather stood there rooted to the spot somehow, praying for a miracle in the form of an earthquake or bomb threat to come to my aid and save me from making a fool of myself.

My mind instantly began spinning with totally outrageous escape plans so ludicrous they were worthy of a Batman and Robin plot. No need to add, I had no more chance of being abducted by aliens than willing my appendix to burst right there and then. I couldn't think straight, probably just as well, because while I was fighting off an impending anxiety attack, Antonio took the initiative and swept me into his arms, leading me masterfully into the middle of the floor while directing the others to follow.

Through my loose-fitting blouse, I could feel the heat radiating from his hands scorching an imprint of his strong fingers upon my flesh. As much as I tried to train my focus on where my feet were supposed to be going, my entire consciousness was consumed with the turmoil of conflicting emotions warring within my vulnerable body.

"Fiona, relax, will you? I promise you I don't bite. Just allow yourself to melt into my arms and let me guide you. If you tense up like this, you won't feel my body directing you where to go."

Well, easier said than done. The more Antonio tried to calm my nerves, the more aware I was of the sensuous feel of his body against mine. Every time he brushed his hips up against my belly or dropped his hands to my waist, a spark of lust shot deep into my womb, awakening a passion that had lain dormant for too long and was now hungry for action. I found it almost impossible to concentrate when his entire aura positively crackled with passion and I desperately fought the urge to give in to my carnal impulses and press myself against him.

God, it was sheer torture.

As the class dragged on, I found it more and more disturbing. I languished in an agony of wanting with every second that passed and Antonio appeared not in the slightest bit affected by the tangible currents of electricity passing between us. Surely, he couldn't be totally immune to the atmosphere building?

Obviously, he was, though, if the benign expression of patience on his face was anything to go by. We crisscrossed the floor, narrowly missing Helen and Joan time and time again, who, still engrossed with the state of their hormones, weren't paying the slightest attention to where they were going.

By the end of the class, I was an emotional wreck. The strain of trying to keep up the false pretense that I wasn't affected by Antonio's close proximity had sapped every bit of strength from my body. So convinced was I that every word to come out of my mouth damned me for the smitten idiot I was, I decided in the end it would be best for all concerned if I just kept my lips zipped.

Over by the flickering Exit sign, the large plastic clock showed there the class was mercifully soon ending. I could have fainted with relief. Only a couple of minutes before I could at last put this whole miserable experience behind me. I had since decided this was definitely, definitely going to be the last dance lesson I inflicted upon myself. Even a visit to the dentist wasn't as harrowing as this!

From this moment on, I would just have to cut my losses and admit to the Oracle I had aimed way too high and therefore would have to learn to be content with pottery or scrapbooking, or at least something a little less threatening than sexy Latin dancing. After all, forfeiting the cost of the other eight lessons was a small price to pay compared to the loss of what little self-esteem I had left after tonight's debacle.

Anyway, I thought, so what if I grow old never knowing the thrill of gliding across a polished dance floor in the arms of a Latin god, at one with the music? It wasn't the end of the world, was it? Merely just one more thing to add to the rapidly expanding list of things I would probably never experience in my sad, boring life. Like winning a Nobel Prize for literature. Or starring in a Hollywood movie with Hugh Grant. Or discovering a cure for cancer. Or finding true love. Or moving out of my parents' house. Or ever having a life at all...

Just then, I noticed Joan and Barry were leaving, closely followed by Helen and Penny. *Quick*, I thought. *Grab my chance to escape before some other calamity strikes.* Making out I was joining them as casually as my shattered nerves would allow, I picked up my bag and keys and scooted for the exit, desperate to make good my escape while trying not to look as though I was fleeing the scene of the crime.

I got almost as far as the door. I could all but taste the freedom of the foyer on my tongue. Then, from somewhere behind me, Antonio's voice rose above the music and for a second my heart stopped dead.

"Fiona, before you go, can I speak to you for a moment?" he called out.

Damn! So close, and yet not quite far enough!

It occurred to me I *could* pretend not to have heard him and make a dash for freedom, but even Helen, walking out of the door in front of me, paused for a second on hearing his voice. I had no real choice but to paste a smile on my strained face and turn around. After all, whatever Antonio had to say, it couldn't be any worse than having to endure an hour and a half of *melting* into his rippling hard chest and him attempting to bring out the *passion* in my tense, uncoordinated body with more than half a dozen witnesses gaping in horror at my total ineptness.

It couldn't have taken me more than a couple of seconds to make my way over to where Antonio stood packing up CDs, but it was enough time for me to realize everyone apart from the two of us had by now left.

I was alone with him yet again.

Shit!

"Fiona, thanks for coming back. I wanted to speak to you away from the others."

I could barely hear him over the sound of blood rushing through my ears.

So I hadn't been imagining things after all. He *had* felt it.

The connection between us. Adrenaline began coursing through my veins, making me feel lightheaded and ridiculously euphoric.

For the first time, I saw Antonio looked slightly embarrassed and awkward as he struggled to find the right words.

"I hope you don't mind me saying so..."

No, I don't. Say it! Say it! I cried out in my head. *I find you totally irresistible as well!*

"But, Fiona, I couldn't help noticing you were finding it very difficult tonight."

Oh, God, yes! As I looked up into his darkened eyes, heavy with seriousness, my stomach turned to liquid and my entire being glowed with warmth. This was it. I could just about taste him on my lips. I mentally willed him to stop with all this unnecessary talking, reach out for me and take me into his arms.

"I realize this is only your second class, but I couldn't help noticing you are still extremely tense, even a little frightened of letting yourself relax into the music and this is stopping you from really enjoying yourself."

Come on, just take me! I'm ready! I've been ready all bloody night, I mentally screamed out as the tension between us reached breaking point.

"So, Fiona, if you don't mind, what I would like to suggest is you meet me here for a private lesson on Monday night. Without the distraction of the other dancers around you, I think you might not feel as intimidated and nervous."

Private lessons! The Latin god and me alone, together, in the same room.

Instantly, I felt faint with wanting. Oh, *obviously* there was more to Antonio's suggestion of *extra tuition* or whatever he wanted to call it. Much more. I couldn't deny at that particular moment I was a little surprised, as well as charmed by him being so coy about our mutual attraction. But then I wasn't exactly laying my feelings out on the table, either.

Not that I would have taken him for being the shy type, but I was more than willing to take it slowly and let Antonio set the pace.

"I'm sorry if I've spoken out of place. After all, you probably have other commitments or a boyfriend waiting for you, I just thought it might help you to overcome your nervousness."

"No! I don't have a boyfriend or commitments," I blurted out, finally finding my voice. "I am totally boyfriendless and commitment-free. I would love to meet you here on Monday night. What time?"

"The same time, say, seven-thirty?"

"Sounds perfect."

"Well that's great, then." He smiled with obvious relief. "If you would just like to fix up the cost with the center on Monday morning, I'll look forward to seeing you Monday night. Right now, I'd better lock up and get out of here before we both get shut in for the night."

The look of mischief on Antonio's face as he said that just about undid me and it wasn't until I was sitting outside in my car did the part of the conversation about fixing up the cost of the private lesson sink into my brain.

Confusion and dumb, sick horror struck me at once and I almost retched. Pay for our rendezvous! Was he serious? Or some kind of a gigolo and, seeing me for the lonely, frustrated woman I am, thought he'd cash in and make a buck on the side?

No! God, how ridiculous am I? All this business with my lying, cheating ex had completely tainted my view of the opposite sex.

When I thought about it a bit more, it dawned on me just how paranoid I'd become of late.

Of course, if we were to meet up under the pretenses of a private dancing lesson, it had to look legitimate, at least until we were both sure of the other's intentions. Anyway, this way it was more exiting. *Just like in the movies!* Secret liaisons disguised as dancing lessons. How incredibly romantic.

Oh, God, I couldn't wait to tell the girls. I hadn't felt this degree of excitement since my teenage years. But then a horrible thought struck me. If I confided in the girls, they would insist on meeting Antonio, and I would be forced to 'fess up to the entire dancing thing. But it wasn't the only reason for my second thoughts. The consequences of the girls getting involved could be disastrous at this delicate, almost embryonic stage of our relationship. Shit, he'd be frightened off before I even had the chance to get into his sexy skin-tight trousers!

No, I couldn't risk them spoiling it all for me. As much as I knew it would *kill* me, keeping it to myself, that was exactly what I'd have to do until such time as Antonio made his move.

Chapter Seven

The weekend stretched out before me, an endless void of almost painful expectation until I could finally see Antonio again. Not even the prospect of Stacey Cooper's bachelorette party that night, which everyone had been talking about for weeks, could completely fill the cavernous weekend I now found myself facing.

Stacey Cooper had almost become a member of our sisterhood in high school before getting all bookish on us. By the middle of year ten, she'd caved in to the ever-present scholastic pressure to get a decent education and, instead of joining us in the ladies' for a smoke at lunchtime, she'd joined the debating team. From there, she'd gone on to become a boring, strung-out overachiever, thus gaining a top place in college before discovering sex and drugs were infinitely more exciting and fashionable than the works of Shakespeare and Yeats.

As a consequence, rather than a high-profile job in journalism as planned, Stacey was *still* 'enjoying a couple of years' break from studying' and worked in center management. On most days, her voice could be heard ringing out in crackling monotone throughout the center, summoning parents of displaced toddlers to the help desk situated behind the food court to collect their wailing offspring.

But for some people like Stacey, despite various setbacks, fate continues to shine on them regardless. Not only had she scored a glamorous job in center management, but in the coup of the century, Stacey had also managed to snare the attentions of the divine Mr. Simon Baker.

Thirty-eight-years old, recently divorced *and* the senior executive manager of the entire shopping complex, he came with the added bonus of being a dead ringer for Pierce Brosnan *and* owning a midnight-blue Porsche, now proudly parked beneath a purpose-built carport behind the center.

So after her having spectacularly fallen flat on her face at college and ended up in rehab for three months, we'd barely had time to gloat before she sported not only a great job but a three-carat diamond engagement ring *and* a fiancé any one of us would have gladly murdered our mothers for the chance of having beside us in bed.

Now, as a crowning glory of her perfect life, she was forgoing the usual bachelorette pub and club crawl for a night of drunken debauchery with Bad Boys Afloat, a troupe of gorgeous male strippers who did their thing wearing very little, or if rumors were to be believed, nothing at all, on a large converted ferry on the harbor.

No one we knew had ever pulled out all the stops like Stacey had with planning this wedding.

Up until now, it'd been considered the height of sophistication to hire *one* sad, scared male stripper for a girl's twenty-first birthday bash. But an entire troupe of glistening, naked muscled men ready and willing to entertain you and your closest friends on this, your last big night out before you're shackled with the chains of matrimony, was something completely unprecedented among our circle of friends. I hated to admit it, but I, along with the other fifty women invited, couldn't help but be impressed by her class.

Of course, when your parents are as rich as Stacey's, being stylish and classy isn't too difficult a feat to pull off. Stacey's father happened to be a prominent member of the local council as well as owning the largest luxury sports car dealership between the city and the mountains, which could have had something to do with her meteoritic rise in status from rehab to center management.

* * * *

"Come on, Fi! What the hell is keeping you, girl? It's only a bloody dress, not an obstacle course," yelled Kim from the other side of the bedroom door.

The girls had been ready to go for ages and I could hear them out in the lounge slowly getting pissed on Janine's rapidly dwindling alcohol supply while I contorted myself into knots, trying to work out how to fasten the multitude of different-length straps that made up the torturous contraption I'd borrowed from Kim, better known as a backless, seamless, halter-neck bra.

Ignoring Kim, I continued my struggle. Twisting and wriggling, I persisted in my quest to pour myself into the embarrassingly short and very, very tight dress I'd been coerced into buying this afternoon. As I at last untangled myself, I made a mental note that in future I'd definitely be leaving my slutty fashion advisors at home.

Appraising the image reflecting back at me from Janine's full-length mirror, I groaned. God, I couldn't be seen in public wearing this. I'm sure there are some people who possess that air of confidence and can pull off a 'look'. But, sadly, I wasn't one of them.

Not this look.

At least, not sober.

"There'd better be some wine left when I get out there or I'm not leaving the house!" I bellowed, regretting now I hadn't had a couple of fortifying drinks *before* I'd started getting dressed.

Instead of giving the impression of sleek sophistication, though, as Rachel in full saleswoman mode had put it, it seemed I was looking at a whore standing there in a backless sequined black micro-mini dress, and as for the new shoes the girls had insisted I also buy, they were so pointy and high that even if I did by some miracle make it to the boat without breaking my neck, I'd be crippled for life before the party got going.

If that wasn't bad enough, adding to my growing unease was the fact my outfit had cost me almost an entire week's pay. Money I could ill-afford to waste. Although, as the girls pointed out, there is also no point dwelling on minor details when you've just made a possibly life-altering investment in a genuine Dolce & Gabbana-inspired creation from Cue.

"Fiona McCrutchen! If you don't get your fat arse out here right now, we are going to miss the fucking boat. Move it, will you!" screamed Rachel and I knew if I put it off any longer, things were going to turn ugly.

Walking out of the house a short time later, I felt everyone in the street was peeking out their windows and whispering in horror, "What was that girl thinking when she chose *that* dress!"

I was wondering the same thing. Just getting out of the house took that much effort it wasn't until I reached the end of the driveway, expecting to see a taxi waiting, that I spotted Jason leaning back nonchalantly on the hood of his car, arms crossed over his chest, eyeing us approvingly.

"You girls look so gorgeous I might see if those Bad Boy dancers, or whatever the hell they're called, will give me a job for the night. I'd hate to see all your efforts wasted on those fruity strippers," he teased before noticing the dark expression creeping up Rachel's face, warning him of an imminent tantrum. "Well, that is, I would, but of course I am a one-woman man myself." Reaching out, he squeezed her butt affectionately. "So I'll just have to be content playing chauffeur tonight instead, won't I, babe?"

By the time we got there, the jetty buzzed with over-excited, over-dressed women of all ages tottering about in high heels. Every few seconds another high-pitched shriek met gales of laughter as someone else stumbled awkwardly, their expensive heels finding yet another gap in the weathered wooden jetty. Aided by the half bottle of Riesling I'd polished off on the drive down here, my confidence level rose dramatically upon seeing more sequins flashing in the floodlit car park than the Gay

Mardi Gras.

If I was going to look like a tart, at least I wasn't alone.

The promised luxuriously appointed cruise boat looked barely seaworthy as it rolled precariously on the small swell at end of the jetty. With just about twenty minutes before we were due to hoist anchor, a steady stream of caterers were filing past on their way to the boat, laden with foil-covered platters of food and weighed down with dozens of crates of wine.

Well, this is more like it. My earlier apprehensions were nothing but a distant memory, along with the dregs of Riesling in the empty bottle to which I still clung for some mysterious reason.

Now that Jason's taxi services were no longer required, Rachel sent him on his way with a peck on the cheek and a dismissive wave of her hand, but not before she extracted a promise from him that he would return sometime around one-thirty to collect us all again.

As soon as we waved Jason off, the four of us made our way over to join the growing crowd of women fussing around bride-to-be Stacey. Decked out in an elaborate costume consisting of a black leather tutu, pink fairy wand, thigh-high white lace-up boots and topped off with a white tulle bridal veil and tiara, she resembled a confused dominatrix.

"Hi, girls, you ready to get blind?" challenged Stacey, loud enough to incite an excited chorus of approval from those around her.

Obviously, the party had already begun, at least for Stacey, who, accompanied by a depleted bottle of Moët, appeared slightly flushed.

She wasn't the only one. Ever since the copious amount of alcohol had been seen being loaded up on HMS Leaky, expectations had almost reached fever-pitch and everyone was desperate to get on board and begin the festivities.

As yet there'd been no sign of the beefy, oiled strippers we'd been drooling over since Kim had discovered a promotional photo of them in the local newspaper, but then, I suppose it would have spoiled their image a tad if they'd rocked up in dirty old track pants and running shoes.

Thirty minutes later, accompanied by a great bellow of diesel smoke, the old clanker lurched noisily into action and we finally inched away from the jetty.

Clutching our plastic wine flutes, it took some time for everyone to find their sea legs as the ferry made its bumpy way toward the middle of the harbor against the chop stirred up from loitering speed boats. Had the water calmed or was it my third glass of wine? Anyway, I discovered I could make it to the bar without clinging to the railings in novice ice skater-style. It might have also been because I'd finally succumbed to the pressure bearing down on my toes and eased those strappy, stylish implements of torture from my throbbing feet before concealing them under a seat at the front of the boat together with my purse.

With a crash, the narrow-paneled door leading out to the front deck swung open and Stacey stumbled out toward us.

"Hi, Stacey!"

"Fuck, I need some fresh air," she groaned and collapsed exhausted on the cushioned bench beside us with a sigh of relief. "You girls all got a drink? Good. Don't let the side down, will you? The way my bloody aunts are tossing it back in there, we're going to have to pull in somewhere and find a liquor store before the blokes even begin the show."

"They're actually on the boat, are they? Now. As we speak?" I asked.

"Well, they're not dropping in by parachute, are they?" Stacey smiled. "They were already on the boat when it picked us up and right now they're downstairs getting ready for later. Aunt Julia thought she saw one of them when she got lost looking for the ladies'."

"I can't believe how lucky you are, Stacey. Simon must trust you heaps if he's letting you go all out like this," commented Rachel, almost choking on her envy.

"Oh, God, don't kid yourselves, girls. His bloody sisters

are in there acting like watchdogs over me. You can be sure every gruesome detail will get back to him. Not that he'll be giving me a rundown of *his* bachelor night. From what I've learned, they've booked a room at the Townhouse down at the Cross. Well, you know what that means, don't you?"

We all looked at her with the naïveté of three-year-olds.

"It *means* Simon, or at least his friends, will be organizing a few hookers to entertain them."

Even we found it difficult to hide our shock at Stacey's bluntness, not to mention her calm acceptance of the idea of her future husband screwing a prostitute only a week before their wedding.

"Oh, my God, how terrible!" I exclaimed. The pain of my own recent betrayal, combined with the effects of numerous glasses of wine, caused me to blurt out the first thing in my head. "I don't know how you can be so calm about it, Stacey. Couldn't you have put your foot down? I'm sure even Simon would agree that prostitutes are a bit over the top."

"Oh, Fiona, don't be too concerned about Simon. I'm not," she laughed. "He's that bloody paranoid about herpes, I doubt if he'll be game to get his dick out in case one of the whores gives him more than he paid for. No, Simon assured me that the girls are more for the benefit of those terminally married blokes. You know, the ones who haven't seen a decent piece of arse since their honeymoon. Anyway, he claims he's so exhausted keeping up with my demands in that area he would need a hydraulic lift to get his pecker up for anyone else."

Oh, yeah, I thought, that's only what he's telling you. From one duped wife to an impending dupe, I could have told her that once the tits are out, their brain goes into hibernation and herpes will be the last thing on his mind, along with his upcoming marriage vows. But Stacey looked confident in her ability to keep the saintly eyes of Simon from wandering I didn't have the heart to disillusion her on that score. I suppose, as my mum was keen to point out, not all blokes are cheating bastards like my ex.

"What are you going to do about the sisters-in-law from hell out there? It'll spoil your whole night if you have to behave yourself," said Janine bluntly, as usual putting into words what the rest of us were only game to think.

"Get 'em both pissed as farts and hope they pass out before the strippers come up," cackled Rachel as she stood up and began stumbling toward the bar for another refill.

Stacey leaned in closer and whispered, "There's the problem, you see, they don't drink."

"Bullshit. Stacey! How could you think of marrying into a family of puritans like that? Next thing you know, they'll have you going to fucking church every Sunday and acting like one of the *Stepford Wives*," bellowed Kim, causing Stacey to wince before checking nervously if anyone inside had heard.

It seemed relations between Stacey and Simon's female relatives were a little strained, going by the sudden look of worry that passed over her usually serene face.

Kim, however, didn't give a stuff who heard. Draining the rest of her half-full glass in one mouthful, she proclaimed to all within hearing range — actually, half the boat — "The drink waiters around here totally suck! I'm off to the bar!" before she took off after Rachel.

"Kim!" yelled Janine. "Bring me back a couple of bottles of vino, will you, luv, my bloody feet are killing me!"

"Well, if you want us to dispose of your problem in-laws overboard, just let us know," I joked in an attempt to lighten the atmosphere, seeing how tense Stacey grew just talking about them.

After a few seconds' thoughtful silence, Stacey turned to me with a big smile.

"Actually, you know what? It's not such a bad idea, Fi."

"Jeez, I'm only joking!"

"No, listen, I just had a great idea. I know it might be a little bit tricky, but I'd be grateful to you forever if you could help me with this one, Fi. *Please!*"

How could anyone possibly say no to the desperate pleas of a whip-wielding Domme wearing a white veil, who at that moment looked as though she was about to burst into tears? Certainly not me.

"Help with what exactly?" I asked cautiously.

"Help me get them a little bit pissed. You know, loosen them up a bit."

"But didn't you just say they don't drink? How are we going to manage that?"

Stacey tapped the side of her nose and winked mischievously. "Well, maybe you can help me with this."

"I don't know, Stacey. I'd hate to get anyone into trouble."

"*I'll* be the one in trouble, with Simon, if those two out there go blabbing, won't I? Anyway, I'm sure they'll have a better time if they have a drink or two in them. Right now they look as though they're at a damn funeral. Pure misery, they are."

This didn't sound good and I was beginning to have serious regrets about bringing up the entire subject.

Janine leaned back on a chair, resting her head on the railing, and I thought she'd dozed off or passed out until I heard her pipe up.

"Come on, Fi. Live dangerously for a change. Go wild! It's just a bit of fun and no one's going to get hurt."

"But..."

"Look, I'm only talking about one or two drinks, Fi, no more," said Stacey. "They won't even know. Then tomorrow they'll look back on it and think it was the best night out they've had in years."

"Yeah, go on, Fi. It would do you good to take a chance for once. And besides, anything to get Stacey off the hook with the guard dogs inside would be worth it."

By this time, Rachel and Kim were back, clutching a couple of bottles of wine.

"Jeez, Stace. Where the hell did you find the fucking drink-Nazis behind the bar? I just about had to promise them my firstborn to get a couple of bottles of wine out of them. Anyone would think it was coming out of their bloody wages!"

"Yeah, sorry about that, Rach. With all this crap now about 'responsible service of alcohol laws', I suppose they're all paranoid about someone falling overboard drunk and suing them. I'll go and have a word with them in a sec," she said, in a bid to calm Rachel down before turning her attention back to me. "What about it, Fi? Are you up for a bit of a challenge?"

"Okay," I relented, "but only if you promise me it won't get out of hand."

With her hand over her leather-clad breast, Stacey declared earnestly, "I promise."

It would have been quite convincing had she not been tottering slightly on her feet with a big wasted grin on her face.

"What the hell is going on with you two? And why don't we know about it?" demanded Rachel to Stacey and me.

Chapter Eight

Stacey owed me big-time for this one. If she didn't go as far as naming her firstborn child after me, I swore to God, there'd be hell to pay.

I managed to stall for just enough time to down a couple of large glasses of Dutch courage before they sent me on my way with chants of *"Go, Girl, You Go, Girl, Go!"* propelling me on toward an entirely new level of stupidity.

As soon as I stepped inside the boat's main cabin from the relative haven of the bow, the first thing that struck me was the noise. Bloody deafening and, oh, my God, the smell. Well, just let me say, if terrorists bombed the Bloomingdale's perfume and cosmetics floor, even that couldn't rival the cocktail of Chanel No. 5, Dior's J'adore and Avon's Lilac Kiss. All that combined with the sour odor of spilled wine filled my befuddled head with the never-to-be-forgotten scent of *Eau de Yuk I Need a Bucket*.

Above the noise of high-pitched shrieks and laughter emanating from almost fifty smashed females, the music sounded like a static mumbling. I found it kind of hard not to stare at Simon's elderly aunt. When I'd seen her earlier, waiting for the ferry to arrive, she might have easily been mistaken for the Queen Mother. Now, though, only an hour later and after God knew how many drinks, she was dancing barefoot on the tiny dance floor with dangerous gusto to Beyoncé's latest hit, just inches from the makeshift tables piled high with food.

The caterers, meanwhile, were looking across at the rising mayhem with open concern at what would become of their edible works of art, which they had painstakingly laid out platters of sometime before, when this mob attacked. They were going to be massacred, for sure. By a horde of red-faced, ravenous women. Well, that was if Simon's aunt didn't keel over and annihilate them first.

It reminded me of a call to the wild and at any moment I expected to hear David Attenborough's disembodied voice coming though the speakers.

"As we can see, a wall of richly plumed females have now sighted their prey and already they are salivating at the sight of so much easily digestible food. As expected in these almost ceremonial surroundings, tension among the tribe members has been steadily escalating and a stampede in now inevitable. Older members of the tribe, disadvantaged by both invalidism and slow reflexes, are only too aware of the precarious nature of their own survival and can been seen snapping at the younger and more virile females as they try to re-establish their authority within the group. The situation is fraught with possible danger as each female fights for the prime feeding position in these final, tense moments before the main attack begins..."

Well, for me, it was now or never. While everyone else stuffed their faces, or in the case of Simon's aunt, stuffed her handbag full of prawns, I slipped past them, and within minutes, had found the narrow door with *No Admittance* written on it. Located between the main bar and the toilets, it was exactly where Stacey had described.

For a moment, I stood there, one hand poised on the polished silver handle, and took a deep breath. Could I go through with it? Through that door loomed the unknown. I couldn't believe I was even contemplating going down there. Behind me, the muffled sounds of eating were interrupted every now and again by those of breaking plates and more high-pitched cackling.

Only one thing was for sure. I knew I wasn't keen to face the anarchy back in the main cabin any time soon, if ever.

Opening the door a couple of inches, I then peered down into the cool darkness below. The hypnotic whirring of the boat's engines felt soothing after the chaos I'd recently left behind, luring me deeper within the hull. Closing the door carefully behind me, I began feeling my way down the dimly lit narrow stairway.

I was well and truly on my own now. Anything could happen to me down here and no one upstairs would hear a thing. My stomach lurched nervously and it was a good job I hadn't eaten anything, for if I had, I reckoned I would've been sick. Stacey's directions only went as far as the door up on deck and, caught up as I'd been in all the excitement of the moment, unfortunately, I hadn't given too much thought to what I would do once I made it past that barrier.

I had only progressed a few feet into the bowels of the boat when, above the pounding of my own heart, the faint sound of distinctly male voices came drifting up to me from the depths. I sent up a silent prayer Stacey wasn't sending me down here to make a complete and utter arse of myself.

My nervousness, however, shrank at the memory of the madness and noise from which I'd just escaped and, well, I figured I really didn't have anything to lose by coming down here except my already tattered dignity. And when I thought about it, even that didn't really bear salvaging after all the abuse it'd received lately.

Considering my current whereabouts, I was grateful I'd been coerced into forking out an outrageous amount of money for what amounted to about a tea-towel's worth of fabric. But still I felt sassy and daring wearing it and, combined with the alcohol I'd recently consumed, it effectively armed me with a healthy measure of self-confidence. That, together with an exhilarating rush of adrenaline, elevated me to an unprecedented level of bravado as a tiny sliver of light guided me toward a door at the end of the short, stuffy corridor.

The deep timbre of male laughter abruptly stopped when I knocked timidly on the faded woodwork.

Suddenly, the door was wrenched open and I was confronted by the sight of six beautiful, tan and incredibly large men with equally large muscles, all of whom glistened in various stages of undress. All of a sudden, my mouth went dry and for a split second I couldn't remember exactly what the hell I was doing down there.

"Hello, beautiful!" said the bronzed Adonis before me with a dazzling smile. "You're a bit early aren't you, honey? The show doesn't start for another hour yet."

"I'm really sorry to bother you, but I was wondering if I could ask a favor?"

"Hey, lady, we're only paid to dance…" came the reply from a deeply tan hunk standing behind Adonis, wearing nothing but army fatigue pants and muscles.

"Oh, God, I don't mean that!" I gasped, instantly feeling the heat rising on my face. "I came down here to ask if anyone…had any…actually if anyone could spare any…"

"Come on, what is it, sweetheart? Out with it. Have you found a bloke upstairs and need a condom, or is it some weed you're after?" prompted a boyish blond impatiently, wearing a shiny black G-string and oiling his pecs over in the corner.

"God, no! I just wanted to know if anyone here had any vodka or gin," I stammered.

I had never felt as stupid in my life as I did right at that moment. I tried self-consciously to yank down the hem of my dress. With six pairs of eyes on me, their expressions ranging from amusement to irritation, the hot sting of tears pricked the backs of my eyes. I felt totally out of my depth. I felt horribly sober as the cold, hard reality of what I was doing suddenly hit me.

Oh, my God, they're practically naked. What the hell was I thinking, coming down here?

"Bloody hell, you hear that, guys? Sounds like the women upstairs have drunk the boat dry already. Looks like we're in for a rough night tonight, boys, that is, if they haven't passed out by the time we get up there."

I started to panic. This was not going well. I got the distinct impression they were taking the piss out of me.

"No, please, it's not that at all. It's for the bride!" I cried.

That got their attention!

"Bloody hell, she *must* be having second thoughts if she needs vodka already," laughed the dark Adonis, winking at the others.

By this time, I'd progressed through nervousness to the edge of really losing it. I felt such an idiot and it wasn't helping matters that they were obviously enjoying my discomfort.

"It's not *for* the damn bride!" I yelled.

My anger ballooned out from my mouth, filling the tiny changing room, charging it with a surge of hostility which felt ugly and out of place in light of the party atmosphere upstairs. I cringed, horrified by my outburst. Why was it that when I desperately needed to take a stand and show some backbone, I retreated like a mute coward, but as soon as a diplomatic approach is required, I turned into a screaming harridan? Their previous good humor instantly evaporated as they all turned to the cranky red-faced tart at the door and I wished I'd never agreed to come down here in the first place.

I had blown it. Utterly.

"Look, I'm sorry, really. The thing is…well, it is a bit of an emergency. Well, kind of, anyway. The bride's future sisters-in-law are as straight as bloody Quakers and up there just waiting for Stacey, she's the bride, to put one foot out of line and they're going to crucify her for the rest of her married life. All we want to do is get them to chill out and enjoy themselves so they'll leave poor Stacey alone to have some fun. But they don't touch wine, or alcohol for that matter, and we were hoping to find some vodka to liven up their orange juice, you know, to loosen them up a bit. Just one drink. We don't want them to do anything silly, mind you. We just want them to enjoy themselves. Otherwise it's going to ruin Stacey's night."

Finally, I'd run out of steam. I had given it my best shot, but by the silence surrounding me, I'd accomplished nothing apart from making a fool of myself.

I half-expected them to shrug, say there was nothing they could do and tell me to leave. To my amazement, though, Adonis, after a few seconds' deliberation, turned to the other guys and said, "Did you hear that, boys? Looks like we have a bit of a situation happening upstairs. What do you say we see what we can do to help out this lovely lady and the unfortunate bride-to-be?"

I couldn't believe my luck.

They didn't have any vodka with them, unfortunately, but for once the gods must have been smiling on me, for they knew exactly where to lay their hands on some. Adonis, or Patrick, as I was soon to learn, went off to raid the boat's storeroom, located a couple of doors up the narrow passage, directly below the bar. Here, spirits were stockpiled, tucked safely away from any marauding drunks upstairs.

Having pulled off what I saw as the coup of the century, I now felt entitled to bask briefly in the elation only success of this magnitude can conjure up within. That was the best part, though. Mission successfully completed, I was surprised to find myself relaxing in the company of these breathtakingly gorgeous men and, unless I'd become totally delusional in the last fifteen minutes, I could have sworn they were quite impressed by my audaciousness, the way they were laughing at what they considered to be my resourcefulness.

"I don't fucking believe it!" yelled Rachel, jumping up and down, as minutes later I casually sauntered across the bow and triumphantly presented a half bottle of Smirnoff to Stacey, who stood slack-jawed with shock for a few seconds.

"Oh. My. God. What a legend! How the fuck did you pull it off?" she screamed, finally finding her voice.

The looks on their faces were priceless. What I would have given to have had a camera handy at that exact moment.

"Well, simple really. I sneaked downstairs while everyone was eating and found their door and, well, I just asked them." By the admiration oozing from their faces, you'd think I'd presented them with undeniable proof Kylie Minogue's tits were in fact made of silicon. "Of course, I also told them if we didn't do something about the sober sisters from hell in there, it would completely ruin the bride's big night out, and I suppose they didn't relish the idea of taking their clothes off for some sad, sober tart in a veil."

"What were they like, Fi? Were they naked?" asked Kim eagerly, no doubt picturing a male harem downstairs.

"Of course they weren't!" I laughed. "Well, not completely naked. One of them was wearing a loincloth."

"Oh, my God," screeched Stacey.

"Fuck it! I knew I should have gone myself," yelled Janine, suddenly wide awake with interest.

"Shut up, you two! Go on, Fi, tell us everything."

"Not much to tell, really. I went down and asked them if they could help, then, while Patrick, he's the one who looks like Vin Diesel — you'll see what I mean later on — well, while he was off raiding some storeroom under the bar, I waited in the dressing room with the other guys."

"And?"

"And nothing. We just talked for a bit and Patrick came back and I came back up here. End of story."

Only then did it sink in what I had done and I felt dizzy with satisfaction. I was a *legend*. It was amazing. I had made it through the entire experience without once making a fool of myself — well, almost, anyway. It was true! Not only that, but from what I could recall, I'd been actually ultra-cool and not the drooling idiot I usually am around gorgeous half-naked men. Not that I make a habit of bursting into the dressing rooms of male strippers. Thinking about it now, it had been nothing short of a miracle.

"Thank you so much, Fiona, you're the best, really," gushed Stacey. For the first time since stepping onto the boat, she actually looked relaxed and reached out to hug me in relief.

The evening was wearing on and the heat inside the

boat was stifling. Owing to this, Simon's older sisters were gratefully accepting yet another glass of orange juice from Stacey and even going as far as complimenting her on being such a thoughtful hostess. No one, least of all them, noticed they were the only ones benefiting from Stacey's newfound attentiveness. True to her word, Stacey had only doctored the first couple of glasses and since then had played it safe, careful not to overdo it. Her plan happened to be working brilliantly, though, and they had finally lightened up and were even dancing with the others on the crowded dance floor.

Operation Watch Dog was deemed a complete success. Stacey was having the time of her life, Rachel and Kim polishing off the rest of the vodka and Janine and I kicking back with a bottle of wine, laughing at the oldies strutting their stuff on the dance floor.

Suddenly, the music stopped and over the speakers a male voice cut through the all-female racket.

"Ladies, if you would like to make your way to the main cabin, tonight's performance from the original Bad Boys Afloat will begin in approximately five minutes' time."

The crush that followed had to be seen to be believed. Not everyone made a mad scramble for the prime positions to gain the best vantage point, though. Many of the more timid guests were equally desperate to move *out* of the line of fire and find an inconspicuous spot where they hoped not to attract the attention of the upcoming hunks of burning love, soon to be strutting their stuff before us all in glorious Technicolor.

It's funny, really, how you never can tell the goers from the flee-ers when you're all standing around chatting politely — that is, before the socially equalizing addition of alcohol enters the picture. Women, who only a couple of hours ago, had given you the impression they would faint with shock, if, say for instance, the subject of oral sex came up in general conversation, after a bottle and a half of chardonnay were violently ejecting interlopers from their prime position at the front. On the other hand, other women who'd previously boasted they would be the first to cop a feel began mumbling their excuses as soon as the announcement sounded and were currently retreating to safer ground on the pretenses of needing to make a desperate dash to the loo.

I must admit normally I would've been making for the hills, hot on the heels of all the other cowards. But alas, with friends like mine, I really had no choice but to put on a brave face and pray I'd get through the evening without having any dangly bits dangled in my face.

The air crackled with excitement as Stacey was led to the middle of the room by her matron of honor and bridesmaids, then promptly seated directly opposite the small cleared dance floor.

"Fi! What are you waiting for?" Janine called to me as I lingered by the bar at the back of the room. "Come on, you're not going to see a thing from there!"

No, I wasn't. And that was kind of the point.

Having recently had a chance to get to know the blokes who would be shortly stripping for our drunken enjoyment, I couldn't now think of them as faceless, nameless bodies. Just the idea of coming face-to-face with the naked, glistening torso of Patrick, for instance, made my insides shrink with embarrassment.

I'm not nearly pissed enough for this, I thought, grabbing two glasses of wine from the fellow working on the bar.

By the salacious looks he was casting over some of the younger and more inebriated partygoers, he thought his chances of getting lucky tonight were better than average. It made no difference that he wasn't exactly Chris Hemsworth, and he knew it. Once the clothes were off and Patrick and the others were once again safely locked up below — for their own protection — any available male above deck would be fair game for the frenzied, frustrated ladies left wanting a little more than an eyeful.

Then I saw them. Pushing their way to the bar beside

me were Simon's sisters, Janet and Sandra, giggling and ordering another glass of wine from the barman. If I hadn't known better, I would have thought they were nightclub veterans. I, for one, was impressed when in one fluid motion they scooped up their glasses from the bar and made their way back to the dance floor without spilling a drop, ready for the show to begin. They appeared to be having a great time now they'd finally let their hair down and, I have to say, I was relieved for poor Stacey's sake. She was free to enjoy herself now.

The morality police were vanquished with one vodka and orange. No one, least of all Janet and Sandra, would be spoiling Stacey's big night.

Above the noise of Ricky Martin's *She Bangs* came the deep male voice of the compère.

"Ladies, may I welcome you to. The one. The only. *Bad Boys Afloat.* All-male dancing extravaganza!"

It seemed as though the entire boat erupted in hysterical female screams as colorful spotlights illuminated the small dance floor, complete with Stacey, who, with her veil askew, sat giggling with nervous anticipation.

"There you are!"

Just as I tossed back the last of my wine, Kim yanked me forward to where the others were standing, just behind Stacey.

Right in the line of fire.

Great!

There wasn't time to react. One minute I was safely hiding at the bar, all set to order another liquid hangover, and the next found me dragged ringside, with no escape from the only show I would ever attend where I would be looking at the ceiling for the entire duration.

Led by Patrick who, complete with a very phallic-looking baton, was dressed up as a policeman, they emerged from the side of the boat and all but exploded on stage as the compère's voice again boomed above the roar of the music.

"Ladies, meet the delectable Patrick, ex-Chippendale and

more than willing to frisk any of you ladies who get out of hand here tonight."

I had to physically hold Rachel back as she screamed out to Patrick, all but begging him to use his baton on her in the most obscene way imaginable.

By the time the compère had finished introducing the other guys, they'd formed a line across the floor in front of poor Stacey who, despite her earlier bravado, looked like a scared rabbit in a trap. For one brief moment, I caught Patrick's eyes and he winked at me and smiled then, without missing a beat, proceeded to straddle Stacey's lap, grinding himself against her breasts while the others continued from one girl to the next, drawing both screams of delight and mortification as they ramped up the dirty-dancing routine to fever pitch, much to the delight of those watching from a safe distance, say, the back of the dance floor. I'd never seen guys dance like this at the nightclub. I doubted they'd make it out of the place unmolested if they did.

It was wild. Pure madness. I couldn't believe these same women, who earlier had been enthusiastically discussing microfiber cleaning mitts, were at this moment almost falling over one another in a desperate attempt to touch the gyrating, sweating guys slowly exposing their buffed and well-pumped bodies. Even worse, among them were Simon's aunt and Stacey's mother! I only hoped they remembered all this next week at the wedding.

After tying up Stacey and rubbing her face in his groin, Tim, who I recognized from downstairs, looked out into the audience, eager to spot his next lucky victim. Suddenly, he lunged into the crowd and a huge cheer went up. Instantly, I recognized Simon's elder sister, Janet, giggling hysterically as she clung onto Tim's broad chest, gazing longingly up at his smiling face. Of course, of all the women eager to manhandle the most delicious male flesh most of us would ever lay eyes on, it wasn't simply a coincidence Janet had been targeted for special treatment and I experienced a twinge of guilt for having landed her in it. Not that she minded, though.

Flashes exploded all around the boat as Tim pushed Janet's hand down his pants and started bucking against her closed fist and rolling his eyes in mock ecstasy.

"Oh, my God, *look!*" screamed Kim aghast, pointing over to a group of ladies on her left.

I couldn't make out what exactly was going on from where I stood, peering through a wall of sweating male bodies, but it looked as though some kind of tussle had started between Simon's relatives. Rather than put the guys off their dancing, though, it appeared to actually spur their performance to more suggestive and risqué heights.

Amid a frenzy of shouting emerged Simon's other sister, Sandra, literally falling out of the crowd, right at the feet of Patrick and another dancer, who by that stage were wearing nothing but the tiniest pairs of shorts which left absolutely nothing to the imagination.

At first, Sandra looked as though she was attempting to rescue party-girl Janet's by now mortally wounded reputation by dragging her from the dance floor, where she remained, eagerly grabbing hold of any exposed male flesh that came within arm's reach.

Unfortunately, by the time anyone woke up to her intentions, it was too late.

Really, considering her condition, it was an impressive feat in itself how quickly she managed to divest herself of what had earlier in the evening been a very prim navy and white pleated skirt and double-breasted jacket. If they gave a prize for speed stripping, I swear Sandra would have had very little competition.

At that point in the proceedings, I admit I was a very long way from being sober, but I found no pleasure in witnessing Sandra make a complete fool of herself. Patrick and the others, rather than getting her off the dance floor and back into her clothes, were encouraging her, simulating some extremely suggestive sexual gymnastics which I swear must be illegal in at least a couple of states. Sandra, meanwhile, was tossing her once pristine white blouse over toward where Simon's aunt and the rest of her family were staring, open-mouthed in shock.

For Sandra and Janet, though, there was no stopping them. Now liberated from their life-long prison of sexual repression and pretentious etiquette, nothing held them back. Thankfully, sanity prevailed and Sandra and Janet were eventually wrestled off the dance floor and to the rear of the boat for some well needed fresh air. Unfortunately, not before at least a dozen cameras captured the moment of their social demise for posterity.

Thirty minutes later, I don't know who was more relieved when the guys finally whipped off the slithers of black Lycra masquerading as G-strings for the last time and vanished in a cloud of tan, oiled flesh to the haven of their dressing room, leaving the audience delirious and breathless.

Chapter Nine

The intensity of the glare raining down on us as we sat at a trendy alfresco café for brunch penetrated even my industrial-strength sunglasses, scorching a painful path right through my brain.

"Oh, God, I feel shithouse," croaked Rachel with the remnants of her voice after last night's madness.

"Tell someone who gives a shit, Rach. We've all got our own fucking problems."

Kim looked in even worse shape than Rachel, if that was humanly possible. This was no friendly get-together over a couple of skinny cappuccinos, but serious misery-sharing on a grand scale. Hangovers seem to bring out the worst in people, and unfortunately, we were no exception.

"I still can't believe what happened last night. I don't suppose anyone's heard from Stacey yet?" Janine asked quietly, carefully nursing her head in her arms.

"The last time I saw her, she was in the gents' with her tongue down the throat of that sleazy barman," mumbled Kim in disgust.

"No way!" I shrieked instantly regretting my outburst as a hot poker of pain seared my head in two.

I couldn't pretend I wasn't shocked, not so much by Stacey's indiscretion as her bad taste.

"What the fuck were you doing in the gents'?" mumbled Janine.

"Well, better that than wade through the vomit in the women's. Honestly, I can't believe one person could be responsible for so much spew."

Unfortunately, the subject of Sandra's dash from the

dance floor to the toilets sparked another memory, this one of Janet passed out cold on the dance floor.

"I hope Janet's all right?"

Even with a hangover of biblical proportions to deal with, I couldn't help feeling guilty about the way the night had ended — at least for those two, anyway.

"Christ, Fi, you worry about everyone. Didn't that cute ambulance man say once she had her stomach pumped, she'd be right as rain?" responded Rachel, sounding like she figured it for no big deal. After all, she'd spent the occasional night curled up on a hospital gurney while some clumsy intern stuck a tube down her throat and it hadn't done her any harm.

"Yeah, I suppose."

"Well, then, stop stressing out, will you? No one held a gun to her head and made her drink that last bottle of wine. Didn't you and Stacey try to get them to swap to orange juice after the show?"

"Yeah."

Not only had Stacey and I tried to curb their drinking, so had Stacey's mum, who'd been far from sober herself. All we'd gotten for our efforts, though, had been a mouthful of haughty abuse from the two of them.

"Anyway, if it makes you feel any better, we can always blame it on the prawns and tell them we were all a bit queasy as well," suggested Janine, in an attempt to be helpful.

Sadly, even the prospect of communal food poisoning didn't dampen down the guilt rapidly rising inside me like a donner kebab after a drunken night out.

"But we didn't eat any prawns," I whined. "God, I feel dreadful now. But how were we to know that after, what, two drinks, they would suddenly go mad like that?"

"Don't be so bloody wet, Fiona. Anyway, who the hell is going to remember what anyone ate or drank? In case you've forgotten, we weren't the only ones plastered last night." Erupting into a fit of laughter, Rachel added, "I don't think I've ever seen anyone that trashed. God, are they going to be sick today."

"Well, I hope for Stacey's sake, it was worth it. At least they might not be as quick to judge her from now on," I mumbled, shielding my eyes from the bright sun.

"I think once they remember what they got up to last night, they'll be horrified, Stacey'll be the least of their worries."

Despite Rachel's reassurances, I couldn't help feeling rotten about my small part in what'd happened with Janet and Sandra. Not that I was responsible for what had gone on later in the night, but still, at the time, I had been mortified witnessing Sandra's impromptu striptease while Janet had indecently assaulted Tim. Only when the compère had been forced to intervene had everyone seen the situation for what it really was and herded Janet and Sandra from the dance floor.

"Well, for Stacey's sake, I wish I could be as sure about that as you are."

"Trust me. I'm absolutely positive," replied Rachel, with a smile.

I looked at her blankly as she waved a little black SD card cryptically in the air.

"What's that?" I asked.

"What does it look like? It's got all the evidence on it from last night. And just to be safe, I'm getting some of the photos printed out this morning. I thought it might be the prefect wedding present for Stacey. If nothing else, it'll keep those two off her back, for a while at least."

Our hangovers must have been abating a little, because bit by bit more of last night's goings on came back to us. Kim nearly choked on her croissant as she recalled probably the most surprising of last night's social degenerates.

"And what about Simon's Aunt Maisie? Did anyone see her grab that gorgeous bloke with the short blond hair, you know, the one who looked like Ryan Gosling."

"Daniel," I offered, the memory of his boyish good looks and impressive body still fresh in my mind, together with the sad realization he was too young, even for me.

"Yeah, Daniel. I swear when she gave him a tonguie, I nearly threw up. Yuck, he'll be rinsing his mouth out with bloody Lysol for a week. Did you get a shot of that, Rach?"

"Fuck, I hope so. By then, I was just snapping everything."

At least I had a clear conscience on that score, as Aunt Maisie only had herself to blame for her drunken display of passion, unfortunately directed toward a now-traumatized Daniel, who couldn't have been too long out of his teens. Poor bloke. I doubt if he'll ever be able to kiss his granny goodbye again without gagging.

The more we spoke about it, the clearer it became that the hangovers that tormented us this morning were a small price to pay for undoubtedly the best night out any of us had experienced in years, and I for one couldn't wait for the wedding next week. Just thinking of last night's antics and the realization that for once I wasn't embroiled in any of the controversy was a relief I'll admit, but from personal, painful experience I knew it was going to be awkward for more than a few wedding guests, when they meet up again the following weekend, this time in the cold, sober light of day. *Somehow, I don't think anyone will be wistfully reminiscing about flashing their fanny or crushing on the odd stripper as they toast the bride and groom over a cold glass of bubbly.*

"Well, don't forget to bring the photos tomorrow night. It might put Stacey's mind at rest, at least," said Kim.

"What's happening tomorrow night?" I asked.

"We're all meeting up with Stacey after work at the Tavern for a post-mortem, *remember*. Come on, you weren't that blitzed, Fi."

"Yeah, I remember now."

I also remembered something else. *Damn it!* How could I have possibly forgotten tomorrow night's lesson with Antonio? For the first time, it occurred to me I hadn't given Antonio a second thought since stepping aboard the boat last night and I felt a twinge of guilt for having so much fun that I'd so easily forgotten him.

I couldn't help thinking it wasn't a very good start to our relationship. Mind you, considering we didn't actually *have* an official relationship yet, I couldn't be expected to sit by the phone in case he called.

All right, I knew then I was getting a little ahead of myself. With all this talk of weddings, I had to stop myself from picturing Antonio in a tuxedo at the altar waiting for me.

"I hope Stacey's heard from Simon's sisters by then. I'm dying to know what happened when they eventually sobered up."

"Don't you mean woke up?" quipped Janine.

"Knowing our luck, they won't remember a thing and it'll spoil all our fun," continued Kim.

"Well, we could always show them the happy snaps at the wedding, couldn't we? That would wipe the smug looks right off their faces."

"Jeez, can we please change the subject? I feel sick enough as it is," I pleaded to the others before digging in my bag for another painkiller.

Coffee soon leaked into lunch, which naturally progressed onto another marathon shopping binge, so by the time I got home it'd gone five and the weekend was almost over.

Sunday night was always an emotional low point as the new working week loomed ahead, promising five days of boredom and drudgery. On the bright side, though, it was also the night Mum and Dad went out to the club for dinner then stayed on afterward to feed Alex's and my inheritance into the poker machines. Unless Alex decided to come home, at least I could look forward to having the place to myself for a change.

* * * *

"Mary! Have you ironed my green shirt? I canna see it anywhere," bellowed Dad, rushing through the house in his bottle-green trousers and undershirt.

"For God's sake, Alistair, open your eyes, man. It's

hanging up right there in the wardrobe, no doubt staring ye in the face," answered Mum from the bathroom, applying more hairspray to an already rock-hard hairdo.

"Where, woman?"

"If I come in there and find it, I swear I'll strangle you with it."

See, this is what I like about my parents — the predictability of their relationship. For as long as I can remember, I've been hearing this very same banter between them. Dad yelling that his shirt-glasses-wallet-favorite pair of slippers has been maliciously spirited away just to spite him, invariably followed by Mum storming in all harassed and indignant and plucking the above-said lost possession right out from in front of Dad's unbelieving eyes.

I swear he thinks there's a conspiracy against him.

Mum just thinks he's blind with a good measure of lazy thrown in.

But behind their gruff words is an affection that has effectively bonded them together for the past thirty years and this warped consistency has come to represent all that's stable and predictable in my sometimes-turbulent life.

On my way through to the kitchen, I called out to Mum, letting her know I'd arrived home.

"Hello, dear. Did you have a nice day out?" she answered from the bathroom, where she remained engulfed in a sweet-smelling cloud of hairspray.

"Yeah, I suppose so," I muttered.

That is, of course, if you don't mind being dragged around countless bargain boutiques when you'd rather be in bed sleeping off a monumental hangover. Seeing as I'd already blown my budget yesterday, I was basically running on fumes, money-wise, and reduced to window shopping while committing further acts of vandalism upon my already-abused liver by popping dissolvable paracetamol into my mouth like they were Tic Tacs.

"Oh, I nearly forgot, darlin', a nice young man rang for you, oh, about an hour ago," Mum called out.

Instantly my face ignited. Good job Mum was still preoccupied with her hairdo.

"Really," I replied, desperately trying to sound completely uninterested when in reality I was in imminent danger of bursting a gasket with excitement. "Don't suppose he left his name?"

"Well, he did, but I can't quite remember it now. I wrote it down somewhere, though."

"Think, Mum, think!" I gritted through clenched teeth.

"Um, let me see. Andrew? Ian? Anthony?"

"How about Antonio?" I yelled, exasperated by Mum's all-too-frequent and ill-timed attacks of Alzheimer's.

"Yes, that would be it. Antonio, nice young man he was. Very polite with a lovely accent! Italian, I think."

"Well?"

"Well, what?"

I swear to God she was doing this on purpose and I tried to calm myself before Mum suspected anything. Why? Because once she got hold of any notion concerning my existent or nonexistent love life, she turned bloody pit bull with a miniature poodle between its teeth. For as much as she would deny to her dying day being a nosy mother, she possessed a unique talent for extracting all my secrets from me using nothing but subtle cunning and, failing that, she wasn't above resorting to emotional blackmail!

"What. Did. He. Say?"

"Let me think on it for a minute."

Holding my breath, I felt my heartbeat ricocheting wildly off my ribs.

"I remember now. He said he might be delayed by a meeting tomorrow night and...wait on, I'll remember in a second..." She paused.

My heart plummeted with acute, almost painful disappointment as I suspected he was experiencing second thoughts and was canceling our rendezvous.

"Um...yes, I remember now. He said he'll meet you at eight-thirty instead of seven-thirty. If there is a problem with that, dear, he left his mobile number."

Suddenly my entire body tingled with exhilaration. Eight-thirty. Who was he kidding? It was more than obvious that eight-thirty was a date time rather than a lesson time! Also, the community center would be more or less deserted by then. *Yippee!*

Glancing across, I saw Mum had by now emerged from the bathroom to stand eyeing me intently with one eyebrow raised.

She didn't say anything. Of course, she didn't have to. She was my mother and, more than anyone else in the world, she knew that sooner or later the silence that polluted the air between us would become too much for me and I would start to run my mouth in a desperate bid to break the tension.

"Don't look at me like that! It's only a dance lesson, for God's sake," I snapped at her.

"Well, if it's *only* a dance lesson, why are you being all defensive about it?" Mum replied calmly, confident as always that she was getting to me. "And, anyway, I thought dance lessons were on Tuesday and Friday nights?"

Where the hell is her bloody Alzheimer's now!

"I'm not being defensive! This is just a private lesson to help me catch up to the other students. Nothing else."

The fact I was banking on it being much, much more than that didn't matter now and, besides, it was none of Mum's business, either.

"I *see!*" she said all-knowingly, raising the other eyebrow to hit me with a double whammy of skepticism.

"It *is* just a dance lesson!" I insisted.

It irked me no end that here I was at twenty-six years of age and I still hadn't outgrown the need to justify my actions to my mother. It didn't matter that I was meeting a gorgeous man, alone, for an hour of close-combat — well, it is the way I do it — Latin dancing and who knew what else. I was an adult, after all, and it was none of her business!

"So I am to gather that these *dance lessons* have become

quite serious, then?"

"I am just doing what that bloody therapist suggested, remember. God, I can't win, can I?" I exploded, my guilty conscience making me irritable. "One minute you and Dad are desperate to get me out of the house and meeting people, then, as soon as I do, you start on at me."

"What's all this shouting aboot?" demanded Dad, walking out from the bedroom buttoning up the same shirt he'd earlier insisted was missing in action.

"Oh, nothing, Alistair. Fiona was just telling me how well the dancing lessons were going."

"Bloody glad to hear it, but then you know exactly what I think about it all," muttered Dad gruffly.

"Yes, Dad," I sighed. "We all know what you think about it. It wouldn't surprise me if the entire *street* knew by now."

By this stage, I'd had enough of being pinned down and dissected under the parental magnifying glass and I turned around to face Mum. "If there are no other questions, I think I'll go to my room and lie down. That is, if it's okay with you?" I finished sarcastically, mentally regressing back to being a petulant fourteen year old.

"Of course, sweetie. You have a nice quiet night now. After all, you do have to get up early for work tomorrow."

I smothered a scream of frustration.

Seriously, why is it as soon as you move back home, your parents start treating you like a child again?

For the past three years, I have successfully dragged my weary butt out of bed to the nauseatingly cheery prattle of early morning wake-up radio propelling me out from under my blankets.

Now I'm living at home again, though, Mum sees it as her parental duty to come into my room at daybreak and lay out my clothes for me before shaking me awake with urgent cries of, "You'll be late, dear, if you don't get a move on."

I honestly don't know what's worse, really, the breakfast radio DJ's innuendo-laced verbal banter, or the sight of

Mum leaning over me, face shiny with cold cream and lop-sided hot rollers tangled in her hair.

At least I can slap the Snooze button on the cursed clock radio and it won't slap me back.

Hearing Mum and Dad's car finally reverse down the driveway immediately evaporated my anger, leaving room for the excitement that had been steadily growing since learning of Antonio's message.

Rolling out of bed, I practically ran into the dining room and made a beeline for the phone. By this time, I was desperate to find Antonio's phone number. I searched frantically through the neat little piles of paper now littering the coffee table that was home to Mum and Dad's one and only phone.

I still find it hard to believe that even in a house of fairly modest proportions like my parents', they only have one phone. And not even a cordless phone, making it impossible to engage in a private conversation without Mum in the kitchen and Dad in the adjoining lounge being privy to every detail of my social life. Once again, I made a mental note to myself to top up my cell phone account. Considering that of late, no one had been calling me *and* I was flat broke, I hadn't been too bothered up until now.

Eyeing Mum's old-fashioned loopy handwriting on the back of an old phone bill, I felt my entire body tingle as I read Antonio's name out loud, savoring the sound of it as it rolled effortlessly off my tongue.

Antonio.

Fiona and Antonio.

Fiona and Antonio sitting in a tree, K. I. S. S. I. N. G...

Shit. I really was losing it.

Staring down at the digits, I couldn't believe it. I could actually ring him right now if I wanted to and hear his voice. It might sound a bit odd, but staring at those ten numbers, I felt a definite psychic connection between us. Then, looking down, I realized with a fright I was clasping the receiver in one hand and I already had the first three numbers pressed before some sanity returned. I threw the receiver back on its cradle in horror.

God, what the hell am I doing? I must be mad. Ringing Antonio in my current state could only result in complete disaster. What would I say to him? Or even worse, what if I couldn't say anything at all and ended up sounding like an obscene caller panting down the phone at him?

Grabbing the piece of paper, I decided a little distance between the phone and me was a must right now and I quickly shut myself away in my room to try to memorize Antonio's phone number.

I couldn't help wondering what was he doing at that moment, picturing him splayed out on a black leather lounge—Italian of course!—sipping a full-bodied red wine while planning his seduction of me tomorrow night. *Shut up – it's my fantasy after all.* Envisioning his soft dark eyes gazing down at me and his gentle practiced hands playing a delicious melody upon my body made all my previous encounters, including those with my ex, seem crude and somehow boorish. With Antonio, I knew without a doubt it would be perfect—more than perfect, actually. Clearly, fate had brought us together and as I drifted off to sleep, I snuggled in Antonio's arms as he slowly lowered me onto his...

Chapter Ten

"What do you mean you can't come? You've *got* to come!" Rachel insisted as we handed over the money for our chicken donner kebabs in the food court.

"I'm really sorry, guys, but Mum rang me at work a little while ago and said Granny wasn't well. Meaning she wants us all to go in and see her tonight. You know what they're like at that age. One hint of indigestion and the next minute they're demanding the last rites and measuring themselves for a shroud."

"I thought you were Protestant?" queried Kim, narrowing her eyes suspiciously.

My heart skipped a beat. I'm a terrible liar and I instantly began to panic, fearing I might have used this excuse one too many times in the past. Taking a deep breath, I tried to erase the telltale flush rising upward from my armpits before it reached my face and I cracked under the pressure of their combined scrutiny.

"Well, we are, of course, but Granny's convinced she's about to die, and she wants us all to say our goodbyes. Unfortunately, there's no way I can get out of it, guys. I'm really sorry, though," I said, adopting what I hoped was a forlorn expression to conceal my lie, while I considered whether to throw in a lone tear for good measure.

"Then I suppose you'd better go and see the old woman in case she does pop off and cuts you from the will," replied Rachel, after a couple of moments' deliberation.

Of course. Like all the other times, Granny wasn't at death's door. In fact, she wasn't even particularly sick. She was only in a nursing home on account of her arthritis and generally declining health, owing mainly to old age. But one thing I've learned over the years is that ailing grannies are very useful at times. Yep, as far as my friends and coworkers are concerned, my granny has come close to death many times only to make a miraculous recovery once the various high school reunions, compulsory work picnic days, or worse still, out-of-hours fire drills were over. I think she ought to have her very own column in the medical journals.

Yes, it was with great relief I found myself off the hook. I wasn't a natural liar and all afternoon it had weighed heavily on my conscience that once again I had taken advantage of Granny's precarious health just to enable me time to get ready for my *dance lesson* tonight with Antonio. And, for the purpose of easing my conscience, I decided to stop in and see Granny for a few minutes after work.

In the two years that Granny's been a resident at the nursing home, I have yet to acclimatize myself to the smell of eighty-five leaky old people which assaults my nostrils every time I walk through the front door. It's urine, basically. Or rather urine tainted even further by the wafting odor of Old Spice and Tweed, used in such copious quantities, I suspect, to divert our attention away from what they are really trying to mask.

It's not as if the place isn't clean. Actually, it looks sterile, with the linoleum floors polished to such a degree the floor's practically a mirror. For the life of me, I can't understand where the smell originates from.

Passing dear old Mr. Sullivan on my way to Granny's room, I recognized the dull look of loneliness in his eyes and my heart went out to him.

"Hello, Mr. Sullivan," I shouted, not because I'm rude but because he's almost deaf.

"Is that you, June?"

Did I mention his eyesight isn't the best either?

"No, it's Fiona, Mrs. McCrutchen's granddaughter!" I yelled.

"Who?"

His memory's going as well.

"Mrs. McCrutchen's granddaughter. The lady in room eight."

"Oh, I remember you now. Did you bring me any beer today?"

"No, sorry, Mr. Sullivan." I sighed. Seeing his disappointment, I immediately regretted that I hadn't sneaked one in, rules be buggered. "You know it's against the nursing home rules."

This I'd learned the hard way about six months ago, after a terse phone call from the Matron informing me it was an infringement of nursing home policy for relatives to distribute alcohol amongst the other residents.

Her call had come after Granny's birthday. Her legitimate one. Not one of the many I've fabricated for my own selfish purposes. When poor Mr. Sullivan had sat across from us in the garden, watching us feed Granny her birthday cake, he'd looked so sad and left out I'd invited him over to join us.

Of course, we'd brought beer. Granny likes a shandy and Dad can't endure a visit to the nursing home without one. Obviously, I'd offered Mr. Sullivan a can. He'd been almost brought to tears with gratitude. Well, I'd never seen him as happy in all the time I'd been coming here. I offered him another three cans of beer when we left. Harmless enough, or so I'd thought.

Well, apparently, I'd been wrong.

It transpired that Mr. Sullivan had polished off the three beers in the short time it'd taken us to reach the car, and by dinnertime he'd been reputedly mooning the kitchen staff and propositioning the nurses, with his trousers down around his ankles. Looking at poor meek little Mr. Sullivan now, with his grey woolly cardigan and tartan slippers peeping out from underneath a gaudy crocheted lap rug, he bore absolutely no resemblance to the sex-crazed social extremist Matron had made him out to be in her phone call.

After chatting to him for a few minutes, I made my excuses

and set off down the corridor toward Granny's room.

"You certainly took yer own fair time in gitting doon herrre!" snapped Granny, turning away from me and crossing her arms in a gesture of sullen defiance.

Huh. Nothing wrong with *her* hearing. She'd heard me yelling at Mr. Sullivan and was now in a right jealous huff. Visitors were jealously guarded here in the home and a resident did not monopolize another's guests. God, it was confusing. Almost as complex as high school social etiquette. Well, people supposedly regress back to their childhood when they grow old.

"I only stopped for a moment to say a quick hello to Mr. Sullivan, Granny. Anyway, I'm here now. How are you?" I said cheerfully, thinking it good tactics to steer the conversation straight around to her.

"How do you think I am, stuck in this bloody hole? In my day, families looked after their auld folk. Not like now where they shut them away and forgit aboot them until they die, when they go oot and whoop it up on the bloody inheritance."

I could see it was going to be one of those visits. The kind where I get an ear bashing and blamed for the state of the world for no other reason than because my generation, according to Granny, all live off welfare and are all drug addicts who bludgeon old ladies to death for their measly pension checks.

"Granny, you know we only want the best care for you. Anyway, if you left, you'd miss all your friends, wouldn't you?"

"What bloody friends? They're all thieves in here. Canna close yer eyes for a minute but someone pinches all yer chocolates. Last week the little buggers only left me the hard centers. They get all stuck in my dentures, though, and I canna get them off. I swear if I catch the bastards, I'll chop off their bloody fingers."

"I'll get you more chocolates, I promise. Would you like creams or those nice sea shell ones?"

"No matter to me now, they'll only git stolen again anywa'," she huffed.

"Well, in that case I'll bring you a box of cream middles in next time."

No point coughing up for expensive chocolates.

"Have you had your dinner yet, Granny?"

"No, did nae want it," she said tersely.

"But you've got to eat something or you'll get sick. What is it and maybe I can get the nurses to heat up some more for you?"

"Irish stew and tatties!"

"Oh!"

Granny has always hated sloppy and tasteless food, and in the home the Irish stew was almost inedible, thanks to the home's no-salt policy. Last time we'd complained about the nasty gruel that in here goes by the name of Irish stew, they'd fobbed us off with some crap about salt being bad for the residents. Seeing as the poor buggers in here were on their last legs anyway, it was about sixty years too late to be worrying about choking up their arteries. If I ever find myself chucked into a nursing home, I'll make damn sure it's one with a Domino's Pizza or McDonald's nearby.

"How about I nip out and get you something tasty to eat, then?" I offered, hoping it might lift her foul mood.

I could almost see her brain ticking over, then, for the first time since I'd arrived, her eyes lit up.

"Ye know wha' I really hae a notion fer?" she whispered, a hint of a smile appearing on her lips.

"What?" I asked, moving closer.

"Chicken Pad Thai noodles and crab cakes."

Having been thinking along the lines of fish and chips or a quarter barbecue chicken, I was a bit taken aback by Granny's new-found culinary sophistication.

"No problems, Gran. There's a nice Thai takeaway about five minutes away, so I'll pop out and be back as soon as I can."

It's amazing the transformation a decent meal makes in a

person. By the time Granny'd finished the very last noodle, residents and staff alike had come from all directions to investigate the delicious smell coming from her room. I suppose, in a place like this, any smell that didn't have the nurses running to fetch a bedpan was worth making a note of.

By the time the crowd had finally dispersed from outside her room, Granny was a changed woman.

"I know how the bloody monkeys at the zoo feel now. Anyone 'ad think they ne'er saw an auld woman eating before." She giggled as I wiped the corners of her mouth with a face towel. "I'll hae to watch ma porridge in the morning."

"Why?"

"Just in case that malicious auld cook slips some poison in it out of spite," she quipped, but her eyes shone with glee.

This was the side of my Gran I really loved, the plucky, no-bullshit, speak-her-mind side. Unless her pluckiness was aimed in my direction, of course. Yeah, it should have come as no surprise when, out of the blue, she turned to me and demanded.

"Fiona, where's that husband of yours? I have'na seen him in ages."

I was kind of hoping Granny had forgotten I was even married in the first place. This wasn't really a conversation I wanted to have with her. I braced myself for the inevitable scene.

"Granny, I'm sure Mum must have told you we're not together anymore. We've separated," I sighed.

"Whatever fer?"

Oh, why couldn't her Thai food begin to repeat on her and I could use the excuse of getting some Pepto-Bismol to bail out of the door before things got sticky? In all senses?

"Well?" she insisted, staring me in the eye.

I knew I wasn't going to get let off easily. "It just wasn't working out, that's all."

My reluctance to explain the circumstances surrounding

the split wasn't simply due to my unwillingness to rehash my recent humiliation. For some strange reason, Granny and my ex had appeared to bond instantly and everyone in the family had been completely flummoxed. Granny had never got on well with any of the in-laws. Mum is still trying to get her to acknowledge she is even married to my father. That said, it had always been a complete mystery why she'd taken to him like she had.

So how, then, could I tell Granny her favorite grandson-in-law was a sleazy, adulterous fuckwit?

"What do you mean, 'not working out'? Nice young men like that don't come aboot too often. At my age, I should hae a dozen wee great-grandkiddies running around by now. What did you do to scare him off, then?" she queried accusingly.

Two minutes ago, I was her savior when I was feeding her bloody Thai, and now I'd manifested into the Antichrist.

Time to set things right, and if Granny didn't like what I was about to tell her, well, so be it.

"I didn't do anything, Gran. *He* cheated on me. *He* slept with one of our neighbors, actually!"

Silence.

More silence.

"*That* bastard!" erupted Granny.

"*What?*"

"I ne'er liked him, ye know. Such a creepy crawler he was. Always sucking up to me he was, saying, 'Mrs. McCrutchen, yur looken lovely today' or 'Mrs. McCrutchen, can I make yoo a cup-a-tea?' Slimy as they come, that one!"

"But, Gran, you always went on about how nice he was and that he was your favorite in-law."

"Well, why wouldn't I?" she said defensively, "when he'd come in here weighed doon with Walkers Toffees and Shortie? I may be a stupid auld woman, but I'm nae one to cut off ma nose ta spite my face there."

And with those last words, at least she had the good grace to look sheepish.

That slimy little brown-nosed bastard, I thought. *Sneaking in here with candies and shortbread in an effort to weasel his way into Granny's affections. Probably thought he'd score a slice of the inheritance for himself when she went. Good thing, then, he couldn't manage to keep his pants on until after Granny had popped off.* Now the game was up and I determined I'd get back at him at some stage.

Pushing vengeful thoughts of my ex out of my mind, I eventually left the nursing home with ample time to get ready for my *lesson*.

Opening my wardrobe later, I stared for a few empty minutes before closing it again. I had nothing at all to wear. Well, nothing decent anyway. I needed just the right balance of sexy, comfortable, casual and clingy. Nothing in my closet came close to matching requirements.

Why hadn't I gone out and bought something to wear? I knew why, of course. I was broke after last week's spending free-for-all.

I had to think. Seeing as, at least for outward appearances, it wasn't an official date, I didn't feel right about getting too dressed up, although I had earlier considered making up some feeble excuse such as I'd just come straight from some function at work. At the time, it had sounded like the perfect excuse to arrive for my lesson dressed to impress. It wasn't until I'd walked in the door after my visit to Granny I realized there were two fundamental flaws to my plan, and they were both sitting in the lounge room watching *Neighbours* on TV.

With Mum and Dad in the house, eagerly following my every move, I knew I'd never make it as far as the front door without arousing their curiosity.

Eight o'clock fast approached and with it, decision time. In the end I reasoned that with Antonio having already seen me at my worst wearing my baggy old Hamilton Island T-shirt, anything else would have to be a vast improvement.

Eventually, after much soul-searching and gnashing of teeth, I emerged from my room wearing jeans and a crisp white shirt. If Mum was disappointed, she did an admirable job of hiding it. But still I could tell she was biting her tongue not to suggest I wear the soft calf-length black skirt and cream camisole top she'd admired when I wore it out to Alex's twenty-third birthday dinner, a month before my split. No, I'm not a mind reader—it was this exact skirt and top I found laid out on my bed for me when I got home.

Pointedly, Mum and Dad said nothing as I left the house, but I'm sure I saw Mum peeking through the lace curtains as I reversed Dad's car down the driveway.

Darkness had fully ascended by the time I pulled up opposite the large, imposing building. It being a Monday night, the community center looked to be deserted save for a very classy Saab convertible parked out the front. It had to be Antonio's. It was exactly what I would have envisioned him driving and, as I walked past, I couldn't stop myself caressing the still-warm polished hood, imagining it to be his bronzed flesh.

Once inside the heavy glass doors, the foyer was uncharacteristically still, bathed in a translucent glow reflected from the security lighting outside. With the absence of human chatter to fill the cavernous void, it took on an almost eerie ambience, transforming the normally bustling meeting place into an intimate romantic grotto, perfect for our clandestine rendezvous.

Once again, I found myself magnetically drawn toward the soulful, timeless music that seeped seductively through the closed door of the studio, inviting and beckoning me to enter with promises of warm flesh and slow, delicious romance. Tonight more than ever, the music created a tight expectation within my chest and a tiny pulse of nervous excitement deep within my belly.

I stopped a couple of inches from the door to the room where Antonio was at this moment waiting for me. Closing my eyes, I drew a deep breath into my lungs to calm my racing heart while I tried to collect my thoughts. I wasn't even sure what I was going to say to him. After all, it had been a long time since I'd been alone with a man who wasn't my husband and I didn't know whether it was merely nervous energy producing that squeezing sensation in my chest or one of those moments that's like saying "I do", when you sense nothing is going to be quite the same ever again.

Suddenly, an image of Antonio appeared in my mind...

Lean and bronzed, he approaches me from across the room with a knowing, indulgent smile playing on his full, sensuous lips. I open my mouth to speak, but he silences me, taking my chin in his hand and pressing his thumb against my lips to halt the words forming on my tongue from escaping. Then, reaching out, he draws me forward into the welcoming circle of his strong arms and lowers his lips to take possession of mine. Slowly, my lips surrender to his skillful teasing and I feel him press farther into my...

"Ah, there you are!"

I jumped, my mouth snapping shut with such force I swear the sound of clashing teeth resonated throughout the center. Oh, Antonio's sexy baritone voice! My face instantly erupted in a fiery explosion of sheer mortification. I didn't have time to dwell on my latest faux pas, because, as if he'd just peered right into my thoughts, Antonio reached out, gently brushing his cool fingers against the fiery flesh of my face.

"It affects me like that, as well, Fiona," he said.

My soul fell helplessly into his dark eyes.

"The music. It is the life force, the heartbeat of Latin dance. Come on, we'll get started now," he whispered, turning around and walking back into the room.

My skin continued to burn where Antonio's fingers had for those few delicious moments caressed my fevered flesh and in so doing started a chain reaction of sharp little spasms of pleasure darting straight to my womb. Caught up as I was in his magical web, I stood motionless while I tried to relocate my senses.

Antonio was well into the studio before he realized I

hadn't moved. Turning back, he saw me standing at the doorway and frowning slightly.

"Fiona, come in, there's no need to be nervous. I'll guarantee by the end of the evening we'll have you dancing on air."

Or with any luck, flat on my back, I thought, unable to banish the wicked thoughts that had taken over my head.

Now, if there's one thing more annoying than a man with no social manners, it's one who's too bloody decent and polite for his—or my—good. And, as the night wore on, I found myself becoming increasingly frustrated. *Story of my bloody life.* When you don't really fancy someone, you find yourself having to scrape them off you with a hot spatula, while the guys who have you almost panting with desire invariably decide to play it cool and treat you like a lady. *I can't win.*

Almost an hour into our *lesson,* much to my frustration, I was rapidly coming to the disappointing conclusion that Antonio fell into the latter category. It's not as though I wanted to be treated like some hooker or anything. Like women the world over, I expect men in general to exhibit a certain amount of respect toward me on account of my gender—after all, what's the point of being seen as the weaker sex if you can't take advantage of it now and again, the perks of possessing a womb being few and far between? But there comes a time when even I am happy to piss respect right off and plunge headlong into toe-curling, butt-clenching, unbridled, frenzied passion.

And, unfortunately, that point came and went almost half an hour ago.

I'm almost ashamed to admit how long it's been since I made any deliberate attempt to ply my charms, so obviously my technique could've used a little polishing. But with the atmosphere all but crackling with sexual tension, I couldn't believe he hadn't made a move by now.

Despite our close proximity and the fact my body language screamed out "throw me down and ravish me now," Antonio continued ruthlessly teasing me with his seductive smiles full of unspoken promises until I almost combusted with frustration.

"See, what did I tell you, Fiona? All you needed was a little one-on-one lesson and look at how much you've improved."

"I have?"

Amazingly, Antonio was right. I found I was moving in time to the music and not bouncing off him in the manner of an out-of-control dodgem car. Strange, really. I'd spent the entire night that worked up, I'd forgotten I was the world's worst dancer, only to make the unexpected discovery I wasn't.

What do you know, miracles do happen.

Instantly, a ridiculous burst of pride at my accomplishment swamped me and I couldn't wipe the smile off my face. For that brief moment, I forgot just how much I fancied him and as a result felt closer to him than ever. I wondered if this was how survivors of earthquakes or train wrecks felt when they were finally pulled free of the rubble in one piece. It must be the elation combined with a sense of camaraderie to have survived a potentially disastrous situation unscathed.

I glowed with happiness. I would savor this moment for the rest of my life. Suddenly, I noticed Antonio had stopped smiling and was looking at me with an intensity that set my pulse racing. My heart did a little flip-flop and something started tap dancing in my stomach as I gazed back into his dark-brown eyes, noticing a stray lock of his black hair brushing against his long, sable eyelashes seductively. As I stared, wide-eyed, I knew this was the moment I had waited for all night. The time had come to stop all this beating around the bush and get down to the business end of the evening.

Reaching out, Antonio took my face in his hands and something instantly dissolved inside me.

"It's so nice to see you smile at last. I think you must be

the saddest person I have ever known."

The tenderness in his eyes warmed me right to the essence of my being and I never wanted this moment to end.

"Tell me, Fiona, what makes a beautiful woman like you this unhappy?"

Without a doubt, the last thing I'd expected to hear. Taken completely off-guard, I opened my mouth to speak, to offer him a lifetime of devotion, but a huge lump lodged itself in my throat and, to my utter horror, a lone tear escaped, scalding a path down my face.

Please, God, why now?

A moment ago, I'd been on the verge of finally getting up close and personal with Antonio, and now he'd effectively thrown cold water over my desire by unearthing the one thought guaranteed to send any thoughts of passion running for cover — my marriage woes.

"Someone hurt you, didn't they? I can tell. Who was it? A boyfriend, maybe?"

"No, husband!" I croaked, the words sticking painfully in my throat.

"What an idiot he is. If I had someone as lovely as you in my life, I would never give them a moment's regret or unhappiness."

That was possibly the single sweetest thing anyone had ever said to me. Unfortunately, his sympathy also re-opened the bottomless well of my self-pity, which up until then had lain quietly, replenishing itself with dark thoughts, but was now set to spurt everywhere once again. I felt completely deflated, my earlier excitement nothing but a distant memory.

No ounce of remaining strength in my body could stop me from trembling as a fresh wave of grief hit me.

Grief for the death of my marriage. Grief for my shattered dreams of a family of my own. And, most of all, grief for all the pain I had carried with me since that awful day when my life fell apart.

Any previous hopes of a romantic interlude between us

tonight were smothered by the resurgence of my misery. As sobs erupted from deep inside me, instead of running for his life from my outburst, Antonio pulled me into his arms and held me against his warm chest while I cried hot tears all over his expensive silk shirt.

* * * *

It was late, very late really, when I eventually climbed into bed. Not late like six-o'clock-in-the-morning-been-bonking-my-brains-out-all-night kind of late, but late enough that by the time I'd gotten home, Mum had gone off to bed in a huff, but not before having turned off every light in the house and locked me out as some kind of petty punishment. To her way of thinking, anyone who stays out later than eleven on a week night obviously has the morals of an alley cat.

Seeing as I'd lost my key over six years ago and hadn't been issued another due to my carelessness, Mum's silent protest had resulted in my rather undignified scramble through my bedroom window.

Fortunately for me, Dad has been meaning to fix it for the past ten years now.

I suppose I should have been exhausted mentally *and* physically after my exertions on both accounts that evening. But, despite my earlier miseries, my mind soared on a high. An Antonio-induced high, that is. Antonio, I discovered, is the best drug on Earth. In fact, you could say he was my heroin, cocaine and ecstasy hit all rolled into one and by now I was hooked, addicted and totally blown away by him.

And what miracle had seen this complete turn-about? No, it wasn't a wild night of orgasmic bonking on shiny black satin sheets, although I still lived in hope on that score. His wonderful, gentle compassion that had eventually lifted me from my dark gloom of despair and dejection.

After I'd recovered from my mini-breakdown and

extradited myself from his soggy arms with what little dignity I could muster, I'd fully expected him to wave goodbye in all haste and make fast his escape, thankful he had survived the all-dreaded female sobbing scene intact. But much to my surprise, he'd instead suggested we go out to a café he knew, not far from the center, for coffee and a chat.

This wasn't quite the evening I had been fantasizing about for the past few days, but then I might add it wasn't part of my grand plan of seduction to blubber hysterically all over him, either.

So with my eyes all swollen and scaly and my face sporting a nose Rudolph would have been ashamed to be seen in public with, I followed Antonio's Saab to a late-night café down the road. As he escorted me to our table, I couldn't help but notice the envious looks thrown my way by the other diners enjoying their after-hours lattes and mochaccinos and my self-esteem finally scraped itself off the floor.

Over a steady stream of cappuccinos, I proceeded to fill him in on my husband's infidelities, together with the miseries I'd experienced over the past few weeks. Naturally, I omitted any mention of my recent sojourn into the sordid world of sexually transmitted diseases, the memory of which even now makes me nauseous.

By midnight, we were the only customers left. Hostile glances came from the direction of the café staff, impatiently waiting for us to leave so they could finally close the place and go home. Antonio, though, was in no hurry to wind up our conversation. It wasn't until they turned off the coffee machine and began cleaning around us we gave in to the mounting pressure to leave and decided to call it a night.

By the time I got home, I'd finally shrugged off the dark, oppressive gloom that had been my constant companion recently and in its place felt a cleansing combination of relief and hope. Relief for finally unburdening myself of some of the dark thoughts of unworthiness which had plagued me for months, if not years. And I prayed that maybe I wasn't a hopeless case after all, doomed to spend the rest of my life alone.

I didn't need to be a psychic to sense something was awry before I even had a chance to sit down at lunch with the girls the next day. Kim glared at me as if I'd arrived sporting a second head and Rachel stared daggers at me. Of the three of them, only a sheepish Janine, who I knew for a fact would prefer to be anywhere else but where she was, said hello as I joined them for lunch in the food court.

It wasn't so much the hostility emanating from Kim and Rachel that set off the warning bells in my head. They always seemed to have the shits about something—naturally lunchtime wouldn't be complete without at least one hissy fit, but Janine's presence today was particularly disconcerting.

You see, these days Janine refused to join us for lunch after her last visit almost got her thrown into jail. Even now I can recall the look of shocked confusion on her face. What a stir she'd caused when, totally oblivious to the fact she still had on her blood-splattered shirt from her morning shift at the abattoir, she'd quickly found herself surrounded by police and ambulance personnel, thinking she'd been the victim of some heinous crime. At the time she had been so shocked with the resulting chaos it had only been as she was being rushed off on a stretcher to a waiting ambulance she'd managed to convince them the blood wasn't hers, or even human for that matter, and she hadn't, in fact, been bleeding from some atrocious but concealed wound.

Not that we'd been much help.

So hysterically had we been laughing at her predicament, the EMS had thought we were in shock and had offered us sedatives, together with warm blankets and sweet drinks. Thankfully we'd had the good sense to decline the sedatives, seeing as we'd ended up spending the better part of the afternoon down at the police station, trying to convince them not to charge Janine with various minor offenses, including disturbing the peace and attempting to incite a riot.

As you can imagine, I took Janine's presence today to be a clear indication that something was seriously amiss.

The girls passed furtive glances back and forth as I sat there, confused by the ugly atmosphere, waiting for the awkward silence to cease. My stomach clenched painfully with dreaded anticipation and I couldn't help but get the impression I was about to be cast from the loop for the second time in recent weeks. In those few seconds, I did a mental retake in an attempt to come up with a possible reason for their portentous mood.

Of course, it was just what I should have expected from a day that had started out shitty, before continuing on in an all-out spiraling nosedive to disastrous.

Initiating my day from hell first of all had been Mum.

Any other morning she can usually be relied on to blast into my room in her best forty-knot southerly bluster manner and wake me at the crack of dawn. But this morning, for reasons known only to herself, she decided to let me have a lie in. *Wonderful!* I wasn't for a minute fooled by her apparent ill-timed consideration, especially when her tight-lipped, cat's-arse look of disapproval scalded me from the kitchen as I raced out of the door, already twenty minutes late for work.

Then, adding further woe to my already shitty morning, I had to suffer the embarrassment of being summoned to appear at an early morning meeting with the various department heads. In keeping with the theme of my morning from hell, my earlier absence had already been noted by some eagle-eyed, brown-nosed junior executive, eager to promote himself in the eyes of the bigwigs upstairs.

Any other time no one would have battered an eye at my tardiness, but apparently, this particular meeting had been called by management to address the worsening crisis of staff punctuality and absenteeism. There I sat, under the scrutiny of the stupid suits upstairs, put on the spot for an explanation for my lateness by the people who can usually be relied on to be at least an hour and a half late for work the morning after their regular Wednesday golfing afternoon.

This, I might add, they tried to justify by referring to it as a Management Team Networking session.

Taking in their hypocritical expressions of solemn disapproval, I had to think quickly – not easy, considering I hadn't yet mainlined my caffeine hit. *Thanks again, Mum, I'll remember this moment when I come to choose your nursing home.* I was standing there, facing the stupid suits, like a prisoner facing a firing squad. Unfortunately, this was dangerously close to the truth.

Hostile stares surrounded me on all sides. Going by the sadistic gleam in their eyes, I suspected they were measuring me for the role of scapegoat as they prepared to make an example of me in a last-ditch attempt to bring the rest of the slackers downstairs in line. I knew then without a doubt that if I was to have any hope of furthering my career in the retail industry, I simply *had to* come up with the most creative and original excuse of my professional career.

The pressure I found myself under was certainly stroke-inducing in its intensity, and as twin trickles of sweat ran down the backs of my knees, I had a sudden brainwave.

Time ticked by and with every second of silence that passed I sank deeper into the no-man's-land of official staff warnings and constant managerial monitoring. It was now or never as I juggled the pros and cons of the words that were about to come out of my mouth.

"Well, Ms. McCrutchen, do you actually *have* a legitimate reason for being...let me see...*thirty-nine* minutes late for work and in doing so setting a very unprofessional example to the younger members of staff?"

If the world in which we lived was a just one, at that moment I would have reminded Mr. Hurst of his own recent 'unprofessional conduct' when he was caught with his personal assistant upon his lap in a moment he glibly referred to as *high spirits*. If office gossip was to be believed, there were certainly spirits involved, but of the Jack Daniel's variety.

"Well, we are waiting!" he added, tapping his pen loudly on the pine laminate conference table.

Only the ticking of the gaudy brass clock perched above Mr. Hurst punctuated the silence surrounding me. Briefly, I considered the chances of it falling off the wall and burying itself in Mr. Hurst's shiny white head.

Slim. At best.

"Mr. Hurst, I'm very sorry I was late today. You can be assured it is not a regular habit of mine to be late for work and I do have a legitimate reason for my absence."

"Well, out with it," he barked.

Taking a deep breath, I knew I had no alternative but to swallow any remaining misgivings and launch straight into my hastily fabricated alibi.

"Well, um, you see, I had a doctor's appointment this morning…" I started.

"Humph," he snorted rudely, all but pinning me to the wall with his scathing look of contempt.

"At my gynecologist," I added. Pausing for effect, I felt an embarrassed hush fall over the mainly male gathering as they instantly developed a fixation with straightening the piles of paper directly in front of them. "You see, I've had terrible problems lately with my menstrual cycle and…"

"It's all right, Ms. McCrutchen, there is no need to explain further…" stammered a red-faced Mr. Hurst through the sounds of rustling paper.

"No, really, I should have checked if the doctor was running on time this morning, I know, but I was almost doubled up with terrible cramps and…"

"Ms. McCrutchen!" he yelled. "We understand, honestly. You can rest assured your lateness today will be overlooked this one time and not recorded on your employee file."

It was certainly a lucky escape, and for the remaining few minutes I stood by the door and did my best not to catch the eye of anyone in the meeting. This wasn't nearly as difficult as it sounded, seeing as not one of the suits present were about to look me in the eye. All the same I decided to play it safe, clutching my stomach protectively and wincing a lot as a sort of insurance.

Not long afterward, Mr. Hurst hastily wrapped up the final points of the meeting to a noticeably subdued and restless gathering, who were by now desperate to escape from any further mention of 'female problems.'

As I walked out from that meeting, I mentally prepared myself to endure a savage bollocking from Joan Clements. Why? Because, being one of the only women in the meeting, she hadn't bought in to any of my lies.

I should have known my short-lived spell of happiness last night would come at a price, and today I was certainly paying for it.

Armed with nothing more than my own weakening bravado, I braced myself for her wrath.

So what if I had used the oldest excuse known to womankind? I was desperate and desperate times call for desperate measures. That wasn't going to placate my fellow female coworkers downstairs, though. Why? Because as anyone with a womb can tell you, using the all-dreaded gyno excuse to your middle-aged, easily embarrassed male boss can only be done on occasions of dire need so as not to dilute its yuck factor effectiveness.

Having survived my earlier inquisition, I now found myself facing another nasty round-table gathering outside the food court's only kebab joint and, if the expressions on the girls' faces were anything to go by, it was not going to be as easy to bullshit my way out of this particularly hostile kangaroo court.

"Well, Fiona, how's your *grandmother* doing? Survive the night, did she?" enquired Kim sarcastically.

Under their intense scrutiny, it was a miracle I didn't crack there and then. Thank God I had Granny's visit to fall back on.

"Yeah, Granny's okay now. Just wanted some attention, I reckon. She's still pissed off, you see, at Mum and Dad for putting her in a home in the first place and now we're paying the price for it. Mum thinks we should call her bluff and ignore her. But then it would be just our luck she'd pop off, leaving us feeling guilty for the rest of our lives."

I was babbling, but—strangely—at this point I found the sound of my own voice weirdly soothing. Not that it seemed to be having any similar effect on the girls, though.

The contempt surrounding me felt smothering and I got the impression that every word that passed my lips merely tightened the noose round my neck.

"How was Stacey last night? Heard anything about you-know-who?" I asked in a last-ditch attempt to deflect the conversation away from me and my hypochondriac grandmother.

"Yeah, yeah, Stacey's fine, apart from a nasty hickey on her neck from that wanker she got off with on the boat," said Kim, referring to the greasy, pock-marked bartender with the raging BO.

"So does that mean the wedding's off?" I asked, in the vain hope Stacey's misfortune would distract them from whatever had got them all in a fury.

"No, the stupid bitch will just have to wear a scarf for the next few days and hope it's disappeared before the big day. I reckon it serves her right for being such a skank—though she did say he had the biggest dick she'd ever seen and..." Kim paused thoughtfully.

Don't stop now, I thought. The juiciest gossip I'd heard in ages and I almost wished I'd been there last night to hear it straight from the be-hickied bride-to-be's own mouth.

"If you'd been there last night, you'd know all about it, wouldn't you?" added Rachel caustically.

I knew she was baiting me, as much as I knew that as punishment for my no-show last night I wasn't going to be getting any more details about Stacey's toilet shag with the well-hung, albeit ugly-as-sin, bartender.

"But you know what's really weird, Fiona..." said Kim, narrowing her eyes. "We rang your place last night and your mum answered the phone..."

Oh, no, not Mum. Anyone but her. As soon as Kim mentioned speaking to Mum, I instantly knew what was wrong with them. Mum, of course, had blabbed. And of all people, she had blabbed to the three most indiscreet people I know. *Shit!* If the morning's near-miss hadn't been bad enough, this was going to be sheer hell, and I immediately sent my brain into warp-six salvage mode, in order to rescue what was left of my reputation after my mother's interference.

"*And* she didn't sound very concerned for your poor *dying* grandmother. You know, she didn't even know she was sick!"

Yep, panic hit and I blurted out, "I did visit Granny, you just ask anyone at the home."

Ignoring my outburst, Kim continued, "She couldn't understand why you thought your granny was ill, but you know what she did say? Now, this is the really funny bit. She said you were at your *dancing lessons*. Now, *why* would she say that?"

I've heard stories on those tacky chat shows of children divorcing their parents, and at that precise moment, I understood what would drive someone to do something so drastic, fourteen hours of labor be buggered. I think, by ruining my entire life in one phone call, she had well and truly paid me back for the hours of excruciating agony I'd apparently caused her by my nine-pound-ten-ounce arrival into the world.

I suppose, in all fairness, it had only been a matter of time before my clandestine new hobby was out in the open. I'd been counting on it being later, though. *Much* later, actually. At my funeral, would have been preferable. Now, unfortunately, decision time had arrived. Was it better to 'fess up about the dancing lessons and put up with the girls taking the piss out of me for the next ten years or until such time as they finally get sick of it, or put them off the scent by confiding my budding romance with Antonio?

Ummm, tough decision.

Well, not really.

"Well, I would have to tell her something like that, wouldn't I?" I stated confidently.

Decision seemingly made…

"What do you mean?" responded Rachel.

I experienced a surge of satisfaction at seeing her earlier smugness falter. "Think about it for a sec," I sighed, rolling my eyes in mock exasperation. "What else was I going to tell Mum, that I was going out on a *date*? After all the drama over the last few weeks, if I tell her I've met someone else, she'd go on and on about me being on the rebound and I shouldn't be getting myself involved with anyone else until I'm over *him*."

It was a lie, of course.

A big, black, filthy lie.

Not only about the date but also the bit about Mum's disapproval. I knew for a certainty she'd be delighted for me to meet someone else in the hope I might move in with them and out of her house and she could reinstate her sewing machine to its rightful spot in my old bedroom. Mum, you see, had barely waved me off at the wedding before transforming my childhood space into her sewing room. Even now I'd moved back in, I still had to compete for space with Mum's piles of scrap material and half-finished patchwork quilts. It's like sleeping in a haberdashery store.

I suppose that any other time, I would have been slightly disturbed at my newfound ability to rattle off such outrageous fibs, not only to the girls, but also my boss and, let's not forget, my parents. In my defense, though, I'd learned recently that the occasional half-truth often proved essential for the preservation of what remained of one's pride.

Kim's eyes by this stage had nearly popped right out of her head. "Are you telling us you were on a *date* last night? With a *man*?"

"Yep! And of course it was a man. Who do you think I'd go out with, a goat?"

Their surprise at my bombshell hung in the air like a child's party piñata, bright with expectation and the promise of the sweet treats within.

"Who is he?"

"When did this all happen?"

"Where did you go?"

Suddenly their suspicions evaporated into thin air as they became desperate for more details of my mystery man.

"Jesus, listen to you three. It was only a date, for God's sake. I have been out on dates before, remember?" I said and laughed, attempting to sound casual while my stomach did a fairly realistic rendition of the chicken dance.

"Yeah, but not since *him*," whispered Janine.

They were completely shell-shocked. So much so, I started to get a little annoyed with them.

Shit, going by their reaction anyone would think I'd just buried my offending ex and, instead of throwing myself on the funeral pyre, I'd started shagging the nearest male contender, within plain view of his corpse.

Nice thought, though.

I must remember that one.

"What do they say about falling off a horse? Leave it too long and you'll never get back on. Well, I'm not about to let my bastard ex turn me off men for life, am I?"

"You still haven't told who he is!" cried Kim. "Oh, God! It's not the bloke from the computer shop, is it? The one who's been perving on you for months?"

"Fuck off, will you! How desperate do you think I am?"

Comparing Antonio to the tall, skinny dork who worked in the center's only computer store was like comparing James Bond to Mr. Bean, and I shuddered at the mere thought of getting it on with him.

"Well, who is he, then?" demanded Rachel.

"All I'm going to tell you at the moment is his name is Tony." *Close enough, anyway.* "He works in the city, and he is gorgeous. I mean, drop-dead gorgeous. Don't get any ideas of meeting him yet as we've only been out once and I don't want you girls scaring him off." Then, looking right at Rachel, I added, "Or stealing him from me."

Rachel smiled back, preening quietly at being acknowledged for her superiority with men.

After that, they all wanted to know when I was seeing him again, what he did for a living, et cetera.

And, in the space of less than ten minutes, it seemed they'd forgiven me for lying to them the night before and the next forty-five minutes slipped by in talk of, what else, sex. Not that I could comment on that score, so I just pretended to be coy and discreet while Rachel gave us a blow-by-blow commentary on her wild bedroom antics with Jason during the past week. Not one dirty little detail was left to our imaginations, and I was both shocked and riveted by Rachel's startling account of Jason's prowess.

By the time we arrived back at our respective jobs, as a legacy of Rachel's X-rated review, we were all feeling a little hot and flustered—not that any of us would ever admit it, ever—prompting more than one person throughout the afternoon to remark on my rather rosy complexion.

Of course, it didn't help matters that by now the rumor mills were in hyper-drive after my morning tête-à-tête with management and the latest breaking news was that, apparently, I was suffering from early menopause? Rather than reveal the real cause of my hot flushes, I had no choice but to put up with well-meaning but still nonetheless embarrassing advice on the many benefits of hormone replacement therapy as opposed to going cold turkey and all the unpleasant effects accompanying it.

This, of course, I already knew, thanks to the ladies from Friday's dance class.

All afternoon, I tried to banish unpleasant thoughts of HRT from my mind by quietly praising myself for possessing the good sense to finally secure a leash on my runaway mouth.

It might have taken twenty-six years, but I'd finally got

the zipper on my mouth working smoothly. Apart from a few hazy details about *Tony* to keep the girls off my back, I hadn't revealed too much, knowing only too well how easily it could all blow up in my face.

Yes, I knew it was a little premature of me to mention him at all, seeing as last night's coffee hadn't strictly speaking been a date and, apart from tonight's lesson, there hadn't actually been any mention from Antonio of repeating our late-night chat. Although I couldn't imagine why not. After all, we had hit it off amazingly well and I couldn't believe how comfortable I felt around him now.

All that remained was to move things along on the physical front. After last night, I was all but incandescent with pent-up frustration and Rachel's lunchtime broadcast of her raging sex life hadn't helped matters. But then, I did have tonight to look forward to.

At least I could now safely go out later without raising any more suspicions. The girls, naturally thinking I'd be spending the night camped next to the phone waiting for *Tony* to ring, knew the only decent thing to do under the circumstances was to leave me to my silent vigil.

And why the sudden burst of decency, you might well ask? Well, I suppose it's another one of those funny *girl* things, really. They've all been in this very same situation, you see, and know from past experiences how agonizing it is to wait for a phone call that quite often never even materializes. So, when every ten minutes one of your well-meaning friends texts to see if the phone fairy has blessed you with a call from the object of your desire, it just amplifies your disappointment when you have nothing positive to report. Universally, all girls know this is the worst kind of torture, so respectfully contain their curiosity until the morning when the phone line runs hot with either excitement or commiserations.

Chapter Eleven

By the end of Tuesday night's class, I had committed to memory every mole, every pitted acne scar and every fine blond hair on Jason's neck.

You might be wondering, why this sudden fetish for Jason's neck?

Rachel's bloody fault, of course.

After hearing all about Jason's impressive, Karma-Sutra-rivalling accomplishments in the bedroom, not only couldn't I look him in the eye, but owing to her graphic portrayal—she'd make a fortune in the phone sex industry—I couldn't banish the image of him naked and screwing the freckles right off my sex-starved body. I'm almost too embarrassed to admit that last part.

I seriously don't know what'd gotten into me lately, but I didn't seem to have a single thought in my head that didn't involve sex. Admittedly, it had been some time since I'd cried out anyone's name in the heat of a toe-curling, screaming orgasmic moment. Well, five months, two weeks and six days in total—in between infecting me with an STD, Bastard Ex had the occasional attack of the droops—meaning it probably wasn't all that surprising I felt more than a little horny.

"It's incredible how much you've improved in just a week, Fi."

"Again, I'm so sorry about last week. How are your toes now?"

"Well, they're not broken, but I have to confess, I wore an extra pair of socks tonight to help cushion the blows."

"You can't say I didn't warn you last week. You knew

I was the world's worst dancer. After all you've seen me in action, remember?" I said thinking of the now-infamous nightclub fiasco.

To that Jason burst out laughing and I lost count and...

"Ouch!" he cried out as I came crashing down hard on top of his right instep. Accidentally, of course.

"Oh, God, I'm sorry, I didn't do it on purpose, honestly. You've put me off my rhythm."

"Fair enough. I get it now. If I laugh at you, you'll hurt me. Right?"

"Yep, right!" I giggled, glancing up into his clear blue, crinkling with suppressed laughter, eyes.

Instantly, a hot bolt of desire shot down my body, taking me completely by surprise. I was shocked as well as disgusted with myself that just looking at a bloke, and not just any old bloke but Rachel's boyfriend no less, could send me off in spasms of wanting. I recoiled at the idea I might have any desire for a man Rachel had clearly marked as her own.

No. No. No.

This is not going to happen. Not now. Not ever.

Besides, I had Antonio almost in the bag. *Almost* being the operative word. I couldn't lose sight of that now simply because my libido was doing backflips as a result of Rachel's love-life broadcast.

Antonio was my future.

My soul mate.

My Latin lover.

But, God almighty, was I horny!

I knew then I really had to find out where Antonio's feelings were heading before I did something totally unforgivable, like hit on Jason. Or even worse, one of Alex's friends, who were beginning to look more desirable for every celibate day that passed, and that would be scraping the bottom of the Himbo barrel, even for me.

"Seriously, though, I have been practicing. Actually, Antonio gave me a private lesson last night."

I hadn't meant to tell Jason. I don't know why I did. Even to my own ears it sounded as though I was boasting. But being flushed with pride for having made it almost through the entire lesson without being the cause of one tear of pain had made me reckless and I couldn't help myself.

Now, Jason was looking at me strangely and I instantly regretted saying anything.

Surely I'm not that transparent?

"You like Antonio, don't you?" he whispered into my ear. Obviously, I was.

How embarrassing.

In one way, it was a relief to actually admit my attraction to someone who wouldn't judge me, and I just knew in my heart Jason was that person.

"Yes, I do," I whispered back and a huge bubble of happiness grew inside me.

It's funny, really—just admitting my feelings for Antonio out loud made them even more real and I knew it wasn't just a silly fantasy, but an intense connection I felt with him.

"Be careful, Fi," murmured Jason. A strange expression, bordering on concern, passed over his face. "Don't get me wrong, he's a great bloke, nicest fellow you'd ever want to meet, but just don't go rushing into anything, okay?"

As soon as the words were out of his mouth, the light, teasing atmosphere between us evaporated and I experienced a pang of irritation toward him for spoiling my moment of happiness. I couldn't understand why he would warn me off Antonio, albeit disguised as friendly advice. Didn't he think I was good enough for him? Or maybe he was a little jealous of the fact we had hit it off so quickly?

Yes, that must be it, I thought, *jealous. After all, he's known Antonio for the past couple of years and I've only known him for a week and already he's taken me out for coffee.*

Suddenly, I felt angry with Jason. He had Rachel, after all. How dare he begrudge me a chance of happiness with Antonio? It was as though now he'd cornered the market on happiness, and, let's not forget, sex, he resented anyone else striving for the same. *Well, if that's the case, he can get stuffed!*

Just then, Antonio called a halt to the lesson and I breathed a sigh of relief, eager to distance myself from the awkwardness that now measured the distance between us.

"Looks like we're done for tonight," I said stiffly. "I don't suppose I'll see you here on Friday night, will I?" I asked, the words sounding sharper than I'd intended them to.

"Actually, I was thinking of coming by," he replied, looking away from me and over toward where Antonio stood speaking to Helen and another woman.

I shot him a look of surprise. "But isn't Friday night *Rachel* night?"

"Yeah, I suppose. But I've missed a few lessons lately and I think I'd better catch up before I start getting lazy."

Very strange, I thought, wondering what would prompt him to pass over a night with Rachel.

"Mind you, I can always meet up with her afterward," he added, almost as an afterthought.

That would be right. *Typical bloke.* I should have known he wouldn't turn down a night of sex, not with the ever-so-delectable Rachel anyway. Oh, for Rachel to develop a huge zit on her nose, or better still a massive cold sore. That last thought came out of nowhere. I had to ask myself why I was so pissed-off with her all of a sudden.

"Well, in that case, I'll see you on Friday night, then." And with that I rudely turned my back on him and headed over toward where Antonio had since begun packing away CDs into his backpack.

I knew Jason was still watching me, but I wasn't about to give him the satisfaction of putting me off what I had been waiting to do all night. So, with my anger fueling my determination, I continued toward Antonio.

"Hi, Antonio. Great lesson tonight," I said brightly.

"Thank you. I've been watching you, Fiona, and I must say I am very impressed by the change in you. It's not just the dancing, either, although you have improved enormously. But you seem…um, I don't know, more confident, somehow. Not so frightened to let yourself go with the music. Did last night help?"

"More than you could imagine. Thanks again, for everything. I'm sorry I was such a headcase and all."

"Don't even think about apologizing. After everything you've been through, you deserve a shoulder to cry on."

I could feel the warmth between us growing, blanketing us in a cocoon of intimacy, and made up my mind to take the risk and be bold.

"Antonio."

"Yes?"

"You were so nice to me last night I'd like to return the favor and take you out for a coffee. What do you say?" I asked shyly.

"Just when did you have in mind?"

"Um, well, how about now? I mean when you've finished here, that is?" I added quickly, not to sound like I was rushing him.

There came a slight pause and I prayed he wouldn't find me pushy.

"You know what, Fiona, I would love to. If you could just give me a minute, I'll finish off in here and meet you out in the foyer."

I felt like skipping out of the room with happiness. But seeing as I'm not five years old anymore, I opted for the more dignified adult approach, calmly sauntering over to where I had earlier dumped my bag and casually swinging it over my shoulder before heading for the door.

When I got out into the foyer, resurrecting my earlier irritation, Jason still stood there, waiting by the glass doors. When he saw me emerging from the room, he came over.

"Um, I didn't see your car when I came in, Fi, so I thought I'd see if you need a lift home?"

It was obvious by the way he avoided all hint of eye contact that even *he* thought it a weak excuse.

Ah, that's his plan. To make sure I didn't loiter around the center, and Antonio, he'd personally drive me home.

"No, it's all right, Jason, my car is just around the corner." For being such a killjoy, I decided to get back at him and added, "There's no need to wait around. Antonio and I are going out for coffee, but, thanks, anyway."

I couldn't read the expression on his face, but by the way the muscle in his jaw twitched, I could tell he was somewhat put out upon hearing my plans for the rest of the evening. Not that I cared. He might be pissed off, but he'd be powerless to stop me. He couldn't even tell Rachel, either, as it would become way too complicated to explain the connection between the three of us. I was safe on that score and riding on cloud nine in the knowledge that within the next ten minutes, I would have Antonio to myself.

By the time Jason had driven off, I was the only one left in the foyer and I wandered over toward the door to see what was keeping him. I peeked into the room to see him tucking his mobile phone back into his jacket pocket. Turning around, he saw me and smiled. God, my heart just about melted on the spot.

"Sorry to keep you waiting, Fiona. I just had to change some plans."

"Oh, God, I sorry. I didn't know. We can make it another time, if you like."

Now I was torn between feelings of guilt, seeing as I had obviously put him on the spot, forcing him to change his plans for the evening, and delight that Antonio felt enough for me he would be willing to do that just to be with me.

"No, it's fine. Anyway, it's nothing that can't wait until later." Then, having picked up his backpack, he turned back toward me and grinned mischievously. "Will we risk going back to the café around the corner? We'll have to careful they don't see us coming or they might shut the doors on us after last night."

Laughing, he put his arm around my shoulders and led me out of the center to my car.

* * * *

Margarita, her round face devoid of any obvious emotion, stared back at me, unblinking. She stayed like that for so long I was beginning to feel a little squirmy and decidedly uncomfortable.

I could honestly say I hadn't felt this uncomfortable since Mum had sat me down for a Mother-Daughter talk at the age of fifteen to discuss the evils of using tampons after discovering a box of them hidden in my underwear draw underneath the pile of big beige grandma undies. *Discreet floral packaging, my arse!*

"Do you really think it's wise for you to get involved in another relationship so soon after the breakup of your marriage?"

What is this? A bloody conspiracy? First Jason and now Margarita? I would have thought she'd have been thrilled for me. After all, the whole point of coming here was, supposedly, to help me get on with my life.

"It's been months now, well, over two months since we split up," I whined. "Anyway, *he's* not exactly living a monk's existence," I added. Even to my own ears I sounded worse than a spoiled eight-year-old child and I could almost hear my mother's voice saying *'I suppose if he stuck his head in an oven, you would, too?'*

Margarita sighed and shook her head, the most animated thing I'd seen her do in all the time I'd been coming here.

"It's not your husband's —"

"Ex-husband!" I reminded her.

"Okay, *ex-husband's* emotional well-being I am concerned about."

I think I preferred it when she simply sat and stared at me.

"Fiona, you've been badly hurt from his deceit and his betrayal of your trust."

"But, can't you see, Antonio has made me see it is pointless to dwell in the past. Even you said it was time to move forward in my life and I can see Antonio becoming a huge part of my future now."

The creases between her eyebrows deepened as she leaned forward, resting her elbows on the desk and concentrating all her disapproval on me.

"Moving forward *is* our ultimate goal. But unless you choose to deal with the issues surrounding your failed marriage, instead of working through the problems of the past, you are doomed to repeat them in future relationships."

"Antonio is nothing, *nothing*, like my bastard ex. He would never dream of treating me badly."

I was incensed that Margarita would even suggest any similarities between the two of them.

"I am not suggesting Antonio would deliberately abuse your trust—"

"What exactly *are* you suggesting, then?" I demanded, my ire rising.

My earlier feelings of buoyant happiness were now replaced with indignant anger that I found myself in the position where I felt the need to defend not only Antonio, but also my own feelings toward him.

Sighing, Margarita changed her line of attack. "Okay, Fiona. Let me ask you this. When did you first become aware that your marriage was in serious trouble?"

"I told you all this the first time we spoke."

"Well, would you mind telling me again?" she asked quietly.

The last thing I wanted to rehash was the whole humiliating STD thing. I could barely cope with thinking about it even now, never mind talking about it again.

"Let me put it this way, then. When did you first become aware of your husband's affair? That first niggling doubt?"

I exhaled deeply and looked up at the ceiling to mask my embarrassment. "Like I said before, I had no idea until the doctor asked me if I engaged in unprotected sex."

The heat rose up from my neck.

"And what was your reaction?"

"Well, at first I had no idea why he'd even ask me such a question. After all, I was married. Why would I need to think about condoms and stuff? I was on the Pill."

"What, then?"

"Then he explained to me the only way I could have contracted it was through unprotected sex with an infected partner. I suppose it only then sank in that I had to have caught it from my husband, and he from someone else, obviously."

"And did that come as a shock to you?"

"What sort of a question is that? Of course it was a shock," I began angrily. "A horrible shock. Why do you think I left him?"

I didn't know where she was going with this, but one thing for sure, I wasn't enjoying this interrogation at all. *Shit.* Anyone would think *I* was the guilty one, not him!

By this stage, I'd become so angry I couldn't think straight. "So what are you trying to say? That it is my fault my husband had an affair? That I somehow *drove* him to it?"

"Of course I'm not!" Margarita replied, trying to calm me down.

"Well, what is it then? Do you think I am only capable of attracting men who are *bastards*? Well, I can tell you Antonio is nothing like that. He is kind and considerate and the gentlest man I have ever met. He hasn't even made a move on me yet!"

Silence.

"Are you saying you haven't slept with him?" she asked bluntly.

I could almost hear the relief in her voice.

"No. Not yet."

And with that, the wind of anger left the sails of my indignation and my previous fury lose its momentum, only to be replaced by niggling self-doubt.

Why hadn't he made a move on me? He was a bloke. Even nice blokes are still blokes who think of nothing but sex.

Shit. I'm not a bloke and even I think of nothing but sex.
What's wrong with him?
Or maybe it's me?

It wasn't until I noticed Margarita staring at me I realized she'd been talking.

"Sorry, I missed that!" I mumbled, suddenly feeling deflated and defeated by her mental onslaught.

"I was just saying it is very wise of you to refrain from taking this new relationship to a deeper level in view of your current emotional vulnerability."

But it wasn't me doing the refraining. It was Antonio. I kept that thought to myself, though. *I do have some dignity left.*

Our hour was almost up and I sighed with relief that I could soon escape from her mental probing. My earlier mood of excitement had been replaced by mental exhaustion and I had a headache coming on.

Margarita's earlier concern had finally receded now she had wheedled out of me the embarrassingly innocent nature of my relationship with Antonio. It was probably my resentment toward her for planting the seeds of doubt in my mind that made me imagine the smug expression on her face. *And why wouldn't she look pleased,* I had to ask myself. She had, after all, mentally whopped my arse.

* * * *

The heat being generated from Antonio's body was having a diabolical effect on my affection-starved senses as I spun across the dance floor in his arms. My body felt on fire with the desire that glowed within, but strangely tonight it didn't bring with it those uncomfortable feelings that had plagued me on other occasions. Tonight, I was thrilled to have Antonio all to myself. Holding me, his attention centered firmly on me, only stopping every now and again to offer advice or encouragement to the others in the class.

Those not so fortunate as to be his partner.

After this afternoon's session with Margarita, I'd felt myself sliding back into that all-too-familiar well of self-doubt and despair. Only when I thought about it did I realize Antonio, although always considerate and affectionate toward me in a sort of brotherly way but minus the name calling and Chinese burns, had never hinted by word or action at deepening our friendship. But now, as I moved within the circle of his arms, I melted into the intimacy that hummed around us like a shimmering force field of lust.

At that moment, I wished Margarita was here to witness the rightness of our relationship and perhaps then she wouldn't be so quick to throw cold water over our budding passion.

Unfortunately, the only thing casting a shadow over tonight's happiness was the tension that remained between Jason and me. Apart from a brief awkward greeting as we'd walked into the center earlier, he had barely spoken two words to me. But despite his stony silence, I remained uncomfortably aware that his gaze followed my every movement as he in turn led a blushing Lorraine across the floor.

Anyone would have thought Lorraine had won the lottery, going by the look of pure delight on her shiny red face. Of course, she had good cause to look pleased with herself. Jason — tall, blond and with lovely clear blue eyes that reminded them all of a young Paul Newman — appeared to have his very own fan club among the middle-aged ladies who flocked to Antonio's lessons.

It's just what every twenty-odd-year-old bloke yearns for, really — a harem of hot-blooded, hormonally challenged senior citizens, complete with super-charged libidos, courtesy of Antonio's Latin tutelage.

So naturally Lorraine had been thrilled to score Jason as her partner and spent most of the night partaking in a strange tug-of-war as she attempted to get up close and personal to a man who was twice her size but at least half her age. I must admit, I found it gratifying to witness his prolonged struggle to keep Lorraine at a respectable distance.

It served him right, though. Yes, I know that sounds bitchy, and any other time I would feel ashamed of myself for harboring such uncharitable thoughts, but tonight, Jason hadn't offered to be my partner like the other nights and I have to admit to being a bit put out at again being the only one without a partner.

All was not lost, though, because salvaging my bruised ego was Antonio. A knight in shining armor, he came to my rescue, pulling me into his arms and out on to the dance floor to begin the class.

This was my fifth lesson and I had finally got the hang of counting *and* talking without inviting disaster upon myself, and more importantly, Antonio's feet. Our easygoing conversation carried on effortlessly from Tuesday's late-night coffee after class. He, in turn, asked me about my appointment with Margarita, about which I had confided in him that first teary night. I did, however, decide to keep certain aspects of this afternoon's heated confrontation to myself, thinking it wiser to stick to the positive. It also occurred to me he might not feel too comfortable knowing he'd been the focus of most of today's session with Margarita.

The class was almost over and after building up the courage all night to ask him out again for coffee, I still hadn't found the right moment. With minutes to go before he ended the lesson, I opened my mouth to ask him. But just then, Antonio called for everyone's attention.

"Ladies, gentleman, before we finish off tonight I want to let you know that, unfortunately, I won't be able to take classes next week as I am going overseas on a short business trip. I will try to reach anyone who isn't here tonight by phone, but classes will resume as normal the following week. I apologize for not giving you more notice, but I've been putting this off for some time and now I have no choice but to follow up on my obligations."

Apart from a couple of disappointed murmurs, no one seemed too put out by Antonio's announcement. No one but me, that is. I felt as though the bottom had fallen out of my world, which was stupid, I know, seeing as he'd only be away for a week, but still, the idea of a week without seeing him felt like an eternity.

Soon everyone drifted away to collect their bags and jackets, leaving just the two of us left standing there.

"Don't look so despondent, Fiona. It's only a week and you're not going to forget everything you've learned in that short space of time."

My unhappiness must have shown on my face, because Antonio put his arms around me and gave me a quick hug.

"I'm sure you can live without me for one week," he teased playfully, flicking me gently on the nose.

No, I wanted to shout, *I can't*, or at least I didn't want to.

"Fiona, I meant to ask you earlier, but I was wondering if you would like to have dinner with me next Saturday? My flight gets in late on Friday night so hopefully after a decent sleep I'll feel human again and won't conk out on you at dinner."

"Oh, I'd love to!" I replied.

Dinner sounded *wonderful*. Dinner implied he had something stronger, more intimate in mind and I felt thrilled as well as relieved that he was finally taking the initiative and our mutual attraction wasn't all in my imagination after all.

Immediately, I started compiling a list in my head. New outfit, haircut and color, leg and bikini wax. Well, here's hoping.

"Fiona, there's one other thing. I hope you don't mind, but I'd like to bring along someone very special for you to meet."

"Of course I don't mind." I beamed.

Instantly my heart swelled to the size of a football. *Someone special* could only mean *his mother*! I suppose anyone else would have been a little put off by the thought of going on a date accompanied by his mother, but as I knew how close these traditional Mediterranean families were, I took this to be a positive sign of his seriousness about our budding relationship. Of course his mother would love me. I was determined she would. Then, when we got her approval, we could finally move things along!

Life was finally looking up for me and not even the fact Antonio had to go home and pack for his flight tomorrow morning instead of sharing a coffee with me could take away the happiness I felt at that moment.

* * * *

"Get out of here!" screamed Kim, laughing so hard she almost spilled her skinny cappuccino all over her skinny brown legs.

"Tell me you're joking, Fi. His fucking *mother*!" cried Rachel.

"You girls can laugh all you like, but I think he might be *the* one, and if he wants me to meet his mum, it means he feels the same way toward me."

Not even their mockery of what I saw as a lovely old-fashioned custom could dampen my mood this morning.

"Where is his family from, anyway? Latvia or something," teased Kim, wiping a dribble of froth from her chin.

"No, of course not. I think he, or at least his family, are Italian."

"I wonder if you'll have to supply a donkey for the dowry?" added Rachel, sniggering.

"Very funny. Ha-ha! I tell you, he has more class than any of those wankers you girls go after at the club. What's more, he drives a Saab and owns his own business in the city," I prattled on, forgetting my earlier resolve not to reveal too much about him.

"Oooh, you're going to be a rich bitch, then, running around in sports cars and stuff. I suppose you won't have any time for your old friends when you're glamming it up with *Tony*," said Kim.

"And don't forget his mother. You'll have to make room in the Saab for her, won't you?" added Rachel sarcastically.

Bitches, the lot of them.

Saturday and, just like every other Saturday for the past ten years, give or take a couple, I was sitting with the girls at our favorite open-air café.

Parkside Café nestled in a quiet street just around the corner from the main shopping drag, or what used to be the main hub of retail activity in our mothers' hat-and-pocketbook days, until the nearby Super Center opened and put most of the older establishments out of business. We met here at our regular spot out the back, alfresco, where we could bask in the sun, surrounded by potted ferns and palm trees, and enjoy brunch. It was here, more importantly, where we would dissect the happenings of the night before and either swap stories of wild bonking in the back of rusty Morris Minis, often backed up by the presence of a neck brace, or totally bitch about the latest new face on the dance floor, who naturally is some feral slut—Rachel doesn't like competition—with absolutely no dress sense.

Very rarely has it been known for one of us to miss the chance to go over the Good, the Bad or the Ugly of the previous evening. Although it would seem of late our talk has been mainly been of the ugly variety, apart from Rachel's reviews of her rampant sex life, which started out as riveting coffee talk of the very, very good variety. I must admit, though, there is only so much one wants to learn of her friend's anatomy before it starts to swing to the ugly.

Even during my brief detour into Matrimonial Masochism, while *he* was away enjoying the company of his mates playing cricket in the summer and footy in the winter, I never missed a Saturday. Okay, *apart* from the odd time after a particularly big night out at the club when I'd spend the morning wearing a trench in the carpet between the bedroom and the toilet, continuously purging myself of the previous night's liquid shame, I've always looked forward to swapping the week's gossip with the girls.

Their reaction to my news didn't come as any surprise to me, so I wasn't overly put out by their teasing and sarcasm. Anyway, I've been on the receiving end of far worse of late, meaning in many ways I've become somewhat anesthetized to the bitchy nature of my friends.

Talking a sip of my full-cream latte — time to live dangerously — I indulged myself in a sly smirk of satisfaction. You see, they may well take the piss out of me about my upcoming dinner date with Antonio, but it gave me a perverse sort of pleasure that, at least as far as Rachel was concerned, I knew something she didn't. Namely, Jason's secret dancing fetish.

"Hey, Rachel, did you have a good night with *Jason* last night?" I asked, trying to hide a smile.

I figured they'd had enough mileage out of me for one morning.

"When he eventually turned up, I did! He was acting really weird, too. He got real shitty when I told him I'd been trying to ring him all night and he had his phone turned off. Said something about it being none of my business at first, but I eventually got it out of him that his boss at the nursery made him stay back late to unload a late delivery of native plants and these new terracotta pots."

"*Poor* Jason! He must have been exhausted," I said, picturing him struggling to put some distance between himself and randy Lorraine.

My sarcasm was completely wasted on them.

"It was all right in the end. Once he got a couple of drinks into him, he loosened up a bit. And later on, much later, when we got back to his place we were all sweaty and horny and he started…"

My brain began its *La, La, La, La…*

"And, Fi, you owe me seventy bucks!"

That snapped my attention back to the present. "What?"

Rachel scowled, Janine rolled her eyes and Kim gave Rachel that 'I told you she'd flake' look.

"Stacey's fucking wedding present, remember? You did agree to pitch in, and now I need the money," she growled, holding out her hand expectantly.

Stacey's wedding. *Bloody hell, that's tonight. How on Earth could I have forgotten?* Well, it wasn't difficult. Considering my recent experiences, I wasn't exactly going all gushy-gooey over what I saw as another lamb heading off merrily to the slaughterhouse of love — known by many as an altar.

"Okay, keep your hair on. I've got your money here. What did we end up getting her, anyway?" I asked, blithely handing over my hard-earned cash.

"Oh, it's great, you'll just love it, believe me," said Kim, all wide-eyed and enthusiastic.

It's weird, but when one of them says that to me, it usually ends up I don't *love* it at all. In fact, I usually hate it with a passion. But, having already paid for it, I have no real choice but to fake rapturous enthusiasm or risk Kim and Rachel chucking another hissy fit over what they consider to be my atrocious taste in everything from clothes to men.

Thinking of my ex, they might just have a point there.

"You know, ages ago when Stacey was telling us how she couldn't wait to have kids but Simon wasn't too keen?" asked Janine, entering the conversation now she'd finally finished her large iced coffee with extra whipped cream and shaved chocolate. A woman after my own heart.

"Yes, vaguely," I answered cautiously, wondering what that had to do with her wedding present.

Surely Stacey wasn't pregnant. *Not that it would be the worst thing that could happen to a girl before her wedding,* I thought, knowing what it was like to want one of those gorgeous little creatures myself.

Babies, that is. Not husbands.

Then I suddenly remembered the well-hung, ugly bartender Stacey had shagged in the gents' in the early morning hours after her bachelorette night. Instantly there came an unbidden image of visiting her at the maternity hospital and having to croon over a hideous mutant of a baby boy with thick greasy hair, congenitally acne-scarred skin and a huge wang.

I shuddered.

"Well, we got her a *Spoodle!*" they screamed in unison.

I frowned, more than a little confused. "What the fuck is a Spoodle?" I asked, somehow knowing I wasn't going to like the answer.

"It's a puppy, you idiot, a cross between a Spaniel and a Poodle, and it is the sweetest thing you've ever seen," gushed Kim, looking dangerously clucky. "All fluffy and curly and its ears are so floppy —"

"You *can't* give them a dog for a wedding present, for crying out loud."

"Why the hell not?" snapped Rachel. "It's a damn sight better than an ugly cut-glass vase."

Suddenly, I had a flashback to my own doomed wedding and the hideous hand-blown purple glass vase *his* cousins gave us for our wedding present, the one that looked a little like a bulbous sex aid. But at least that was within society's accepted limits, even if it did resemble a big purple dildo.

"Because it's a *dog*, that's why!" I yelled. "How do you even know they want a bloody dog?"

"No one ever rejects a beautiful puppy. Not once they see it," answered Janine.

"See, I told you we should have waited until tonight to tell her," Rachel said to the other two, pouting. "Now she's going to go on and on about it all fucking afternoon."

I knew the futility of pointing out to them what an inappropriate wedding present it was, as they obviously couldn't put the bloody dog back where it came from.

Shit, if this was their idea of the perfect wedding gift for poor unsuspecting Stacey and Simon, what would they come up with if and or when Antonio and I decided to make it official? A life-sized stuffed crocodile to go beside the pool, or a year's supply of Lean Cuisine in case I let myself go and balloon in marital contentment, or maybe even a couple of tons of chicken manure for the garden?

The mind boggles, really. Not that I would have to worry about our wedding plans any time in the near future. I still had to sort something out with my ex before I was free to officially commit myself to Antonio.

Just then I had a terrible thought. *What if Antonio is a strict Catholic?* I had no idea, really, but then I remembered he always wore a tiny gold crucifix on a chain around his neck. I groaned. *This could complicate matters.* Not only would I have to change my religion, but also they might not let us marry if I'm divorced. With that in mind, I knew the only way around this little dilemma would be to convince my ex to agree to an annulment. Of course, I'd have to make out *he* was impotent and we'd never consummated the marriage in the two and half years we'd been hitched. That one could be a little tricky, I realized, but it was worth a try.

I'm getting off track here.

Oh, of course, the dog!

"Okay," I sighed, resigning myself to the fact that like it or not we were now hauling a fucking *Spoodle*, and an outrageously overpriced one at that, to the wedding with us later on that afternoon. "But if Stacey and what's-his-face don't want it, it's your problem, not mine. Agreed?"

"Agreed," they chorused.

Chapter Twelve

I bloody hate weddings!
I'm willing to go on record saying that, too.

Fine, I'll admit I wasn't always so jaded. In fact, I used to love the romance and magic that comes with being part of a couple's special day, but with my own marriage disaster still fresh and painful, I suppose I can be forgiven for being a bit of a kill joy.

And as I sat squished in the back seat of Janine's RAV4 next to a desperately whining Spoodle shut away in a large silver gift box secured with a huge purple bow to match the bridesmaid's dresses – thank God I'm not one of them – I couldn't help ponder over the memories of all the nuptials I've witnessed over the years.

To date, I've lost count of the number of weddings I've attended. Cousins' weddings, friends' weddings, work mates' weddings – always a good excuse to get shit-faced and embarrass yourself in front of colleagues, second only to Christmas parties in that respect – and even friends' cousins' weddings, the latter to even up numbers. Oh, then there are the invitations to my parents' friends' children's weddings!

Talk about six degrees of separation.

But my recent cynicism isn't just due to the fact that so little consideration is given to the fifty or whatever years of marriage that come *after* the big day – the till death do you part bit – it's all the hysteria that attaches itself to anything bridal-related I now find difficult to tolerate, given my current circumstances.

Take, for instance, the wedding dress. I've known girls

to spend more on a dress they will only wear once than they did on their first car — which, I might add, is still faithfully getting them from A to B five years on, long after the groom has packed up his PlayStation and *Terminator* DVDs and moved on to greener pastures. There also seems to be a conspiracy between brides the world over to make their bridesmaids look as hideous as possible while almost plunging them into bankruptcy with the exorbitant costs involved in hiring BO-stained, pea-green taffeta dresses straight from the set of *The King and I.*

Having said that, I would like to go on record in saying that I *did not* go all draconian on *my* bridesmaids. Therefore, I take no responsibly for the eclectic assortment of getups they choose to present themselves in on my big day.

I'll never forget the look on my mother's face when she saw them.

Kim had opted for the Hollywood sex-siren look and in honor of my big day had even gone to all the trouble of dying her hair platinum-blonde as the final touch to her Marilyn Monroe homage.

Rachel, also fancying the mega-star theme, had gone for a Madonna look. Unfortunately, *not* Madonna's brief but memorable Marilyn Monroe phase—that would have been too much to ask—but her hard-arsed, lesbian-bitch phase complete with conical pointed bra, suspender belt and towering platform shoes.

At least I could usually depend on Janine to bring some sanity and decorum to an event. But apparently not on that particular day, though. Having taken a solemn vow at the age of eight never to wear a dress again after a bad experience at her Confirmation, she arrived wearing a suit. What's that you're thinking? That sounds all right? Normal? Well, I might add, it was a man's business suit, and not any old suit, but a very old suit. To my abject horror, it turned out to be a pale-blue safari suit she'd found at the local charity shop and, to add that special touch, she'd decided to dress it up with a huge floppy orange hat.

I swear my mother almost had a stroke when she saw the three of them. To this day, she's never forgiven them for attempting to upstage me, the bride dressed in a simple but classy 1960s-inspired strapless A-line satin gown that wasn't boring, no matter what the girls said.

Any sane person would have seen this as an omen for my short-lived marriage, but not me. Instead I was followed down the aisle by what looked like the drunken cast members of some weird Broadway salute to stardom. Needless to say, the gasps that rippled in the wake of my stroll down to the altar toward my slack-jawed husband-to-be were not so much in appreciation of my ethereal beauty but more the result of my bridesmaids' noisy conga-line procession down the red carpet before me.

At least everyone agreed they were unlikely to forget this wedding in a hurry.

Under the circumstances, I don't think it's considered a good thing really.

Little wonder I was experiencing certain difficulties summoning the appropriate enthusiasm for this upcoming nuptial extravaganza.

Rounding the corner at breakneck speed, I screamed. The Spoodle yelped and Kim swore.

"Jesus, Janine. What the fuck are you trying to do, kill us or something?"

"Sorry, guys, didn't see the turn off until it was almost too late."

She didn't sound in the least bit sorry, though.

The whining increased until the Spoodle sounded as though he was singing along to 1990s-inspired grunge music on the stereo. The poor thing, he didn't sound very well, or happy about his continuing confinement in a box which had never been designed to hold livestock.

"Can't we let him out of this box, at least until we get to the church?" I asked, retaining a firm hold on the jumping, yelping wedding present.

"No, you can't! Rachel spent ages getting him in there

and she'll kill us if we let him out," Kim replied bluntly, turning up the volume on the stereo in an attempt to drown out the puppy cries coming from the backseat.

My heart went out to poor little no-name beside me. In our short but life-altering, almost life-ending, drive to the large Episcopalian church, the venue for Stacy's wedding, I'd found myself bonding with our noisy little wedding present. I suppose it was inevitable, seeing as I was beginning to think none of us were going to reach the church alive, thanks to Janine's kamikaze-inspired road skills.

Despite my earlier misgivings, I really love animals, especially dogs. As children, my brother and I had continually begged Mum to let us have a dog, but the answer had always been the same. "No!" she'd say. "You two can't even clean up after yourselves, never mind a dog, and I'm no' going to git left with all the feedin' and pickin' up of the dog dirt."

Mum never said 'shit', not even when describing shit.

You see, Mum is not a *dog* person, but a cat person. Yes, there *are* two distinct types of animal lovers and Mum is definitely of the latter persuasion. When I was younger, she'd had this massive black Persian that she positively doted on. It was called Cinda, short for Cinderella, but my brother and I referred to it as Satan. Evil by name, evil by nature.

It was without a doubt *the* most spiteful creature I have ever known. I still bear the scars down the backs of my thighs from its well-timed and vindictive assaults. How? Well, the malevolent little bastard would lie in wait until I'd get up in the middle of the night to go to the toilet. Then, out of nowhere it would pounce, burying its razor-sharp claws in the back of my bare legs before using my tender flesh as a human scratching post.

Naturally I'd scream, waking up the entire house. But would the fucking cat be thrown out into the back yard? No! Mum would race out of the bedroom all in a fluster and scoop up 'her poor wee darling', leaving me, her poor *bleeding* darling to limp back to my room while Satan got to sleep at the end of Mum and Dad's bed for the remainder of the night.

The injustice of it all!

Mind you, like the saying goes, what comes around, goes around. And Satan's wicked nature finished up being the end of her when she picked on one bird too many. Satan lived off a diet of Australian native birds – some endangered, some just tasty.

We were up the coast at my Aunty Margaret's and as usual Satan was accompanying us. By the time we arrived, I could barely walk for sneezing and my eyes were all but glued together due to the fact I was obliged to cradle the cat basket despite being severely allergic to cat fur.

I swear that fucking cat could shed on cue.

After getting settled in at Aunty Margaret's where we were spending a couple of days, Mum let Satan out to explore.

Satan's exploring led her upstairs, where she soon spotted fresh prey, in the form of a flock of king parrots gathered in the tree outside Aunty Margaret's bedroom window. To Satan, it must have been like walking into Willy Wonka's chocolate factory. Unfortunately, her insatiable appetite for rare Australian birds proved to be her ultimate downfall when she leapt out toward the hapless birds, all fangs and fur a-flying, and found herself frantically scrambling in thin air. Within seconds she had dropped like a rock twenty feet down into Aunty Margaret's free-form swimming pool.

Poor Satan was a sadist, not a swimmer, and we found her at the bottom of the pool soon after.

Mum instantly went into mourning and we went home to what could almost be described as a state funeral for Satan, and my nights once again were terror-free.

"Oh, look," Kim cried out, as Janine swung into the car park of St Benedict's and screeched to a halt in the only remaining space available, cutting off someone who I suspected was the groom's mother, "there's Rachel and Jason over there by those lovely old tombstones."

Kim had a thing about tombstones that bordered on creepy. Strike that. It *was* creepy.

She couldn't pass a cemetery without wandering through it oohing and aahing over the graves of entire families of toddlers wiped out by measles or whooping cough epidemics more than a hundred years before. Or she'd make us run around looking for the oldest person buried in the graveyard. To date, I hold the record after coming across some poor old codger who'd hung in there until the ripe old age of one hundred and nine, only to die in a bullock train accident. At the time, I did have to ask myself what the hell a one-hundred-and-nine-year-old was doing that close to a team of bullocks in the first place. But, well, you've got to die somehow.

So it was no surprise really that, as soon as the car came to a halt, Kim jumped out and made a beeline toward where Rachel and Jason were waiting by the entrance of the decaying graveyard. Janine, being of the opinion that her role of chauffeur exonerated her from any further guest-related duties, went off in search of the powder room, leaving me to struggle with the present that was becoming increasingly animated and difficult to hold.

Bloody hell, what was I going to do with him? It was too hot to leave him in the car—he'd surely dehydrate before the end of the ceremony, especially one of these long drawn-out Episcopalian affairs. Stacey had assured us we wouldn't have to get down on our knees for the duration of the service, but she hadn't made eye contact as she'd said it, making me understandably apprehensive.

I couldn't bring myself to leave him outside the church, either, concealed under a large nearby hydrangea. That reeked too heavily of leaving a baby on the doorstep of an orphanage in the middle of the night for my liking. Anyway, I'd never forgive myself if some passing dog-hating sicko spotted the silver and purple box and nicked it. What if he dumped my poor Spoodle in some lonely, out-of-the-way dirt track at the mercy of wild animals when he discovered the contents of the above said wedding present were not the ugly cut-glass vase they secretly hoped for but a poor scared little puppy!

Just then I felt something small, wet and cold against my hot, clammy palm—his cute little Spoodle nose poking through one of the neat little air holes Rachel had cut in the box—just prior to callously stuffing his furry protesting limbs into it, that is.

When his little nose disappeared and a tiny pink tongue emerged and licked my hand, my heart instantly liquefied into a big ball of mushy love. I knew then I'd be sneaking him into the church, and well away from potential puppy-hating thieves with an ugly cut-glass vase fetish.

* * * *

Well, who could blame him? I bloody hate hymns, too.

But when his whining threatened to drown out the organist, I was left with no other alternative but to sing louder and louder. I sounded like a contestant on the Eurovision song contest belting out a tune in a language completely alien to me.

Rachel, Kim and Janine kept nudging one another and snickering in my direction as they mouthed the words printed out in the well-thumbed hymn books. Obviously, they found my newfound enthusiasm for church music a welcome diversion from the big fat baritone directly in front of them, who reeked of BO and sang like he'd personally written the hymn and therefore had every right to sing it louder and more off-key than anyone else in the church.

Having slipped in a good fifteen minutes before the bride was due to arrive, I managed to conceal our boxed Spoodle undetected in a corner at the end of an elaborately decorated pew at the back. Thankfully my prayers had been answered—I was in church after all—and the puppy remained quiet once more, having finally fallen asleep from the rocking motion of being carried from the car to the building.

Soon after, the girls, tailed by Jason, joined me in the rapidly filling church. I quickly explained the presence of the by now less-than-pristine box at my feet, but they didn't seem to be the least bit concerned about possible puppy thieves or the dangers of dehydration.

Heaven help any poor baby who finds him or herself saddled with one of these three as a mother.

Eventually, I began to relax. All was well. The Spoodle was sound asleep. The bride was beautiful. The groom looked just like Pierce Brosnan in *Die Another Day*, leaving most of the women in the church almost choking on their envy. The bridesmaids were coping well with their humiliation even though purple crushed velvet should be universally outlawed and the girls were behaving themselves. Even Aunt Maisie had reverted back to her Queen Mother persona, having put her short-lived but nonetheless scary ambitions to become the next Beyoncé to rest, thank God.

Everything would have remained smooth cruising had it not been for the fucking organist. This woman looked as though a small puff of wind would have flattened her. But as soon as she sat down at the organ—and not just any old clapped-out church organ, but one of those serious kick-ass organs with the twenty-foot pipes shooting out from the top—she turned into the Mr. Hyde of organists.

So how could I blame the poor puppy for yelping when the first blood-curdling notes of *Jerusalem* all but shook the church's foundations? The only guests who didn't jump up and clutch their chests as the place shook to the rude booming were either deaf or regular church-goers who obviously knew what was going down. The rest of us were left debating whether to make a run for it or not, half expecting bits of the ceiling to come crashing down on our heads.

Eventually the noise started him off, yelping and whining.

At first, no one noticed, but as the organist settled into the hymn, those of us who were initially startled into singing soon gave it up as a bad joke and gradually began miming, first every second or third word until we were simply opening and closing our lips like starving goldfish. As we were seated among mostly non-church-going heathen, soon the only sounds were the above-mentioned big fat baritone and our cruelly incarcerated Spoodle.

My first instinct was to pick up the Spoodle and make a dash outdoors, but, as I was soon to discover, that proved to be less than desirable seeing as the bottom of the box was by now a soggy pulp of puppy piss. *Yuk!* No way was I going to be able to make a discreet exit with dog piss trailing behind my retreating form, hence my sudden enthusiasm for hymn singing.

In one way, I prayed for the damn singing to stop as my throat was beginning to feel like I'd swallowed a mouthful of diced cactus and, apart from that, I suspected I was seriously scaring those unfortunate enough to be sitting within a five-pew radius of me. But then the horrible thought lingered that, as soon as the organist stopped the racket, the puppy's whines were going to echo incriminatingly throughout the church.

When I felt sure he had calmed, I was game enough to turn down the volume of my own crude salutations to the almighty, to the obvious relief of the girls, who were finding it difficult to compose themselves from the shock of my profound religious experience.

Deathly silence.

"Ladies and gentlemen, we are gathered here to solemnize the union between Stacey and Simon in the eyes of God and with you as witnesses…"

The minister's voice restored a certain kind of calm among the shell-shocked wedding guests and thus the business end of proceedings began.

From beneath me, I was vaguely aware of a muffled scratching coming from the box. At the time, I was so relieved he had stopped crying that I paid little or no attention to it. There would be plenty of time later to regret my complacency. Besides, almost certainly no one else had heard it.

"Do you, Simon Edward Horace Baker…"

Kim sniggered loudly beside me, resulting in a couple of dirty looks from Aunt Maisie and her elderly sidekicks. I struck out at her with my elbow, silencing her. The last thing I wanted was to draw attention to our general direction.

"Take this woman, Stacey June Taylor, to be your lawful wedded wife…"

I sighed. My emotions were all over the place. The years rushed back to greet me head-on. It felt like only yesterday that I'd been standing there in Stacey's place, a picture of wide-eyed naiveté and blinded by love. A lump of raw emotion rose up toward my throat and I stifled an urge to shout out to Stacey to think again before she committed herself to this man. But then, she already had a nice normal-sounding surname, so that ruled out one possible reason for rushing into a hasty, ill-matched marriage unprepared.

I know people say they often cry at weddings, but I don't. You see, I'm usually too busy eagerly anticipating the free alcohol at the reception. But sitting there in that cavernous church, watching Stacey and Simon pledge their undying love to one another, brought back memories of all those feelings of hope, excitement and euphoria that had washed over me as that plain gold ring had been slipped onto *my* finger.

Instantly, I was back in that stuffy, dour Presbyterian church, where as a child I would sit squashed between Mum and Dad, while Granny sat next to Alex rolling barley sugars noisily around her dentures. I could see it as if it was yesterday. I was about to pledge myself body and soul to the bastard at my right. And what do I remember most about that portentous moment? The love shining from my intended's eyes, or the scent of roses wafting freely around the church, or that chest-swelling sensation of overwhelming love?

Most of all, I remember trying to decide whether to add a little twirl after the second *L* when I signed the wedding register, Fiona Morgana Maxwell.

Thinking back on it now, of course, I feel ashamed. But at the time, the addition of the little theatrical twirl at the end of Maxwell symbolized the realization of my dream of a magical life of wedded bliss.

My eyes were beginning to mist over. Stacey and Simon were barely more than a blur as the minister called for the rings. *There goes singlehood and here comes a lifetime of married misery.*

I know I sound cynical, defeatist, even mean-spirited. I didn't begrudge Stacey her stab at happiness, really.

I took in a big bitter lungful of forced optimism and tried to focus on something positive in my life, something to lift my sagging spirits.

Antonio.

Although we'd only known one another for a short time, in my heart of hearts, I felt it was only a matter of time before I married Antonio and became part of his huge, warm-hearted, extended European family. Then I could finally put the memory of my first marriage—my starter or entrée marriage as I'll refer to it henceforth—where it rightfully belongs. That is, in the part of my brain together with all the other stupid things I've done, regretted, then consequently gotten over.

That particular corner of my mind is getting a little full of late, mind you. Of course, marriage number one fills a fair portion of it. There is also the nightclub fiasco, something not easily forgotten. Then the time I took up smoking at thirteen because I considered it to be ultra-sophisticated, and spent the next three weeks feeling like I was about to throw up any moment. Apart from that, the list goes on. The time Kim had a huge fight with her parents and ran away, dragging me along with her, where we spent a memorable night hiding in a disused train carriage, freezing our arses off until the transit police discovered us and called our parents.

"I now pronounce you husband and wife!"

It was at that exact moment in time everything seemed to happen at once.

The groom kissed the bride.

The wedding guests cheers and clapped.

Rachel yelled out, "Stick ya tongue down his throat, Stace!"

And something wet and fluffy brushed past my bare ankles and flew out into the aisle before hanging a sharp left and making a frantic dash up to the altar, barking madly.

Sure, he was small and fluffy and, looking at it one way, I could see how one or two of the more shortsighted guests could have mistaken him for a baby bear. But it still didn't explain the chaos and hysteria that burst forth as the Spoodle made a beeline for the bewildered bride.

At once, my heart went all fluttery and I felt decidedly nauseous. If I was ever going to faint in my life, I prayed it would be now to save me facing the coming recriminations.

No such luck, though.

I remained stubbornly conscious.

Looking down at my feet to where the puppy had until recently been perfectly safe and inconspicuous, I saw the tattered remains of one soggy silver gift box and what was left of the horrible purple ribbon that had once secured it.

Fuck. Fuck. Fuck!

All the time I had been busy indulging myself in a little self-pity, it never occurred to me that the Spoodle had also been busy, effectively digging his way to freedom out of the damn box.

People were screaming and shouting and trying to catch the slippery little bugger as he repeatedly dodged and twisted his way out of everyone's reach, ears flapping and tiny lightning-fast legs skidding this way and that, like a scrum half going for the winning try.

I knew I couldn't just sit there and do nothing. So as much

as I wanted to make good my escape now, I decided to swallow my pride and do the right thing. I jumped up in pursuit of the little doggy fugitive.

Unfortunately, I was too late. Way too late.

Stacey screamed loudly and I instinctively cringed and closed my eyes, not game enough to watch the disaster about to unfold before me.

I stood there, unable to move, halfway down the aisle where on one side a ten-year-old cousin of Stacey laughed hysterically and on the other side some old relative of Simon's sported a hat that defied gravity was crying, again hysterically.

Stacey's screams died down and instead she began calling out, for help, I imagined. By the time I opened my eyes, curiosity easily outweighing my dread, I couldn't believe what I saw. There stood Stacey, at the altar, with her husband of all of twenty-five seconds, cradling the puppy in her arms, calming the by now very frightened little creature.

Just then, looking up, Stacey saw me standing frozen in the aisle, and I in turn saw the trail of grubby, pissy puppy paw prints all over her hand-beaded one-off designer wedding dress.

I thought I was going to vomit all over the plush crimson carpet that stretched out in front of me to the altar. Not only had I ruined her wedding ceremony, I had also ruined her staggeringly expensive wedding dress.

Nightmarish!

I couldn't speak. I'd actually been rendered speechless. A first, I assure you. But then, this was also the first time I'd single-handedly destroyed someone's wedding. I felt as though I stood in a long tunnel and the only way out was the very place I didn't want to go. And right now Stacey stood at the end of that long tunnel with her doggy-soiled wedding dress, cradling her yapping wedding present.

I wanted to die.

But nothing prepared me for what was to happen next.

"Oh, my God, Fiona!" Stacey cried out. Tears of mortification instantly began welling in my eyes. "He's *gorgeous!*"

Instantly relief hit me as Stacey put two and two together. Of course, it helped that Janine by now stood behind me with the remains of the silver box at arm's length between thumb and forefinger. I itched to point out that the damn box was fuck-all use to us now, but at least she was making an effort to be useful. More than I could say for Rachel and Kim, who together with poor Jason stood, mouths gaping, like they'd just witnessed a horrific car crash.

"Fiona, I can't believe it. You got us a puppy! I just love him," Stacey cried and held up the squirming bundle of fur to Simon. "Look, Simon, a puppy!"

Simon smiled and reached out to pat the fluffy head affectionately. But then he wasn't really in a position to do anything else. He could hardly order us to take the dog away, and in the process, break his new bride's heart. And thus it appeared as if the Spoodle was staying—for the time being, at least.

Chapter Thirteen

"I bet you sink you're soo fuckn' clefer?" slurred Rachel, adding more wine to the rapidly growing moat of alcohol surrounding her on the table as she tried yet again to get it past her lipstick-smeared lips.

I could almost track the words as they formed in her brain before making the long, difficult journey to her mouth. Like a three-second delay on a bad overseas phone line.

"You made out like it was all your idea. You *hated* the idea," she continued vehemently, drawing attention from those unlucky enough to be seated close to us. "All you had to do was bring the fuck'n dog to the wedd'n an' you couldn't get tha' right witho' fuck'n it up! Now fuck'n Stacey thinks you're soo great. Well, you can *kiss my fuck'n arse!*"

Rachel was way, way past ugly drunk and rapidly zeroing in on obnoxious, fisty, paralytic drunk. She had already sharpened her vicious tongue on various other innocent wedding guests, most of them unknown to her, but that had obviously been just her way of warming up for the grand finale, the mother of verbal assaults she was to soon unleash on me.

Thank God the meal and speeches were over at last and the lights had dimmed. She wasn't a pleasant sight at all. Her normally smooth blonde hair looked as if it had seen artillery or mortar fire somewhere in the Middle East, with her forty-dollar blow wave basically massacred. Adding to her recently unearthed Cruella de Vil persona was the remains of her usually immaculate makeup, by now migrating to new and better pastures. That is, her mascara stained her cheeks and her lippy, the divine Dior pink I'd been dying to try, was now well on its way to saying hello to her ear.

Kim and Janine weren't far behind her, I might add. So, of course, I had to stay sober in order to drive Janine and Kim home. It hadn't been planned this way, but after Janine'd polished off the second carafe of house white before we'd even begun the main course, I was fairly sure which one of us would be the designated driver tonight. Usually, there is nothing I hate more than being the *only* sober one among us at the end of the night. So, I should point out at this stage I was more than a little relieved that Jason had also been press-ganged by Rachel into driving. Apart from the fact it would need more than my muscle power to get these three prime candidates for AA out of the Function Center and into the car in one piece, I was glad to have a coherent conversation with someone, anyone, even Jason.

Right then, compared to the volley of venom shooting out of Rachel's blotchy mouth, the ceremony fiasco and what had followed seemed like little more than a passing diversion.

After the service ended, Stacey and Simon had been whizzed off for wedding photos, of which Romper was a feature.

Why Romper? Well, shortly after all the fuss died down, Stacey decided to call the Spoodle Romper, as in *Romper Stomper*, due to the carnage and mayhem his appearance had caused.

Well, with Stacey and Simon safely outside, it cleared the way for everyone who was anyone to converge in my direction, where they proceeded to verbally beat the shit out of me. First in line — Stacey's mum, who, I was soon to discover, had paid for Stacey's now slightly soiled wedding dress. In fact, her tearful rantings and recriminations only subsided when I promised to foot the dry cleaning bill. I had a horrible suspicion, though, that it was going to set me back a nauseatingly large sum of money and briefly considered my chances of getting the girls to contribute. Deep down, though, I knew I had more chance of having them donate a kidney than coming up with the necessary moolah. Yes, I was basically on my own with this one.

Then next in line came the minister, who went on and on for a full fifteen minutes about my blatant lack of respect for the almighty and the holiness of marriage. In my defense, I did try to point out that puppies were also God's creatures, but this religious zealot steamrollered all my attempts to lighten the ugly atmosphere I found myself at the center of.

Not to be left out was Simon's aunt, who elbowed her way through the throng to deliver unto me a right bollocking. That was until something twanged in her rapidly deteriorating short-term memory and she recognized me from the *bachelorette* night. Or, more precisely, she remembered *I* was one of the number who'd witnessed *her* impromptu lap dancing at Stacey's bachelorette night before poor Daniel had been rescued by the compère and herded downstairs to safety. How a woman of her advanced years knew that much about the art of lap-dancing is a mystery I have no wish to delve into. But one thing's for sure, it certainly put me off considering a career change in that direction. There is nothing more bile-producing than a geriatric debauchee.

Anyway, as the veil of recognition lifted from her mind, Aunt Maisie's pompous, Victorian bubble of self-righteousness was irreparably punctured. With the knowledge that I knew what she undoubtedly would prefer never to remember, she rapidly lost her momentum. Puffing out her matronly bosom, she scampered off to rejoin the other likewise matronly bosomed women wearing loud floral royalty-inspired frocks, over by the marble christening font. There they stood together under massive hats of all styles, fanning themselves with wedding programs, making a big show of being outraged over Romper's dramatic arrival.

Strangely, the only people who weren't lining up to have a piece of my by now well-chewed arse were Rachel,

Kim and Janine, who had bailed out at the first available opportunity, fearing they would be set upon as well by Stacey and Simon's scandalized relatives.

Eventually, sanity returned when the photographer poked his head around the church door and summoned the parents of the bride and groom outside for photos. It was at that moment they were forced to put aside their hostility as they turned their attention to the happy couple.

So, in the spirit of the day, they decided to bury the hatchet, and not in my head, thank God.

By the time I made good my escape from the church, the girls were already in the car and waiting for me. After all, the reception and free alcohol were only a short drive away.

After Rachel had exhausted herself screaming at me, she staggered off to the toilet with Kim and Janine in tow.

"Jesus, Fiona, what can I say? I'm so sorry about Rachel. I had no idea she could get that *nasty*. Or that *drunk*! I'm sure when she sobers up, she's going to feel really bad about being such a bitch to you," said Jason.

In the past hour or so, poor Jason had really had his rose-colored glasses snatched from his face and stomped into oblivion right in front of his disbelieving eyes. Actually, he looked positively shell-shocked at what could possibly have been rated as one of Rachel's more vicious verbal assaults.

What amazed *me* more was not so much the volley of vindictiveness I had just been pelted with, but more the fact Rachel and Jason had been going out together for a month now and she'd managed to keep this particularly ugly facet of her personality contained for that long. *Shit, she must really love him.* Usually the honeymoon phase of her many, many relationships rarely lasted longer than a week, at most, before the bitch in her escaped.

I'm sure, had it not been for the copious amounts of alcohol consumed by Rachel, she would have remained safe and adored in her ivory tower for at least a little while longer.

"Don't *you* go apologizing for her, Jason. Sometimes

Rachel needs a handler rather than a boyfriend."

Jason just sat and stared glumly into his tasteless light beer.

"How can you be so forgiving, Fi? She's a complete bitch to you. Don't you ever just want to say, 'stuff this, I'm off'?"

"It's just the way she is. I try not to take it personally. Anyway, she's always been a bit temperamental."

"*Temperamental!* That little display of hers goes way past *temperamental*, don't you think? *Psychotic* is more like it!"

I suppose when I thought about it, it did. But, over the years, I had become immune to Rachel's poisonous temper, meaning tonight's little episode didn't shock me as much as it probably should have. She did have her good points, as well. Not that I could recall any at that particular moment, but they were out there somewhere, just waiting for my memory to trip over.

"You can tell me to shut up if I'm out of line here, but I think you can do a lot better than to hang about with those three. They treat you like shit sometimes. I've seen it myself and —"

Jason was suddenly silenced by the sight of Rachel bearing down on us, flanked by Kim and Janine, as they returned from the ladies'.

The girls were all brandishing fresh drinks, which had thankfully restored some civility in them once more.

"Hey, Rach," said Jason quietly. "Don't you think you've maybe had enough?" He nodded to the brimming glass of merlot in her hand.

And *on* her hand.

And dribbling down her wrist onto the carpet below.

"Shut up, Jason," she snapped. "Don't be such a boring shit. I'm just having a good time with my friends here."

And to demonstrate the depths of her drunken camaraderie, she swung her arms around Kim and Janine and staggered back slightly, promptly spilling her wine right down Janine's back.

"Fuck, Rach!" screamed Janine as the sticky red liquid

coursed down her spine, rapidly forming very unbecoming red stain across her butt.

"Oops, I suppose I'd better go and get myself another drink then," she giggled, not in the least concerned about Janine's plight.

Throwing her now-empty glass down on the table, Rachel then spun around and headed off on a mercy dash to the bar for a refill, leaving Janine hurling black looks in her direction.

"Look at me," cried Janine. "Fucking bitch is what she is," she continued as she took off back toward the toilets with a fistful of serviettes, closely followed by Kim.

Jason groaned and I laughed. I couldn't help myself. It was funny.

Well, at least it was better than being yelled at.

"Oh, God, it's all right for you to laugh. But I've got to go home with her tonight," he said, watching Rachel stumble her way toward the bar, looking as though she was trying to make it up the gangplank of the QE2 in the middle of a freak cyclone.

"Well, someone's got to hold the bucket as she throws up," I responded in a feeble attempt to lighten Jason's mood.

Jason just looked at me, his expression that of a condemned man facing the scaffold.

This wasn't like him at all. I supposed I'd become so used to seeing the besotted look on his face whenever he merely glanced in Rachel's direction that it was a shock to discover all was not well in the Rachel-Jason love camp.

"It can't be that bad, surely?" I laughed, looking up to where Rachel rested at a table near the bar, deep in some meaningful conversation with Simon's mother, who was frantically looking around for any means of escape possible.

I probably shouldn't have stuck my nose any further into Jason's Rachel woes, but I was more than a little curious. Okay, *dying* to know what was going on between the two on them. Especially considering Rachel had only this week been sighted sneaking out of the convenience store with a bridal magazine tucked under her arm and a guilty expression on her face. This interesting snippet of information I had gleaned from Tanya, with whom I shared the duties of junior assistant sales manager in the Ladies' Fashion department at work.

"I sometimes wonder what I've got myself into as far as Rachel goes. Some of the guys at the club warned me at the beginning that she was high-maintenance, but I had no idea just how demanding she is. Shit. I'm sorry. I shouldn't be telling you this. You're her friend, after all. It's not fair of me to dump on you."

Yeah, yeah, yeah.

Friends, friends, friends.

Blah, blah, blah.

More, tell me more, I thought, terrified he'd clam up on me now in an ill-timed attack of decency. Rachel was still chewing Simon's now-desperate mother's ear off, the band had moved on to hits from the eighties and as the other two were nowhere in sight, I decided to press Jason for more info.

After all, this was just too good to pass up.

"It's okay, Jason. If you want to talk, I'm a great listener. Remember, we've salsa danced together—there are no secrets between us now."

Jason slowly looked across at me and our eyes locked. Granted, the lights *were* dimmed, but I could have sworn his pupils darkened in a spectacularly *non*-platonic manner.

My face ignited into a fiery ball of intense awkwardness. Never have I been so grateful for blush-friendly lighting as I was at that moment.

My God! I was flirting with him. I hadn't actually meant to, but regardless of that, Jason knew and I knew, and more embarrassingly Jason knew that *I* knew I was flirting with him.

Shit, where did that come from? In a flash the atmosphere between us shifted, akin to polar ice setting off an avalanche. Jason leaned closer to me. I held my breath, wondering what the hell I was going to do if he tried to kiss me.

Thank God neither of us were drunk.

"If we hold no secrets, can I ask you something?" he whispered, with a half-smile lifting the corners of his mouth.

I wasn't dreaming this now. *He* was flirting with me. I was as sure of it as I was sure this could only lead to disaster.

"Okay," I squeaked, swallowing a huge lump of caution that had risen in my throat.

Why? Why is this happening?

Confusion had suddenly become my middle name.

Jason wasn't my *one*. *Antonio* was.

Despite this, a rush of lust filled my head, quickly draining down into the rest of my body. I was burning, dissolving with desire and the desperate need for Jason to press his lips to mine. The soft mood lighting, the romantic atmosphere, the strains of Bryan Adams playing in the background. There were only a couple of inches separating us by now and I smelled his aftershave and felt the heat radiating from his tan flesh.

Caught up in his presence, I prepared to throw all caution to the wind and let my body guide me.

Jason's face wore a mask of intense longing. This was it. He put his arm around the back of my chair and leaned closer. I held my breath, waiting for him to kiss me. *Five, four, three, two, one.*

"What's going on between you and Antonio?" he asked bluntly.

Fuck!

"What do you mean?" I sputtered. The lungful of air I held escaped, wheezing out punctured balloon-style. This was not exactly what I'd been expecting.

"Well, Rachel's been telling me all week about this hot new bloke of yours — *Tony*."

The name hung in the air like one of those little cartoon explosions and Jason raised an enquiring eyebrow in an almost identical fashion to the one my mother unleashes on me when she knows I'm hiding something.

My disappointment threatened to overwhelm me. Antonio's beautiful smiling face danced before my eyes and I experienced a nasty sharp stab of guilt.

I knew then the game was up. Jason had put two and two together and figured out *Tony* was really just a pseudonym for Antonio.

Instantly, I wanted to kick myself for not choosing another name like Bruce or Terry or even Malcolm. *Tony* had been stupid. A dead giveaway.

My face went from red to an even more unflattering shade of mortification — magenta.

"Okay, okay! Tony *is* Antonio," I confessed, feeling more than a tad pathetic.

"So, there really is a thing going on between you two?"

Had I been a sensitive kind of person, I might easily have been offended by the tone of utter disbelief in his voice.

"Yes, I suppose there is," I replied haughtily, in response to Jason's rather insulting reaction. "We've become really close in the past few weeks. Yes, he's taking me out to dinner to meet his mother next weekend."

So there!

Stick that in your pipe.

Jason didn't say anything, but sat looking at me really strangely. I must admit, I was a little confused.

"His mother, you say?"

"Yes, what's wrong with that?"

"Well, nothing, nothing at all."

"I know it must seem sudden, but we just clicked. I can tell him absolutely anything and he understands. I even told Antonio about my bastard ex, and he was very sweet and supportive."

I might have been mistaken, but it was about then I could have sworn Jason breathed a sigh of relief when he spotted Rachel returning from across the other side of the room.

"Look, Fiona, I realize you have had a really rough time lately. I'm really pleased you're finally getting your life together again. Believe me, I really, really hope things work out between you and Antonio."

There was certainly no mistaking *that* for anything but a brush-off. I suppose I was relieved in a way. I'd started to feel strangely uncomfortable talking to Jason about Antonio. Considering Jason had known Antonio for a lot longer than I had, it might have been a little awkward for him to see Antonio in another light.

"Jason, baby, I don't feel very well at all," whimpered Rachel, wobbling while turning about five different shades of green.

"Okay, okay," Jason sighed. "I'll go out and get the car."

"Pleassse. Hurrrrry, I really feel sick."

Oh, Jesus! Good luck, Jason.

Chapter Fourteen

My peaceful slumber was rudely shattered by a masculine voice calling my name somewhere very close by. It was pitch-black outside and at first I thought I was dreaming. Men quite often cry out my name in my dreams — usually that's a good dream, though. Then it happened again a second later. Now I knew it wasn't a dream, because the male voice had a broad Scottish accent. None of my dream lovers had Scottish accents. That would be just plain creepy.

"Fiona, git in here right now!" bellowed Dad, the almost hysterical urgency in his voice propelling me out of my nice cozy bed.

About five hundred awful thoughts raced through my head at that moment. Like…

He'd rolled over and found Mum stone-cold dead in the bed beside him. A horrendous thing to imagine, but I couldn't help it.

Or he'd smelled something burning in the house and we all had to evacuate. Terrible thought, but still preferable to Mum being dead.

Or Granny had suddenly died in very compromising and shameful circumstances — naked under Mr. Sullivan, gripped in a passionate embrace, good on ya, Granny!

Or the police were at the door, demanding to know my recent whereabouts, because my bastard ex had woken up minus a penis.

Or my brother had just come home and announced to Dad that he was gay and moving in with his hairy lover, Brian. Not that there's anything wrong with that, but I know Alex isn't gay. Well, he hadn't been the last time I asked him. It has been some time since he's had a girlfriend.

Then I heard a very surprised female shriek—a young, female shriek. I prayed it was the sound of Alex being castrated by Dad.

I couldn't be that lucky, though.

"*Ffffuuuccccckkkkkk!*"

Suddenly my legs launched me down the hallway to my parents' room, where all hell had broken loose in the last twenty seconds.

Dad was screaming.

Mum was screaming.

Kim was screaming?

By the time I fell into the room, they were all yelling and pointing at one another, Dad trying to look dignified in his green stripy pajamas, Mum on the verge of tears in her floor-length pink nylon nightie and Kim, to my abject horror, standing between them, naked but for a ridiculous excuse for a G-string, which covered absolutely *nothing* whatsoever.

Right then some primal instinct inside of me urged me to run. *Anywhere, just run!*

This couldn't be happening.

Was Dad capable of having an affair with Kim?

Was Kim capable of sleeping with my dad? *Yuk!*

What the fuck were they thinking having an affair—*double yuk!*—right there in front of Mum's eyes?

How *could* he?

How could *she*?

Oh, my God...not a *threesome*?

I thought I was going to be ill all over their hallucinogenic swirly green bedroom carpet.

Then, like a phoenix out of the ashes, their scattered wits seemed to group together and they turned their combined wrath onto *me!*

"Fiona, what the hell were ye thinking, telling Kim here... oh, for God's sake, girl, get some clothes on...she could sleep in my bed?"

"What do you mean? I never did!" I protested, incensed I was somehow being blamed for their sleazy affair. Oh, God, even the mere word *affair* made me feel sick.

"You did!" insisted Kim, not bothering to make any effort to cover her nakedness. "You told Janine and me to sleep anywhere comfortable."

"I meant the bloody lounge. Not in my parents' bedroom, you idiot!"

Sudden understanding illuminated the situation and profound relief flooded over me when I realized Dad and Kim were not carrying on in some kinky illicit hookup.

Once everyone had calmed down and stopped shouting and screaming at each other, I learned what had actually transpired. It wasn't quite so dramatic as Dad and Kim having a liaison. It was really very benign, if not acutely embarrassing for those parties involved — that is, everyone in the room bar me.

You see, not long after Jason left the reception with Rachel, who by this stage was puking up her guts in an ice bucket, I drove the girls back to Janine's place. Unfortunately, it wasn't until we arrived that Janine discovered she'd left her house keys, together with her handbag, back at the reception. Consequently, not only was she locked out for the night, but so was Kim, who'd been planning on staying at Janine's for the night.

By this stage, the alcohol had finally caught up with Janine and she had become very maudlin and teary. So, naturally, she sat down in the cold gutter and started to cry. I found this very unsettling, as Janine was not one to get all emotional like that. Even Kim looked a little rattled.

Considering it was fast approaching one in the morning by then and I faced a thirty minute drive back to the reception, I offered to let them crash at my place tonight, it being only ten minutes away. Tomorrow morning Janine could go and pick up her keys and bag and life could go on as normal. Simple.

It was very late and I just wanted my own comfy bed and

a few hours' sleep. God, I must be getting too old for this crap. After letting us into the darkened house – my mother, had thankfully not locked me out this time – I gathered up a few pillows and blankets for the girls, told them to keep their voices down so as not to wake up Mum and Dad, then suggested they find somewhere comfortable to sleep.

Never in my worst nightmares would I have imagined that in the middle of the night Kim would awaken, cold, still inebriated and therefore slightly disorientated, and decide to fumble her way through to Alex's room, not caring if Alex was there or not. To Kim's reasoning, a shag's a shag, no matter who the shaggee – any port in the storm.

So that's how it happened that Dad woke to find himself in bed with Kim after she'd crawled in beside him and curled her as-good-as-naked body around his for warmth. It was only when she stole the bedclothes off him that Dad woke to find Kim's hand underneath his pajama top and stroking his nipples in a very suggestive, not to mention very inappropriate, manner. Apparently, Kim had mistaken Dad for Alex, who had crashed at a friend's place after a party.

Janine naturally slept right through all the ensuing drama.

I might add at this point I didn't learn these intimate details from Dad, thank God, but from Kim the next day, when she had recovered from the shock sufficiently to find the entire experience unbearable funny.

"Jesus, Fiona, you should have seen the look on your face when you walked into your parents' room," laughed Kim. "Did you really think I'd been boning your dad?"

"What else was I supposed to think?" I replied gruffly.

"Dunno. Mind you, I have to admit he did look particularly sexy in those stripy grandpa pajamas. I really had to hold myself back."

Ha-ha! My sense of humor was still at home, catching up on lost sleep – unlike me.

Sunday afternoon and the first time we'd had to get together after this morning's rude awakening. Dad still walked around with a face like thunder even though Kim had immediately woken Janine and made good her escape, leaving me to cope with his ongoing rantings.

"Well, what would you have thought if you'd walked into *your* parents' room and found me almost naked on the bed next to *your* dad, then?" I answered hotly.

"I'd say your taste in men was in your arse, for one," responded Kim glibly. "My dad's revolting *and* he doesn't even have the decency to cover his flabby white body with pajamas. He says the body should *breathe*. Disgusting, is what it is."

That was a mental picture I was in no hurry to cultivate.

"But if that's what you fancy, hey, feel free to go for it, girl!"

I was in no mood for this today. The thing that really pissed me off was Dad blaming the whole thing on me. The bloody injustice of it. Not my fault Kim was so used to climbing into unfamiliar beds it didn't seem to matter whose bed she climbed into as long as it was warm and preferably occupied by a man.

All morning, I'd tried my best to avoid Dad, who was having difficulty looking me in the eye. Believe me, the feeling was mutual. By lunchtime, the atmosphere in our house was that tense I was desperate to escape, even to Janine's place. The only saving grace was that Rachel wasn't there, but considering the state of her last night, no one expected her to surface for the next couple of days at least.

This was also the first chance I'd had to think over what Jason had said to me last night, and I must admit my curiosity was getting the better of me.

"Hey, guys, has Rachel mentioned anything to either of you about how Jason and her are getting on?"

"Why?" asked Kim.

"Oh, nothing, it's just by now she is usually whining to us about how bored she is and looking around for someone else."

"Not this time, she isn't," added Janine.

"How so?" I asked, intrigued by the hint of interest in Janine's normally indifferent manner.

"Don't you breathe a word to anyone, but Rachel thinks Jason might just be *the* one! Of course, she says he'll have to get a better job, trendier clothes and a decent place to live before she moves in with him, seeing as Jason's granny and her haven't exactly hit it off," said Kim.

No surprises there.

"But has Jason actually asked her to move in with him?" I queried, more than a little surprised in light of our discussion last night. I could have sworn he was having serious second thoughts about their relationship. Mind you, I might well have been reading too much into that. After all, don't all couples have their up and downs?

"No, not yet he hasn't. But Rachel reckons that she can't stand living with her mother for too much longer and she's begun to look around for somewhere for the two of them. She's planning on surprising him with it once she's found a place."

"What if Jason doesn't want to move out of his granny flat?" I asked Kim.

"Get real. He's hardly going to refuse, is he? Anyway, Rachel reckons he's that into her, it's only a matter of time before he pops the question."

I couldn't deny I was shocked at hearing this startling new revelation. But then I remembered Rachel *had* recently been spotted with a bridal magazine tucked under her arm. The pieces began to fall into place.

At that moment it hit me.

The girls were actually serious.

"Christ, they've only been together, what, a month?"

"Six weeks. Anyway, who are you to talk, what with *Tony* and all? And talking about *Tony*, when are we going to meet him? You can't hide him forever, you know," said Kim.

"Yeah, come on, Fi! We're beginning to think he doesn't actually exist, or is he so ugly you don't want to let him out of the cupboard?" pressed Janine.

"Or is it *us* you're ashamed of?" added Kim suspiciously.

"Oh, of course not. Don't be so paranoid."

"Well, when is it going to be, then?"

I knew I couldn't put it off for too much longer, and in one way I was looking forward to showing him off. So, against my better judgment, I relented.

"Okay, I'll talk to him about it on Saturday night, and we'll organize something maybe for the end of next week. That is, if he's not too busy. Remember, he does have a business to run and I'd hate him to think I was becoming demanding or anything."

The girls were going to die with envy when they saw him and I felt a rush of excitement at the mere thought of being seen out with him as a couple. Or for that matter just being part of a couple again. It wasn't as though I missed my ex, but I did miss that easygoing intimacy, of having someone to share my day with and, more especially, someone to share my nights with.

That last thought came at me out of nowhere, and it started me wondering what Antonio was like in bed. The thought had crossed my mind before, but if things went the way I was hoping they would on Saturday night, maybe I'd find out sooner than later.

Obviously, not until Antonio's mother leaves, of course.

That goes without saying.

Only then did it occur to me I didn't even know where Antonio lived. Surely, not with his mother. No, I was sure one of the ladies from the dance classes had mentioned something about him living in the city somewhere. Presumably, that was reason I was meeting him in the city, at a cozy little Italian restaurant there. Knowing he'd be working late, I'd offered to meet him in the center, therefore saving him a long, tedious drive through the evening traffic.

I'd been dreaming about this moment since the first time I'd laid eyes on him. Now it was actually happening, I couldn't help but feel nervous—after all it *was* a dinner date. And with any luck, following that, I'd be sampling an extra-large serving of Latin god for dessert, dished up on a king-sized bed. Mind you I'm not fussy — table, floor, car, in fact anywhere would be fine by me.

Dinner, of course, posed no particular problems. I could handle that standing on my head. All I had to do was open my mouth and put food into it. *Very difficult to screw that one up*. No, the post-dinner production was causing my stomach to churn nervously.

It's true I'm not exactly swimwear model material. I'll admit it. I'd also left it a little too late to start dieting and exercising. God, only a week to go and here I was facing the very real prospect of getting up close and personal with Antonio, looking like a complete heifer!

It's always a lot less daunting in my fantasies. Mind you, in my fantasies, I am always tan, svelte, graceful, not to mention ultra-sophisticated and sexy. There are no embarrassing rolls of unwanted flesh waiting to pop out and say "hello, remember me? I'm that pizza you scoffed last week" as soon as I let my guard down. Or my breath out, for that matter.

The more I thought about it, the worse I felt.

Instantly, I made a mental list. Firstly, and most importantly, I'd have to remember to suck my stomach in at all times. Then it was always a good idea keep my head tilted ever-so-slightly back to eradicate any hint of a double chin without looking like I'm peering down my nose at him. I still hadn't decided what to wear, either. If it was just the two of us, I'd aim for ultra-sexy and maybe take the impossibly expensive dress the girls talked me into buying for Stacey's bachelorette night out for an airing. Mind you, I'd be airing more of me than the dress. The presence of his mother complicated matters somewhat. After all, I wanted to make a good impression and arriving looking like one of the local streetwalkers was not going to create one with my potential future mother-in-law.

I knew it was going to be a fine balance between sexy and

sedate, but, after all, I *was* trying to seduce Antonio, not his mother.

Seduce. *Shit, there's that bloody word again.* In my short-but-tragic marriage, seduction featured prominently. My ex's idea of romantic foreplay usually came by way of the sudden appearance of a bottle of bourbon, accompanied by "How about a shag? I'm so horny my balls are about to explode."

Enough to make a girl swoon, isn't it?

With Antonio, though, I instinctively knew he'd take his time. After all, hadn't he proven just how much patience he had, teaching me to dance? Not once had he tried to rush me or become frustrated when I messed up over and over again.

Of course, that was Latin dancing.

Sex was another thing altogether.

Oh, God. *What if Antonio sees me naked and takes off in disgust?* The shame would just kill me. But, no, he was far too nice to do something like that, but I could just imagine his previous girlfriends were probably supermodels, or at the very least, gorgeous, sultry and cultured, what with him being in the antiques business. And I'll bet my life they were willowy slender. That would be it, tall and slender with perfect hair and flawless skin.

I was being pathetic. *Just first-date nerves?* It'd been that long since I'd been on a first date I'd forgotten how truly excruciating it all was. Finally, I could see why people might see marriage, even a bad one, as being infinitely better than the agonies of single life.

It had never been like this when I'd met my ex. Of course, I'd only been twenty at the time, meaning I didn't have to worry about cellulite or spare tires — in fact, I never thought about cellulite at all. Ever! What twenty-year-old does? When you're that age, cellulite is merely a word women use to cover up the fact they've let themselves go and now sport thighs resembling slabs of cottage cheese. Looking back, I wish I'd appreciated my youthful days of carefree eating without the worry of rapidly approaching obesity.

Sadly, now I have matured, the scary reality of saddlebag thighs and everything that goes along with them has completely shaken me out of my youthful complacency.

My ex was always suggesting I go on a diet, hinting I was piling on the pounds. Even when on the rare occasion I felt good about the way I looked, he'd point out that my butt was getting big or my tummy stuck out and complain I didn't have a rake-thin figure like Rachel's. Not that I consider myself to be vain, but I must admit it might've been nice to hear the occasional compliment.

"What's up, Fiona? You've gone all white and sickly looking," said Janine.

"Oh, no, it's nothing. I just remembered I have to pick something up at the shops, and if I don't get out of here now, they'll be closed before I get there."

"Fuck, it couldn't be that important, surely?" mumbled Kim as I raced out of the door.

Yes, it was that important. A matter of life and death I thought, as I raced off to the local supermarket to stock up on a week's worth of Lean Cuisine.

I was desperate and it was the only thing I could think of on such short notice. And with less than a week to turn big fat Fiona into svelte sexy Fiona, I sorely needed divine intervention, or maybe a forty-eight-hour debilitating stomach bug.

Chapter Fifteen

Well, what could I possibly say in my defense? Margarita was my own personal car crash – as much as I wanted to run away and never look back, to my shame, I found myself to be one of those morbid, rubber-necked motorists who just can't resist one more peek at the mangled wreck and ensuing carnage.

Unfortunately, the mangled wreck in question just happened to be my life. Or at least Margarita seemed to think so.

By now, I had learned the basic rundown of this whole therapy deal.

Come into Margarita's office at the designated time. Sit down in the appointed standard beige vinyl, very sticky and butt-numbingly hard chair, then proceed to spill my guts to her as she sits impassively categorizing all my hopes, fears and disappointments into two distinct neat piles.

The first pile – usually my hopes and wishes – she totally dismantles and scatters to the wind and the second pile – fears and disappointments, naturally. What else is left? – she drags out and parades before me, just in case I'm not entirely convinced of my capacity for attracting disaster to my otherwise mundane life.

Next, I thank her profusely for granting me an hour of her precious time, hand over another eighty-five dollars, then make another appointment for the same time next week where I can once again look forward to having my innermost thoughts surgically dissected without even an aspirin to anesthetize the pain.

I'm sure it would be just as effective and cheaper to

have myself locked in a medieval pillory, naked, right in the middle of town and have passersby throw rotten fruit at me. But being the masochist I am, I choose to return to Margarita week after week.

Margarita took off her glasses, then slowly, deliberately started her ritualistic wiping of the small half-moon panels with a tissue, seemingly deep in thought, before replacing them on her podgy face. Then, only when she was completely satisfied I had stewed long enough, did she choose to acknowledge my presence before her.

"Well, from what you've just told me, I'd say you have had a very busy week."

I'd learned by now that the psychobabble translation of Margarita's words was actually "How the heck could one person possibly find themselves caught up in so much shit in the space of seven days?"

"I suppose it's had its ups and downs."

Highs and lows. Mountains and valleys. Peaks and troughs. Yada, yada, yada. Jeez, this therapy thing is tedious.

"You must have found the incident at the wedding very upsetting, I'm sure."

"Which one?" I asked.

When everyone is yelling at you from all directions, it's a little hard to differentiate where one ugly scene ends and another begins.

"For now, I'd like to begin by discussing the altercation between you and Rachel at the reception."

Of course she did. Margarita wasn't a person to pass up an opportunity like that, was she?

"Have you any idea what might have prompted her outburst?" Margarita questioned.

"Well, apart from the fact Rachel is a nasty drunk, and always has been, I imagine it had something to do with the puppy."

"What makes you think that?"

Only that she mentioned "the fucking dog" at least once every five seconds while she was balling me out.

"Because Rachel had it in her head that I'd deliberately let the puppy out at the church for no other reason than to take all the credit for thinking of such a *fantastic* wedding present. She thought I purposely upstaged her, even though it turned out that all I got was a slamming from everyone there. Except Stacey, of course, who was absolutely thrilled with Romper."

"Romper?"

"The puppy. Stacey named him Romper, as in *Romper Stomper*."

Margarita looked at me blankly. God, she really was stuck in a sixties time warp. "The movie? With Russell Crowe? Where he's part of a gang of skinheads who go around terrorizing people? Same reaction Romper caused when he got loose in the church."

"Then am I right in thinking you weren't very happy about giving them a puppy for a wedding present?"

"It was a *dog*, for God's sake! They never even considered the fact that maybe Stacey and Simon might not appreciate being lumbered with a puppy on their wedding day. Yeah, you could say I was not happy about the puppy, the most inappropriate wedding present I had ever heard of, except for the last wedding we went to, where my ex wanted to buy the poor couple a bloody Christmas tree – in the middle of August! Thank God we couldn't find one anywhere and he had to be content with a boring old crystal vase instead."

Not that it'd mattered much in the end. The happy couple had barely been speaking by Christmas and separated by Easter.

"If you were so against the idea of a puppy, why were you concerned about the puppy's welfare at the church?"

Oh, we were back at the dog.

"I never said I hated dogs, just it was wrong to give one as a wedding present. Like giving someone an adoption certificate and a tiny Romanian baby and saying, I hope you like it, we picked it out especially!"

"Bearing that in mind, then, why did you agree to pay

your share of the cost? You could have simply bought them something else, couldn't you?" pressed Margarita.

She obviously wasn't expecting an answer, because, perhaps sensing my growing unease, she went for the jugular. "*Or* are you too intimidated by your friends to stand up for what you believe to be right?"

Ouch!

"Of course I'm not intimidated by them. That's ridiculous!"

"Is it?"

"Yes!"

"Then why didn't you simply tell Rachel you didn't agree with her choice of present and you would buy your own?"

Oh, God, I didn't even want to imagine the ugly scene that would have followed had I stood my ground. Standing up to Rachel was unthinkable. Not that she intimidated me, mind you.

By now, I knew exactly where Margarita was going with this and I was getting tired of playing her little mind games.

"Well, Fiona! *Does* Rachel intimidate you? After all, you are what…twenty-five years old?"

"Twenty-six, actually."

"Well, don't you think as a grown woman you should be allowed to make up your own mind about something as trivial as a wedding present?"

I chose not to answer that question, fearing my answer would incriminate me for the social coward I was. Actually, I'm not a coward. I just hate unpleasant scenes. Which I know sounds funny considering I spent most of last weekend stumbling from one unpleasant scene to another.

Anyway, it's not my fault I'm not an aggressive person. I never have been. I find the very thought of losing my temper in public just too horribly humiliating to contemplate. This social inhibition can probably be traced back to a childhood listening to Mum's favorite mantra—"What would the neighbors think?" Not that it seems to bother the girls one iota. They feed on drama and, if no dramas are evident, they're not above creating one just for their own entertainment.

"Okay. Obviously, you didn't feel comfortable standing up for what you believed to be right concerning the wedding present, but what about other times? Have there been instances where you *have* made a stand? Do you always buckle under the pressure to keep the peace, or is it just out of habit you let them walk all over you, Fiona? Because it seems to me that is precisely what they are doing, walking all over you, and you appear to be allowing it to happen."

God, I wished she would simply shut up. As much as I tried to shut out Margarita's persistent prattling, bits and pieces of it penetrated my shell of denial, painfully piercing my ego.

"Look, Fiona, I can tell you're not keen to talk about this today, but I would really like you to think about what we have been discussing here, and maybe next week we can talk about it further."

Yeah, right! Not if I can help it.

If Margarita considered my friends to be bullies, maybe she should sit back and listen to herself hammering into me. I knew who the damn bully was and I was paying her for the pleasure. The girls might not be perfect, but at least I didn't pay them to pick on me.

Of course, I said none of this to Margarita, coward that I am, and meekly made another appointment for Friday for my weekly dose of pain and metal abuse.

* * * *

"Wha' don't ye go out with yer brother t'night?" suggested Dad, looking up from the newspaper.

"Because I'd rather rip out my fingernails one by one than torture myself putting up with his pathetic friends. That's why!"

Oh, God, and wasn't that the truth. I couldn't believe Dad would even suggest such a thing. Did he really think I was that desperate?

Well, probably, yes.

Margarita's words still hovered in my mind, and as much as I wanted to ignore her cruel implications that I was a living, breathing doormat, it was difficult. The girls were off to the club later and with no dance lessons to fill the void of a long, lonely Friday night, I decided to spend a quiet evening in front of the television with Hugh Grant. Well, obviously, not in the flesh, but the next best thing. Escapism at its best and desperately required after this afternoon's session with Margarita, the therapist from hell.

There you have it. *Bridget Jones's Diary*, *Notting Hill* and *Four Weddings and a Funeral*.

A Hugh Grant-fest, in truth. Five hours of back-to-back floppy dark hair and charming English stammer, guaranteed to lift the spirits of even the saddest socially inept single gal.

I suppose it could have been the ominous sight of the pile of chick flick DVDs I'd walked in with that had prompted Dad to suggest I expand my social experiences.

But if he thought for one moment I would choose a night at the raceway being jostled by a pack of plaid-clad Neanderthals until my ears bled from the noise of pistons being blasted through the top of big block V8 engines over a night of gentle wooing by Hugh Grant—okay, I know it's just pretend wooing, but a girl can dream after all—in the English countryside, he must be totally gone in the head.

"It'll doo you tha' world of good to git oot and enjoy yerself in the fresh air," pressed Dad, glancing with concern over to where the pile of DVDs waited by the telly.

"What do mean, fresh air? The only thing fresh at the raceway is the pile of dog shit I always manage to stand in. Oh, I forgot, there's always the delightful smell of nitrous oxide and petrol fumes in the air and, if that isn't bad enough, I can always breathe in the stench of BO that wafts from hundreds of unwashed Rev Heads! Oh, I'm certainly tempted, I tell you!"

"There's noo need to git smart-moothed with me now.

I was just suggest'n yoo go oot and hae some fun wit' yer brother."

And far, far away from those Hugh Grant movies, I guessed by the fleeting look of desperation on his face.

"Go on, Fiona, yer brother was only say'n tha other day, he nev'r spends any time wit' ya," pleaded Dad.

"No! Forget it. And I think I can safely say Alex wouldn't appreciate having his big sister hanging around. I'd only cramp his style."

Okay, my brother has no style to speak of, but it was the only thing I could think of at the time.

Dad seemed to quiet down after that and I thought he'd finally reconciled himself to an evening reading the latest Matthew Reilly novel in his room, leaving me free to gorge myself on potato chips—if I even look at another Lean Cuisine, I swear I'll vomit—while feasting my eyes on the delectable Hugh Grant with a good measure of Colin Firth thrown in—yum, yum!

I sensed victory was near when Dad folded his newspaper and stuffed it down the side of the recliner. Great, he was leaving me to my movies.

How wrong could I be?

Very wrong!

Now, as I might have mentioned before, Dad isn't one of those modern New Age fathers who makes it their business to bond with their daughters on an emotional level. So, bearing that in mind, it made what came next even more surprising.

"Fiona, dear."

Dear? Where the hell had that come from? Dad's never called me *dear* before. I should have guessed there and then something was up. And with no Mum at home to soften the weird factor because she was across the road sewing Mrs. Evans's curtains for her, I had an ominous feeling about what was coming.

"I'm worried aboot you, and so is yer mother."

Shit, I must be dying or something and no one's told me.

"Don't be stupid, Dad, I'm fine."

Well, not *fine* fine, obviously. After all, I'd just experienced the worst couple of months of my entire life. But with the appearance of Antonio, things were looking up. Not that I was telling Dad any of this. How embarrassing would that be?

"We don't think yoo are. Yoo nev'r go out unless it's with those girlfriends of yers, and I don't think they are good fer yoo. That's why I thought yoo might goo out with Alex and his friends and meet new people."

"I go out to dance lessons," I offered, trying to relieve Dad of his ill-placed concern.

"I don't want to talk aboot bloody dance lessons."

Well, that made two of us, because I didn't want to talk to Dad about Antonio, either. If he was so enraged over me learning Latin dancing, imagine his reaction to me shagging the gorgeous Latin instructor. Well, hopefully by tomorrow night I would be, anyway.

Not that Dad was a racist. No way! Well, maybe a tiny little bit. A smidgen. A tiny weenie almost inconsequential racist. He considers himself a patriot instead.

My ex had only just got through the screening process because it was uncovered that his great-great-grandmother hailed from Edinburgh. Even then, there'd been a little grumbling as Dad considered Edinburgh too close to the border for his liking. Practically English, he'd insisted. And he'd almost refused to pay for the wedding when he'd discovered my intended refused point blank to wear a kilt. It'd been one of the few times I'd actually felt sorry for my ex. After all, having to face Dad's wrath as he ranted on and on about us turning our backs on our proud heritage had been excruciating even for me, and I'm his daughter.

"What exactly *do* you want to talk about then?" I asked.

Not that I wanted to have a deep and meaningful chat with Dad at *all*, but time was creeping on and Hugh was waiting, so I thought it better to get this uncomfortable *chat* out of the way.

By the ominous way Dad kept clearing his throat and rubbing the bridge of his nose, I knew I wasn't the only one feeling the stress of this father-daughter moment. Fuck, I prayed this wasn't going to be a 'safe sex' talk. If he pulled out a condom and started demonstrating how to use one—on a carrot or some other vegetable of course. Dad's embarrassing, but he's not some sicko—I'd be left with no other choice but to leave the country for good, as I'd *never* be able to look at him again. Ever.

"Well, ye know yer mother and I love having ye here with us..."

I suspected that was pushing the truth a little, but I let it slide.

"An' yer welcome to stay as long as yee want. It is yer home, after all."

"Yes, Dad, I understand."

"But, eventually we'd like to see you settle down with a nice fellow."

"So would I, Dad."

"One tha treats yoo like the lovely young woman ye are."

Now I was getting seriously freaked out. Dad hadn't even told me I was a lovely young woman when I'd been all decked out in my wedding finery!

"Dad, what's going on?"

Like it or not, I had to get this hideously embarrassing exchange over with, and quickly.

"I dinnae know whether ta tell ye or not, but ye have a right to know."

"Know *what?*"

A sick dread fell over me, but pride wouldn't let me back down now.

"I was in town today and I ran in tae Brian."

"Brian?" Which Brian?

"Brian Maxwell."

"Ahh!" *That* Brian, my ex father-in-law. "How is Brian?"

"Fine, fine. Said to say hello to yoo, and ta tell yoo how sorry they all were aboot everythin'."

As fathers-in-law go, Brian was not bad. In truth, I'd gotten on better with him than my ex did. Most likely because my ex was one of four boys and, with no daughter to dote on, Brian had taken to spoiling me from the moment we met. Pity I couldn't say the same about my mother-in-law, though. No one was good enough for any of her boys and she resented any female who tried to take away any of the attention they lavished on her. A spoiled bitch, my mother called her, which'd shocked me mute because I'd never heard my mother utter anything stronger than a "damn," and even that was reserved for times of intense outrage.

"Did he mention *him* at all?"

I knew I had to bring the subject up, or risk Dad blathering on all night.

"Actually, yes, he did," stammered Dad.

"Well!"

"Darl'n, I don't know how ta tell you this?"

There was the *darling* again. Now I really felt sick.

"Just say it!"

"Brian told me…and mind yoo, he wasna too happy aboot it."

"What, Dad? Just spit it out, will you!"

Dad looked like he was about to be sick himself and I braced myself.

"Brian told me that bastard ex of yers had gone and got that floozy up the pole!"

"What, she's pole dancing? Why the fuck should I care?"

"She's not bloody *pole* dancing. Fiona, she's pregnant, and yer *Troy's* the father!"

Suddenly, the taste of bile hit the back of my throat and I ran from the room.

* * * *

I thought the retching would never stop. Wave after wave of painful convulsions assaulted my shuddering body until the initial shock purged itself from my soul. Then later, as I lay on my bed, I felt as though a huge hole of nothing had opened up inside me. A void. A cavernous void of painful nothing.

I felt empty. Empty of emotion, empty of thought and empty of everything I'd once held dear. Suspended as I was in that numb void, I was grateful in a way that my body had graced me with a brief mental respite from my earlier torture. Had it been left up to me, I would have stayed in that safe place — my own custom-made padded cell — that corner of my mind where I felt secure, protected from the cruel reality of life outside my head.

My respite was short-lived, though. The hole inside me suddenly replenished itself with a surge of throbbing, blazing outraged anger. Suddenly, I felt cheated, robbed, not only of the years of my life I had wasted on my bastard husband, but robbed of my dreams.

Only Troy had known how much I wanted a baby. It'd never been the right time, though. Either he'd been between jobs, or we'd needed to buy a house first, or he'd wanted us to spend time on our own, or we couldn't have afforded it. There'd *always* been a reason to delay starting a family. But in the end, it'd boiled down to the fact *he* hadn't been ready.

I'd agreed to wait. After all, we had years and years ahead of us — or so I'd thought at the time.

It was such a private yearning I hadn't even confided in the girls about my desperation to start a family. Sure, we would all gush over the new tiny fashions that graced the shops, trying to imagine the little bodies that would fill out the various outfits as we dreamed that one day we might acquire one of these accessories for ourselves—a baby, that is. But I didn't want to wait until I was older. I wanted to be a young mum and enjoy my kids while I had the energy to keep up with them.

Now I was left with nothing and that fucking bitch was having the baby that by rights should have been mine.

Though the blood-red haze of my fury, I pictured some

poor, innocent, hungry baby desperately trying to fight its way past a mountain of cold, impersonal silicon searching for its mother's milk and I felt a fresh wave of tears building for a baby deprived of *my* warm, motherly mammaries.

I don't know what hurt more, her living *my* dream, with *my* fucking husband, no less, or my ex being willing to give her what he'd adamantly refused to give me. *A baby!*

Poor Dad had been distraught, knowing the anguish I was in. In desperation, he'd called Mum home from Mrs. Evans' on the pretext he couldn't find his angina medication. Dad doesn't have angina, so, of course, she knew it was an emergency and immediately rushed home, leaving the entire street peering through Mrs. Evans' naked lounge window at Mr. Evans snoring in his tatty recliner with his false teeth half hanging out of his mouth.

There was no need for her to leave the Evanses exposed like that, though. My grief was an intensely private one and endurable only on my own. Anyway, no amount of sympathy was going to turn back time or block out the knowledge that my ex was going to be a father while I remained childless and heartbroken.

Suddenly, I wondered how he was feeling about the coming event. Had it been planned? God, I hoped not. That would be too much for me to bear. But, like they say, there's no such thing as an accident. Of course, that left the question of if *she* deliberately allowed herself to fall pregnant, which immediately stirred another wave of anger within me.

Naturally, I had been tempted. A fait accompli. It would have been so easy to 'forget' to take a couple of pills and risk fate intervening. Don't think I hadn't considered it. The way I saw it, once the deed was done, surely, he'd come around. And when he held his infant son—it was always going to be a boy first— for the first time, his heart would swell with pride and love and the circumstances surrounding the conception would be but a distant memory.

By now Mum and Dad were in bed and my Hugh-fest was well and truly forgotten. Emotional fatigue caused by hours of crying had taken its toll on my body and I ached all over, but my mind was loath to give up its hold upon my hurt and let me submit to the mercy of sleep.

Initially, I had focused my anger on poor Dad. Talk about shooting the messenger! But once I'd settled down a little, I realized it would never be easy, no matter how the truth was revealed. When I did eventually open my door to Dad's pleadings, the look of distress on his face shocked me from my selfish self-pity and I understood how hard it must have been for him to break the news to me. Better my dad, though, than, say, one of the girls. Or, worse still, the *bitch* herself wandering around the baby section at work with her swollen stomach on show for all to see.

At least now it would hurry along the divorce, and hopefully I would be able to put this whole miserable mess behind me, once and for all.

Glancing over to the illuminated clock radio beside my bed, I realized it was now Saturday. Gradually, the thoughts racing in my head began to slow and soften around the edges as I felt myself sliding back into the comfortable world of my inner consciousness, far away from Troy and his betrayal.

It must have been a result of the shock, but I slept dreamlessly and only stirred when the next-door neighbor started up his noisy hedge trimmer, effectively rousing me from my healing slumber.

It was well after ten o'clock and, to my surprise, the house was completely silent. I wondered if Mum and Dad had gone out. Mum always had a radio on, or music of some description, preferring it to the empty sound of silence. It was as though someone had died. For a second, I allowed myself a tiny glimmer of hope that my prayers had indeed been miraculously answered and Troy had suffered a heart attack, brought on by an overdose of Viagra—but not before his penis had swollen to roughly the size of a prize-winning marrow and exploded, leaving him to be buried a eunuch.

No, that was too merciful. Now I prayed he *hadn't* died

of a heart attack and had to live a life of an ever-increasing girth, accompanied by squeaky soprano voice.

With that final thought, I found the strength to throw back the covers and crawl from my protective cocoon.

Although my tears had ceased, my eyes felt raw and swollen and I could just imagine how awful I looked — and the mirror proved me right.

As always, my timing was up the shit. Tonight, I was meeting Antonio in the city for dinner and here I was, looking a right hag. A scaly, swollen, pale hag at that. For the past few weeks, despite my ups and downs, the only thing that hadn't gone to pot had been my skin, remaining as always smooth and blemish-free. My skin is probably the only part of my body that can usually be relied upon not to give me any grief. Not so much the rest of me, though.

Bad hair days. I've had more than my fair share.

Bloating. I can usually count on that to make me look five months pregnant whenever I want to wear something sexy and figure-hugging.

Split and broken nails. Well, enough said, just there. Like a spoilt child, the more attention I give them with the buffing, filing, undercoat, top coat, super-strengtheners, the more they rebel. It's a never-ending pursuit, and I gave up any hope of having ten nails of equal length years ago.

But at least I could eat chocolate till I puked and throughout my teenage years I was the only one of my friends who didn't spend the Easter holidays with their head submerged in a bucket of Clearasil. Sure, I'd been the fat one, but at least I'd been blessed with a peaches-and-cream complexion.

Until now!

Overnight my peaches-and-cream complexion had turned rancid. Yuk! I was all spotty and lumpy and generally not a pretty sight at all.

All my crying last night had purged me of more than my misery. By the scary woman staring back at me in mirror, I'd say it had also purged me of at least fifteen years of toxins, including nauseating amounts of chocolate, enough alcohol to satisfy even Charlie Sheen on a bender and every ounce of fat I have ingested in my entire life.

For a split second, I contemplated ringing Antonio and putting off our date for another evening. But, thankfully, sanity returned and swiftly slapped me, restoring my scattered senses.

What am I thinking?

Here I'd been so engrossed in mourning my past, including my perfect skin, I was ignoring the fact that as of tonight, I would be leaving behind my past and embarking on a new future with a man I adored, and who I was almost certain adored me. Regardless of how spotty I looked, the shock of last night's discovery now seemed bearable in the bright light of a new day. I felt as if I'd broken through the final barrier and mentally torn myself away from my ex. Anyway, I had survived the initial shock with only a few pimples to show for it, and no amount of hiding away was going to change the past. With that last thought, I got myself dressed, raided Mum's cache of skin cleansers and toners and decided to face the world.

"Hi, Mum," I said cheerfully, entering the quiet kitchen.

"Oh, you're up. Did Jim next door wake you with that noisy trimmer?" Mum frowned, clearly annoyed at the poor old man next door who just wanted to get in some gardening while the sun was out.

"It's fine, really. I should have been up ages ago."

"How are yoo this morning, dear? Yer Dad and I were really worried aboot you last night," said Mum.

"I'm fine, Mum. Sorry about last night. It was the shock more than anything else. I feel a little better today. I promise, I'm not about to throw myself under a train or anything stupid like that."

For the first time, I noticed how tired Mum looked, and realized the strain I'd placed on both her and Dad as a result of my recent problems. Suddenly, I felt ashamed of myself for causing them so much worry over the past few months.

"Are yoo sure yer going to be all right?" repeated Mum, obviously thinking I was merely putting on a brave face for her benefit.

"Yeah, don't worry about me, Mum. I know now I'm well rid of Troy. I almost feel sorry for any child who ends up with his DNA swimming around inside them. It's just this was the last thing I expected to hear, that's all. Where's Dad, anyway?"

Mum looked a bit sheepish. "Oh, he's just gone out for a bit."

Immediately, the warning bells sounded in my head. I knew I had to ask.

"Oh, God, don't tell me he's gone over to confront Troy," I cried, imagining Dad bashing down his door and clobbering him. That would be just too horrible to contemplate. Not that I cared if Troy got hurt, but I'd never forgive myself if something happened to Dad. He's not as young as he used to be, after all.

"No, don't worry, I'm sure it's not what he has in mind," reassured Mum.

"Where did he go then?"

"I don't really know exactly, but I shouldn't think he'll be long."

Something was going on. I knew it. Mum was too quiet and my suspicions were aroused.

Glancing up, I noticed the time. Whatever Dad was up, to it would have to wait. The girls would be expecting me at eleven for our usual coffee and yak, which only left me half an hour to get dressed and find a bus, seeing as Dad had pissed off with the car. Not that I was really in the mood for their bitching, but if I failed to show, they would start to ask questions, especially considering they all knew that tonight was the night as far as Antonio went.

I'd already decided not to tell them about last night's drama. Not yet, anyway. After all, I had months of public humiliation ahead of me, so I couldn't see the point of denying myself a little respite until then. Apart from that,

I also needed some time to get my own head around it, to work out how I was going to deal with it before the world. Because, like it or not, it would soon be out in the open. A baby is not something that can be kept a secret for long, after all.

I knew no one would blame me if I immersed myself in self-pity. Being the wronged wife, I had every right to do so. But I couldn't help but feel I'd already overdone the whole Sobbing Susan act. Sure, it would be satisfying to wallow in the sympathy offered by others, but having used up my lifetime quota of tissues in the past couple of months, I realized that, if only for the sake of my self-respect, a different approach was required.

With that in mind, I determined to pull myself together and try to be adult about it all. Not that my hurt lessened, but it was humiliating enough to have my husband's infidelities on show for all the world to see without adding my own personal torment to it, no doubt to the amusement of those who thrive on other people's miseries. No, I would deal with Troy's betrayal privately, gracefully and most of all with the cool contempt it truly deserved.

* * * *

Rounding the corner, I saw the girls huddled together at our usual table beside the huge potted palm in the far corner of the small courtyard, solemnly staring into their cups of coffee.

No one was talking.

Wow, a first. Usually I heard their high-pitched squeals or bursts of, well, bad language well before I sighted them. The more I thought of it, the more I understood why the other patrons preferred to keep a wide buffer between us and them, solving the age-old mystery of why our regular table always appeared to be available for our convenience.

And here we thought we just had incredibly good luck.

Even at their worst, hungover and pissed-off, they were

never this subdued, and my curiosity was instantly aroused.

Maybe someone had died?

Instantly an image of Troy, stone-cold, gray and dickless sprang to mind and I smiled.

At least I could rest assured last night's news hadn't reached them yet. How did I know that? Well, had it been the case, they would have been beside themselves with scandal-inspired rapture, waiting for me with bated breath to hear the inside gossip.

"What's up, guys?" I asked pulling up a seat.

Kim continued to stare into her skinny cappuccino, while Rachel and Janine looked on with concern.

"Okay, what dickhead did Kim get off with this time?"

Kim winced and Rachel shot me a 'how could you be so callous' look. I knew I was on the right track.

Mind you, a dickhead involved in this somewhere was a fair bet, going by the look of shame on Kim's face. That, plus the general air of doom and gloom hanging over the three of them.

"Dave," Janine whispered, casting a worried glance across in Kim's direction.

"Dave who?" I whispered back.

"*Dangerous Dave*," mouthed Janine, before cringing.

"Oh!"

No wonder they were all in mourning. They were in mourning for the loss of Kim's taste in men.

Dangerous Dave.

Yuck!

What the heck had she been thinking, or drinking? She did look a bit pale, but of course it could have been a result of the post-shag horrors.

This went way beyond that, though.

This was post-shag *Nightmare on Elm St.* with a good measure of *Amityville Horror* and *Night of the Living Dead* thrown in.

Dangerous Dave was considered socially radioactive on a grand scale. Even Chernobyl hadn't been as toxic. Once news of this leaked out, poor Kim wouldn't get another bloke to look at her for years. At the very least. She'd be nuclear waste.

Shit!

"Bloody hell," I sighed.

This was tragic, worse than death. If I were in Kim's shoes right now, *I'd* be wishing *I* was dead.

For the first time since Dad had dropped the bombshell concerning Troy and his slut, I didn't feel like the saddest person on the face of the planet. For now I had a rival, Kim. Actually, she was way ahead of me on the loser scale, toppling even me from my summit of shame.

Never in a million years would I have imagined Kim—or any female with their wits about them for that matter—*having anything to do with Dave*, never mind actually having sex with him. Naturally, we all assumed he was a virgin. He had to be. Who'd have him?

Well, Kim, obviously.

I'm not sure exactly how to describe Dave.

To start with, Dave'd gone to school with us. Although he was about the same age as us girls, he'd been held back a grade, not once but twice. Unfortunately, he never really caught up socially. Not that I would ever mock the intellectually disadvantaged—there but for the grace of God and all that crap—but Dave possessed bigger problems than his inability to grasp even the rudiments of basic education.

Maybe it was a result of his academic problems, but by year eight at high school, when we'd entered year ten, he lived in a fantasy world with Sylvester Stallone, Jean-Claude Van Damme and Steven Seagal his constant companions. You don't have to be bloody Freud to work out that a fifteen-year-old boy living in a parallel universe of *First Blood* movies was seriously scary.

As a result of his unhealthy infatuation with anything military, he was convinced he was a lean, mean fighting machine. When in reality, he was a five-foot-four, hundred-and-ten-pounds gnome, complete with a shock of red hair that to this day continues to clash horribly with the army fatigues he's been wearing constantly since high school. Apart from his disastrous fashion sense, his carroty-red hair springs up in coils from his scalp, gracing him with an uncanny resemblance to Ronald McDonald. We used to joke that if he did find himself involved in some sort of military operation, he wouldn't last an hour. Why? Because his hair effectively acted as a navigation aide, a flare that could be spotted no doubt from the bloody space shuttle.

Got the general picture yet?

Not pretty, is it?

Dave had only secured the job as a bouncer at the club because his grandfather was a Second World War hero, before landing in a Japanese prison camp where he sat out the remainder of the war. It was no doubt out of respect for his grandfather that the board of directors at the RSL club had agreed to employ Dave in the capacity of junior trainee doorman, a position he has held for the past four years.

For his own personal safety, Dave is never left on his own. Usually Jason or one of the other guys on the door is forced to spend more time keeping him from being beaten up by drunken louts of both genders than they do actually policing the mob inside.

"Oh, God," whimpered Kim. "I don't know how it happened."

She sounded like a wounded animal and my heart went out to her.

"It's going to be all right, Kim. We're here for you," comforted Rachel as she put her arm around the by-now-sobbing Kim.

I'd honestly never seen her like this before and I had to admit I was shocked by her emotional meltdown.

"What the hell happened?" I asked Janine.

Rachel continued to hold Kim, whose noisy sobs were by now attracting the concerned attention of the other diners.

"We're still trying to work it out," Janine whispered. "She was fairly pissed last night, but none of us thought she'd do anything like this."

In the end, it took more than an hour and three rounds of hot chocolate before we could get any kind of coherent conversation out of her at all.

A horror story, all right.

Out on the dance floor, the dim lights were working their magic and Kim was getting particularly cozy with a really, really cute but vertically challenged guy called Dean. His head only came up to her chin so Kim, as a measure of her eagerness, removed her shoes to help stabilize the discrepancy.

The night was moving on and Kim becoming increasingly horny. It had been a long dry spell for her sex-wise, hence the lowering of height restrictions. Unfortunately, owing to the fact Kim was in between abodes at the moment—she and Rachel had been recently evicted and their bond withheld because of an incident involving a small fire in the kitchen—she was languishing at home with her parents, and Dean was currently sharing a house with six other blokes, meaning they had nowhere to act upon their rapidly escalating carnal impulses.

It was about that time Kim's alcohol-soaked head recalled Rachel telling her about a storage room directly behind the DJ's booth where Jason had taken her once for a private moment. With no other alternative available and facing another long, lonely night of sexual frustration, Kim suggested to Dean that he grab a packet of condoms and wait for her in the storage room until she returned from the ladies'. No more encouragement was needed for Dean, and he took off obediently to get some condoms from the vending machine in the men's toilets.

It was about this stage where it all began to go wrong.

Kim returned to the dance floor after having a pee and stopping off at the sacred table in order to throw back the rest of the rum and cola she'd left earlier. Having taken what she considered to be ample time to allow Dean to procure the above-mentioned condoms, Kim casually made her way over to the DJ's booth before slipping unnoticed into the storeroom.

As soon as Kim had closed the door behind her, she quickly flicked off the harsh fluoro lights, so as not to scare off her prey with the stark reality of the one a.m. uglies. The storeroom was plunged into darkness and Kim's need for a shag peaked. The noise from the disco made conversation all but impossible, but on the plus side it had the added advantage of obscuring any sounds of rapturous orgasms — faked or otherwise from the people out in the nightclub.

Within minutes, Kim had successfully located her pint-sized fuck-buddy in the dark. Then, after a brief but frenzied struggle with clothes and panties and the like, things started to get hot and steamy in the cramped storeroom, chock-full of stacked chairs and folded tables.

Maybe it was the alcohol, or her recent bout of enforced celibacy, but Kim swore it was the best fuck she'd had in years and to express her appreciation of Dean's skills she apparently treated him to quick post-fuck blow job as a measure of her gratitude. She swears it couldn't have taken more than ten minutes tops, but it was ten minutes of pure heaven with her pocket-sized sexual dynamo.

Who could have anticipated the gut-churning reality that was about to be cruelly thrust upon her, though?

For it seems, just as Kim was straightening her panties, the door to the storeroom was wrenched open and in staggered Dean, red-faced and fighting for breath after racing around every toilet in the club in search of the elusive condoms because every condom machine was either empty or jammed with foreign money or chewing gum.

Confused, Kim spun around and to her abject horror saw Dangerous Dave sagged against a stack of plastic orange chairs, his fatigues down around his ankles, totally shagged out and grinning like a fucking simpleton. She felt as though she'd been dropped into someone else's nightmare. This couldn't possibly be happening to her. She wanted to scream, but no sound would come out and she tried to run, but her legs felt like wood—not even light balsa wood, but heavy, water-logged oak.

So what did she do?

She threw up. Right there on the storeroom floor. Eight rum and colas and a serve of chicken nachos laced with a topping of gnome cum, bridging the gap between her and Dean.

Dean naturally saw everything. He might have been short, but, unfortunately, he wasn't blind. Immediately he put two and two together and...

"Oh. God, you should have seen the look on his face," wailed Kim. "He was totally grossed out. If you could have seen the way he looked at me. I revolted him. And before I could explain what an awful mistake it was, he staggered back out of the door and took off. Oh, God, it was horrible, just horrible. I wish I were dead," she sobbed. "I don't know if I can live with the memory of fucking that...that... Oh, Jesus and to think I went down on him after... *Arrrggghhh!*"

Then poor Kim completely lost it and started sobbing all over again. That was it. After that we couldn't get anything else out of her.

No one knew what to say. We just sat there, stunned and feeling slightly nauseous. Well, it was a particularly sickening tale, after all. I had to admit, this was without a doubt the most catastrophic thing that could ever be delivered upon a girl. Possibly even *worse* than my ex getting his floozy knocked up.

Like they say, there is always someone worse off than you. It kind of put my own dramas into perspective.

I'm loath to admit it, really, but at that moment I was extremely glad I'd put on a brave face and decided to meet the girls for coffee, because after listening to Kim's tale of woe, I felt a whole lot better about my own problems. After all, compared to Kim shagging the truly hideous Dangerous Dave, my ex's recent indiscretions were relatively tame.

Still, it didn't explain what Dave had been doing in the storeroom in the first place. For that, I had to wait until

Rachel drove Kim home, with her not in any fit state to be seen in public. Once Kim was safely out of the way, Janine filled me in on rest of the Dave-shagging incident.

It seemed, as fate would have it, shortly before Kim had slipped into the storeroom for her horny rendezvous, Jason, working on the door last night, had asked Dave to fetch some extra ashtrays from the storeroom. Not so much because an inordinately large number of smokers came in the nightclub that night, but because he had been forewarned by the girl on the front desk of a large group of army reserve blokes about to converge on the nightclub.

Last time these same so-called trained killers had visited, Dave'd only escaped from enduring a savage beating because of Jason's quick thinking. At the time, Jason had had the good sense to lock Dave in the disabled toilets until the danger had passed. By then, the marauding psychopaths had been incapable of anything more harmful than crawling about the floor and pissing themselves laughing at their mates' pathetic attempts to chat up the very unimpressed and very sober girls behind the bar.

I think in retrospect, Kim would have preferred to see Dave broken and grievously wounded by the local grunts than grinning back at her with his disproportionately large wang hanging out of his stained Y-fronts.

It's not an image that will be easily scrubbed from my mind, I can assure you.

Chapter Sixteen

Kim's mini-breakdown and subsequent departure had effectively put an end to our regular tête-à-tête. Janine was rostered to work the afternoon shift at the abattoirs and left soon after, leaving me rather unexpectedly with the afternoon to myself.

An hour later, and with nothing better to do, I found myself wandering around the large shopping center on my own.

Excitement plus!

On some wild impulse, I decided to treat myself to some new lingerie. My current panties held all sorts of bad memories of my ex, and if tonight's date did by some miracle reach its logical conclusion, I could well find myself in the position where I might have some use for sexy underwear. With this in mind, I didn't want to risk tainting the experience with recollections of mediocre gropes at the hands of my bastard ex.

Mind you, the fantasy of wearing these figure-hugging, dainty creations of lace and silk, falsely guaranteed to make any able-bodied man fall at my feet while declaring his undying love, usually falls far short of expectations.

To date, every item of lingerie I possess — ranging from sedate oyster camisole tops to a blood-red lace bra and G-string combination complete with matching suspender belt and garters — has proven to be not only totally impractical, hook and eye crotch fasteners a prime example, but require a super-human tolerance for itching and scratching.

I suppose this might account for the fact my fancy panties

collection is languishing in three polystyrene bags on top of my wardrobe, while taking pride of place in my top drawer are the female friendly, one-hundred-percent-cotton, non-itch, wedgie-resistant boys' shorts.

I must admit, I never did find the courage or the motivation to wear the slutty red ensemble apart from one time when my ex begged me to dress up for him when he'd got himself all worked up after perving on some tacky porn magazine.

Despite my reservations—I felt silly prancing around the house in my fuck-me-now panties with cricket blaring out on the telly—I took myself off to *glam up*. His words, not mine. By the time I wrestled myself into the damn garter belt, ruining three pairs of stockings in the process, I was almost blue with cold, every crevice of my body had developed synthetic lace-induced rash and I felt such a right stupid cow walking around in my bare essentials.

The only thing that convinced me to walk out of the bedroom and toward where he and his hard-on were waiting in the lounge, was the knowledge that, although I wasn't a supermodel, I was flesh and blood, and therefore, a damn sight more appealing and attainable than the air-brushed tarts in *People* magazine. It had to count for something, surely.

Consequently, it was a mammoth blow to my ego to discover my other half glued to the sports and yelling at his brother on the phone about some disputed high tackle penalty.

No adoration.

No flattery.

No pervy leers.

And, ultimately, no sex.

His favorite team lost the quarter-finals and he locked himself away in the garage with a six-pack of beer to mourn the end of their semi-final dreams.

The next day, he was nursing a hangover and I was covered from head toe in anti-rash powder.

Romance.

What's romance?

With this in mind, I decided put these bad experiences behind me and go all out, forking out an obscene amount of dosh for a blindingly exquisite jade green, satin, half-cup Versace bra and matching high-cut bikini brief. Simple but classy, with a lifetime anti-wedgie guarantee.

Perfect.

Sickeningly extravagant.

Divinely comfortable.

Sold to the lady with the desperate need to feel sexy and loved, just once before she dies.

Me!

Walking out of the lingerie boutique, a wave of exhilaration washed over me. My post-purchase high felt *great*.

The center was filled with weekend shoppers. As I was pushing my way through walls of screaming toddlers and packs of scary-looking teenage boys with their boxer shorts on show for all to see, together with evil expressions on their spotty fourteen-year-old faces, someone called out to me.

"Fiona, over here!" yelled out a familiar voice.

I spun around to find Stacey running over to me.

"Oh, my God! What are you doing back this early?"

She was supposed to be enjoying her honeymoon at the Port Douglas Sheraton Mirage for another week yet, not trailing around town on her own.

"You wouldn't believe it. Simon got a call yesterday to say his little boy Dylan had fallen off the veranda and was in hospital with a broken arm. Poor little darling. We caught the next flight back, and Simon's at the hospital with him right now."

"Oh, my God, how awful! Is he okay?"

"Yeah. Simon rang from the hospital about half an hour ago and Dylan should be home by tonight. I thought it might be better if I kept my distance, though. The situation between Simon and his ex is still really tense and me being there will only make it worse."

"What about your honeymoon? Are you going to head back after Dylan gets home?"

"We thought about it, but Romper's wearing out his welcome at Mum and Dad's. Apparently, he's demolished Mum's garden and piddled in every room in the house. The cat's taken off and he's even chewed through the TV cables. From what I gather, Dad's well and truly pissed-off."

"Shit, I am *so* sorry about that. Believe me, I told the girls I thought it was a bad idea. But you know what they're like," I said.

"You don't have to tell me. I know exactly what they're like," Stacey said, rolling her eyes. "Don't worry about it. Honestly, Dad will get over it. Anyway, what are you doing now?"

"Nothing much, just killing time and spending money," I answered, holding up my bag as evidence.

"You've got time for a coffee, then?" she suggested.

"Sounds great!"

For the rest of the afternoon, Stacey and I caught up and relived the happenings of the wedding the previous weekend. In turn, I filled her in on most of last week's dramas, including Kim's disaster, which had Stacey in stitches laughing.

I suppose it *was* funny in a way. Not for poor Kim, maybe. But as Stacey was quick to point out, if you shag as many blokes as Kim does, sooner or later you're bound to come across the odd dork. Looking at it like that, I had to agree with Stacey that it had only been a matter of time before something like this happened.

Then suddenly I remembered. "Stacey, whatever happened with Simon's sisters after that night out on the boat?"

Stacey colored slightly and self-consciously covered her neck where the hickie had long since faded.

"Oh, God, those two. Didn't you know, we are best buddies now."?"

I raised my eyebrows, not sure if she was taking the piss

out of me.

"It's true," she laughed.

"So they never found out about you know what?"

"I think they have their suspicions, but they have no way of proving anything. I, on the other hand, have a shit load of photos to prove what *they* got up to with those hunky strippers."

"What did Simon have to say about it all?"

"Well, the best part is, Simon has *no idea*, and I think that is why they're being so nice to me. They'd absolutely die of shame if he found out, especially after all the crap they heaped on him when he first left Debra—all but called in an exorcist to release him of his evil intentions. Talk about zealots—they even got the priest who married them to talk to him. At the time, he was furious. Mind you, I did let it slip that I had some very interesting photos of the bachelorette night. Now they're living in terror I'll blab to Simon and show them up for the hypocrites they are."

"And will you?"

"No. I think they've suffered enough. But I'm sure eventually someone will. They won't stay nice for long, though. Those two have had it in for me from day one, so I really owe you for helping me out that night."

I'd forgotten how well we got on together away from Kim's, and especially Rachel's, catty influence. After chatting to Stacey for an hour, I realized how much I'd missed having someone to confide in who wouldn't judge me or laugh at my misfortunes. That must have been why I eventually decided to tell her about Troy and the baby—but not before swearing her to secrecy.

Stacey was suitably horrified when I spilled what I'd learned the night before and agreed wholeheartedly with my decision to not only keep it from the girls, but also to play it very cool as far as everyone else was concerned. As she pointed out, everyone would be waiting for me to fall apart, why should I give them the satisfaction of knowing Troy had wounded me to that degree?

For a few moments, we sat there, enjoying the comfortable silence that had settled between us, before Stacey licked the froth from the top of her third cappuccino and laughed. "Do you remember what awful bitches we were back in high school?"

"Yeah," I responded, thinking of all the times I had blindly followed Rachel and Kim in their weekly vendettas. "God, it seems like only yesterday we were standing outside the principal's office, waiting to find out if we were going to be suspended for flooding the girls' toilets that time."

"*And* the art block, as well, remember," added Stacey with a grin. "At the time, we didn't consider the art block was right underneath the ladies'."

"Christ, all I remember was being shit-scared at the time. Mum and Dad would have killed me if I'd gotten myself suspended. Hey, if I'd got busted for half the stuff Rachel and Kim did, I'm sure they would've packed me off to some stuffy private boarding school. They did threaten to once or twice."

"Didn't appear to bother Rachel and Kim," said Stacey.

"They were used to it, I suppose. You know what, though? I reckon they used to do it on purpose to get suspended."

"What?"

"Really. Think about it. It was always a couple of days before the school holidays when they would go on one of their rampages. They'd nearly always get suspended and they'd kick back and relax until the school holidays began. They thought it was a hoot."

"How did you manage to keep out of trouble, then?"

"Janine and I used to steer clear of them for a few days when we knew what they were planning. That way, we wouldn't be roped into whatever they had in mind."

"Fiona, I always wondered why you got caught up with them in the first place. Janine's okay, I always got on well with her, but Rachel and Kim, well, back in high school they were both nasty pieces of work."

I sighed. *Not a lot has changed since then, unfortunately.*

"I have to say I was always surprised you didn't just find another group to hang about with. Not all the girls at school were bitches like those two were at the time. And now…"

"You used to hang about with us, too, remember."

"True," said Stacey, taking a sip of her coffee. "Even now I have trouble figuring out what it was about Rachel especially that attracted us to her. Sure, they were fun. But sometimes their idea of fun was a bit over the top."

"Well, for a start, she was the prettiest girl at school."

"I suppose she was, but it was more than that at the time. When I was in rehab, I had a lot of time to think about not only my life but also about the way we were back then. I think the only reason why Rachel was popular back in high school was because everyone was terrified of her. No one was game enough to face up to her, fearing they'd become her next target. I reckon it had nothing to do with the other girls actually liking her, but it was purely out of fear they pretended to worship the ground she walked on. Think about it, Fi. How many of the girls we went to school with have anything to do with her now? None. And why would they want to? I reckon they'd cross the street to avoid her these days."

True. Since we'd all made the transition from school to work, I hardly ever ran into anyone from school. Suddenly, I saw myself through Stacey's eyes, and it wasn't pleasant. Surely, the other girls I'd gone to school with weren't also scared of me? No, they couldn't have been. I was never nasty like Rachel. But still, Stacey had uncovered a cache of memories I'd kept hidden away for years.

Could it possibly be I was I still caught up in their net because I was too gutless to stand on my own two feet? No. Ridiculous. Rachel, Kim and Janine — well, we'd been friends forever. You didn't just forget your friends, leave them in the gutter like unwanted rubbish when the going got tough.

Still, chatting with Stacey was bringing back feelings I had tucked away in an iron vault of my conscience. Memories of having been a sad, scared child in a new school, surrounded by what could only be described as hostile forces. I'd found it terrifying at the time. Nothing in my quiet, sheltered upbringing had prepared me for the jungle of adolescence. I'd been lost in a frightening new environment until, like a miracle, I'd been pulled into Rachel's group and for the first time since beginning high school had been able to relax, safe in the knowledge I was at last one of the cool girls.

"But at least *I* got away from them," said Stacey, drawing my focus back to the present.

"Yeah. What happened? I never did find out. One day you were part of the group and next thing you seemed to just disappear."

Stacey took a deep breath. "I'm not sure whether I should tell you. It's not really any of our business. Mind you, it was years ago when it happened."

"What?"

"Look, I would normally never mention this to anyone, meaning you have to promise never to repeat this to anyone."

"Sure," I said.

"Back when we were in year ten, I was staying over at Rachel's place one weekend. Mum and Dad were having guests around for dinner and Rachel and I were going to the Blue Light Disco in town. Rachel had been acting a little bit weird, but I didn't pay any attention at the time. She was always shitty about something. Well, not long after we got back from the disco, something happened. I hadn't seen her father before we left to go out. Apparently, he'd been at the pub. Well, just as we got into bed, he came in."

Stacey took a deep breath. "God, it was horrible. He was drunk. Really drunk. He began yelling and screaming at Rachel's mum. I could tell Rachel was really embarrassed so I tried to, like, ignore what was going on out in the house. But things got even worse and a little while later, I could hear stuff breaking. He was smashing up the place. Poor Rachel looked really frightened then and I couldn't pretend to ignore it anymore. Her father was yelling about everything, most of which I couldn't understand because he was that drunk."

"Oh, my God. Stacey, I had no idea. What did Rachel do?"

"Nothing. It was obvious by then her dad was belting the shit out of her mother. We could hear everything that was going on. But Rachel just lay there, not moving, not speaking. She was terrified. *I* was terrified. Eventually, I couldn't stand it anymore and reached out for her. She just lost it and started crying hysterically. It was a nightmare. I didn't know what to do. I think her father must have heard her crying, because he began banging on the wall and screaming at her to shut up. Honestly, I thought he was going to come in and attack us. He was totally out of control."

I felt as though the breath had been knocked from my body. Never in my wildest dreams would I have imagined Rachel had suffered at home like this.

"He didn't hurt you or Rachel, did he?" I felt sick with dread of what I would learn, but I knew if I didn't ask now, it would torture me until I found out.

"No, not me. I climbed out of the window. I honestly thought he was coming in to lay into us. I got out of there, ran to a phone booth and called Mum and Dad. I could hardly talk to them for crying. They rang the police and came straight over."

"Poor Rachel," I whispered. "What happened to her father afterwards?"

"I think he was charged with assault. Rachel's mum was in a real mess and they took her away in an ambulance."

Tears pricked the backs of my eyes as I thought of Rachel and what she must have suffered. No wonder she was extremely aggressive and angry. Life for her must have been one big nightmare.

"Mum and Dad were totally freaked out. I have never seen my dad as angry. I think if Rachel's dad had actually touched me, he would have killed him. After that, Mum and Dad made me promise I'd stay away from Rachel."

"But, surely, it wasn't her fault her dad was a violent bastard."

"Of course not. I knew, and so did they. But still my parents felt responsible for allowing me to be there in the first place. They'd never met Rachel's folks. Probably if they had, they might not have let me stay. Mum was never really fond of Rachel, thought she was a bad influence. She was, of course. Mind you, after seeing first-hand what she had to put up with, I reckoned maybe it wasn't all her fault. After that night, I decided to concentrate more on my schoolwork rather than making trouble. Rachel and I never discussed what happened. Not even a word. But from that day on, she avoided me, wouldn't even look at me. Soon, I found another group to hang about with and I moved on."

As I waved goodbye to Stacey, I couldn't stop thinking about Rachel. She never spoke about her dad. Ever. He and her mum weren't together anymore. I couldn't actually remember when they'd split up. Not that it mattered. By then, the damage had already been done.

What a day. First Troy, then Kim's fall from grace and now Rachel. And I still had my date with Antonio tonight. Before Stacey and I had parted, she'd made me promise I'd never mention what I'd learned about Rachel's home life. Not that there was any need. I would never tell a soul. If Rachel ever wanted to talk about it, I would, but more than anything else, it was up to her.

Since spending the afternoon with Stacey, I had to admit, I felt more at peace with the horrible news that had landed painfully on my empty, childless lap last night. If nothing else, learning the awful truth about Rachel had only served to remind me I certainly wasn't the only one to face crises and heartbreak and, most probably I wouldn't be the last either. Moping around wasn't going to get my life back on track. The shock of Troy's recent betrayal still stung, but I knew it would eventually pass.

It was almost four o'clock before I finally got home, thanks to our local Dodgy Brothers bus service. As a rule, the fat middle-aged bus drivers saw it as a gross inconvenience when they were called upon to actually pick up passengers, never mind having to drop them at the specified destination. Service with a smile—not.

I began the short walk home, feeling slightly disturbed and befouled by the ugly vibes emanating from the sullen driver. I tried to remind myself *again* of the reasons why I'd decided not to buy a car.

One. Apart from the fact I can't afford to buy one, they're horrendously expensive to run, insure, park and keep on the road.

Two. Dad already has one, meaning I can always borrow his if I'm desperate. Mind you, the convenience of being independently mobile only just outweighs the annoying ritual of groveling and pleading beforehand.

And three. Being without means of transport comes in handy when going out for a night on the town. Exhibit A, Janine. Owns her own car and is therefore always expected to ferry us home from the pub or club after a few drinks. Considering I'd been the poor unfortunate one forced into driving home from the wedding, maybe it wasn't such a good example now.

I did have a car once—sort of. But after I'd walked out on Troy, and our only means of available transport, I'd been so wrapped up in my own misery I hadn't given a second thought to the fact I'd been without wheels. At the time, it hadn't mattered, because I'd never been going to leave Mum and Dad's lounge ever again. Even if I had found cause to leave the house, unlikely, seeing as I had been robbed of my life, lowly public transport would fulfil my humble needs. Now, as I found myself rushing home to scrub off the evil taint of another perilous bus journey, I couldn't help wondering if I might have acted a tad hastily.

I suppose, in all fairness, the car was technically Troy's to begin with. I also hated being seen out in it. If it had been left up to me, we would have had a sensible, economic Hyundai or Mitsubishi, not a testosterone-fueled red V8 Holden.

I was almost home and the distant sounds of traffic and the odd dog barking struck me as being strangely out of place. An eerie stillness had settled over the street and it took me a few minutes to work out what was wrong.

Then it hit me. *How could I have missed it?* Not a bagpipe to be heard. Not even a single drum roll or hint of chanter. The neighbors must have been beside themselves with relief at not having to endure another Saturday afternoon in the Highlands.

As I'd tried to explain to Dad on many occasions, not everyone was as fond of pipe music as he was. Not even the mysterious appearance of a set of headphones in the letterbox a couple of years back had managed to get through to Dad the damage his musical preferences were inflicting on neighborly relations.

The car was in the driveway, meaning Mum and Dad were home. *Very curious.* Something was going on. I sensed it. I just had no idea what.

Coming on top of Dad's unexplained errand this morning and Mum's vagueness concerning his whereabouts, I figured I had good reason to be nervous as I made my way toward the front door.

Inside, I immediately headed for the kitchen, thinking if I was going to be confronted with more disaster, it was best to be within striking range of some form of comfort food to soften the blow.

This was where I found Mum, grinning wildly and looking in danger of bursting a gasket with excitement.

"What's going on?" I asked, confusion compounding my unease. "And where's Dad?"

"Oh, he's out the back. He'll be in soon, though. How about you sit down and close your eyes?"

"*What?*"

"Just doo as yer told and close yer eyes."

"This isn't going to be one of those weird intervention things, is it? You know, where you get all my friends to come around and tell me how crap my life is and how I'm screwing up?"

Mum, never having been a *Seinfeld* fan, looked genuinely perplexed and I allowed myself to relax on that score.

"Just do it, close your eyes. Your dad has a surprise for you."

"Not Troy's head on a sharp pike, I hope?"

Mum was so excited I didn't have the heart to spoil her fun. Instead I closed my eyes and prayed it was one of those good surprises, say, a new car or tickets to an exotic overseas holiday, and *not* an announcement that Granny was moving into my room with me or Dad had just treated himself to a flash, state-of-the-art toupee and wanted us all to go out to celebrate — in public.

"Yes, Alistair, she's right here," Mum yelled out through the kitchen window. "No, she has noo idea, either."

Suddenly I heard the back door open and Dad stomp in to the kitchen.

"Yoo can open yer eyes now," Dad said.

When I did, what do you imagine was sitting in front of me on the kitchen table? The tiniest ball of white fluff! I could have cried with the instant jolt of pure love that leapt from my heart to encompass the sweetest miniature Maltese Terrier I had ever set eyes on. I was speechless.

"I hope yoo like him. He was the last of the litter and the smallest, from what I'm told."

Instantly tears welled in my eyes and I couldn't speak.

The darling little puppy then opened its tiny pink mouth and yawned and that was it. I was in love.

"I know it doesnae make up for what that bastard ex did, but yer mother and I thought it might cheer yoo up some."

"Oh, Dad," I choked. "I don't know what to say. He's beautiful! I can't believe you went out and bought me a puppy. And here I thought you were off beating the shit out of Troy."

Dad grunted. "I would nae waste my breath on the bastard."

"Well, dear, what are ye going to call the wee little treasure, then?" asked Mum.

Scooping him up from the table where he had fallen asleep, I snuggled his tiny little body into the crook of my neck, breathing in his delicious puppy smell. His heart beat strongly against my throat as he flicked a wet little tongue out of his tiny mouth and licked my chin.

"Oh, I don't know."

He looked so small and vulnerable. *Maybe Fluff or Pocket?*

No, if he was ever going to grow up to be a strong, kick-ass dog with spunk and attitude, he'd need a little more help than that. Then it came to me. The perfect name.

"Arnie. Yep, I think I'll call him Arnie."

And why not? My own little *Terminator*.

Hasta la vista, baby!

Chapter Seventeen

Well, this was it. Before me stood Alberto's Restaurant and, on the other side of the heavy ornate doors, Antonio and my future happiness were waiting.

All around me the city hummed with the energy emanating from thousands of people intent on having a great time. The lights and the noise pouring from the hundreds of tiny pubs and clubs set the place alive with a carnival-type ambiance. Walking through the city, I felt as though I was living another life, far away from my recent dramas, not to mention those of my friends.

I was on a high. I'd spent the last couple of hours playing with Arnie and now here I was about to meet Antonio at last. I didn't think my day could get any better.

If I died tonight — that is, after the much-anticipated sex and not a second before — I'd die a blissfully happy girl.

I took a deep breath and did one last mental check of my appearance.

Hair. Fine, opted for the safe approach and put it up in a sort a half twist, half roll — all the better to shake out later in the evening, affecting a sexy, disheveled look.

Makeup. Went easy on that score as not to look too much like a tart, leaving room to show a little leg and cleavage while not too much as to offend Antonio's mother.

Clothes. In the end, I'd decided to go for the sexy look, balancing it with subtle makeup for maximum effect, and had worn my black leather skirt. It was the same one I'd previously sworn never to don again after that fateful night at the club. It was a measure of the new, improved, confident me that I'd decided to laugh in the face of past miseries, *ha, ha, ha,* and once again wear my favorite skirt. Especially as it cost forty-five dollars to dry-clean after the vomiting incident. Then, completing my new confident, sexy Fiona look, I'd picked out a lovely chocolate-brown wrap-around top and soft knee-length brown suede boots.

I had to admit, I felt like a million bucks and prayed Antonio would be totally knocked out by the new sexy me. After tonight, I was chucking the Hamilton Island T-shirt in the Goodwill bag, never to be thought of again.

I looked at my watch. A few minutes past eight. By the time I'd dodged the millions of taxis and the dirty-looking buses that plagued the streets I would be just in time — respectably ten minutes late.

I took a deep breath. Time to go in and meet my gorgeous Latin god — and his mother!

Inside, the maître d', an impossibly good-looking young man with a disparaging air about him, eyed me standing there before him and to my utter amazement promptly ignored me, rudely turning his attention back to the large, well-thumbed reservation book. Anyone would imagine I had just crawled in off the street, twitching, with hypodermic needles sticking out of both arms. I experienced a moment of self-doubt. Had it been that long since I'd entered a trendy inner-city restaurant I'd forgotten some vitally important piece of protocol? A secret hand signal or sly flash of cash, perhaps?

No. This was just an exceptionally snooty maître d' — actually just a glorified waiter if we're honest. Yes, he was probably a frustrated actor whose only acting job in the past year and a half had been dressing up as a toilet roll for a Cottonelle commercial. Hence the shitty waiting job.

I had two choices here. Either I stood there politely, looking like a complete doofus and waiting for him to acknowledge me, or I went pro-active and announced myself.

Going against the grain, I settled for the latter.

"Excuse me!"

The little prick looked up, gave a perfect plastic smile and pretended he had only just noticed me standing there.

"I'm meeting a friend for dinner. He has a reservation for eight o'clock."

"I'll just check the list. What name is the reservation under?" asked the rude waiter.

"Antonio…"

Rolling his eyes with obvious contempt, he smiled smugly and asked, "And does this *Antonio* have another name, by any chance?"

Shit! I'd never thought to ask him. *What kind of an idiot am I?*

"Umm…" I mumbled, trying to stall for time as I frantically racked my brain for any mention of a surname.

"I'm not a mind reader, madam. You. Will. Have. To. Say. It. Out. Loud," he enunciated, like I was deaf or stupid or both.

Fuck, I wanted to slap him. The only reason I didn't was because my desire to gain entrance into the restaurant and meet Antonio was stronger than my urge to put this asshole in his place.

"I'm sorry but I can't remember his surname right now, but his name is Antonio and I *know* he made a reservation for tonight. If I could just have a quick look in the restaurant, I'm sure he's waiting in there for me as I speak."

The arrogant prick of a waiter shot me a look of scathing contempt and shook his head slowly.

"I'm sorry, madam. Maybe you could phone him — if of course you have his phone number?" he added sarcastically.

Behind me, the heavy doors opened and a cold night breeze hit the backs of my knees. I knew my time was up. Someone else entered the restaurant behind me and I began to panic. I couldn't believe I was going to be turned away by the oik in front of me, leaving Antonio and his mother thinking I'd stood them up.

What a total arse-up.

I did have Antonio's number, but unfortunately at home, safe and sound in the top drawer of my bedside table, ironically enough so I wouldn't bloody well lose it. Safe it may have been, but it was fuck all use to me at this most crucial moment in time.

Quickly, I considered my options. I *could* ring Mum and asking her to find it for me. Not that I wanted Mum rummaging around in my drawers, but I was desperate. I calculated it was worth the risk of her stumbling across the vibrator the girls had given me as a joke for my last birthday, seeing as I would never be able to face Antonio again if I stood him and his mother up tonight.

"Fiona, I'm *so* sorry I'm late."

Recognizing Antonio's voice as he entered the restaurant behind me, I could have cried with relief.

Like a knight in shining Armani, Antonio's sudden arrival turned what might well have been a horribly embarrassing moment into something entirely different. For a second, the waiter's expression hovered between annoyance at being thwarted in his endeavor to evict me from the premises and alarm that he had come to within a sneer of making a rather colossal error in judgment.

"Mr. Fiorelli, what a delight it is to see you here tonight," gushed the waiter, his previous churlish attitude now nothing but an unpleasant memory. "And this *must* be your charming guest," he added, presumably referring to me, the slime who had just crawled in off the street not five minutes before. "Don't you worry, Mr. Fiorelli, I've been taking good care of your guest while she's been waiting."

Could this be the same arrogant asshole who barely thirty seconds ago had been gleefully preparing to eject me from the restaurant? I was flabbergasted, speechless with shock at the transformation Antonio's appearance had triggered in the cowering out-of-work actor before me now.

"Will your other guest be joining you tonight or are just the two of you dining this evening?"

"No, my *other* guest is parking the car and should be here in a moment," responded Antonio flatly, not at all impressed by his craven sycophancy, putting his arm around my shoulders and leading me into the restaurant.

At the time I was so impressed by Antonio's handling of the offensive waiter I gave little thought to the fact he'd left his mother to park the car. My relief that he'd arrived when he had was immense. Another couple of minutes and I would have been history as far as this waiter was concerned.

"Very well, Mr. Fiorelli. Allow me to show you and your *lovely* guest to your table and I will *personally* show the rest of your party when they arrive."

I was still in a state of shock as Trystan—he wasn't christened Prick, after all—draped the crisp white serviette across my lap with all the exaggerated flourish of an eighteenth-century royal courtier.

When he was out of earshot, Antonio turned to me, taking my clammy-with-nerves hand between his warm and dry ones and smiled apologetically. "I have to say you look absolutely stunning tonight. I'll be the envy of every man here, I'm sure. Again, I can't tell you how sorry I am to be late. Since I got back yesterday, I feel as though I haven't been off the phone for more than five minutes. Then I had a late meeting this afternoon with some of my suppliers and, well, I thought I was never going to get out of there."

"Don't worry about it. As it happened, you arrived just in time," I said, nodding toward where Trystan busied himself giving another poor bastard a hard time at the door.

Instantly Antonio put two and two together. "I hope he wasn't too rude to you?"

I had to laugh at his perceptiveness. "How could you tell?"

"Oh, don't worry, he's rude to everyone. Don't take it personally."

"Well, he wasn't rude to you. In fact, as soon as you walked through the door, I reckon he could have hoovered the carpet with all the sucking up going on."

Antonio laughed. There were those perfect white teeth again—in casual clothes he was gorgeous, but tonight, wearing a charcoal-grey Armani suit perfectly complemented by a black silk shirt, he was nothing short of breathtaking.

"For some strange reason, he's got it into his head I'm some underground crime boss." Noticing the surprised look on my face, he winked. "I don't know where he got that impression, honestly, but while I continue to get star treatment and a table at my disposal, I think I'll leave him to his active imagination."

Looking into his dark, bedroom eyes—you may well scorn but they *were*, although it does sound dangerously Harlequin-esque—I felt giddy with desire and desperate for his mother to make her appearance, pronounce me perfect for her adorable son, then piss off, leaving us free to get on with our night of romping around doing the wild thing with energetic abandon.

Thinking of his mother, I wondered just what could be keeping her. I hoped she hadn't been mugged on the way in here or something equally inconvenient like being run down by a taxi or lured into a sleazy opium den. It would be just my luck we'd spend the evening either sitting at the hospital waiting for her to emerge from a bloody coma or bargaining with the Chinese triad for her release, rescuing her from a life of human slavery. Yes, I could see that might just place a damper on the evening.

Still, Antonio didn't appear in the least worried about her absence. I decided to forget those thoughts of doom and gloom and sat back, determined to enjoy our last private moments together before she arrived.

"I'm glad you asked me out tonight."

"I'm glad you came. All those late-night coffees were keeping me awake," he teased.

This was going well. My earlier nerves had fled and the warmth of Antonio's easy intimacy wrapped around me like a cozy blanket.

"I have to tell you it's been a long time since I've been taken out to a lovely restaurant in the city—it's a wonderful treat."

"Well, in that case I'll definitely have to make a point of taking you out more often, then, won't I?"

My heart did a little victory dance. If I'd died right then, I would have gone out a very happy, if very horny, girl. Yes, I could definitely get used to this. Antonio's sexy presence was doing diabolical things to my libido and if I didn't try to put a lid on my escalating frustration, I feared I might just jump him right there in front of everyone.

"How about we order some wine? What would you prefer, white or red?"

My knowledge of fine wine was fairly basic at best. I knew cask wine was generally evil and normally produced hangovers of catastrophic proportions, but at a push I had to admit I wasn't really fussy. After all, if you survived the first couple of glasses, you got a taste for it—eventually. The image of me slurping sweet wine from a box via its plastic nozzle wasn't a side of my personality I wished to acquaint Antonio with, so I decided to play it safe.

"I think I'll let you chose."

Catching the drink waiter's eye, Antonio beckoned him over and, after a rapid exchange in Italian, ordered something that appeared to impress the man no end, if the finger kissing and rapturous eye rolling were anything to go by.

Alberto's wasn't a large restaurant by city standards, and it was already almost full. After our wine arrived, in an elaborate wicker-encased bottle, Antonio explained that Alberto's was owned by a wonderful Italian family and quite a lot of the dishes were actually old family recipes. Originally, nearly all the cooking had been done by the matriarch of the family, Mama Torrisi, but in the last couple of years, the business had grown to the stage they'd been forced to bring in a couple of chefs to take over the ever-increasing work load. Mama Torrisi still had a say in the menu, though, ensuring the authenticity of the cuisine.

I could have sat there all night listening to Antonio's sexy burr. The alcove where we were seated ensured us a certain amount of privacy and Antonio's company, together with the wine, had kindled a warm humming sensation deep in my belly.

But I was getting ahead of myself. I still had to face Antonio's mother. Looking down at my glass, I was a little shocked to find it empty. The heat creeping up my face and the fuzzy feel-good sensation swirling around my head reminded me I had barely eaten a thing today, apart from a small slice of pecan pie with Stacey. I knew I'd better put the brakes on the vino or I'd run the risk of passing out on Antonio before the night was out. And, of course, I still had to get around his mother yet — if she ever got there — so a clear head was definitely required for the next hour or two.

"And this *special* person you wanted me to meet, I'm really looking forward to…"

"Ah, and talking about that, look who's finally arrived."

I swiveled around in my seat as a large group of diners entered the restaurant en masse.

Among the new arrivals were a couple of very sophisticated older ladies, but not one of them could I immediately identify as the type of woman who could possibly be Antonio's mother. None of them were wearing black ankle-length sack-type dresses with heavy orthopedic shoes and a headscarf. Going by the big hair, even bigger breasts and designer clothes, it seemed as though I was laboring under a false impression as far as Antonio's mother was concerned. Could it be possible she was *not* the traditional village-mama-type, but more the chic Sophia-Loren-type? I had only *assumed* she was the former. Maybe it was wishful thinking on my behalf and I possessed a subconscious yearning to be tearfully drawn into to her matronly bosom and warmly welcomed into the family. Considering the reception I usually received from my ex-mother-in-law, little wonder I'd been busy cultivating fantasies involving harmonious family relations.

Then, among the knot of diners waiting to be seated, I

spied a familiar face. Patrick, the stripper from Stacey's bachelorette night. I could have combusted with sheer mortification.

Oh, please God, don't let him see me. I didn't know what I was going to say if he recognized me or, worse still, strolled over to say hello. How was I going to explain to Antonio how we'd met — oh, my God, and his mother of all people? *'Oh yes, I make a habit of walking into dressing rooms full of half-naked male strippers.'*

Yes, I'm sure that *would impress them. Not!*

I spun around in my chair and grabbed the menu, feigning intense interest in the extravagant array of culinary delights before me, despite not having a clue what any of the dishes were of course — with them being written in Italian and all.

My heart beat wildly and the noise in the restaurant seemed to instantly amplify. Straining to be heard above the manic burst of *Happy Birthday* coming from a nearby table, Antonio leaned across to me and said, "Are you okay, Fiona? Don't be nervous. I'm sure he'll adore you."

Did Antonio say he? I couldn't hear him properly over the noise, but something turned in my stomach just then.

Beside me, I heard an unnervingly familiar voice and groaned inwardly.

"What an amazing coincidence. Fiona, isn't it? Maybe you don't remember me."

It was Patrick, and even the unfamiliar sight of him with clothes on couldn't erase the memory of his Adonis-like beauty. I knew I'd have to say something and hopefully he'd move on before Antonio's mother reached the table and I was forced to introduce them.

I pasted a smile on my face and answered politely, "Of course I remember you. Patrick, isn't it?"

"You *do* have a very good memory."

And right then my memory was busy conjuring up images of his well-buffed and sexy oiled abs, not to mention the rest of his equally impressive body, every orgasmic inch of which was ingrained indelibly upon my eyeballs.

Instantly my womb leaped, enthusiastically responding to the memory of him whipping off that last strip of Lycra, leaving most of the women on the boat positively agog at his raw, naked beauty.

How the hell can this be happening? I swear my embarrassment was all but cremating my carefully applied makeup, not to mention the damage it was inflicting on the cringing flesh beneath.

"Do you two know each other?" asked Antonio, plainly taken aback.

"You could say so," replied Patrick, then, to my abject horror, he sat down next to Antonio.

How rude was that? And how was I going to get rid of him before Mama Fiorelli arrived now? I was so occupied with my current dilemma I failed to notice the look that passed between Antonio and Patrick.

"Well, it seems there's no need for introductions after all," said Antonio, beaming with obvious delight as he poured Patrick a glass of Chianti.

I was confused.

Very confused.

"Sorry," I stammered, looking from one to the other, "have I missed something here?"

"Fiona, it's Patrick I wanted you to meet. I can't believe you already know each other. Patrick is my partner."

"What, business partner?" I blurted out inanely, stalling for time while I tried to get my head around it all.

Where the fuck is his mother?

Then, as if to clarify any possible further misunderstandings, he very discreetly placed his hand over Patrick's and squeezed it affectionately.

"No, my *partner*, partner," he added gently, smiling warmly at Patrick.

Instant, horrifying understanding blotted out everything around me and the blood drained from my face before returning in a tidal wave of undiluted horror.

The restaurant and all the other diners ceased to exist,

leaving just the three of us frozen in a hideously awkward moment. My hair shrank back into my scalp in shock as I suddenly developed trauma-induced tunnel vision. In that critical moment, the only thing I could actually focus on was Antonio's hand placed ever so intimately over Patrick's.

Oh. My. God. How could I have gotten it so devastatingly wrong?

Suddenly, everything fell into place with a sickening crunch.

Antonio's perfect fashion sense, his perfect manners, his perfect rhythm, his perfect good looks, his perfectly manicured nails, all leading up to his perfectly delectable boyfriend — Patrick!

Here I'd been living in a fantasy world, believing he was being considerate and gentlemanly by not immediately attempting to jump into my pants.

He wasn't being gentlemanly.

He was being fucking *gay*.

Antonio sat smiling at me and, by the light in his eyes, I could tell he was in love.

And not with me, unfortunately.

I didn't know what to say.

Congratulations, I am very happy for you both, might have been a good start. But, at that exact moment, I didn't think I had it in me to conjure up the kind of sincerity needed to pull it off successfully.

"Fiona, honey, you *did* know I was gay, didn't you?"

Oh, God, this was it. The rest of the evening—the rest of my life actually—hung on the next thing to come out of my mouth.

"Of course!" I laughed. Or at least I hoped it sounded like a laugh and not a strangled cry of disbelief. "Gorgeous man. Dance instructor. *Hello!*"

It was weak, I know, but it defused the moment and Antonio visibly relaxed.

"Well, isn't this the most *amazing* coincidence," said Patrick brightly, breaking the tension. "When Antonio told

227

me about this gorgeous new student in his dance class and how much I would enjoy meeting her, he had no idea you were the same girl who'd burst into our dressing room that night looking for, what was it again, vodka?"

"Oh, God. He told you about that?" I asked, turning to Antonio.

Antonio was the last person on Earth I wanted to know about my uncharacteristic sojourn into the seedy below-deck world of male strippers, begging for vodka. Not that it *had* been seedy, mind you, but people do tend to jump to conclusions when alcohol and naked men are involved.

"Of course! He thought you were really…what was the word — sweet," he answered, confirming my dread. So much for imagining myself to be the epitome of casual sophistication. "Mind you, it sounded as though by the end of the night he and the other guys only just escaped by the skin of their teeth from a horde of horny old ladies."

Antonio laughed and I wanted to die.

"You know, Patrick is really a classically trained dancer," he continued proudly. "He should be on the stage performing with one of the local dance companies rather than wasting his talent on some tacky boat."

Patrick playfully slapped Antonio on the back of his hand. "Don't you listen to him. For years, I performed in various contemporary dance companies, and I must say, mostly it was extremely hard work and very little fun. The reason why I enjoy working with Bad Boys Afloat so much. It's minimum pressure, maximum pleasure."

"*And* he gets a kick out of all those women drooling over him," teased Antonio. "Go on, admit it!"

God, the air of intimacy around them all but crackled and the neglected glass of wine in front of me just cried out to be polished off.

Being the obedient sucker I was, I immediately complied and downed it in one mouthful.

The warm fingers of alcohol beelined for my mouth, loosening my tongue. "I thought they said you were an ex-

Chippendale? Or was I just pissed at the time?"

God, I wished I was pissed right then—wasted and completely legless. Noticing my empty glass, Antonio leaned over and refilled it and I murmured my thanks. A couple more glasses of wine and I might just be able to look Antonio in the eye—I hoped.

Patrick laughed. "No, you're right, they prefer to announce me as an ex-Chippendale. You have to admit, it sounds a hell of a lot better than introducing me as a gay ex-ballet dancer."

He had a point there.

"Is that how you met then, dancing?" I asked, desperate to appear cool in the shadow of Antonio's shock announcement.

"Nothing quite so romantic, I'm afraid. I bought this *fabulous* late-nineteenth-century hall table from Antonio's shop. Then the idiots who delivered it dropped the bloody thing, snapping off one of the legs. I was absolutely livid at the time and threatened to sue the arse off them. Antonio came to my house to smooth things over and personally apologize for the incident, and, well...he didn't leave for two days. Of *course,* I didn't end up suing. It was almost three years ago now and we've been together ever since. And there you have it. No dancing, no gay bars, just broken furniture and a lot of yelling brought us together."

"Seriously, Patrick, you make it out like I bribed you with my body."

"Well, didn't you?"

Antonio at least had the good grace to blush, and I cringed inwardly, desperately trying to figure out how I'd thought he fancied me.

Of course, neither of them could ever be described as camp. Not in a million years. Manly, drop-dead gorgeous, staggeringly sophisticated, perfect skin—they obviously saw the inside of a beautician's more than I do—wearing clothes no married bloke with a mortgage and kids could *ever* afford to look at, never mind buy.

They were definitely T.I.N.Ks, two-income-no-kids.

Gay in other words.

Very, very gay.

In hindsight, it couldn't have been more obvious if they'd had G-A-Y stamped on their foreheads.

I felt like such a fool.

My initial mortification had mostly worn off by now. As much as I wanted to be angry with Antonio for leading me on, in hindsight, I had to take responsibility for leading myself on and I found, much to my surprise, I was enjoying myself too much to dwell on the fact I had come within a whisker of making the faux pas of the century. Thank God I hadn't found the guts to make a pass at Antonio yet, but believe me, it was next on my list of things to do.

When Antonio had made his life-altering announcement, the only thing stopping me from fleeing the restaurant and throwing myself under the nearest bus had been the realization he honestly had no idea I'd fallen for him like some stupid lovesick teenager.

By the time our meal arrived, I had to admit I was beginning to appreciate and enjoy their warmth and honesty — it was like having two Antonios for the price of one, and I basked in the attention they lavished on me. Though watching him and Patrick together now, I couldn't help feeling a stab of envy for the love that radiated from both of them.

Why can't I find someone to look at me like that? Someone who isn't gay, preferably.

Did this mean I was a gabe, a gay babe?

It seemed so.

Life wasn't fair. In fact, it sucked, big-time!

Chapter Eighteen

Lying naked on cool, rumpled sheets, my body is sated, aching and raw from a night of frenzied sex. The primal scent of spent urges lingers in the room, melding with the pungent smell of freshly brewed coffee, bringing our passion racing back to boiling point once more. Looking up, I see him approaching me, his naked beauty summoning my tired yearnings to the surface afresh. All our previous inhibitions have been obliterated by our night of exploration, discovery and our delight in our mutual love.

Instantly our need for sustenance is forgotten. He places the streaming cups beside the bed and reaches out for me, trailing a lone finger down the length of my spine. I shiver. Not from cold, but for the jolt of pleasure his touch has initiated deep within my womb.

He leans over my prostrate, naked body and traces a line down my back with his warm tongue.

I am burning up, melting. I try to move away, but he pins me down and flattens his tongue, lapping up the taste of my flesh like a starving man.

I groan, unable to stem the primitive sounds coming from my love-swollen lips.

He rolls me over and continues feasting on my flesh. Moving up my belly, he lingers over my breasts until I think I can stand no more of his erotic torture and cry out to him.

Tenderness, warmth and softness. He looks into my eyes and kisses my eyelids. Slowly, very slowly, he searches for my lips and plants tiny little kisses upon my parted lips…

"Ouch!"

A needle-sharp stinging sensation pierced my left nostril, wrenching me cruelly away from my faceless lover. Desperate to retrieve my vision, I tried to ignore the pain and return to my delicious love-fest. My body was humming and I could feel the weight of him pressing against my body. I could almost smell the rough masculine aroma of his warm, sated body — male earthiness laced with a hint of sandalwood.

"Shit!"

I screamed as another splinter of pain sliced through my nose. Dream lovers weren't supposed to bite, at least not my bloody nose, at least.

Suddenly, the pain disappeared, only to be replaced with a yucky squelchy wet sensation up and down the side of my nose. Definitely not sexy or particularly pleasant. My dream lover stomped off back to the land of nocturnal fantasies in a right huff and I opened my eyes to find Arnie sitting on my pillow, licking my nose by way of an apology for the pain he had caused.

I was torn between delight and disappointment. Delight at my early morning affection delivered by Arnie, and disappointment that here I am, a twenty-six-year-old woman in her sexual prime just gagging for a beautiful man to fill her bed — as well, as other more pressing orifices — and here the only affection I can get, apart from my sexy phantom lover, is from a baseball-sized bundle of slightly pissy-smelling fur.

Damn!

Arnie looked at me, his disproportionately large brown eyes filled with unconditional love, and I couldn't bring myself to be angry with him. After all, he was irresistible. Totally adorable. My heart swelled. I hadn't felt like this since — Antonio.

Shit! It only took a microsecond for the awful truth of last night to come racing back to kick me in the guts.

Why couldn't I have died in the arms of my sexy apparition last night? Where are all the natural disasters when you need them? I know, in bloody South America tormenting poor Brazilians — *lucky bastards!*

Despite the shock of Antonio's bombshell, I had to admit, albeit grudgingly, that I'd had a fabulous time with him and Patrick last night, once I'd recovered my scattered wits.

They'd made me laugh. They'd deciphered the menu so I didn't end up ordering marinated eels. They'd got me well and truly plastered on that deceptively potent Italian wine. They'd flirted shamelessly with me and sadly each other, as well and to cap it all off, they'd even picked up the bill and driven me home in the Saab.

Who could complain?

They'd been simply wonderful and I couldn't imagine anyone I'd rather have spent the evening with.

Unfortunately, I was *supposed* to be waking up this morning on cool satin sheets, stretching my aching body with a horny Italian wedged firmly between my spread thighs.

Instead, I woke to find myself being mauled by a miniature Cujo.

What a monumental cock-up!

Oh, God, how was I ever going to face anyone ever again? My life was over, *again*!

The girls were expecting a blow-by-blow account of my night of a thousand sex acts and I couldn't bear the idea of them knowing what a fool I'd almost made of myself. If I confided that Antonio was, in reality, gay, they'd laugh themselves stupid and within an hour everyone within a ten-mile radius would be privy to my shameful secret — I'd lost my head and heart to a man who sadly only has eyes for other men.

No, I wouldn't be telling them anything of the sort, that was for sure. Besides, Antonio's personal life was none of their business.

I only wished *my* personal life fell into the same category.

I cringed every time I thought of the way I had all but thrown myself at Antonio.

What had I been thinking?

How could I have ever imagined he had fallen for me? At least seeing them both together, all happy and relaxed, had forced me come to terms with the cruel fact that Antonio was absolutely, definitely, categorically *not* romantically interested in me.

How embarrassing!

My only saving grace was it appeared he'd had no idea I'd fallen head over heels in lust with him, thank God. Had he suspected anything, I'd have never be able to look him in the eye ever again.

Wallowing in my puddle of self-pity, I wondered just how I long I could put off explaining it to the girls. Then, just as I thought my life couldn't get any worse, the house phone rang. I dived back under the blanket, wishing I could miraculously disappear. Of course, if my recent run of bad luck was anything to go by, I knew it had to be one of the girls ringing to see how last night had gone. When Mum knocked on my door, my suspicions were confirmed.

"Rachel's on the phone fer yoo," she said, opening the door. She stuck her head into the room and I rolled over in an attempt to block out the rest of the world, including my mother and my friends.

The last thing I wanted to do was talk to Rachel. In my current mental state, she would sense something was amiss before a single word left my mouth. Suddenly, I was reminded of one of Rachel's pet sayings.

Never bullshit a bullshitter.

Rachel was certainly a bullshitter, especially when it came to the opposite sex. Half the male population in the area were still scouring back issues of *FHM* magazine for Rachel's elusive pictorial spread after she'd *kind of* boasted to a few blokes at the nightclub of her brief, but nonetheless successful, career as a centerfold model.

Pure wishful thinking.

She'd given up any hope of a modelling career years ago after unsuccessfully attempting to screw her way onto the catwalk. She'd lost heart, though, when she'd finally discovered only after countless *auditions* — blow jobs in dark rooms—that set designers and assistant photographers didn't really pull much weight when it came to hiring models. Apparently, by all accounts, she'd left a good impression, though.

No, I couldn't face a cross-examination right now.

"Mum, tell her I'm sick and can't come to the phone. Please!"

Then I had a vision of the three of them landing on the doorstep to visit and I panicked. "No! Mum, wait. Just tell her I haven't come home yet."

"Why would you want Rachel to think that?"

"Please, Mum, just do it," I pleaded.

Mum gave me a strange look, but thankfully didn't press the issue—for now, anyway. Going by her expression, I knew I was going to cop one of her motherly inquisitions later on.

I was pushing my luck. I also knew it was only a matter of time before I'd have to face the girls and either admit my shameful secret, or lie like I'd never lied before.

In the end, the decision was not all that difficult.

I chose to lie.

* * * *

"You bloody knew, didn't you?" I challenged Jason, while keeping an eye on Antonio, who was on the other side of the room, taking a group of new students through some basic steps.

It was Tuesday night and the first time I had left the house since my *date* with Antonio. So far, I had managed to fend the girls off, firstly by telling them I'd spent the weekend locked in a shag-fest with *Tony*. Then, by conjuring up a sudden attack of laryngitis brought on by all the orgasmic screaming—another lie, but who's counting—I bought myself two more days' respite to pull myself together.

If I failed to turn up at class, though, I worried that Antonio might think I was freaked out about him and Patrick.

I was, of course. But not because I'm homophobic — I'm a gabe now, so how could I be — but because every time I thought of Antonio, I cringed, reliving every embarrassing moment I'd spent fantasizing over him.

Watching him now with a group of new students comprised of three middle-aged sisters and a funny-looking bloke wearing baggy beige corduroy trousers, a short-sleeved business shirt and a thin leather bolo tie — yes, a bolo with a large lapis lazuli fastener — every sexy swivel of Antonio's hips, every rhythmic twirl of his still gorgeous body, every graceful slide across the dance floor just screamed out *gay, gay, gay*.

Of course, it's blatantly obvious now, what with hindsight being just another word for *I fucked up yet again but it's not my fault*.

Still, watching the three giggling sisters drooling over Antonio, I allowed myself a small smile of satisfaction.

Been there, done that!

"What the hell was I supposed to say, Fi?"

"Well, how about *don't waste your time on Antonio, he's gay*? That might have been a good start, don't you think?" I replied though clenched teeth. "But no, you just let me carry on like a complete idiot, thinking Antonio had a thing for me. Great. Stupid Fiona louses up — again, ha-ha!"

Seeing as Jason was the only one who'd known about my infatuation for Antonio, it seemed fair he took some responsibility for the fact I had been making a complete fool of myself over him.

"Even if I had said something, would it have made any difference? Really. You were so into him, I bet you'd have thought I was just making it up because I was jealous or something."

Ouch, that hurt.

"Well, thanks for nothing. God, you must have been laughing your head off."

"No, I wasn't, honestly. And, if you remember, I did try to warn you," Jason said quietly.

"When?"

"A couple of weeks ago, just after your *private lesson*. At the time, I told you to be careful and you got all shirty at me."

Yes, I remembered it all too well, unfortunately. Just like Jason had predicted, I had thought him jealous that Antonio and I had hit it off quickly. *What an idiot.* All the signs had been there, flashing in front of me the whole time, iridescent and neon. Blinded by the whole *happily ever after* dream, I'd failed to notice any of them.

I felt like a right bitch. Jason didn't deserve to be treated like this. The only thing he was guilty of was trying to shield me from my own stupid actions while keeping Antonio's confidences private. He was merely an innocent bystander, trampled in the stampede of my rampant romantic notions.

"Shit, I'm sorry, Jason. I know it's not your fault, and I'm not trying to blame you, really. I just feel like the world's biggest fool and you're the only one I can talk to about it."

For a brief moment, I could have sworn Jason's hands tightened around my waist and a weird tingling sensation spread through my flesh.

"Don't worry. I'm pretty sure he didn't suspect you had a thing for him. I reckon every female here has a crush on him, anyway, so I wouldn't beat yourself up over it."

It didn't help. I still felt a complete fool.

"I honestly thought you'd figure out for yourself he was gay. But still, I'm sorry you had to find out about it like you did. It's just I didn't think it my place to go telling people about Antonio's private life. I will say this, though, he must really think you're something special to introduce you to Patrick."

Up until now, I'd been so consumed feeling sorry for myself it had never occurred to me what a big step it'd been for Antonio to open up his private world to me.

"Oh, you've met Patrick?"

"Yeah, a while ago. I ran into them one day at the nursery and he introduced me to him. They were looking at indoor plants and I got the impression he had no idea I worked there. I kind of guessed then he was gay, and a few months later he dropped it into a conversation about his partner, Patrick. Like I said before, though, Antonio's a genuinely nice bloke. Why should I care who he chooses to sleep with?"

Right then, I realized just how special Jason really was. Not too many blokes I knew were that easygoing and accepting of others. God, I didn't want to even imagine my ex's reaction if I'd told him I'd gone out to dinner with two gay men. He'd immediately round up a posse of his redneck homophobic mates and go out gay bashing, I bet. Of course, he was so into himself, he thought every gay man was just aching to come on to him. What an asshole. No self-respecting homosexual would give him a second look, what with his pseudo-mullet and burgeoning beer-gut. Comparing him to Patrick was like comparing a clapped-out Cortina and a brand-new Maserati.

Sad to admit it, but Antonio definitely has better taste in men than I do, or did, at least.

Just then, Jason laughed. "Check out the boy scout over there."

The weirdo in corduroy stared at Antonio with an openly adoring expression plastered on his face.

"Poor Antonio," I laughed.

At least I wasn't the only poor sucker to fall for his Latin charm. Mind you, the weirdo in beige corduroy stood on the right side of the fence, even if he didn't know it.

* * * *

It was Wednesday lunch and the first time I'd seen any of the girls since Kim's meltdown following the Dangerous Dave incident. Poor Kim had spent the remainder of the weekend in a state of shock, and apparently, she'd completely written herself off on a bottle of vodka at Janine's on Saturday night, Janine having arrived home from her afternoon shift, tired and bloody, only to find Rachel and Kim waiting for her, armed to the teeth with enough alcohol to ensure they wouldn't so much as remember their names by midnight.

As a result, Kim had been violently ill and, together with her poor abused liver, had lain in bed detoxing ever since. That is, until this morning, when after a brief struggle she'd been dragged out of bed and ordered back to work by her very unimpressed mother.

At first, Rachel had been positively venomous that I hadn't returned any of her calls on Sunday. But on hearing my fabricated tale of unbridled lust and the unfortunate rapture-induced laryngitis that followed, it appeared all was forgiven, on the proviso that I loaded their imaginations with enough juicy details to keep their curiosity well fed.

"You filthy whore!" teased Rachel. "I can't believe you spent the entire weekend doing the big ugly with this Tony bloke."

"Believe what you will, I don't care. I will say this, though. By the time I got home, I was sore in places I never knew existed before Saturday night."

I'd decided to go all out on the description of a weekend lost in the pursuit of satisfying our mutual desires and animal lust. As a result, by the time I'd finished divulging all the sordid details, a few of which Rachel was quick to point out were possibly illegal in some states I had them slack-jawed and in awe of my libidinous encounter. Rachel and especially Janine were almost cross-eyed with envy and, now I come to think of it, I was, too, desperately wishing I had actually been there to enjoy it in the flesh and not just in my imagination.

"You lucky bitch," sighed Janine, whose curiosity had far outweighed her previous resolve never to return to the scene of her past humiliation.

Ignoring Janine, Rachel launched into phase two of her interrogation. "Okay. Now when do we get to meet this sex bomb? You can't put us off forever, you know."

"Yeah, come on, he might have some really hunky rich friends he can hook us up with, so don't be selfish," whined Janine. "God knows, I'm not having any luck around here."

Sadly for Janine, before I could successfully set her up with any of Antonio's circle, she'd first have to grow a penis.

Poor Janine was desperately hoping to be rescued from a long string of dating disappointments. Not that she had any problems picking up guys. She was a bloke magnet. Her tall, athletic build, together with her generously sized tits, usually ensured a never-ending stream of willing partners. But generally, once they found out what she did for a living, they soon hit the road, cupping their genitalia protectively. After all, there is nothing more emasculating than a chainsaw-wielding woman. Janine's relationship crisis had become so critical of late she hasn't been able to face the thought of getting it on with any bloke. "What's the point?" she'd said recently, "there's no one out there for me. I might as well give it up now as a bad joke."

Yes, she was in a poor way.

"You can leave me out. I am never looking at another man — ever again," groaned Kim.

"Okay, Kim, we've all heard that one before. I bet you don't last a week. Hey, when's it going to be?" insisted Rachel, pouncing on me.

"When's *what* going to be?" I responded vaguely.

"Don't be a bitch. You know. When are we going to meet this Italian stallion of yours?"

I had to think quickly. After all, Rachel was practically salivating in her eagerness to check out my mysterious lover.

"Hmmm, Friday night's out as he has a meeting in the city. And Saturday night he's arranged to get us a table at that brand-new restaurant in the city. The one that's been on that TV show."

"Bullshit!" they screamed in unison.

"I don't believe it," cried Rachel. "That place's supposed to be next to impossible to get in to. They reckon you practically have to be boning one of the production crew on the show just to get on the waiting list."

"Oh, I don't know about that, but we have a table booked for Saturday night. When I spoke to *Tony* last night, though, he said he might have a window open in his schedule on Sunday night — that is, if we're out of bed by then," I added for good measure. A girl can dream, after all.

"Bloody hell! It sounds like all he does is work, swan around in posh restaurants and bonk. Where the fuck did you manage to meet a bloke like that?" asked Janine, awed somewhat by *Tony's* daunting sophistication.

Janine considered a bloke sophisticated if he could use a knife and fork and speak in complete sentences.

Picking up my diet soda, I sighed, feigning boredom. "I'm *sure* I must have told you the story."

"No, you haven't, actually," said Kim, finally showing some interest in the subject.

"Well, it was after I'd been…"

And off I went, fabricating a tale of numerous brief but completely innocent encounters years ago when I'd been married, through a friend of a friend of my cousin, who they naturally had never met. Then a chance reunion outside my local chemist in the main street had brought us back together a few weeks back when I stumbled off the curb, teary-eyed after purchasing my weekly tissue supply, and he'd almost run me over in the brand-new Saab he'd just picked up from the dealership. I was on a roll, here! After he'd scooped me up off the road and checked I wasn't injured, we'd suddenly recognized each other and fallen into each other's arms, our shock being all-encompassing. Then he'd insisted I accompany him for a restorative cup of coffee. Only after he'd been satisfied I was all right did he tentatively bring up the delicate subject of my ex. I, of course, had told him the whole sorry state of my marriage. At least that bit was true so I won't go to Hell for lying. We'd sat talking for hours before he'd insisted on driving me home, in case I'd gone into a belated state of shock from my near miss.

On and on I went until I had almost woven together the plots of *Sliding Doors, When Harry Met Sally, Serendipity* and almost every other 'boy meets girl' movie I had watched in the past ten years.

The girls were *riveted*!

Having successfully bluffed my way thus far, I just had to keep them satisfied until I could implement phase two of my plan.

Phase two involved my dramatic break-up with Tony and, for that finishing touch, I decided to coordinate the big split with our upcoming *date* on the weekend.

Several versions were in contention.

One. He was a secret agent. For my personal safety, he had to end it as the Russian mafia had taken out a contract on his life and he would not be able to live with himself if I got caught in the crossfire and something happened to me.

Two. He'd just received word he'd inherited an ancient princedom in Italy. But, as part of the inheritance, he had to marry the hideous, middle-aged heiress of a rival *famiglia*. If he refused his call to honor, a war would almost certainly break out between the two opposing families. Thus he was left with no other choice but to sacrifice his future happiness with me and return to the land of his birth to marry, ultimately martyring himself to stop what would otherwise result in a complete bloodbath.

Three. A SWAT team drops down from the ceiling of his bedroom just as we're in the throes of yet *another* ferociously toe-curling orgasm and physically drags him from my panting body. Then, a big beefy and very nice-looking Marine tenderly wraps my naked body in a warm rug and gently explains to me that *Tony* had been eluding capture for months on charges of drug trafficking and human sex-slave racketeering. I, of course, am stunned and promptly faint in his arms from the shock. When I awake, *Tony* is securely bound in both arm and leg irons and I am cradled in the arms of the hunky Marine as he croons reassuringly in my ear to soothe me.

And four. I discover *Tony* is a right sicko when he suggests how I might enjoy a wild romp in the sack with him, his best mate and two hookers he hired for the night! His best friend was kind of cute, but I had to draw the line at hookers, mainly on moral grounds — and the fact they both had far better figures than I do.

So far, option three was favorable, closely followed by option four.

If my plan went smoothly, I'd be off the hook by Sunday afternoon and I could finally put this whole disastrous infatuation behind me with my dignity intact.

Perfect!

To my immense relief, this proved far easier and a damn sight more enjoyable than I'd expected it to be. Over the previous few weeks, I had been gorging my imagination on a banquet-size portion of Antonio for breakfast, lunch and dinner, so it was no effort to recall some of the events that had, in truth, only been consummated in my fantasies.

"Excuse me, can we change the fucking subject, now, or I think I'm going to hurl. I *am* trying to eat here."

Considering Kim's recent doings, no surprise that she was the only one not goggle-eyed with rapt curiosity at my weekend sex-fest.

Taking in the sight of her now, she might well have been going around in a hair shirt. As it was, she looked like she had her mother's clothes on. Her new look comprised stained blue jogging pants and an oversized black jumper, and was capped off by the crummiest running shoes I'd ever seen, plus her brother's mangled baseball cap. Had she slept in a garbage bin for a month? Not that her mother looked like she frequently camped out in garbage bins, but, then again, *she* could never be described as a fashion icon, either. Today, though, Kim had a hopeless, shameful aura about her, all but advertising her recent social demise.

There was, of course, another reason why Kim had switched her customary provocative, slutty attire for her new, uncool grunge look.

She was in hiding – from Dangerous Dave.

It seems after his recent initiation to the heady delights of carnal pleasure, to which Kim had unwittingly exposed him, Dave had developed an unquenchable taste for clandestine storeroom shags. In other words, Kim had well and truly lit his wick and he was now *desperate* to repeat the experience.

Kim was horrified beyond belief. Especially when Dangerous Dave had started phoning her, first at home, and later leaving messages at work, begging her to go out with him. Not even the savage knock-backs she repeatedly screamed down the phone, and ultimately a wall of stony silence appeared to get through to him, convinced as he was that they were a match made in Heaven.

Bearing in mind my recent conversation with Stacey, I found it quite a trial to keep myself from laughing as Kim relayed her humble return to work this morning, via the back door of the salon in order to avoid Dave, who'd waited in vain for her every day that week outside the main door, clasping a by-now wilting bunch of flowers.

Janine suggested that Kim take out a restraining order against him for stalking. We all agreed it was a fabulous idea – very *now*, actually. Didn't everyone who was anyone have a stalker or two lurking around? Unfortunately, that wouldn't work, seeing as there'd been no threats or violence involved. Yet. Kim *had* briefly considered beating the shit out of him but loathed the thought of actually having to touch him again. Plus, there was also the added suspicion he might just get off on it. *Yuck.*

By now, Rachel's patience was beginning to wear thin. In truth, I'm surprised she'd lasted this long.

"For God's sake, Kim, lighten up, will you? Just because you're never likely to have sex again doesn't mean we all have to suffer along with you. Honestly, you're going to have to deal with the ugly little troll once and for all, and the sooner the better, because if he comes into my shop one more time, begging me to put in a good word for him, I swear to God, I won't be responsible for what happens—to either of you," she adding, leaving no doubt that Kim was seriously pushing the friendship.

"*Thanks* for your understanding, Rach," cried Kim tearfully. "It's fine for you. You have a gorgeous *tall* boyfriend, and here I am, a total laughing-stock and never likely to get another bloke unless I leave the country and move to say...fucking *Iceland* or something. But don't let that worry you. You just go on rubbing it in and you can carry on with your *perfect* life and your *perfect* boyfriend and just forget about me, your best friend."

Possibly it was Kim's mention of Jason, but instantly Rachel's mood plummeted.

"Hey, what's up, Rach?" asked Janine.

"Oh, nothing really... Well actually now you've asked, it's Jason. Something's going on with him and I'm not sure what it is."

Kim snorted derisively. "Oh, my God, Rach, can't a girl have a crisis without you having to home in on her misery? What could possibly be wrong? He's the perfect boyfriend. Hangs on your every word and would kiss your bloody feet if you asked him to."

Rachel looked a little sheepish.

"If you even start going on about him sucking your fucking toes or anything of a similarly disgusting nature, I swear I really *will* throw up," Kim promised.

Things were beginning to get ugly and, for once, I was relieved. Kim's continuing woes had hijacked interest away from my imaginary weekend shag-fest.

And thank God for that.

I was beginning to run out of steam. Imaginary sex proved even more exhausting than the real thing.

"Don't listen to her," Janine interrupted, obviously fearing an all-out brawl was brewing between the two of them. "She's hurting inside and has to take it out on someone. Now, what's going on with you and Jason, then?"

"Like I said, I don't know. Last night I tried to ring him and got no answer. Then, I tried his mobile and *that* was switched off. I decided to go around to his place and surprise him with a little spontaneous sex — you know a little teasing, some kinky underwear with a hint of bondage. It all helps to keep them in line you know, keeps them guessing…" Noting the dangerous narrowing of Kim's eyes, Rachel wisely didn't dwell on the subject. "Well, he wasn't home, was he? The old bag wouldn't tell me where he was *or* when he was coming back so I thought I'd just wait for him. After all, where the Hell could he have gone off to on a bloody Tuesday night?"

I knew exactly where he'd been. *With me.*

"Where was he, then?" chipped in Kim.

"That's just the thing, isn't it? I waited there for almost two bloody hours. He didn't get home until almost *ten o'clock*, and when I asked him where the fuck he'd been all bloody night, he refused to tell me."

"What! Just like that?"

"Yes, just like that. He got all defensive and, when I pushed him for an answer, he said I wasn't his bloody mother and he didn't have to ask me or anyone else for permission to leave the house."

We all sat there, suitably stunned.

I couldn't believe she'd waited for two hours.

"Then what? I hope you told him to go fuck himself?" queried Kim, clearly outraged on Rachel's behalf, her own problems briefly forgotten.

"No. Well, I thought about it, but I didn't get the chance. He walked straight past me into his flat and, when I went to follow him, he stopped me at the door and said he was really tired and was going to bed. Alone! And that was it. With me left standing there like a complete idiot."

"Jesus. What the hell's got into him?" Kim wondered.

"I don't know, but I'll tell you what, I swear I saw that hag of a grandmother of his smirking out of the window at me as I got back in the car. I bet she knew *exactly* where he was, too."

"What are you going to do?" I asked.

I couldn't help myself. This was just too juicy.

Rachel took a moment to think.

At any other time, even something as trivial as a bad haircut or wrong choice of shirt could trigger the ousting of any one of Rachel's many boyfriends back into the Rachel-free abyss whence they came. So it was going to be very interesting to hear what nasty retribution she would devise to deal with Jason's brush-off last night.

He was history, that was for sure, and I had a feeling the end would be bloody.

"Well I've been thinking about it all morning and…"

"And what?" demanded Kim.

"*And*, I've decided — it's time we moved in together. That way, I'll know exactly where he is."

"What!" we all cried out.

"Yep, I'm pulling a sick day tomorrow and I'm going to look at a couple of places. Then, as soon as I've found something decent, I'll tell Jason to pack his bags and we'll move in together, well away from his interfering bitch of a grandmother."

This was a side to Rachel I'd never seen before.

She was scared.

Scared of losing Jason, that was.

Yes, this behavior was that of a desperate woman, even if she was the only one who didn't realize it yet.

Obviously, Jason's unprecedented rejection of her last night had pushed the panic-sequence button in Rachel's brain, overriding all rational thought. Never before had she been treated in any other manner than open adoration and it was without doubt the first time her ego had suffered a direct hit.

Welcome to the real world, Rachel.

* * * *

"Fiona, phone for yoo," yelled Mum from the lounge.

I threw down the magazine I'd been flicking though and gently made a nest in my blankets before placing a very dozy puppy into the protective hollow.

Dragging myself from the bed, I groaned.

God, if it was Rachel *again*, I would scream.

It was only Thursday evening, but since her shock announcement at lunch on Wednesday, not only *her* life, but ours as well had begun to revolve around her never-ending search for the perfect love nest in which to finally imprison poor ignorant Jason for a life of sexual slavery. Jason didn't know it yet, but his manhood now belonged to Rachel, only to be let out on a good-behavior bond if he proved his ongoing devotion.

Rachel now saw it as her calling in life to haul Jason back into line after his unforgivable digression away from her emotional domination.

I had never seen her so focused, so determined, so affronted, so *monomaniacal.*

A sight to behold.

And seriously scary at that.

"*Hello,*" I answered cautiously, frantically trying to come up with a viable excuse to escape yet another hour of listening to her increasingly diabolical schemes.

It was sadly obvious to all of those around her that she was beginning to unravel. The very idea she might be in danger of losing Jason was, to Rachel at least, unthinkable.

Not for a moment did I think she truly loved him, but, for Rachel, it was the principle of the situation. To her way of thinking, she was the top dog, the prima donna, *the one*. No one treated her like that and got away with it. As a result, she saw Jason as a prisoner trying to escape and she wanted him back. After all, if anyone was going to be dumping anyone, it would be her, not Jason.

"Oh, thank God you're home!" sighed Janine, the weariness in her voice hinting of things to come. "I've just come off the phone with Rachel…"

No surprises there.

"And someone's got to have a serious talk with that girl. I swear she's losing it — "

"Well, you can rule me out," I interrupted, thinking it better to make it plain before I found myself coerced into confronting Rachel. "There's no way I'm getting involved with her sick plans. You do agree, don't you? She's gone way too far."

"It's why I'm phoning. I tried to talk to Kim about it, but she won't listen. I really think someone should at least warn Jason what she's planning."

I had already thought of that. Sadly, I wasn't entirely certain Jason would thank me for sticking my nose into his business. Anyway, had he taken it upon himself to warn me about Antonio? *No.* This had nothing to do with me. My decision to stay well out of it wasn't because of his reluctance to forewarn me of Antonio's romantic leanings. Not at all. Sometimes people have to find out these things for themselves. Unfortunately, Jason was about to come face-to-face with the real Rachel. The Rachel we all knew. The Rachel who would stampede over her own granny to get what she wanted out of life.

"Warn him about what, exactly? Rachel might be acting a little freaky, but she's not going to hold a gun to his head and *force* him move in with her, is she?"

A horrible thought struck me.

"Oh, fuck, Janine, tell me she hasn't got a gun, has she?"

"No, of course not!"

I breathed a sigh of relief. After all, considering the way she'd been behaving for the past couple of days, it wouldn't have surprised me.

"Look, I can't see the point of overreacting at this stage. Jason's a grown man, after all, and I'm sure he can make up his own mind whether he wants to move in with her or not. For all we know, he might jump at the chance."

Not that I believed it for a second, but the last thing I wanted to do was get involved, and the last place I wanted to be was standing on the landmine of Rachel's love-scorned rage when it detonated.

"Listen, Janine. How about we leave it for a couple of days and, hopefully, she'll calm down a bit?"

I could sense Janine's frustration coming through the phone.

"I'm sick to death of waiting for bloody Rachel to calm down. I feel as though I've been tiptoeing around her filthy moods ever since high school."

"You and me both," I sighed.

"Jesus, we all have problems and issues of our own to deal with. Not that *she* would know. When was the last time Rachel asked *you* how you were coping, what with that bastard husband of yours doing a runner and all?"

"I don't know."

Never, in point of fact.

"Exactly my point. She doesn't care about anyone but herself. Honestly, I think it might do her the world of good to experience what it's like to be dumped. She's been doing it to guys for as long as I can remember and she doesn't give a damn who she hurts."

"We don't know if Jason is planning on dumping her."

"No. But if he stays with her, or worse still, moves in with her, he's an idiot, honestly."

I had never heard Janine vent like this, and especially about Rachel.

She was seriously pissed off.

The worm had turned.

Over the years, there'd been numerous occasions when Rachel's dramas had become hard to take, but I'd thought Kim and Janine looked on her outbursts and moods indulgently. *'Oh, it's just Rachel, you know how she is, ha-ha.'*

No one was laughing now, especially not Janine.

Two solid days of Rachel ringing continuously with her problems had eroded even Janine's legendary patience.

"Look, why don't you take your phone off the hook tonight and turn your mobile to silent? At least that'll give you some peace. There's nothing we can do tonight. With any luck, she'll come to her senses in a couple of days. If not, we'll worry about it then."

"Okay. I suppose you're right. What could possibly happen in the next day or so?"

Yeah, what can happen?

Almost fucking anything, is my bet.

Chapter Nineteen

Here I was again, strolling into the torture chamber for my weekly dose of emotional flagellation.

Every instinct in my body screamed out to run. Run like the wind. Escape while the exits were open.

I, possessing a hefty proportion of lemming in my DNA, though, passively followed Margarita into the room-where-no-one-can-hear-you-scream, meekly making my way over to the solid beige chair whose callus-forming qualities were gradually turning my once wobbly soft buttocks into something resembling the colorful, hardened derrières of those exotic-looking baboons on the nature channel.

Arse-numbing it might be, but at least today I was mentally prepared.

All afternoon, I'd been rehearsing my opening speech. For the past few weeks, Margarita had held the upper hand while I continued to blubber incoherently, treating her to a six-volume saga of the life and times of my pathetic existence.

Not today.

My mind was, after all, my own, despite my treacherous and cowardly body leading me in here in the first place. But don't they say all self-improvement must start from the inside? Well, once I'd wrestled back control of my self-will, I felt fairly confident the rest of me would follow obediently — hopefully thinner and with thicker hair.

Anyway, I didn't *have* to tell her anything if I didn't want to. Nothing. After all, *I* was the one doing the paying. Okay, so Dad was technically financing this extravagant Freudian jaunt, but let's not dwell on frivolities. Bearing that in mind, it was entirely up to me if I spoke or not. I could very well sit there in complete silence and count the dead bugs trapped in the cold strip lighting. Or read a book — *The Bride Stripped Bare*, for example. That would certainly give her some good psychological fodder to chew on — bored, neglected wife goes a bit screwy and embarks on an illicit and kinky love affair with a virtual stranger before vanishing over a cliff, leaving her salacious past in writing, resulting in every would-be academic frantically trying to weave some sort of esoteric message from her wretched and by now very *un*anonymous scribblings.

But, I digress.

This wasn't about some book.

This was about self-empowerment.

My self-empowerment, to be precise.

Over the last couple of days, I'd finally made peace with myself over the Antonio sickness that had taken hold of me during the past few weeks. Now I'd successfully exorcised the carnal beast of that unrequited love, I was free to take hold of the reins of my mental health once again.

So that was my state of mind as I eased myself into the chair opposite my beige nemesis. Tensed to do battle. Well, my butt was tensed anyway, in preparation for the torture to come.

My strategy was this.

To demonstrate my newfound emotional maturity, I would begin the session by telling her of the wonderful grown-up, *platonic* evening spent with Antonio last weekend, with no mention of Patrick — naturally. Then I *might* slip into the conversation a mention of Troy's further misdemeanor—if an unexpected pregnancy can be considered a misdemeanor—if for no other reason than to stress my capacity for abundant forgiveness.

Not, I repeat, *not* that I'd forgiven him. But you get the general picture.

Then, when I've finished giving her the rundown of my very uneventful *normal* week, I might just treat her to a short account of the tragic self-inflicted woes of my friends so she can see I am emotionally healed, psychologically strong and mentally firing on all cylinders.

At least, compared to Kim and Rachel.

I'd been psyching myself up for this all afternoon and as I watched Margarita sink down in her divinely comfortable plush leather chair—I suspect the ergonomic perch is propped up next to the Dumpster awaiting collection and confusing would-be garbage scavengers—I took a deep, fortifying breath and centered myself.

Quietly, I waited for my cue.

This was, by now, a familiar ritual. First, Margarita makes herself comfy, or ties herself up in knots in the ergonomic apparatus. Then she takes her tiny little glasses off her incredibly large, fleshy face before wiping and polishing them so vigorously I fully expect the glass to be reduced to a contact lens by the time she's finished. Then she straightens the single piece of paper on her deck—apparently there to take notes on—and finally she nudges the box of tissues in my direction until they are within arm's reach, pre-empting my emotional weeping. Cheeky bitch.

Lights. Camera. Action.

I opened my mouth to begin.

"Fiona, before you start," interrupted Margarita, holding up her hand to halt the flow of words all ready to march confidently from my mouth. "I want to begin today's session by discussing your early relationship with your ex-husband."

"What?"

Usually we start with my week in review and only *then* does she bombard me with sly, curly questions, hoping I'll unintentionally drop some remark that she can jump on, ravenously tearing it apart until I crack under pressure. Then, when I'm a complete babbling headcase, she books my appointment for the following week. By the time I've recovered my equilibrium, it's usually too late and I'm ensnared in Margarita's psycho-web for another seven days.

Hence my resolve to turn the tables on her. Primarily by pre-empting her kiss-kick-kick method of clinical practice.

So, naturally, I was a little thrown by her sneaky pre-empting of my obviously not sneaky enough pre-empting, but determined not to let it rattle me too much.

"Your courtship, if you like. Tell me, how did you meet your ex-husband?"

This was fine. I could deal with this.

"Actually, Rachel introduced us, at a party. He was a friend of her older brother. She'd known him for a couple of years beforehand and thought we might hit it off."

"And what was your first impression of him?"

"Not great, I suppose. He was a bit of an arsehole, really. It's funny, but I thought he had a thing for Rachel at the time, so I didn't really take it too seriously when he started flirting with me. Then, later on, he asked me out to the movies. Mind you, when I think about it, every bloke there had a thing for her."

"But you went out with him regardless of your initial reservations?"

"Yes. Obviously. I did end up marrying him, after all." *What a dumb question.*

"No, what I meant was, if you weren't attracted to him, why did you agree to go out with him?"

I sighed, exasperation making me impatient. "I never said I wasn't attracted to him, just that he came across as being a bit of a...I don't know, a ladies' man, a bit of a chauvinist. Still, girls seemed to flock around him, regardless."

"So you were flattered by the attention he paid to you?"

"Yeah, I suppose so," I answered glumly, wondering how I could have been so gullible.

When she put it like that, it made me sound desperate. Looking back on it now, I probably was. But how could I have known what a bastard he'd turn out to be? Back then, Troy was popular, good-looking and bore enough of a resemblance to Keith Urban in his Levi's and standard-issue plaid shirt to prompt any girl to throw her panties at him. Hey, half the girls at the party that night would have killed for a chance to go home with him. In light of that, I had to admit it was a much-needed boost to my ego when he spent almost the entire evening outrageously flirting with me and cracking jokes about my luscious — yes, that was the word he used — luscious body. I think he was mostly referring to my tits, though.

Those were the days when *Baywatch* and push up-bras were all the rage, despite the fact a push-up bra was the last thing my C-cup boobs required, or appreciated for that matter. I remember now, I spent most of the night vigilantly rescuing my wayward tits from spilling out of the top in their desperate bid for freedom. No wonder Troy was so bloody fascinated. He probably thought I was playing with myself for his viewing pleasure.

Damn.

Margarita straightened in her chair and wrote something down. I tried to make it out. I almost turned my bloody eyeballs upside down with the effort of trying to fathom her sharp, purposeful script.

Call me paranoid but the words *loser* and *hasty* assaulted my straining retinas, but then, of course, maybe I was just imagining it.

"And what movie did you go and see?"

Jesus, that was a tough one. It'd been years ago.

I racked my brain. "Um, some big budget, loud, blow-them-up flick."

Margarita paused for a moment's deliberation before responding, "And was that your choice of movie?"

"God, no! I hate those blood-and-guts, guy-type movies."

"Why didn't you choose something different, then?"

"Jesus, I don't know. It was a long time ago."

"Think about it for a moment," suggested Margarita benignly, leaning back in her chair as if she had all the time in the world.

At eighty-five bucks an hour, I don't suppose she was too

keen to rush things, now.

I hadn't thought about this for years. Then I remembered I'd gone out and bought a pair of flares especially for my date. They had only just come back in for the first time since the seventies and I felt so reckless and sophisticated, wearing the latest cutting-edge fashion. Of course, I could get away with it back then. I was slim and lacked the self-consciousness a few extra pounds had since inflicted on me. At the time, I couldn't wait to see the look on Troy's face when I arrived to meet him in my trendy new outfit.

Difficult to believe it had been only six years—and roughly twelve pounds—ago. It felt as though a lifetime had passed since then.

And flares were still in vogue!

Not that mine still fit me.

"By the time I got to the cinema, Troy was already there with his mates. Seeing as he'd already paid for the tickets, I couldn't exactly complain and tell him I'd rather see *My Best Friend's Wedding*."

My words hung in the air. They may as well have been waving a white flag, passing her the gun and reaching for the blindfold. Immediately, I knew I'd handed my fate to her on a silver platter.

"He brought his *friends* along with him on your first date?" she asked incredulously.

I shrugged. What could I say? For our first big date, instead of taking me out to a nice restaurant where we could get to know each other over a candle-lit dinner, Troy had opted for a night at the movies with three of his mates, where I spent an hour and a half picking popcorn out of my hair—popcorn *I* paid for—while they laughed, instigated an impromptu food fight, again with my popcorn, and wrestled with one another throughout the entire movie, in the process annoying the shit out of the people sitting near us. It wasn't a very impressive beginning to our evening, but compared to the sleazy pub I was dragged along to afterward, then subsequently ignored in, the movie debacle had to be considered a high point.

"What's a movie got to do with my ex having an affair?" I snapped.

I grew increasingly nervous watching Margarita enthusiastically jotting lines and lines of what I now recognized as shorthand.

Alarm bells were hammering away in my head.

Danger. Danger!

By now, my grand plan of mental manipulation was retreating at breakneck speed in the shadow of her Machiavelli-inspired tactics. I had to admit, I'd become seriously unnerved.

"Fiona, your early relationship tells me a lot about the dynamics of what was later to become your marriage."

Oh, great! Time to batten down the hatches. The destructive forces of typhoon Margarita were gaining momentum.

"And from the little of what you have told me of your early relationship, I have to say it seems it didn't start out looking very promising. In fact," she continued, glancing down at her notes, "you said yourself that your first impression of Troy wasn't particularly a positive one — even then he had a reputation of sorts for womanizing."

Before I could open my mouth to protest, she continued. "Then, and feel free to correct me if I am wrong, he didn't appear to go to any lengths to impress you the first time you went out together."

What else could I do but sit and listen? Protesting at this stage would be futile, as I knew any further hint of defensiveness would only spur her on. I sat there mutely while she continued to perform an autopsy on my life.

"Don't you agree most women would have been more than a little put off by the thought of a man they had only just met inviting his friends along to their first date?"

I nodded sullenly then resumed inspecting my nails. They were in a shocking state. I really had to think about either regular manicures or a set of acrylics, but unfortunately fakes were so expensive to maintain and eventually were all doomed to snap off in car doors and while trying to locate house keys after a night on the town...

Not working.

Unfortunately, she was not at all perturbed by my childish sulking and plowed on regardless, "And how did *your* friends get along with him?"

Finally, something positive to report.

"My *friends* thought he was wonderful." I boasted.

The lofty ideals I'd walked in with earlier had now plummeted headfirst into the hard, barren dirt and died a truly hideous death. With a shock, I realized I was now *defending* him!

"They weren't concerned about his previous reputation?"

"No."

"So *they* didn't think him an 'arsehole'?"

"No! Like I said, they loved him. Rachel, particularly, was thrilled we were going out together and used to say what a perfect couple we were. Oh, not just Rachel, of course. They all loved him and he came everywhere with us."

"Even after your marriage?"

"Just about. On Friday nights I still went out to the club with the girls, as he was usually at the footy."

"With his friends?"

"Yes, with his friends!" *Who else would he be at the footy with, his granny?*

"So most of your time together was in the company of either your friends or his?"

"Not all the time. I mean, there are *some* times when even your girlfriends are in the way," I added, trying to sound worldly and mysteriously seductive.

God, did I have to spell it out? The way she was going on, anyone would think we all slept in the same bed, all ten or twelve of us, and indulged in ritualistic group sex.

"I see."

I wondered if she did though.

"But, generally, you didn't spend a lot of time together, just the two of you?"

"I suppose not." I couldn't see where she was going with this, making me decidedly uncomfortable. Any minute something nasty was going to jump out at me, I could just feel it.

"Why not?"

"We just didn't. It never bothered me, though. Troy got on with my circle and enjoyed hanging out with them. I didn't hate his friends — much, so I tolerated their drunkenness and general obnoxiousness. His mates were continuously trying to come on to my friends and they in turn continuously told them to fuck off back into the hole they'd crawled out of. They kind of enjoyed it really. It was a game. You see, never a problem."

"So, is it fair to say your life didn't really change much after you were married?"

"Well, I didn't turn into my mother overnight and Troy didn't start wearing beige cardigans and falling asleep in front of the TV, if that's what you're getting at."

I knew from past experiences in Margarita's hot or, rather, hard seat, that at this point I had to remain calm and keep a check on my anger. If I allowed her to get to me, I knew my temper was not the only thing that would spew out. Because accompanying it, my mouth tended to pour forth many incriminating facts and foibles for her to latch on to afterward.

Easier said than done.

I felt myself being pushed into an emotional corner with the only way out fight or surrender.

Foolishly, my mouth reacted against direct orders from my brain.

"This is all crap. You go on and on about stupid things like what bloody movie we saw on our first date and implying I should have been home baking cakes and knitting sweaters after we were married instead of going out with our friends like any normal twenty-three-year-olds would. I'd just got married, not jumped straight into middle age. What do you want from me?"

The backs of my eyes were beginning to burn. Unshed tears of defiant anger were building. But I resisted the urge to stretch across to the tissues. I knew as well as she did that the tissue-reaching stage of the session usually marked my defeat. I dried my threatening waterworks with the heat of my growing resentment toward Margarita and her barrage of insidious questions.

"I know," I began caustically, my voice rising in both pitch and volume, "you want me to admit I was so insecure at the time I rushed into a marriage I had no real faith in because he was the first good-looking bloke to overlook my attractive friends and pay me any real attention. You want me to say we never had much in common apart from our friends and that's the reason he was always finding fault with me and telling me to lose weight, grow my hair or be sexier. In other words, he wanted me to be more like *them*."

My chest heaved painfully and dark spots of rage appeared before my eyes. I sat there, seething, while my brain caught up with my runaway mouth. By that time, I didn't even know what I was raging against.

The silence following my outburst hung like a dank, poisonous cloud.

Margarita sat quietly waiting for me to calm down before slowly leaning across the table and saying softly, "Is that how you're really feeling, Fiona, deep inside?"

I couldn't speak. The sympathy reflecting from her eyes heralded my final undoing.

I quickly reached out and snatched up the box of tissues. After all, I was already heading for the scaffold, so why deny myself one last indulgence?

What had I done?

* * * *

Mum and Dad couldn't help but notice my foul disposition when I stormed through the door as soon as I could leave the torture session. I mean, it was like trying to ignore a guided missile blasting its way through the front door, screaming down your hallway and hanging a sharp left before making a beeline for the kitchen.

My head pounded, my anger sending my blood pressure hurtling skyward — I expected my eyeballs to pop out of their sockets any second.

As I stomped past the lounge room, I shot Dad a filthy look for sending me to that Freudian bitch in the first place. A look he missed, I might add — I even suck at that. Then I picked up Arnie and headed straight for my room. I was in no fit state for company and the malevolent cloud of my filthy mood ensured no one would be volunteering to approach me any time in the near future.

I must have been truly scary, because it wasn't until an hour later Mum finally thought it safe to tiptoe into my room bearing a tray, on which sat my favorite dinner of spaghetti Bolognese topped with a mountain of grated cheese. After carefully placing the abovementioned tray down on my bedside table as not to startle the crazy woman — me — Mum informed me quietly that Dad had offered me the use of his car to get to my dance lesson tonight.

No groveling or arse-licking required.

At any other time, I would have seen this as being the ultimate achievement, the culmination of years spent learning the age-old art of progeny manipulation. Oh, I'd often dreamed of this very moment. A triumph of sorts over Dad's notoriously stingy attitude toward availing my brother and me of the family chariot. Had my head not been so fouled with resentment toward the world in general, I would have been hard-pressed to stifle a smirk of satisfaction, seeing it as an unexpected boon to be quietly celebrated and privately gloated over. Bearing this in mind, I made a mental note to consider re-establishing my long abandoned teenage habit of storming into the house and slamming doors and cupboards. It obviously has more impact when you're an adult.

"I'm not going!" I snapped like a truculent five-year-old,

and you can't make me, I thought, but didn't say.

For the next twenty minutes or so Mum tried everything to talk me into going, short of frog-marching me out of the door. I wasn't about to budge, not for her, or anyone else. I needed time alone to reassess the damage my outburst had caused earlier. In truth, I couldn't remember exactly what I'd told Margarita, and in a way, that bothered me most of all.

In the end, I relented slightly and, if only for the sake of my conscience, decided to ring Antonio to let him know I was giving the cha-cha the big heave-ho tonight in favor of sitting at home alone kicking the shit out myself for being a right stupid bitch with an out-of-control oratory dependency.

I caught up with him on his mobile just as he was leaving the city. Antonio had been so wonderful toward me in the last few weeks I didn't have it in me to lie, pretending to be laid up with a stomach bug or some other equally lame excuse. I decided to tell him the truth—I'd just got in from a nightmare session with Margarita and as a result felt completely gutted.

He was so sweet, even going so far as offering to meet me for a coffee later, if I wanted a shoulder to cry on and a sympathetic ear. At any other time I would have jumped at the chance. But I figured my mouth had done more than enough damage for one day, so I asked if I could take a rain check on his empathy instead. Besides, if *I* had someone as gorgeous as Patrick waiting at home for *me*, the last place I'd want to be would be sitting listening to some sad female moan on about how miserable her life was.

No, it was sweet of him to offer, but I couldn't.

Antonio's voice was balm for my shattered nerves. The only negative to finally calming down was that the lessening of my anger allowed room for the ghastly finale of my recent session with Margarita to squeeze its way back into my head.

Even now, thinking about it, I cringed. Had I really said

what I thought I'd said or had the gods been merciful and it'd just been a bad trip? Not that I have ever partaken of drugs of that particular chemical nature, but, if I had, I couldn't imagine it being any worse. Still, now those fateful words had been spoken, there was no more chance of Margarita forgetting them than there was the chance of me suddenly catching the eye of Prince Harry and being whisked away to the palace to bond with the Corgis and try on a tiara or two for size.

The real impact of my outburst was beginning to materialize into a truth I had no wish to delve into...

* * * *

It wasn't long after we arrived home from our honeymoon that I experienced the first of many niggling doubts. Oh, not just that Troy had chucked in yet another job—personality differences with the boss apparently, oh, and the six a.m. starts—leaving me to scrounge more and more overtime to keep food, and particularly beer, on the table, but more that the harsh reality of being a modern wife was beginning to dawn on me. By that I mean, while I worked all the hours God put on this Earth, Troy whiled away the time watching sport on telly. But then I'd come home, cook his dinner, clear away a mountain of empties and on top of that, I was expected to perform all manner of exotic sexual acts in the bedroom for his pleasure, when all I really wanted to do was sleep.

For the first few weeks, despite constant weariness, I obliged and indulged him in what he described as a well-deserved rest after the rigors of planning the wedding, although what planning he'd done was a mystery to me. But by the time the third month rolled around and he hadn't shown any sign of recovery from the strain of saying, "I do," I was left with little alternative but to make a stand.

My overtime had dwindled to almost nothing and more and more I tended to arrive home to be greeted by the sight of Troy and his mates sprawled out in front of the telly surrounded by a sea of empty beer cans. Oh, I wasn't expecting to be swept off my feet and treated to a candlelit dinner every night, but to be greeted at the door by shouts of "Run down to the corner store and pick us up a case, luv," as I returned from a hard day at work rubbed me up the wrong way after a while.

The incident that brought things to a head occurred not long afterward. I arrived home after working twelve days straight—I'd since begun working weekends as well— to find not only the house in a shambles and six of Troy's mates sprawled out with their feet on my new sofa, which had been a wedding present from my parents. They were clearly pissed off their faces on beer that I had paid for, *but* I was treated to the sight of Kim and Rachel giggling their heads off as they paraded around the lounge room in *my* clothes. They appeared to be having a great laugh at my shoddy fashion sense after availing themselves of the contents of my wardrobe.

Our first actual head-on, clashing-of-horns, screaming fight occurred soon afterward.

The next day, Troy picked up a job bricklaying for a mate.

I thought he'd finally settled down. Mind you, I was still responsible for all the washing, cleaning, cooking and general arse wiping, but the little of Troy's wages that survived after his daily drinking session at the local pub helped to alleviate some of our financial woes.

This certainly wasn't how I'd envisioned our life of wedded bliss.

Then, as well as later on, I rationalized these feelings as being merely teething problems—after all, don't all newlyweds have the occasional spat as part of the process of acclimatizing themselves to marriage?

It would be wrong of me to blame my growing resentment entirely on Troy, though. His family, or I should say, his mother, didn't help matters.

She had an uncanny knack of arriving on the doorstep

completely unannounced at the worst possible moments. Her visits usually occurred either the minute I walked in the door from work, or more often than not, obscenely early on my rare days off. Then, if that wasn't bad enough, she'd proceed to do a room-by-room inspection of my house, pointing out every cobweb or grain of dust so I would know to clean it up after she'd gone. *Poor* Troy, she informed me, was terribly allergic to dust mites. *Pity he's not allergic to beer,* I wanted to reply. But if only for the sake of family harmony, I'd bite my tongue.

Naturally, I thought Troy considered her visits to be every bit as intrusive as I did, until the day I'd overheard him apologizing to his mother for my slack attitude toward housework and bad manners, seemingly for not kissing her feet at the door.

I was livid. Actually, what I felt went way beyond livid, to irate, seething with injustice. I felt completely betrayed by him…

We'd been married almost a year by then and it hadn't been easy to adjust to the stresses and strains, not only of married life but our ongoing financial woes—Troy was once again unemployed. Coupled with the fact I was working like a slave, both at work and home and copping all sorts of flack because I insisted, well, demanded, his mates be gone by the time I got home from work, as their all-night drinking binges were the last straw. I was sick of hearing I was a killjoy and a fat one at that.

Could have been because I was so exhausted by the time I got in from work, or because the gym cost money—money we didn't have—I hadn't had the inclination or the energy to exercise for months and consequently I'd gained a few pounds since our wedding.

I don't think a day passed that Troy didn't have a go at me because of it, either. Anyone would have thought I'd grown a second head, or a moustache. I hadn't, just in case you were wondering.

Where was the fun, the romance, the staring into each

other's eyes as we made plans for our future and the future of our children—when they eventuated, which I was hoping would be sometime before the onset of menopause.

Every time I brought up the subject of starting a family, Troy harped on about us not being able to support ourselves, never mind a child. I itched to point out if he held down a job for more than a couple of weeks, our financial situation might not appear so desperate. Of course, I kept my gripes to myself as the fights that followed any mention of his erratic employment status had escalated from loud to very, *very* ugly.

Not long afterward, when I broached the subject of starting a family again, he began dropping snide remarks about me losing weight before he'd even consider it. As he was quick to point out, "No one wants to be seen with an obese wife."

I admit his comments hurt, especially as I was anything but obese. Looking back now, it was hardly any wonder I rarely wanted to have sex with him anymore. With his cruel taunts ringing in my ears, I felt anything but sexy.

I suppose it didn't do my confidence any favors that Rachel and Kim continued to flirt with Troy and he, in turn, did everything to encourage them. Originally, I had seen it as kind of endearing, in a way. Troy liked my friends and they thought he was gorgeous. It was a boost to my ego they considered my boyfriend to be flirt-worthy at all. But now he was my husband, it was beginning to get old. *Real* old. Especially when he lavished more attention and compliments on them than he did me.

Any protests on my behalf were generally greeted with laughter, or, worse still, accusations that I was possessive and paranoid, which of course only made me feel even more possessive and paranoid…

* * * *

Arnie scratched at the door, whimpering to be let out. As I

took him outside, an overwhelming sense of sadness rushed through me. Try as I might, I couldn't conjure up one happy memory of my time together with Troy, prompting me to wonder why I'd married him in the first place.

Of course, things were always going to get better. That was the eternal optimist in me speaking. Ignore a problem long enough and it will eventually resolve itself — my motto of denial, or at least it had been until recently.

Things don't always get better.

Sometimes they get a whole lot worse, as I was soon to learn.

As I fumbled my way in the dark through to the kitchen, an urgent thumping on the front door startled me. It sounded as though someone was trying to break the damn thing down. Mum and Dad were in bed, asleep, so after placing Arnie outside, I quickly made my way to the front before whoever it was woke the entire street. Silently, I swore. If it turned out to be Alex, pissed and unable to find his key, he'd get a right earful.

As I reached the hall, the pounding increased and I experience a brief sense of foreboding. What if it was a home invasion? The news had reported an alarming increase in the crime of late. But, surely, they wouldn't knock first? Maybe they were extremely polite felons? No, it was unlikely to be home invaders. Anyway, we had nothing worth stealing — besides Dad's spoon collection. And if it was just the spoons they were after, I figured it would be well worth a mild concussion and swift bludgeoning to finally rid us of those cursed implements.

By the time I got to the front door, I knew for a fact it was neither Alex nor a gang of home invaders. I almost wished it was.

I recognized Janine's voice arguing hotly with Kim. This was not good. This could only mean something dreadful had befallen one of them. Then I heard thin, high-pitched keening sounds coming from farther afield and I felt an ominous sense of impending disaster.

As I reached for the knob, Dad stuck his head out from his bedroom and shouted, "What tha' *hell's* goin' on oot there? Sounds like a cat's getting murdered somewhere."

"Go back to bed," I whispered. "It's just the girls. I think. Don't worry. I'll see what they want and get rid of them."

This had better be good, I thought. If they had woken the entire house just to tell me that one of them had broken a bloody nail or something equally trivial I was going absolutely ballistic.

I turned the key in the lock and the door almost flattened me as they barged into the house.

"How bloody long does it take you to answer the fucking door?" barked Kim.

"Jesus, what the hell is going on?" I replied.

"It's Rachel," cried Janine, looking deathly pale.

Now I felt alarmed. Janine was usually unflappable and the only one who I could rely on not to panic over stupid things. "Oh, my God, is she hurt or something?"

Instantly, I pictured Rachel lying bleeding on a hospital bed, tubes coming out of her.

"She's in a terrible state," cried Kim, her eyes brimming with tears.

"Where is she?"

Both of them just stood there.

"For God's sake. Is she in hospital? Has someone at least rung a doctor?"

"A doctor? Why would she need a bloody doctor?" queried Janine, looking confused.

"You just said she was in a terrible state. If she's been hurt, we'd better get her to a hospital."

I could have throttled them. Hopeless, they were.

"Where is she now?" I repeated a little louder, in an attempt to get through to them.

Kim's bottom lip trembled. "Outside, in the car."

"You left her outside, on her own? What the hell were you both thinking?"

Someone had to take control and, going by the looks of

helplessness and confusion clouding their faces, it seemed once again it was up to me.

Out of the door I ran, my heart pounding with dread.

Under the dim streetlights, I saw her, slumped over in the gutter next to Janine's car, and my breath caught in my throat. Then I heard a thin whining sound and thanked the Lord I wasn't too late. At least she was breathing. Silently, I prayed Janine had recovered her wits and phoned for an ambulance. Unfortunately, it had been years since I'd sat though the one-day first aid course at work and now I regretted sneaking out before they got to the resuscitation part. All that simulated blood and tying of tourniquets had finished me off and I didn't think I could have sat through an afternoon of airway clearing and mouth-to-mouth without passing out.

The moment I touched Rachel, she began howling. Yes, howling, like a dog. My relief I wouldn't be required to give her mouth-to-mouth was immense. I read somewhere that if it was not done exactly right, you could actually cause the patient's lung to burst. A horrific thing to imagine.

Unfortunately, Rachel's ungodly howling was getting progressively louder and louder and I saw the odd light flickering on up and down the road.

I had to do something before half the street came out.

"Rachel. Rachel. Listen to me. Tell me what's wrong," I pleaded.

"*I'm dying*," she moaned. Well, that was what it sounded like, anyway. It was difficult to tell with all the sucking and gasping noises coming from her as she clutched her stomach and rocked back and forward. She stared blindly into the distance, her eyes, red from crying.

Just then Kim and Janine came running toward us.

"Has someone called a fucking ambulance yet?" I yelled.

"Fiona, listen to me," began Janine, trying to catch her breath. "There is nothing wrong with her!"

"*What!* Listen to her, she's in agony!"

Beside me, Rachel flung back her head and cried, "I'm

dying… The pain… Someone just kill me…"

It certainly sounded like she was in torment. It reminded me of a program I'd watched recently on natural birth and I winced. No one should be allowed to give birth without a plethora of drugs, if for no other reason but for the consideration of those poor unfortunates, otherwise known as the support person who has to endure the screaming and general hideousness of the whole procedure. How anyone can describe it as a wonderful, spiritual, *beautiful* experience is beyond me. Yes, I did want children one day, but after witnessing that, I think I'd rather import one from overseas.

By now, I was fairly certain Rachel was not about to give birth to some phantom baby in the gutter outside my parents' house, and I struggled with how to move her to somewhere not so public.

"What the hell is going on?" I demanded.

"*It's Jason! He's gone!*" Rachel keened, her voice rising in hysteria.

I felt as though I had been kicked in the chest. For a moment, I couldn't draw breath. Jason was dead! I couldn't believe it. My eyes began to burn and I choked back a sob.

Chapter Twenty

"Jason's *dead*?" I whispered.

I could barely bring myself to form the words.

"Don't be fucking stupid, Fi," Rachel snapped, suddenly sounding anything but a grieving girlfriend. "Dying is too fucking good for that...that...*bastard*!"

No sooner were the words out of her mouth than Rachel commenced lashing out at the closest object to her at the time, which unfortunately happened to be Janine's car, kicking and punching it with surprising vigor.

"What? So he's *not* dead?"

"No, he's not dead. He's only dumped her!" Janine informed me flatly, while looking on with growing concern at the damage Rachel was inflicting upon her poor, hapless vehicle. "*Rachel*, for God's sake, stop kicking my bloody car. Jesus, it's in a bad enough state as it is."

Janine's I'm-not-messing-around-here tone seemed to get through to Rachel, because she stopped assaulting her transport, only to focus her rage on my dad's carefully nurtured grass. She began pulling out huge clumps of it and hurling it onto the road, each clump accompanied with vile threats aimed primarily at Jason's genitals—or more precisely the removal of.

Dad was going to freak tomorrow morning when he saw the many pits of exposed earth and I knew I had to get Rachel back in the car before she started ripping into Mum's newly planted flowers.

"What the hell made you bring her here?" I barked at Janine. "Why didn't you take her home or back to your place?"

"Sorry," Janine replied, dodging a stray clod. "We didn't know what to do with her. She's been like this ever since he told her and, well, I was afraid to have her in the house in case she started smashing the place up."

"Oh, you thought you would bring her here to rip up my parents' lawn instead? Great!"

"I just thought you could maybe calm her down. We've tried everything and, well, look at her. It's not working."

Janine was right. I'd never seen Rachel in a state like this before. I had witnessed countless savage outbursts over the years, but I had to agree with the girls that this was without doubt the worst we'd encountered.

Hadn't Rachel ever heard of the concept of dignity? Looking at her now, thrashing around with stray blades of grass sticking out of her hair, I knew *I* wasn't about to suggest she pull herself together, fearing she'd turn on me.

She resembled a woman possessed.

No wonder they were scared. Anyone in their right mind would be. For a second, I considered ringing for an ambulance. At least they had tranquillizers, which was a damn sight more than we had to deal with her psychotic rage. Only out of fear they might head straight for the nearest Psych Unit made me decide to scrap the idea. Still, we couldn't stand here all night and watch her annihilate Dad's lawn. Something had to be done. And soon.

"Here, Janine, give us a hand to get her back in the car, will you?"

It was a struggle, and not without the odd kick and slap being administered by Janine, who by this stage was way past caring what the consequences would be when Rachel discovered all the bruises tomorrow. Finally, we manage to haul her into the back seat and while I ran back to the house to get some clothes on—my lovely satin pajamas were covered with dirt—I left Kim and Janine to control the fizzing headcase in the car.

The ten-minute drive to Janine's place proved to be nothing short of perilous. Rachel was quite a handful and, for someone so skinny, she possessed a surprising amount of strength. Every time Janine slowed down at a corner or set of lights Rachel tried to throw herself out of the car until both Kim and I were forced to sit on her, if only for her own safety.

An hour later, aided by a healthy measure of bourbon and a couple of spliffs Janine had been saving for a special occasion, Rachel finally calmed down, much to everyone's relief, and stopped trying to smash everything in sight.

"What happened?" I asked. "I thought things were going well between you and Jason?"

Well, I didn't really, but this was a girl thing. In times of crisis the number-one rule was never point out the obvious—like, we could all see it coming. And rule number two, if the situation warranted it, lying was perfectly acceptable.

"I can't believe it, Rach. You two were so in love. Maybe it's just a big horrible mistake?" added Kim, rubbing Rachel's back.

Rachel howled, her eyes awash with tears, "This was no fucking mistake. He said he never wants to see me again!"

"But why?" asked Kim. "You were so good to him. *And* you went to all the trouble of finding a place where you could both be together. He should have been grateful."

"No, he wasn't fucking grateful. He was furious. Called me an interfering bitch and controlling and all sorts of nasty things."

"No way! You're not controlling. He's the control maniac, not you," soothed Kim.

I looked at Janine and we both rolled our eyes. Shit, Kim was laying it on a bit thick.

"Maybe the whole moving-in together thing freaked him out," I suggested diplomatically. "I suppose it's understandable. Lots of guys get cold feet when it comes to the big decisions in a relationship. When he has had time to think about it more, I'm sure he'll come around."

No, I didn't believe it for a minute, but it was worth a try.

I desperately wanted to get some sleep.

Rachel began to cry again. "No, he won't."

"You don't know that for certain," said Kim, looking about to burst into tears, as well.

"Yes, I do, because he told me he's fallen for someone else."

"*What!*" we chorused.

This was certainly news to us. Instantly, I was wide awake.

"Oh, my God. Who?" gasped Kim.

"The coward wouldn't fucking say, would he. But I tell you this, when I find out who the whore is, I'll fucking kill her, I will."

"So will I," seconded Kim.

"And me, too," added Janine quietly.

I mumbled something unintelligible and tried to look inconspicuous.

Vigilante hunting isn't exactly my preferred weekend pastime.

* * * *

By Sunday night, it was obvious to all that Jason was in hiding. Mind you, he had very good reason to be.

In order to protect Janine and her house from any further damage in the event of another violent Jason-induced relapse, I stayed on at Janine's Friday night and most of Saturday. There, in round-the-clock one-hour shifts, the three of us took turns keeping an eye on her. Thankfully, Rachel seemed calm for now, but there was no predicting what might happen when the drugs and alcohol wore off. Just to be on the safe side, we slipped her a tranquilizer as well.

By Sunday morning, she'd finally ceased with all the sobbing, wailing and gnashing of teeth, but only when pure demonic hate finally possessed her. Had I been a religious person, I would have rung for a priest in the faint hope the devil could be lured from her love-scorned body. Sadly, this was not a case of demonic possession, just Rachel learning how it felt to be on the receiving end of the cold, hard reality of the rejection stick. Personally, I'd have preferred spinning heads, projectile vomiting and disembodied voices coming out of the walls.

As a result of her recent new-life experience, instead of espousing a dignified philosophical approach toward it, Rachel had decided to embrace it in the only way she knew how to. By throwing it down on the floor, stomping the shit out of it and ripping its head off for good measure.

Needless to say, it wasn't a pretty sight. In fact, it was ugly.

Very, very ugly.

Rachel was well and truly on the warpath.

First on the list to cop a super-sized serving of Rachel's wrath with large fries and soda was Jason's granny. I wasn't there, thank God. My own granny had suddenly developed a shocking case of eczema and I *had* to visit. Sadly, my physical absence did not grant me a much-desired respite from learning the grisly details.

By all accounts, Rachel had given the poor woman a right verbal thrashing, accusing her of ruining her life, Jason's life *and* almost everything else that was wrong with the world until the neighbors finally rang the police and they ordered Rachel from the property. Not before threatening to have her charged with trespassing, though.

That was just a warm-up, however. Accompanied by Kim with Janine was at work — lucky Janine had offered to work a double shift—they went around and confronted each and every one of Jason's friends, trying to find him. If any of them did know his whereabouts, they were not about to tell her and Rachel's hostile quest yielded nothing but further frustration.

The masculine cone of silence had been well and truly lowered.

Jason's friends had closed ranks.

I can't say I was particularly surprised. Most of them

had at one time or another been granted the rare pleasure of becoming one of Rachel's chosen ones and, as a result, they were well-acquainted with her almost legendary spitefulness. I have a suspicion they were all quietly pleased that the tables had been turned on her at last.

During the days following, every single girl she came across was a potential boyfriend stealer and copped a menacing look. Consequently, Rachel's shop sales fell drastically as her need for revenge increased.

It was rumored in the center that more than one Chick customer had been seen fleeing the shop in tears following Rachel's third degree on why they were needing a new outfit. If, Heaven forbid, one of them hinted at a new love interest in their lives, they only escaped a near savaging because the junior sales staff were more afraid of being fired by head office than they were of Rachel's fury.

By now, I was becoming increasingly worried about Jason. No one, and I mean no one, had seen him since the big bust-up. First of all, I worried Rachel had secretly paid a hit man to take him out. But then, I reasoned that if she had, in her current frame of mind she would have taken out a full-page ad in the local paper boasting of it as a dire warning to any others out there who might in the future contemplate breaking her heart.

Adding to my concern was the fact he hadn't shown up at work, the first place Rachel looked for him — how better to get back at a bloke than to ridicule him in front of his workmates?

But I suppose it wasn't until I arrived at dance lessons on Tuesday night and discovered his absence I got *really* worried. The class was larger than usual, with a further influx of new students. Apart from a quick hello before the lesson began, I never got a chance to speak to Antonio privately.

By the time the class ended, I was exhausted and therefore didn't fancy fighting my way through the three-deep crowd of new Antonio devotees to ask him if he had heard anything. It was a long shot, anyway. Besides, I didn't want to worry Antonio needlessly. At least not at this stage. I headed for home.

No sooner had I walked in the door than the phone rang. It was almost ten at night and I immediately wondered if someone had died. I've found phone calls after nine o'clock rarely offer good news and my stomach twisted itself into a tight, hard knot.

"Fi, where have you been?" demanded Rachel as I put the receiver to my ear.

"Excuse me?"

I felt like slamming the phone down on her. Her rudeness was beyond belief!

"Doesn't matter. Now listen. I heard something very interesting tonight down at the Tavern — about Jason."

"Really!" I said, trying my best to sound interested.

It was becoming harder and harder of late to conjure up the required mental stamina to cope with Rachel's all-too-frequent phone calls.

"Yes, really. This bloke I got speaking to knows him from the club. Apparently, he used to work on the door with him a couple of years back before he took off up the coast. Anyway, *he* reckons he saw Jason a couple of weeks back standing in front of the community center, of all places, talking to some bitch with light-brown hair."

Suddenly, I felt sick.

Community center. Light-brown hair. Friday night.

The bitch in question? Was me.

"Shit!" I squeaked.

"That'll be her. I'm sure of it. I'd never be caught dead near that weird center for social retards, so I know it wasn't me. All we have to do is hang out until we spot the whore. Then she is all mine. Once I'm finished with her, I swear she'll think twice before stealing someone else's bloke."

A cold sweat of fear broke out all over my body.

I knew no good would come out of lying to the girls about those bloody salsa lessons. I should have known I'd

278

be caught out. Couldn't lie my way out of a damn paper bag.

This was excruciating.

What was I going to do? I couldn't exactly admit *I'd* been spotted outside the community center as it would not only blow my dancing cover, but Jason's as well. Another horrible thought came to mind then. But what if she proceeded to barge her way into the center to confront Antonio, demanding answers? For Rachel, interrogating total strangers wasn't completely beyond the realms of possibility. The thought of Antonio being dragged into Rachel's sordid world of revenge turned my insides liquid with shame. *What a mess!*

"Are you there?" she screeched down the phone.

"Yes," I croaked, not trusting myself to say any more.

"Now, listen carefully, because this is what we're going to do. This bloke reckons it was a Friday night he saw them together—I can't believe he'd come to me straight after seeing his whore, but, anyway, what I was going to say is, I'll pick you and the girls up at around seven on Friday night and we'll wait outside the center for them."

"Don't you think it's a bit over the top? How do you even know they'll be there? Jason might have just been wandering past at the time."

By now, I was sweating torrents.

"No, this bloke definitely said he saw them walking *out* of the center—together. I'm certain it wasn't the first time, either. Remember all the times I tried to ring him and he had his phone switched off? I reckon he was with *her*. Why there, I have no idea. Then the other night, when I waited for him for hours and he wouldn't tell me where he'd been? Again, ditto. It was her. I'm absolutely certain."

"I don't know, Rach. It sounds a long shot to me."

Rachel's voice deepened slightly. A sure sign of her becoming pissed off. "Don't be such a flake. I need you there."

"Why?"

"What do you mean *why*? For support, that's why," she snapped.

This was exactly the thing bothering me. By *support* she could be thinking of moral support or it could also mean she expected me to hold the poor girl down while she beat the shit out of her.

What was I thinking? *I* was the poor girl in question. How could I have forgotten?

"Hey, Rach, I'm really sorry but I'm afraid Friday night's not really good for me. I have other plans — with *Tony*."

Thank God I hadn't got around to faking our break-up yet. A phantom boyfriend was an even better alibi that an ailing Granny.

"*Break them!*" she demanded in a voice that clearly warned any insubordination would be dealt with swiftly and severely.

Could poison be administered through the phone lines? I hoped not, or I was a dead girl walking.

"But I can't!" I persisted bravely.

"You bloody well can, and you will. I need you there and this is more important than any stupid Italian shag, I can tell you!"

By the determination in Rachel's voice, no way was I getting out if it tonight, so I considered my best tactic for now to be procrastination, leaving me time to sort out something tomorrow.

"Look, I'll ring Tony tomorrow and see if I can change our date to Saturday. I can't promise anything, mind you, because he might not be able to swap our reservations, but I'll try to let you know before the end of the week."

Yet another lie, but I figured I was waist-deep in Hell already, so I had very little to lose.

"Okay," she growled, "but just you remember one thing, Fiona. After Troy dumped you, we were there for you. We didn't desert *you* when you needed us. No one else would have put up with all your crying and whining and crap. So think about that before you decided to turn your back on me for this so-called *boyfriend* of yours. Because if you do, when he dumps you, and it's my bet he will, you'll be on your own — guaranteed!"

Then she hung up.

I didn't know whether to laugh, cry or ring her back and give her a piece of my mind. *What a bitch.*

Anyway, Troy *didn't* dump me. I walked out on him. And as for *being there* for me afterward, I suppose they were, in a fashion. But then I never insisted they form a lynch mob and track Amanda down, did I? I can even remember a couple of times Rachel and Kim actually broke ranks and attended Amanda's step class — *after* she'd got together with Troy. At the time, all they could come up with as a defense for their treason was she was the best step class instructor at the gym. The firmness of their buns rated higher on the scale than my marriage agonies.

Support. Yeah, support, my flabby, sagging arse!

My increasing resentment toward Rachel and the girls had triggered a whole avalanche of unpalatable memories. Little incidents that up until now I had chosen to overlook. Like when they'd wondered if I'd be returning the wedding gifts. They'd figured, seeing I was now single and living back home, I'd have no further use for the deluxe cappuccino and espresso machine they'd been eyeing ever since our wedding. They'd tried to argue that they desperately needed one because it was infinitely classier than the instant crap they've been drinking up until now — apparently, they had suffered enough.

And they hadn't even bought us the bloody cappuccino machine in the first place!

They weren't at all happy when I refused to relinquish the machine, despite offering to return the concrete birdbath they *had* bought us — an offer they refused, I might add. No, the cappuccino machine or nothing.

Talk about rape and pillage. I'm sure the Huns weren't as cold-blooded as those three were when they'd tried to divvy up the spoils of my defunct marriage.

By that stage, I was so mad I almost wished I *was* Jason's other woman. Wouldn't that wipe the smugness right off Rachel's perfect pouty lips? Beautiful, sexy Rachel gets dumped for plain, mousy Fiona. Not that it would ever happen, but pleasant to imagine. Still, it started me wondering just who Jason's mysterious new love could be. One thing was for sure, she must be an absolute stunner to have turned Jason's head away from Rachel.

Lying in bed a short time later, I couldn't stop thinking about it. Over the past few weeks, I'd come to think Jason and I had built up a certain amount of trust and closeness, to the point I even told him things I wouldn't normally tell the girls. Therefore, I was a little hurt he hadn't confided in me about this new girlfriend of his. Out of nowhere, I felt a pang of inexplicable anger toward Jason. Why would he have kept something as important as this from me? *Huh.* I was as confused about my anger as I was about Rachel's blatant ultimatum.

Somewhere inside my head came the unwanted notion that maybe, just maybe, the anger swirling around me was masking another less noble emotion – jealousy.

Immediately, I buried this unpalatable idea under a steaming, smelly pile of scorn. How ridiculous was that. *Jealous of what?* I thought.

Jealous of Jason's new love, bellowed an annoying little voice in my head.

The realization brought a surge of hot, acrid nausea rising to my throat.

No, this wasn't going to happen. Not again. Especially so soon after the entire Antonio fiasco. I'd only just managed to extract myself from that particularly embarrassing farce with my dignity intact and I wasn't about to put myself through another fanciful unrequited crush, this time with Jason.

What, exactly, was wrong with me?

Unbidden, an image of Jason appeared in my head. His open smile and generous lips. His strong hands on my waist, pulling me into his body. His clear blue eyes, crinkled at the corners as he laughed. With a sinking heart, I realized it was too late. I was sliding out of control on the slippery ice toward yet another heartbreak. My epicenter shifted closer to the image and a spark of intense longing flickered inside my belly.

In a last-ditch effort to halt my rampant foolishness, I tried compiling a mental list of all the things about Jason I disliked, in the vain hope it might turn me off him. Trouble was, apart from the undeniable fact he had been intimate with Rachel—and God only knew where she had been before him—my list fell well short of the required mark.

Why do I always do this to myself? Of late, it seemed as soon as a guy shows me any compassion or attention, I immediately launch my affections into hyper-drive. Then, before I know it, I'm fantasizing about wedding dresses, flowers for the church, baby names and all that goes along with the elusive, mythical happily ever after dream.

The words *needy* and *pathetic* immediately sprang to mind.

How could I *not* have seen this coming a mile off?

But, it had started out innocently enough. Then, before I could get a grip on myself, I'd really begun to look forward to seeing him at dance lessons—even more so than Antonio! I couldn't remember exactly when it had happened. Maybe after Stacey's wedding? Rarely did he mention Rachel, though, and I, in turn, wasn't keen to bring up the specter of her role of Jason's girlfriend and bedmate to dilute the intimacy that had sprung up between us.

Up until now, I hadn't given it a lot of thought. Maybe I should have examined my own motives in secluding Rachel from our conversation a little more closely. But there was always so much to talk about that bumped Jason's love life down on our verbal agenda. Ever since Stacey's wedding, his relationship with Rachel had been a subject both of us pointedly avoided.

Considering current circumstances, I should have seen this as a sign of the trouble brewing between them.

The next day, I was still unable to shake the bitterness Rachel's late-night phone call had sparked inside me. I tried to remind myself that I was probably over-dramatizing the entire thing, but the weight of injustice refused to budge from my heavily burdened shoulders.

As a measure of my simmering discontent, that day I chose to eat lunch alone in the staff room at work rather than joining Rachel and Kim in the food court — well, as alone as I could be with thirty-odd other people munching away around me. For once, I envied Janine working at the abattoir, with nothing but dead cows to keep her company. At least she didn't spend her lunch hour dodging social landmines. I'd have been happy to have joined her if only I could overlook the blood and stench of death. Unfortunately, I was stuck there in the center with them, whether I liked it or not and, as I was to discover later, you can run but, sadly, you cannot hide.

If I were honest, in light of last night's revelations concerning my latent yearnings for Jason, another reason I'd chosen to avoid Rachel and Kim was because I didn't know if I could look Rachel in the eye without giving away the thoughts spinning in my head.

It was mid-afternoon and I was busy unpacking the latest delivery of new season swimwear when the hairs rose up on the back of my neck — a malevolent presence loomed nearby.

"Where were you at lunch?" asked Rachel, stepping out from behind a rack of sarongs.

Here goes…

"Um, I had to work through lunch. Two big deliveries arrived together and we wanted to clear the dock. No biggie, I'll grab something to eat later on. Thanks for your concern, though."

A cloud of confusion passed over Rachel's face as she tried to gauge whether I was being sarcastic or not.

"Well, it was really inconsiderate of you, all the same. We had things to discuss, you know, about Friday night. Have you called Tony and changed your plans?"

"No," I replied lightly.

"Why not?"

"Well, maybe it's because I'm not sure if I want to, that's why!"

Instantly the air between us turned chilly with hostility, a Mexican standoff of wills, and I half expected the racks of clothes to part and a ball of tumbleweed to roll down the aisle between us.

I don't know who was more surprised by my sudden rebelliousness, Rachel or me. It certainly hadn't been planned, but as soon as the words spilled from my mouth, I knew my course was set in concrete.

No going back now.

"*What* did you say?" she asked with more than a hint of menace in her voice.

I took a deep breath. "I said, I'm not going. I have plans with Tony, and I'm not going to break them to follow you out on some crazed witch-hunt for some poor girl who probably won't even be there."

The expression on Rachel's face changed from shock to total disbelief and I experienced a surge of exhilaration. Right then, I didn't care what she did. I had made a stand against her regime of terror for the first time and it felt wonderful. Besides, I knew the security cameras would be recording everything — easy to be brave knowing backup was only a yelp away.

The blood drained from her face as she stood there, swaying slightly, clenching and unclenching her white-knuckled fists. I could tell she was trying to formulate a spiteful retort, but her outrage appeared to have robbed her of the power of speech.

"Anyway, good luck on Friday night," I said brightly, as though nothing had passed between us. "I've got to get all this put out on the racks ASAP, so if there is nothing else you wanted to say, I'd better get on with it."

And with that, I turned my attention to the boxes of bikinis waiting for hangers, dismissing her in no uncertain terms. I could never have found it in me to so rude to anyone else, but right then, I considered it far better than what I really wanted to do — wrap one of the hangers around her scrawny little neck and strangle her with it.

If she had hit me right there and then I wouldn't have been at all surprised. But then the strangest thing happened. She opened her mouth, no doubt meaning to hurl a string of abuse my way, but faced with my uncharacteristic stand, all the bravado seemed to drain from her body. She silently turned around and walked out of the shop without a single word being uttered.

What an anti-climax.

Adrenaline pumping furiously through my veins, I was almost disappointed our brief conflict was over. After putting up with all her abuse lately, I was ready for a fight. Strangely, I felt robbed. I knew it wouldn't last long, though. Once Rachel'd had time to regroup her scattered wits, she'd come back at me in full force.

I kind of looked forward to it.

At least now I knew what I had to do.

Chapter Twenty-One

"Patrick. Hi, it's Fiona. I'm sorry to bother you guys at home, but I really need to speak to Antonio if he's around?"

Since my earlier confrontation with Rachel, I'd decided to ring Antonio after all. Not that I held any hope of him knowing Jason's whereabouts, but I felt obliged to warn him about Rachel, nonetheless. By the steely look of determination on her face as she'd stormed out of the store that afternoon, she was still holding firm to her plan to stake out the community center on Friday night. With this in mind, I thought it only fair to give Antonio prior notice he was dealing with a crazy woman.

"Hang on, he's right here."

Antonio answered, "Fiona, what a coincidence. I was just about to ring you. You sounded really down last week and I was a little worried. Then with all the new students on Tuesday night, I didn't get a chance to speak to you. By the time they'd left, you'd gone as well. Are you feeling any better, hon?"

"Well, yes and no. But the reason I'm ringing is because, well, I have a problem and I'm worried it could easily blow up and become your problem as well. I really hate to land this on you. It's to do with Jason and his ex-girlfriend, Rachel."

I didn't quite know where to start. What Antonio would make of my psychotic friends worried me. He and Patrick were so together. Not just in the physical sense, but they appeared to have their act together in every area of lives. The way Rachel was carrying on made me flinch in embarrassment, especially when I remembered all the times I'd meekly allowed her to bully me into joining her on one of her childish escapades. But if Rachel thought for a minute I'd sit back and allow her to walk all over Antonio like she did with everyone she came across, she had another think coming.

"Sounds exciting, really. I'm all ears."

I laughed. *Trust Antonio to see it that way.* "It's serious, so stop laughing."

"Serious, you say. Um, let me guess now. Jason's finally found the good sense to rid himself of that blonde bitch."

It wasn't put to me as a question as such, and I immediately sensed something strange going on.

"How did you know?"

God, if it turned out he was a closet telepath, I swear, I'd be left with no other alternative but to kill myself.

"Well, didn't you just mention Jason and his *ex*-girlfriend? And, besides that, he's sitting here next to me right now."

"Who, Jason?"

"Yes."

"What!" I blurted out.

My relief was only fleeting before a big lump of annoyance jumped the queue and kicked it out. "What the hell is he doing at your place? Jesus, I've been worried sick about him for days and now you tell me he's been there all this time with you guys?"

The lingering waft of my building hysteria hung suspended between us for a moment and I could have bitten my bloody tongue off.

"Worried sick, were you?" repeated Antonio, knowingly.

Shit. I could almost see his smirk on his face through the phone. My own stupid fault though. I *had* laid it on a bit thick, I suppose. Now it was time for a little damage limitation.

"Well, of course I was concerned," I began, trying to sound convincingly indifferent. "Who wouldn't be? No one has seen or heard from him since the weekend, including his mates, and he wasn't at class on Tuesday night, so naturally, I began to get a little bit worried. And now you're telling me he's been hiding out at your place all week. What's wrong with a simple phone call to let me know?"

So much for indifferent. I sounded like a neurotic nagging wife.

"Hiding out? What do you mean, hiding out? Hiding from whom?"

"Well, from Rachel, of course!"

Antonio burst out laughing.

"Is that what you're all thinking? That he's running scared?"

"Hey, no one would blame him. Rachel's gone absolutely mental since he dumped her."

By now, Antonio was laughing so much I could barely hear what he was saying. The blood began pounding in my ears and I grew more incensed by the minute.

"It's not funny, you know!" I insisted.

"Oh, I'm sorry, Fiona. I'm not laughing at you — honestly. But you should see the look on Jason's face. I've just told him everyone thinks he's run away because of a bust-up with his girlfriend and, well, you could say he's not particularly impressed."

Right then, I didn't know what to think. Obviously, something was going on, and by the uproar on the other end of the line, I realized I'd once again made an idiot of myself by overreacting.

In the background, everyone was talking at once before Jason's voice reached me. Antonio had been right. He didn't sound at all amused.

"Fiona, what the hell has that bitch been saying?"

Hearing his voice, I struggled to compose myself. Shit, was I going to say to him? I hadn't a clue. The combination of immense relief and nervousness propelled my mouth into attention before my brain gave the green light. "Oh, my God, Jason, are you all right?" I blurted out in the absence of anything intelligent.

"Of course I am. Why wouldn't I be?"

"When you disappeared like that, everyone went almost demented looking for you."

"You mean Rachel is demented and that is why you all presumed I'd buggered off."

I didn't know what to say, so for once I listened to my head and kept my mouth shut.

"Fi, I've been staying at Antonio's this week *landscaping his garden*. That's all. I haven't taken off and I am definitely *not* in hiding from bloody Rachel, regardless of what she's been saying to everyone. I didn't tell anyone but my gran because, well, I didn't think it was anyone else's business."

"I'm sorry, Jason. I've been an idiot again, haven't I?"

"No, *I'm* the one who should be apologizing, Fi. I shouldn't be taking it out on you." Jason sighed. "It's just I know Rachel's been all over the place, out for my blood, because Johnno rang the nursery and left a message. Is she as bad as he's making out?"

"Worse. I'm sorry, Jason."

"Fuck!"

For a few seconds, there was silence while the awful truth of Rachel's declining mental state sank in.

"You'd better tell me what going on," said Jason, finally breaking the silence. He sounded as though he faced the death sentence.

"It's not so much what's she done—that's bad enough, but, apparently, some bloke she got talking to down the pub saw the two of us walking out of the community center and told Rachel."

"So?"

"*Sooo*, the thing is Rachel has no idea it was me and is so convinced the woman you left the center with is your new girlfriend that she has all but rounded up a lynch mob to track her down to beat her to within an inch of her life."

"Bloody hell."

Again, more silence.

"Jason."

"Yes."

"Who *is* this new girlfriend of yours?"

I heard Jason sigh.

"Fi, we have to talk."

That awful gut-curdling feeling once again returned to torment me. This time wearing full battle armor and ready to go to war. My stomach had become a combat zone, all right, and I felt sick with dread at what horrible truth Jason was preparing, albeit reluctantly, to land on me. He didn't elaborate any further on the phone and I, being the total coward I am, didn't press him for more details. After all, I can always wait for bad news, and it was obvious by the tone of his voice I wouldn't like what he had to say.

In the few awkward minutes that filled the gap between "Fi, we have to talk" and "So I'll see you then", we arranged to meet on Friday night at the very same café Antonio had taken me the night of my *private lesson,* timing it purposely to coincide with Rachel's stakeout of the community center. At least then we'd know where she'd be. Antonio assured me he could handle Rachel on the unlikely possibility she did go as far as gatecrashing his salsa class – being a gay Italian, he'd had to deal with foes far scarier than one hysterical blonde bimbo.

Unfortunately, my imagination was going berserk. I had long ago given up on a happy ending to my otherwise sad, empty existence. Ever since I'd woken up from my denial and realized my feelings for Jason were light-years away from being platonic, I'd been waiting for the inevitable disaster to strike.

All night I lay in bed, thinking of worst-case scenarios in a futile attempt at desensitization to what I felt for certain had to be something cataclysmic. I couldn't help myself. It was the only coping mechanism I could think of to calm my nervousness.

First, of course, I imagined Jason declaring himself to be gay – well, it had happened to me once already, so why not again? – *and* he was in love with my brother. That would be just my luck, finding myself spending the rest of my life having to watch the man of my dreams going all gooey over my unworthy sibling. Dad would probably embrace Alex's newfound sexuality, invite Jason to live with us then begin a campaign to bring about equal rights for queers and lesbian ladies. "Not that there is anything wrong with that," to quote Jerry Seinfeld.

Then I pictured him valiantly trying to put on a brave face while explaining how he'd been forced to dump Rachel because he had recently been diagnosed with a rare form of penis cancer brought on by all the mad shagging she'd inflicted upon him – against his will, of course – you could even say she'd practically *forced* him. His only chance of survival depended on him having his wang amputated with the operation booked for that very night – not even time for one last screw. I, being the humanitarian I am, would offer anyway. What harm could it do? As a consequence of his new life as a sad eunuch, he was preparing to enter the priesthood, where he hoped to spend the rest of his days in isolation and quiet contemplation. This would be doubly tragic as he isn't even Catholic, or religious.

Then, just as I reasoned it couldn't get any worse, I pictured him confessing that he too was secretly in love with Amanda, the home- and heart-wrecking slut, and was going to be moving in with her and Troy to begin a ménage-à-trois existence, together with their love-child. But to prove there were no bad feelings between us, he wanted me to move in with the three of them – as their au pair. Poor, precious Amanda couldn't possibly be expected to change shitty nappies.

Thankfully, by then, I had run out things to torment myself with. Mind you, I was practically comatose with the depth of my depression, which in a way was the only thing stopping me from hanging myself with the lavatory chain.

When I finally drifted off into a fitful, restless sleep, oblivion from my recent problems remained elusive. My dreams just carried on where my imagination had left off, punctuating my slumber with bizarre images. Most of these revolved around me being either stranded naked in the middle of some unknown but public place, or equally disturbing, my hair and teeth falling out just as I was about to renew my marriage vows with both Troy and Amanda at a blood-soaked altar. Seriously scary stuff. Especially the marriage vows.

I hadn't heard a thing from either Rachel or Kim since our spat yesterday afternoon and their continuing non-appearance was, in a way, more unsettling than the thought of them converging en masse. Still, to be on the safe side, I avoided them for the second day in a row and remained within the relative haven of the staff lunch room.

By now, it was mid-afternoon and I had started to cast furtive glances behind me every two seconds. Even my workmates noticed my growing edginess whenever the loudspeaker came on to announce a lost child or new in-store promotion. It wasn't until after four o'clock that I began to relax a little. At the time, I had thought it was too good to be true, and unfortunately for once I was right.

Exactly half an hour before I was due to leave work for the day, I found myself confronted by Kim at the entrance to the ladies' changing rooms. Hemmed in. No escape impossible. Although, having said that, I could have locked myself in a changing cubicle until she got bored and left, but there are some limits to which even I am not prepared to stoop. That left me with no other option but to stand my ground.

"What the hell is wrong with you?" she challenged, loud enough to attract the attention of one or two nearby shoppers.

"What do you mean?"

Not that I had any doubt what she was referring to, but in the past I had found it a useful stalling technique while I considered my range of possible responses.

"Poor Rachel is facing the worst crisis of her entire life and here you are being a selfish bitch and thinking of nothing but your own happiness."

If being dumped by her boyfriend of barely two months counts as the worst crisis she'd had to date, I figured she must have done a deal with the devil. God, if that was the worst I'd lived through, instead of going all Glenn Close, I'd be thanking God for being so merciful, cutting my losses and moving on to the next waiting shag.

"And exactly *why* do you think I'm being selfish?" I challenged, putting aside a pile of T-shirts and crossing my arms in one of those standing-my-ground-type stances usually seen on wrestling shows, accompanied by a don't-mess-with-me stare.

I was trying not to react to Kim's blatant antagonism, but as a result of the little sleep I'd managed to get the previous night, together with my growing unease over Jason, I struggled to maintain my composure in the face of her unwarranted accusations.

"You know damn well why. You've turned into one of those bitches who drops their friends as soon as they find a boyfriend."

I have?

I should wish!

"And," she continued, "ever since you started going out with this Tony guy, you've become a real snob."

"A what?"

"A snob. Like suddenly you're too good to been seen with us," she sneered.

By now, I'd well and truly had enough of listening to Kim's ranting accusations. I had a mountain of unwanted merchandise to return to stock before I could finally leave for the day and... Oh, shit, I'd almost forgotten I had an appointment to see Margarita after work. Consequently, I didn't have the time or the patience to put up with Kim's crap today – or, for that matter, any day.

"Look, Kim. I don't know exactly what your problem is with me going out with *Tony*, but if you think I am going to ditch him just to tag along on some stupid witch-hunt because precious bloody Rachel is half out of her mind, you can go and get stuffed."

The sneer of contempt on Kim's face, was, I'm sorry to say, my final undoing and something inside me snapped. "*And*, while we're on the subject of *poor, precious Rachel*, let me tell you this. Rachel wouldn't be in this situation if she'd shown Jason even a micron of respect. The way she treats blokes in general is nothing sort of disgusting. Jason is one of the nicest fellows around, but Rachel is such a nasty, possessive bitch it's little wonder he dumped her. *Everyone* could see it coming but Rachel, oh, yeah, and you."

Somehow Kim managed to find her voice — once she'd picked her jaw up off the floor.

"That's where you're wrong," she spat. "Everything would have been fine between them if it wasn't for that whore who stole Jason from her. But once we get hold of the bitch, I'm telling you, she'll regret throwing herself at Rachel's man."

"Regret! I think the only person who has reason to *regret* anything is Jason," I screamed. "I reckon he must be *regretting* the moment he first laid eyes on Rachel. For his sake, I'm glad he's finally seen Rachel's ugly side. As far as I'm concerned, she deserves everything she gets. After all, if you fling enough shit at people, sooner or later, they're going to start throwing it back at you."

By now, our raised voices had attracted a growing ring of curious spectators and pushing her way through the throng was Mrs. Clements. As always with perfect timing, for at that exact moment, Kim launched herself at me, teeth and nails bared to strike. As I staggered back under the shock of her unexpected physical attack, all around us racks of clothes came crashing down. Like dominos, once the first rack of black one-hundred-percent linen trousers hit the neighboring rack of delicate silk shirts, it took only seconds before every stand in the immediate vicinity was swaying precariously and clattering noisily to the floor, shirt and pants and jackets flying. The noise of swearing, screaming and rending fabric filled the air. Pure bedlam, and my only thought at the time was to defend myself.

By the time Mrs. Clements recovered from the shock of witnessing the demolition of the Women's 'After Five' department, our frenzied hair-pulling and bitch-slapping episode had fizzled out as suddenly as it had started. Before I had time to recover my breath, Kim was storming out of the shop, much to the amusement of the crowd of on-looking shoppers.

"What on *Earth* is going on here?" Mrs. Clements screeched hysterically, almost in tears as she took in the pile of debris surrounding me.

Mrs. Clements's arrival heralded the end of the show. With their bloodlust still unsatisfied, the crowd of mumbling people quickly dispersed, disappointed that the unexpected entertainment had been diffused.

"Ms. McCrutchen," she glowered, "*after* you clean up this mess, I want to see you *in my office*! You have exactly twenty minutes!"

And with that said, she stormed off, leaving me half-sitting, half-lying across a mound of pure wool twinsets, hair askew, and burning up with mortification.

Immediately Tanya and Julie, the trainee, began scooping up armfuls of ruined merchandise, solemnly separating them into what would be written off as damaged stock and what would be next week's in-house clearance stock, all the time quietly eyeing up the not-so-ruined articles they would later be smuggling back to the staff room before stashing them away in their bags.

I was seething. First of all, Kim barges her way into my workplace and proceeds to bawl me out, then, when I respond, as I had every right to do, she attacks me. And *I'm* the one who's held accountable?

* * * *

By the time I arrived to keep my appointment with Margarita, my head was awash with a veritable menagerie of emotions. In the face of adversity, I had proven to myself once and for all that I was capable of sticking up for myself and for the first time in my entire life I hadn't buckled when the shit hit the fan. Instead of being a doormat, I'd shown some spunk, some courage and some real maturity — well, apart from when I'd been rolling around the floor trying to rip out handfuls of Kim's over-dyed, brittle-as-shit hair, that is.

And the result?

Self-respect. Empowerment. Release.

And…

I'd been fired!

It wasn't even one of those, *'I'm really, really sorry, it pains me to let you go,'* kind of firings, but a full managerial, all-gloves-off, high-decibel, this-is-how-you-fire-someone, *'Clean out your locker immediately and security will see you to the door,'* type of dismissals. You know, one of those normally saved for postal workers who go crazy and slaughter entire floors of coworkers.

As I was escorted out of the store, tears flowed freely, the sound of weeping heralding my final farewell to a long, and if I'm going to be honest, *not* very illustrious career in retail. Surprisingly, none of the tears were mine. It was as though I walked out of the gloom to embrace the warmth of the sun again — or the chilly blast of the center's air-conditioning, as it happens.

I should have been devastated. I'd just been thrown out of my place of employment in the worst possible manner and now had no visible means of supporting myself. It was a disaster, a complete and utter balls-up. So why wasn't I sobbing disconsolately? I should have been.

I wasn't even sad or angry or worried or anything resembling the normal range of emotions one would usually be confronted with in this situation. I put it down to shock, the same kind that enables car accidents victims to walk five miles to seek help with a broken leg and compressed fracture of the skull. I suspected by later tonight I would be crying my eyes out and picturing a life of homeless desperation with nothing but a cheap bottle of plonk and a musty blanket to keep me company.

But right then, I had to admit I felt relief. It was just a job. One I'd landed in soon after leaving school and I'd never had the courage to try anything else. While I'd been married to Troy, it had been unthinkable I would throw in my job for the chance of finding something better. After all, one of us had to work, and that responsibility had always landed on me. Now I was free. Free to do what exactly, I didn't know.

Talking it up, that was what I was doing.

The only thing I was free to do was join the unemployment line come Monday morning.

Margarita sat there, beaming. Her big fleshy face almost split in two with a smile that could front an amusement park. Where was the outrage, the sympathy, the shoulder to cry on? Not that I *was* crying, but an offer would have been nice. Maybe she hadn't understood. Shit, when I want her to *mis*understand, she's sharp as a tack. I was still waiting for her to launch into a counterattack from last week. But now that I actually *wanted* her indulgent sympathy, what does she do? She sits there grinning like a loon.

"This has been quite a breakthrough for you, Fiona."

"What? I lose my job, and this is a good thing? Is this what you're saying?"

"Getting fired is traumatic, I'll admit. But think of it as an opportunity to expand your horizons."

Coming from someone with a master's degree, a recognized profession *and* their own successful psychology practice, that was rich. Very rich. No doubt Margarita would see the bright side of losing a limb. "Just think how strong your other leg will become with all that hopping!" I wondered then if anyone had ever slapped their shrink? Then I also remembered with a certain degree of shame that slapping was what had landed me in the unemployment line in the first place.

"So, you offering me a job, then?" I responded.

Margarita chose to ignore my caustic remark.

"Fiona, I am *not* pleased because you lost your job. I *am* pleased that, for the first time in your life, you stood up for what you believed to be right. And that is something you should be proud of."

"*Hello*! It got me canned, remember!"

"It also gave you back some measure of self-esteem."

"How do you figure that one?" I asked.

"Okay. Let me ask you this. How do you feel right now?"

"Pissed off, obviously. I've just been bodily ejected from my place of employment. Flung out onto the street."

"Apart from that. Deep down, what emotions are you experiencing as a result of this afternoon's events? Tell me the very first thing you felt as you walked away?"

"You mean as I was frog-marched out of the door!"

"Okay," she conceded, "but what was your immediate response once you left?"

I thought about it for a minute. Talking it through just now had clarified my earlier conflict and I began to realize getting fired maybe wasn't the disaster I had first imagined it to be. Actually, it felt quite liberating, in a weird out-of-body-experience kind of way.

"Relief," I admitted. "Yes, I suppose I *was* relieved. I felt clean, for some weird reason, like I'd been rinsed of years of stress. It's like a weight has lifted from my shoulders."

"I think what you're feeling at the moment is a certain degree of release. You mentioned once you worked a lot of extra hours while Troy was unemployed, and from I gather, that was quite a lot of the time. So it is only natural to associate your job with the stress and anxiety you were experiencing at that time, considering the declining state of your marriage."

I smiled weakly. "Then you don't think I'm a nut case after all?"

Margarita straightened in her chair defensively and cast me a disapproving look. "Of course I don't!"

Considering I *was* sitting in a therapist's office, the use of the term *nut case* could be seen by some to be a little indelicate, I suppose.

Margarita cleared her throat. Obviously, we had covered the actual firing sufficiently, and it was time to get back to the real nitty-gritty.

"Tell me, how exactly did this argument arise with Kim in the first place?"

For the next fifteen minutes, I filled Margarita in on the ongoing soap opera that masquerades as my life. Such a shame I only had a supporting role in it, though, what with Rachel, Kim and, to a lesser degree, Janine hogging the limelight all the time.

"And the catalyst to the actual physical violence? What triggered that?"

"I think it was me telling Kim no wonder Jason dumped Rachel after the way she'd treated him, and if anyone had any reason to regret anything, it was Jason, who must be regretting ever getting involved with Rachel in the first place."

"So you were defending Jason?"

"Yes, I suppose so. Someone had to. But it wasn't just that. I'm sick of being told by them how selfish and unworthy I am and I don't deserve to have such wonderful friends. God, they act as though they are doing me a favor by treating me like shit and yelling at me all the time."

"*Did you*, in the past, feel grateful they allowed you to enter into their little circle?"

"In a way. They were so popular and beautiful and always part of the in-crowd when we were at school."

"And you didn't think of yourself as beautiful, then?"

"Well, compared to them, I wasn't. They had all the guys at school falling all over themselves to go out with them, whereas I was more or less left out."

"Until you met Troy?"

"Yes, until I met Troy!" I repeated solemnly.

"So being with Troy made you feel worthy of their

friendship because you had proven to them you could also attract a good-looking boyfriend."

After a pause, I exhaled. "Yes, I suppose I did."

Put like that, I could see I had been a fool.

"Is it possible, Fiona, that was perhaps one of the reasons why you married him, despite knowing deep down the relationship between the two of you was anything but stable?"

There was no point denying it now. I knew with a sinking feeling that Margarita had read me like a book while I'd been trying to muddle through it all in an altogether different language. The language of denial — like reading one of those condensed novels that skim over the really important parts to get to the exciting ending.

I remembered then how jealous the girls were when I announced our engagement and the thrill I'd experienced at the time to have something they didn't — a real-live fiancé. Not that he went down on one knee and proposed to me with tears of love in his eyes. Our engagement had been more of a housing-solution proposal than an undying-love one.

Troy wanted us to move in together. But I knew my parents, being quite old-fashioned, would never speak to me again if I 'shacked up' with a man without being married, or engaged at the very least. At the time, Troy also lived at home with his parents and three younger brothers. As a result, their small weatherboard house bulged at the seams with the volatile combination of testosterone and over-inflated egos. Fights were commonplace in a house where merely glancing at a TV guide was considered provocative. Any sudden move toward the remote control when there was sport on the telly quite often resulted in bloodshed.

Considering Troy's home life and Dad's insistence we legalize our union before God — Mum and Dad were all but ostracized at church when word of their harlot daughter's living arrangements leaked out — needless to say, it wasn't a very long engagement. Actually, it was so short that numerous elderly aunts on both sides of the family monitored my figure with great relish for any sign of an expanded girth in the months following the ceremony.

You can imagine their disappointment, therefore, when the much-awaited bump didn't eventuate.

I imagine planning a wedding is always stressful, but to plan one in less than three months had been nothing short of harrowing. I think at the time the only thing that saved my sanity was my abject joy at being the first one to bag a man. In all the hysteria surrounding the months before the big day, Rachel and Kim had embarked on a quest to find themselves a fiancé, and ideally *before* I got married so they, too, could use their walk up the aisle as my bridesmaids as some kind of prelude for their own big day—a practice run, so to speak.

At the time, I remembered loving their enthusiasm for following in my matrimonial footsteps. Imitation being the sincerest form of flattery, or something like that. We even went as far as planning the barbecues and dinner parties we'd have together once we were all hitched. Thanks to the joy of wedding gifts, I had the grill and the eight-place dinner setting. All they needed to complete the picture were the required husbands. Unfortunately for them, word soon spread that three husband-hungry girls were on the loose, prompting a sudden drought of eligible male candidates.

Mind you, I can remember being less than flattered at the wedding rehearsal.

It was held on the eve of our wedding. The entire wedding party had assembled at the church for a practice run-through when Rachel, supposedly as a joke, pushed me none too gently from my place beside Troy at the altar and playfully suggested she play the part of bride for the rehearsal. As if that wasn't bad enough, Troy'd thought it a great lark and insisted she have her way—for a laugh, of course, a way of lightening the nervous atmosphere, he hinted. Their lingering kiss at the 'you may now kiss the bride' part of the mock-rehearsal had been anything but funny at the time. I thought the minister was going to have a stroke when forced to physically separate the two of them.

Shortly afterward, the sounds of raised voices shattered the spiritual tranquility. Our first serious married fight — and it preceded the wedding by a full twenty-four hours.

"Fiona, sometimes it's easy to get so involved in the planning of the wedding that the actual reality of marriage is somehow overshadowed. You are the only daughter in the family, aren't you?" Margarita asked.

I nodded. "Yes."

"And your parents no doubt wanted to give you a lovely wedding with all the extras?"

Again, I nodded glumly, thinking of the stretch limo that must have set them back a bundle. Guilt washed over me.

"I imagine the wedding must have cost them a lot of money?"

"They took out a personal loan to pay for it," I added. A loan they're still paying off, even now. If it were possible to die from remorse, I swear I would have drawn my last breath right there and then.

"What would have happened, if say, you had, for whatever reason, changed your mind about marrying Troy?"

"They would have lost thousands of dollars. Because we booked everything so late, most of the costs had to be paid up-front in full."

Margarita sat back and considered this for a moment.

"Fiona, *did* you have second thoughts about the wedding?"

"Yes, of course I did. But everyone assured me it was perfectly normal for a bride to get cold feet, almost expected. They said it would be more of a worry if I didn't experience some kind of doubt."

"Was it just wedding nerves, though, or something more?"

Out of nowhere, a memory came back of the many arguments between Troy and me that had seemed to spring up out of nowhere in the months before the big day. He was so snarky and sullen all the time, but the girls claimed it was merely his way of dealing with the stress of everything. In the end, I couldn't even discuss the wedding plans with him without a huge row blowing up. It was also around this time Dad developed shingles, a mild case, thankfully, but serious enough to see him off work for over a month. During this time, I knew they were experiencing financial difficulties, but all my offers to contribute toward the cost of the wedding out of my own small savings were shouted down. I was their one and only daughter, Dad would say, and if they couldn't do this one thing for me, they had failed as parents.

"At the time, I hoped Troy would change after the wedding and things would start to settle down. But I think deep down I knew it was a mistake and by the time I admitted it to myself, it was too late. It would have killed my poor Mum and Dad if I had canceled the wedding. Apart from the money they stood to lose, their humiliation would have been dreadful."

Margarita cast me a quizzical look.

"You see, a lot of the guests had flown in especially from Scotland for the wedding and I couldn't put Dad through the agony of meeting them at the airport to tell them the wedding was off," I added, by way of an explanation.

"You went ahead to save your parents from heartbreak."

I nodded.

"What about your own heartbreak, Fiona?"

"I tried not to think about it too much. Besides, I think I'd convinced myself that everything would work out in the end."

"It didn't, though, did it?"

"No. It didn't."

Chapter Twenty-Two

I must say, it felt kind of strange returning to the very same café where I'd spent many an evening going all gooey over Antonio. Back then, in the time before I'd discovered I was making a fool of myself over a gay man — albeit a lovely one and with an equally gorgeous boyfriend — the place had sung with romantic warmth and intimacy. It'd been shiny and classy and oozed sophistication.

More than once, I'd gone home after our late-night chats and dreamed of a time years from now when Antonio and I would revisit this very same café on our wedding anniversary to reminisce fondly about those first heady days when we'd fallen in love over a Danish pastry and mochaccino. I'd even gone as far as imagining a small framed photograph of the two of us up on the wall, taken on our wedding day when we'd stopped the limo especially to have our picture taken posing out on the front of La Palazzi. Everyone would greet us fondly by name when we called in for a coffee and a smooch.

Could I have been such an idiot?

Need I ask!

Walking back into La Palazzi, I experienced a sensation of déjà-vu. Sadly, this time, the lights were switched on in my starry-eyed head. For the first time, I noticed the faded upholstery on the very un-chic coffee-brown chairs, the dust gathering in the corners and the nicks and scratches on the cheap wooden tables where teenagers had carved their names, no doubt as some kind of dare — ten years ago, it might have been me. Okay, five years ago. It was as though the place had wilted and decayed since our last visit. Like the absence of our glowing warmth had robbed the café of its vitality.

The staff were still the same surly, arrogant college students I remembered, though. Did they remember me at all? Probably not. Last time I'd been here with Antonio, I couldn't help but notice they'd never taken their eyes off him, while I'd been merely the coffee-drinking lump of bone and corpuscles who happened to be taking up valuable space next to him. I could have sprouted horns and they wouldn't have noticed in the blinding glare of his masculine beauty.

As I walked past the same girl who'd served us probably half a dozen times in the past few weeks, I gave her a weak, shy smile of recognition. A smile she completely ignored as she looked back at me blankly, a stony expression frozen on her pretty but eternally bored face. Nope, she had no recollection of me whatsoever. But it was my bet she would have recognized Antonio by the sound of his breathing.

I still felt emotionally raw after my session with Margarita. Then, following that, I'd had the unenviable task of breaking the news to Mum and Dad that I'd been canned. They'd been shocked, of course. No one in our family had ever been fired, not even Alex. It was as though someone had died. Worse still had been explaining the circumstances leading up to it.

Mum was livid. I'd never seen her so mad. As a measure of her fury, she even let loose with the bitch word — twice — and although it may well have been an auditory hallucination on my part, I swear she uttered 'fucking bitch' under her breath. I couldn't have been more shocked if she'd discovered a liking for vodka and cigars. Note — I've never witnessed my mother sip anything stronger than Earl Grey tea. Even Dad was a little shaken by her outburst. Her profanities were not aimed at me. She was no doubt saving them up in case I ever burn the house down or get arrested on drug-running charges.

Kim's involvement provoked Mum's wrath. In a bizarre

twist of fate, I actually found myself in the unique position of having to talk Mum *out* of going around to Kim's and blasting her from here till next week for causing me to lose my job. Not that I didn't contribute, but all Mum and Dad could see was once again the girls had proven to be high-caliber bitches.

Who was I to argue with them?

Now, I tried to steel myself for more unpleasantness. You know it's got to be bad news when it can't be revealed over the phone. Public places are always the preferred locality for dropping a bombshell of the worst kind. I think most men figure their chances of having to endure the much-dreaded female emotional scene of sobbing, screaming or anything in between are lessened by the addition of a room full of strangers.

I can honestly say that in my short but dramatic existence on this Earth I have yet to meet a girl who isn't provoked beyond all measure of reason by said room full of strangers being privy to her heartbreak and or humiliation. I know for a fact most women would rather be seen as a screaming harridan throwing empty glasses at a bloke's head than a poor pathetic loser left sobbing on her own to pay the bill after being fed the much-dreaded line, "It's not you, it's me."

Men. They have no idea.

I saw him the moment I stepped into the café. Jason's height and bulk, together with his sun-bleached spike of blond hair, seemed to attract more than one appreciative female look. The booth he was crammed into further accentuated his height. It was right at the back of the café and I suspected he had chosen it for the privacy it afforded. My heart sank. Obviously, Jason didn't want anyone eavesdropping on our conversation.

He looked up and saw me as I passed the counter. The same girl behind the cappuccino machine who not three seconds before had looked straight through me now snorted in disbelief when she realized I was heading over to meet the hunky blond bloke she'd no doubt spent the last ten minutes perving on. If the expression on her face was anything to go by, she was thinking along the lines of, *She must be his sister, why else would he give her a second look?* Maybe I was being oversensitive there.

"Hi, Jason!" I said as I slid into the booth across from him. Lumpy and uneven, it felt as if it'd been stuffed with oranges. I wondered why I'd never noticed it before. Then I remembered my thoughts at the time were usually focused on Antonio and what sort of children we'd produce. Would they be dark-haired and exotic like him or Caledonian with sturdy legs and scrubbed-pink complexions like me? Especially the sturdy legs — *flagon legs* my dad used to call them? I had more pressing things to worry about, but still I granted myself a quick mental slap for being such an idiot.

Across from me, I could feel the manly heat radiating from his equally manly body. *Oh, God, hold on to your panties. Here I go again!*

Jason looked as nervous as I felt and I glanced around the café for something to comment on to lighten the atmosphere. A funny poster. A strange light fitting in the shape of Tasmania. A disfigured head. Anything at all.

"Thanks for coming, Fi. Hope you don't mind, but I ordered you a cappuccino. Is that okay? I can change it if you want something else," he said awkwardly.

Anyone would have thought *he* was the one bracing for bad news. "No, that's fine. Cappuccino sounds great, thanks."

"That chick behind the counter kept giving me a filthy look so I thought I'd better order something before she kicked me out," Jason offered by way of an explanation.

"You must be blind." I laughed. "That wasn't a filthy look — it was a leer. She was having a right old gawp. I saw her at it as I walked past."

Jason looked genuinely surprised. "Do you think so?"

Bless him, he doesn't even recognize a girlie ogle when he sees one.

"So, how are you?"

"Okay, I suppose." I shrugged, frantically trying to think of something intelligent to say. I knew I'd come up with a million witty responses on the way home, but by then, of course, it would be too late. *Life is a bitch, after all.*

Thankfully, our cappuccinos arrived then, rescuing us from one of those embarrassing silences dreaded by all, but especially me because I always seem to panic and blurt out the most inane shit just to fill in a conversational flat spot.

I can't say I was surprised when the surly waitress simply dumped my coffee in front of me, while Jason's was presented to him like the keys to the bloody city. Going by her attitude, I half-expected to get to the bottom of the cup and find a cockroach winking up at me.

As soon as she was out of earshot, Jason leaned over and whispered, "Jesus, talk about service with a smile. Did any of your coffee stay in the cup?"

I looked down to see most of the froth dripping down the sides of the mug. I reached out for a serviette to mop up the worst of it before I ended up with sticky froth all down my arm.

"Well, I hope she's not expecting a tip when we leave."

"Don't worry, I think she'd settle for your phone number instead."

Why did I say that? I wanted to slurp the words back into my mouth. Only a masochist plants an idea like that in the head of a man she fancies. God, the only thing worse than having to stand back and watch the object of my desire with my best friend would be to see him going out with a girl who openly hurled scorn and coffees at people she considered to be her physical, intellectual and social inferiors. An intellectual snob, and probably a raging coffee snob at that.

"Ha, ha. Have you heard anything from Rachel today?"

"Not Rachel, but I did have an interesting run-in with Kim. She came into work and blasted the shit out of me for being a selfish bitch, you know, for not joining their jolly little lynch mob tonight."

I tried to laugh, but there was nothing funny about it at all and I ended up sounding a touch hysterical.

Frowning, Jason took a sip of his coffee before responding, "I gather Rachel's still out for my blood."

"You could say that."

"That must have made your day. The perfect end to the week. I bet you're glad to have the next couple of days off, then?"

"*Ha*, what a joke."

"Why? Do you have to work over the weekend?"

"Not very likely, seeing as I got fired this afternoon!"

Jason's sexy stubbled chin almost hit the table in shock. "You're joking, aren't you?"

"I wish I was."

"Jeez, what happened?"

For the umpteenth time, I told what had by now become 'the firing story'. Maybe with less emphasis on me defending Jason and more on Kim's virtually unprovoked, not to mention vicious, physical assault. By the time I'd finished relating all the ugly details of what had transpired later in Mrs. Clements' office, my nervousness had abated a little.

Jason was shocked by their shoddy treatment of me. A slap in the face after eight years of loyal service. "You are going to fight it, aren't you?" he asked. "They can't can someone for being attacked by a customer. Shouldn't you be out on workers' comp or something, with the stress and all?"

I didn't feel up to mentioning the fact the security cameras had caught it all on tape. A tape, unfortunately, I'd been forced to watch in the grisly lead-up before I'd finally been fired. The memory of that grainy black-and-white footage caused me to cringe even now. Needless to say, it wasn't pretty or graceful. Not that two grown women kicking and slapping one another with the skirts up around their waists and buttons flying off their shirts could ever be described as elegant. It could easily have been part of one of those tacky

TV specials, *Women Behaving Badly*, or *When Good Girls Turn Bad*. Or worse still, a badly dubbed porn flick.

Furthermore, I had a sneaking suspicion the tape had been seized by one of the senior male managers for further scrutiny after hours. *Yuck.*

It was a mystery to me how the girls on *Charlie's Angels* managed to look like stunning ballet dancers while beating the shit out of their opponents, when all I could manage was something akin to a baboon suffering an epileptic fit.

"I don't think it would make any difference," I responded.

"Of course it would. What about your union reps? Where the hell were they at the time?"

"I don't know. There were so many people in the room I'm not sure who was there. They might as well have televised it throughout the store. As it was, I'm sure they could have heard all the yelling out in the center," I said, reddening with the memory of my humiliation.

Jason placed his hand over mine and squeezed it in a reassuring gesture. "Shit, I'm sorry about your job, Fi. I really am. I feel kind of responsible for it all, in a way."

"You? Responsible? How do you figure that out?"

"Well, if I hadn't split up with Rachel, she wouldn't be hiding in a car somewhere waiting to ambush me — and you — as we speak, *and* it wouldn't have stirred up all this trouble between you and the girls."

The look of misery on his face was adorable. Not that I enjoy seeing people in emotional torment, but his concern for me was touching. Pity I had to fuck it all up by fancying him. Had I not fallen for Jason, I might have indulged myself with a few moments basking in the warmth of his concern. But considering the state of my own emotions — dangerously out of control, a public nuisance, a danger to myself and others — I knew I had to pass up on that one or risk inadvertently revealing my true feelings toward him.

"Don't beat yourself up about it," I said with a smile. "I'd put up with their crap for years only because I was a spineless wimp who never said anything before now. You were right, though, at the wedding, remember, when you said I deserved to be treated better by them. I think after this afternoon's fight it's a fair bet I won't be hearing from any of them anytime in the near future, unless of course it's in the form of a letter bomb."

"Fiona, again, I am really sorry. But you're absolutely right. You do deserve better than that. It still sucks that Kim made you lose your job. What are you going to do now?"

"I don't know. I could go to community college or something and try to get some decent qualifications. I haven't thought much about it yet. But you know what, I'm beginning to think maybe she did me a favor. I'd been stuck in that awful job so long, I swear to God I was becoming institutionalized."

"I thought you liked working there."

"It was all right, I suppose. But I reckon if I'd stayed there for too much longer I would have turned into another Mrs. Clements. A scary thought, believe me. Mrs. Clements is a lot like that Mrs. Slocombe off *Are You Being Served* — except for the purple-colored hair. But you were right about the girls, though. What's that saying, with friends like that, who needs enemies?"

We both laughed, grimly.

"What went wrong between you and Rachel, anyway? You know she's completely lost the plot, don't you? What happened?"

Jason winced.

I immediately regretted being so blunt. "Look, don't answer that if you don't want to. It's absolutely none of my business," I added quickly, feeling like a nosy bitch.

A heavy silence descended over us. Across from me, Jason began shifting in his seat, fiddling with a stack of sugar straws. "No, it's all right. Considering all the trouble it's caused for you, I think you have every right to know what happened last week. Um… It was my night off and Rachel had left a message on my mobile to meet her at the Tavern. Apparently, Kim had refused to set foot in the club

312

in case she ran into Dave."

The pained expression returned and I sensed he wasn't finding it easy. "Fiona, you've got to understand, things hadn't really been working out too well between Rachel and me."

This I had already guessed, but hearing the genuine regret in Jason's voice, I knew it must have been difficult for him to come to terms with the fact that the girl of his dreams, the girl he'd secretly worshiped for years, was in reality a nasty, self-centered bitch.

"I couldn't move without her wanting to know where I was going and with who," he continued. "I felt as though I was slowly being suffocated by her. Honestly, Fi, she's some sort of emotional sponge. It didn't seem to matter how much attention I gave her, she wanted more and more. And, wow, you should have seen her tantrums if she didn't get her own way. It was awful."

I smiled reassuringly and he sighed, running his fingers through his hair.

"I don't have to tell you what she is like, do I? I was exhausted trying to please her. I think I knew even before Stacey and Simon's wedding it was never going to work out between us. I just didn't know how to tell her. She was so bloody intense. I suppose the final straw was the way she treated you. Remember, when she went off on you at the reception? I had to wonder what kind of a person would treat their friends like that. Then, for the next couple of weeks, every time I tried to bring up the subject about having some time apart, she would either fly off the handle and burst into tears, *or* she'd plan it so Kim or someone else was always around so I never got a chance to actually sit down and gently break it off. When she told me to meet her at the Tavern, I decided I just couldn't pretend anymore. I'd have to get her alone and somehow make her understand we were finished. It just wasn't fair to let her go on thinking things were okay between us."

"Surely, she guessed *something* was wrong?"

"I don't know. Maybe she did? Or maybe she's just so used to getting her own way with guys she thinks putting up with her crap is simply the price us poor blokes have to pay for the privilege of going out with her." He shrugged. "I don't know."

I sort of guessed what was coming next.

"Well, as soon as I walked into the Tavern and saw her sitting with Kim and Janine, I had a horrible feeling something was up. For a start, she looked about to burst a gasket with excitement. Seeing as the last couple of times I'd seen her, she'd been in a shit mood, I reckoned I'd every reason to be suspicious. My first thought was she'd guessed somehow I wanted to dump her and was about to tell me she was pregnant or something."

My shock must have been obvious.

"Fiona, it's happened to a few blokes I know. Either their girlfriends have deliberately got themselves pregnant, hoping to pressure the poor bloke into marrying them, or they've done it just to get a pay-out. Most of these blokes are up to their necks in child support payments and still don't get to see their kids. I don't think I could live like that. It would just break my heart. Mind you, the rate she was tossing back the Bacardi, I soon dropped that idea. Even then, I couldn't shift the feeling in the pit of my stomach that I was about to be floored by something, and soon. After a few more drinks, she was getting more and more flirtier and I was desperately trying to think of a way to get her on her own so I could break it off before she got too pissed to remember. *Then*, and, oh, God, Fiona, I'll never forget it, she stood up and announced to practically half the Tavern that we were moving in together. She all but hinted we were as good as engaged. I nearly died."

I suddenly found myself unable to look Jason in the eye.

His eyes narrowed. "You knew about it, didn't you?"

"Not about the engagement bit, but I had a fair idea she was planning on you and her moving in together."

"You could have at least warned me, Fi. Seriously, I

couldn't believe it. Did you know she'd actually put down a bond on a place and told them we'd be moving in that weekend?"

"She didn't, did she?" I gasped. "I never imagined she'd go that far. You know what she's like. Always shooting her mouth off about something. That's why I didn't really take her too seriously. I mean, I knew she was looking at places," I offered, feeling guilty.

"When?"

"Um, after she waited hours at your place for you to come home the other week. You were at classes with me and she was in a filthy mood because you had given her the cold shoulder."

Jason looked like he'd been slapped. "She told you about that?"

"Yes. She figured if you guys were living together, at least she'd know where you were," I said, shamefaced. I felt about two inches tall.

Running his hand through his hair, Jason looked completely shell-shocked by the true extent of Rachel's scheming. "Jesus, what else did she tell you all about us?"

Instantly, I recalled the countless times Kim, Janine and I had sat in stunned silence over lunch or a coffee as Rachel related the intimate details of their staggeringly active sex life. Considering he had already started to go off her, I had to admit I was impressed. How amazing would he be in bed with a woman he was actually in love with? I turned red and in those couple of seconds I prayed harder than I had ever prayed in my life for my face to return to its normal pasty hue before Jason guessed what was going through my head.

The anguish of being fair-skinned and easily embarrassed.

"Oh, just the usual things. Girly things. That's all."

Jason didn't look at all convinced and I was fairly certain my glowing face didn't reassure him much.

"And tell me, did *you* actually think I'd agree to move in with her?"

"God, no. Not for a minute. That's why I decided to stay right out of it. After all, it was playing on my mind that if things did blow up with you two, I didn't want to be caught in the middle and forced to take sides."

I realized then what I'd just said and couldn't help laughing at the irony of it all. Who was I kidding? I was in it up to my neck already and in urgent need of a snorkel. "What did you do when she made her big announcement?" I'd already heard Rachel's version in all the gory detail, but in light of recent events, I suspected her perspective to be perhaps a little poisoned — at the very least.

"Honestly, I was so mad I didn't trust myself not to start yelling at her in front of everyone in the Tavern, so I asked her to come outside with me to the car for a talk. Can you believe she honestly thought her *little surprise* had thrilled me so much, I was dragging her out for a quickie in the car park to celebrate?"

I had no trouble whatsoever believing she would have been thinking exactly that, especially after a few Bacardis.

"Looking back on it, I suppose, I should have handled it better," continued Jason, staring bleakly down at the table. "But by then I was so mad and way past caring. Once we reached the car, I simply turned to her and told we were through and I never wanted to see her again. Can you believe Rachel thought I was joking and actually started laughing? That was it. I just lost it, didn't I. I told if she wanted someone to push around and treat like shit, she'd have to find another bloke to fill the role, because I'd had a gutful of her tantrums, her demands and her spite, and I wanted out. It must have sunk in, because then she suddenly went ape-shit. Started laying into me with her fists and screaming at the top of her lungs that I was a bastard and didn't deserve her and she only went out with me because she felt sorry for me. According to her, I was going to regret treating her so badly because she was the best thing that had ever happened to me. Then she started screaming I'd end up on my own because no other decent girl would give me a second look when word got out that I was a complete loser *and*, apparently, a dud in the sack."

I almost burst out laughing on hearing this last part. God, at that very moment he had half the girls in the café ogling him over the tops of their lattes, earning him a few filthy looks from who I suspected were their boyfriends or husbands. I'd have bet my life that as we spoke, half the single girls at the nightclub were waiting for Jason to make an appearance, and the race would be on to see who could fill Rachel's role as his new girlfriend. Rachel really must have been off her rocker to suggest he would never find another lady.

Then I was taken back to a time when I remembered Troy saying much the same to me. Every time we'd have a fight, he'd tell me I should be grateful he'd overlooked me being fat and ugly and agreed to marry me in the first place. And if it weren't for him, I'd never find a bloke who was willing to take on a whining bitch like me, so I ought to be down on my hands and knees thanking him, rather than complaining all the time about nothing. According to him, I was a spoiled bitch who needed putting in her place.

"I hope you didn't believe a word of it, Jason. Rachel was just trying to hurt you, that's all. For what it's worth, I know exactly how you must be feeling. I used to cop the same treatment from Troy all the time, until he almost had me believing him."

Suddenly the truth of what I'd revealed sunk in and Jason reached out and took my hands in his. "Jesus, Fi, I'm sorry. I had no idea. You must think I'm an insensitive prat, carrying on about all this."

"Don't be silly. I'd never think that. Anyway, you shouldn't worry too much what Rachel says. After all, at least *you* know you're not going to be left on your own for the rest of your life."

"What makes you say that?"

"Well, Rachel said you'd met someone else."

Jason didn't make any move to deny it and any hope I

had for us sank.

I had to ask, even though I knew it would break my heart. "Is it someone I know?"

Suddenly his face flooded with color. After a brief pause, he lowered his head and sighed. "Yes."

Every part of my body, from my toes to my hair, tensed, ready to endure another painful emotional blow. It was like losing control of a car on a wet road and being about to collide with an oncoming truck.

"Who is she?"

Jason sat silently for what felt like minutes before eventually looking up from his cappuccino and into my eyes with an expression of pure misery that made my breath catch in my throat. Taking a deep breath, he then sighed again.

"Fiona, I'm so sorry to add to your burdens, after everything you've been through, but...I think...I'm falling for *you*."

Chapter Twenty-Three

I was still trying to get my head around what Jason had just said when the café erupted in an explosion of hostile profanities.

"You fucking skanky whore. I should have fucking known it would be you!"

Like a rabid dog, Rachel stood at the doorway, bristling with what could only be described as apoplectic fury. Her long blonde hair, usually immaculately coiffured like one of those girls on the shampoo commercials, stuck out all over the place and her bulging eyes were almost oscillating in her head. She was white with rage and all but frothing at the mouth. I'd never seen anything like it. I couldn't help sending up a silent prayer that I'd been caught up in some kind of weird movie shoot, maybe a cheap remake of the *Body Snatchers* featuring Rachel in the lead role.

Oh, how the mighty had fallen.

"You bitch. You fucking whoring, dirty, man-stealing bitch," she shrieked hysterically from her position at the entrance, where, unfortunately she had a clear view of Jason and me, and perhaps even more incriminating, our hands clasped intimately across the table.

Throughout the café, every conversation abruptly ceased and more than a dozen heads swiveled from Rachel to me and back again.

I couldn't move. I was literally frozen to the seat, the shock of Jason's declaration compounded tenfold by Rachel descending on us out of nowhere like a madwoman. Opposite me, a white-faced Jason looked as if he'd been shot.

How the hell did she know we were here?

It was akin to a scene straight out of one of those embarrassing farfetched comedies. The ones that have you cringing in sympathy for the humiliation about to be landed on the poor hapless fool in the middle. Had I not been the hapless fool currently center stage, I might have been riveted to the drama unfolding before my eyes, too.

Everyone in the café sat aghast as Rachel advanced toward where Jason and I sat motionless, too horrified by her transformation to do anything but stare. I barely recognized her. Her face was contorted into a grotesque parody of some possessed doll I vaguely remembered from an old horror flick.

There was absolutely no time to react.

Before I could even think of defending myself, Rachel lashed out at me. A fiery bolt of pain exploded down the side of my face. My vision turned red, and as the initial shock receded, I felt the full fury of her anger through the ringing in my ears.

"I'll fucking kill you, I will!" she screeched, before landing another stinging blow on my burning flesh.

My head snapped backward as she swung her arm again in preparation for another strike. With no time to think, I braced myself for a further attack, instinctively covering my face and closing my eyes, tensing for the by now unavoidable strike about to descend.

A deep, throaty roar filled the space between us and I buckled down.

One second passed, followed by another. Rachel continued to spew forth more poisonous barbs, though by now they were hardly more than a stream of jumbled animalistic grunts and screeches. I could barely make out what she was saying, though the loathing and vile contempt in her voice was a fair indication of her current frame of mind.

Only when I realized I was not about to be punched again did I open my eyes to see Antonio and Patrick restraining Rachel while she attempted to kick out at them.

"Fiona. Are you all right?" panted Antonio, struggling to keep Rachel from breaking free of his arms. "I'm so sorry, Fi, she must have followed us here. I had no idea."

All Hell broke loose then as customers, fearing further violence, started leaving the café en masse. Then the waitress, who I might add had a set of lungs on her to rival Rachel's, began screaming at us to get Rachel out of the place or she'd ring the police.

What a hideous mess.

Behind Antonio, I suddenly caught a glimpse of Kim and Janine standing at the door, their mouths gaping as they took in the scene of utter mayhem before them.

Less than five minutes later, we were all outside. I immediately recognized Antonio's Saab parked in front of the café and it dawned on me that while waiting for Jason at the center, Rachel and co must have somehow remembered Patrick from the bachelorette night and decided to follow him and Antonio here, hoping to catch the eye of the hunky dancer.

Rachel was by now half-sobbing, half-snarling and standing between Kim and Janine while Antonio and Patrick positioned themselves between Rachel and me, ensuring she didn't make any more sudden lunges in my direction.

It wasn't until that point the events of the last five minutes began to sink in. My head throbbed. Intense pain rose from my jawline to travel northward, where it continued stabbing hot shards into my temple. The side of my face must have been twice its normal size. A mixture of emotions converged on me all at once. As the shock softened, something slowly crumbled inside my chest and I burst into noisy gulping sobs.

Before the first tear hit the pavement, I found myself surrounded by Antonio and Patrick. Horrified by what they'd just witnessed, they rushed over to comfort me just as Jason emerged from the café with a handful of ice for my rapidly swelling face. I was almost crushed between the three of them as they all tried to console me at once.

It was like a scene from one of my more adventurous sexual fantasies. Pity, though, it had been spawned by my abject humiliation and physical pain.

Sadly, there was nothing remotely erotic about it at all.

Not ten feet away Rachel stood alongside Antonio's car and, with the lack of a suitable audience—Kim and Janine didn't count—she ceased her theatrical bawling.

Suddenly something must have twigged in her memory—what had led her here to the café in the first place. Looking across at Antonio and his flashy sports car, it all seemed to come back to her.

"*This* is Tony?" she yelled, her expression pasted with disbelief as she pointed to Antonio. "*This* is the man you've been telling us about?"

Instantly, Rachel turned about five different shades of green and her face hardened with hatred. A hatred aimed right at me! "*Why?* Why would anyone who looks like *him*"—she nodded toward Antonio—"want to have anything to do with a dog like you, Fiona? You must have fucking paid him. Is that why you threw yourself at my man, is it? Thought you were suddenly so fucking hot you'd notch up another bloke?" She laughed maliciously, pausing for effect. "Mind you, any bloke will jump in if you open your legs wide enough, won't they, Fiona."

Antonio had slung his arm around my shoulder and he tensed on hearing Rachel's offensive innuendo. His expression narrowed ominously and he shot a look of loathing at Rachel. "Why, you must be that nasty slut Jason's been telling us about. Rachel, isn't it?" Turning to Jason, he quipped, "Jesus, Jason, whatever did you ever see in her? Hard-arsed nasty piece of trash, she is."

Rachel's mouth dropped at Antonio's well-aimed and even-better-timed insult. I could have gladly kissed Antonio for coming to my defense. For Rachel, being insulted by a bloke was bad enough, but make that a man of Antonio's league and it had all the impact of a savage punch to the face.

Before my eyes, Rachel seemed to gather all her hate around her like some kind of security blanket. Antonio's contempt, rather than putting her in her place, had only fueled her spite. Right then, I could tell she was gearing up to fire her final heinous bullet—a bullet aimed right at me.

"You can fuck them all, for all I care, Fiona," she snapped, throwing back her head defiantly. "Good luck. But let me tell you something before I go. Troy wasn't the best screw I ever had, but at least he was always up for a good time, unlike that loser," she snarled, looking straight at Jason.

What? Suddenly everyone froze in shock. Even the air around us stopped moving. Rachel certainly had everyone's attention now.

She laughed before casting her malice back in my direction. "You know what? At first, I actually felt guilty for fucking Troy behind your back. But then he used to tell me you were a dead loss in the sack—you hadn't a bloody clue. I can't believe I actually felt sorry for you at the time. He couldn't even bear to look at your fat, flabby body, he'd tell me. Just the thought of fucking you made him want to puke. No wonder he always came running to me."

I thought I was going to be ill.

Rachel and Troy. Together. How long had it been going on for?

Nothing at all could have prepared me for what Rachel had revealed. I tasted bile. Taking big gulps of night air, I willed myself not to throw up. *Not here. Not in front of Rachel.*

"*You bitch.*" I hissed, doubling over in pain.

Rachel laughed, a horrible tight nasty snigger. "You can't really blame him. If you were a *real* wife to him, he wouldn't have come running to me for sex after you guys married. I thought he'd give up begging me for it after you two got hitched, but I'd been wrong, hadn't I? Pity, though, he had to go and fuck it all up with that slut Amanda—*everyone* knew she was a filthy tramp."

Suddenly, my lungs began to burn. The more air I tried to

draw into my body, the harder it was to catch my breath. Rachel and her vile words slowly receded as my desperate struggle to breathe wiped everything else from my mind bar the burning pain searing a path inside me.

* * * *

Rising from the murky depths of unconsciousness, the first thing to hit me was the smell. Disgustingly antiseptic. I could almost taste it at the back of my throat and my first instinct was to gag.

The only sensations I could grasp onto were muffled, swirling chaotically in and out of my head. Before long, my confused state was further addled by the awareness of splintering pain running laps around my brain. My head pounded, my mouth felt lined with sandpaper and my chest raw and scratched. For a moment, I lay there, wondering if it was possible I was dead.

I couldn't remember a thing. The pain in my head, together with the pressure bearing down on my chest, effectively chased away the fragments of color that flashed through my head intermittently. Was I pissed? I must be. I couldn't even remember drinking anything, but I was obviously in bed and suffering major alcohol-induced spin-out. Images of Jason, Antonio and Rachel were swirling around in the back of my head, but nothing seemed to make any sense at all.

This feeling of disembodiment wasn't entirely *un*pleasant, but it was unnerving.

"Fiona. Oh, thank God you're awake!"

I recognized Jason's voice instantly. He sounded really weird, though, quite tremulous and hollow.

Blind panic struck as it dawned on me that *I was in bed with Jason*. How had this happened and why couldn't I remember? Oh, Jesus, I must have been pissed off my head — legless, blotto, smashed, totally and utterly annihilated. I felt nauseous with post-binge dread. *What* had I done — and with Jason no less? Every primal instinct in my body urged me to sink back into the warm, inky depths of oblivion, where I wouldn't have to face the consequences of my excesses — whatever they had been. I silently pleaded with the gods, armed with promises that I would never so much as look at another strawberry daiquiri again if only they'd just make it all go away.

Alas, oblivion was not going to rescue me this time. Clearly, I'd used the 'I'll never drink again' plea bargain once too often. With no other option available, I realized that hiding away in my dreams was not going to get me out of Jason's bed and into a taxi home. So, ruling out divine intervention, I had no alternative but to ignore the pain currently squeezing my gray matter out through my ears and remove myself pronto before I heaped further disgrace on myself.

The usually simple art of opening my eyes proved to be more of a challenge than I'd expected. My eyelids felt as though they had been glued together and it was a struggle to pry them apart at all. Great, not only was I hungover and in a bed I shouldn't be in, I had crusty eyes as well. *Very glamorous!*

"Don't worry, Fi. You're okay now. I've rung your mum and dad and they're on their way over."

"Mum. Dad. Why? Where am I?" I croaked, trying to sit up.

Oh, God, I'd never hear the end of it. Mum and Dad having to collect me after a night of drunken debauchery, like a juvenile delinquent caught shoplifting makeup at JCPenney. How had my life been reduced to this? I'd be committed to some Home for Social Degenerates for sure. The only thing I knew for certain was I had to get out of there before they arrived or I would never be able to face them again.

A splice of pain shot through the side of my head, forcing me back again. I groaned.

Even that hurt.

Maybe I'd give myself another five minutes.

"Fiona, relax, you're safe. You're in the hospital."

"What!"

I forced my eyes open and willed them to focus. *Hospital?* At least that accounted for why I felt so ill. *And* the smell. *And* the horrible green curtains surrounding the bed.

Whatever was wrong with me, I hoped it was terminal.

Sensing my growing alarm, Jason quickly began to explain, "It's all right now. The doctor thinks you started hyperventilating, which brought on some kind of a panic attack. Then you passed out. Scared the shit out of everyone. We rang for an ambulance and they brought you in here. I think the doctor's given you some kind of a sedative to keep you calm, so that might be why you're feeling a bit woozy. Christ, we were so worried about you, Fi. We thought you were having a heart attack or something."

Then the events of the past few hours came rushing back to me in nightmarish Technicolor horror.

Jason's declaration of love. Rachel's attack. Antonio and Patrick's arrival at the café. Rachel's bombshell about her and Troy. Then falling, falling into a net of blackness.

I wished it *had* been a bloody heart attack — and a fatal one, at that. I don't know what was worse. The embarrassment of going all Victorian in front of everyone and collapsing was completely overshadowed by the knowledge that not only had Rachel been sleeping with my husband, but they'd been laughing at me behind my back. Troy's affair with Amanda suddenly paled into insignificance in light of Rachel's vindictive confession.

An ominous burning sensation rose from the pain in my heart to fill my eyes with hot tears of misery. I hadn't any strength left in me to fight the wave of anguish that was crashing down on me as a result of Rachel's betrayal. At least I had come to terms with the fact *he* was a complete waste of space and I was better off without him. But all these years I'd considered Rachel to be my friend. Part of my inner circle. My support network. A sister of sorts. Of course, I am not denying she could be temperamental and a monumental pain in the neck at times. But I'd considered her a friend all the same, a friend I thought I could trust and rely on.

Then I remembered the horrible things she had said about me, and worse still about what Troy had disclosed about our sex life, in front of everyone and especially Jason. I thought I would drown in my humiliation.

A choking sob erupted from deep within my burning chest.

"Aw, Fi, don't cry," soothed Jason, stroking my arm.

For the first time, I became aware that Jason was holding my hand. How long for, I hadn't a clue. That one simple gesture of sympathy threatened to tear me apart. I couldn't bring myself to look at him, imagining the pity in his eye for poor, sexless, hopeless-in-the-sack Fiona.

What must he be thinking about me, especially considering Rachel's very public broadcast that my own husband had thought me a dead loss in bed? I felt as though all my femininity had somehow been obliterated the moment those dreadful words left her snarling lips. Troy's nasty taunts returned to torture me some more with a fresh wave of shame, bringing further tears with every cruel word I remembered him throwing at me.

"Fiona, look at me, please," begged Jason.

But I couldn't. I doubted I would ever be able to look at him again without reliving that last awful scene outside the café.

"I can't," I sobbed.

"If it makes you feel any better, I don't think Rachel will be game to show her face after that. Even Janine and Kim were horrified and, well, you should have seen Antonio. He went completely mental and absolutely blasted the shit out of her. I never thought he had it in him."

I allowed myself the luxury of a smile, picturing Antonio, my avenging angel in full flight.

"Patrick and Antonio are outside in the waiting room

now. They've been so worried about you, Fi. The nurse wouldn't let them come in. She wasn't going to let me stay, either, but I told her I was your boyfriend."

Boyfriend? That one simple word hung shyly in the air between us, as if testing the temperature before it dived, headfirst into our lives. I tried out the phrase in my mind. *'My boyfriend, Jason.'* They were by far the loveliest words I'd heard in such a long time. I wanted to wrap them up and lock them away somewhere safe where I could bring them out and cherish them when I felt in need of comfort. An instant rush of warmth coursed through my limbs, awakening a tiny flicker of something deep within my body. Something I vaguely recognized from a lifetime ago. *Love.*

Mistaking my silence for disapproval, Jason slowly released my hand. "I hope you don't mind. I couldn't bear having to wait outside, not knowing if you were okay or not, so I told them we were a couple."

Jason gently touched my chin with a finger, drawing my face around to meet his. "I know you've been through hell these last few months," he began, solemnly, "but I promise I'll never, ever let anyone hurt you again. I want to be with you, Fiona, all the time. I can't begin to tell you how sorry I am about tonight, and especially about Rachel and your ex. But if you'll let me, I'll prove to you that not all blokes are complete bastards like Troy. What do you say? Will you give me a chance? Give us a chance?"

For the first time in months, a little cautious bubble of pure bliss rose within my chest. Maybe it was the drugs, but after spending so long in the cold depths of my misery, I now floated upward toward the surface and the warmth of the sun on my face once more.

Taking hold of Jason's hand, I smiled. "I think you're worth taking a risk over."

Relief softened the lines of weariness around Jason's eyes and he leaned across and kissed me lightly on my forehead.

* * * *

I barely had time to calm Mum down before the doctors decided I was going to live after all, and so shunted me out of my warm bed as if I was some kind of serial hypochondriac in order to make room for someone worthier of their attention. After being given what looked like a year's supply of diazepam and instructions to take it easy for the next few days, I was deemed fit to rejoin the rest of society.

Outside in the over-crowded waiting room sat Antonio and Patrick, flicking through old issues of *National Geographic* and *Cosmo*. They were almost completely surrounded by a sea of screaming toddlers, old men in stripy pajamas and young blokes fresh in from various brawls sporting bloody noses and rapidly swelling eye sockets. It was now after midnight and happy hour was in full swing at the hospital's emergency department.

As soon as I emerged, they both leaped on me at once. Such a touching scene. Anyone would have thought I'd just woken up after being in a coma for six years. Thankfully the painkillers I'd been given had started to kick in by that time, so apart from possessing a head like the elephant man, I must say, I felt pleasantly mellow.

Mum and Dad were noticeably shaken by the entire episode and were eager to shuttle me off home and tuck me into the safety of my bed. But, after various introductions accompanied by what I suspected was a little girly flirting from Mum as Antonio and Patrick treated her to a full five-course banquet of shameless flattery — I couldn't wait to tell her they were gay, that would teach her to hint she'd been a teen bride — I convinced them I wasn't about to collapse and die and would be perfectly safe in Jason's protective custody.

Dad, of course, being Dad, gave Jason a wary look and made him promise he'd have me home post-haste. Yep, I was fifteen all over again. Jason, to his credit, took it quite well and further managed to charm his way into Mum's good books when he sided with them over my protestations at being treated like a child, promising to escort me right to the door and protect me with his life. God, *embarrassing*. Antonio and Patrick hovered around like two aging aunts, giving advice on what to put on my poor battered face to ease the bruising, before finally leaving. But not until they extracted a promise from me that I'd let them cook me and Jason dinner the following weekend.

Subtle?

Not!

Jason avoided any further mention of Rachel as he drove me home from the hospital. I was trying not to think of her, either, determined as I was not to let her spoil another moment of my life. She had been responsible for so much misery of late I figured she'd used up more than her fair share of space in my head.

With the absence of traffic, the drive from the hospital took only half the time that distance normally would and in no time at all we were turning into Mum and Dad's street. When I thought about climbing into my cold single bed again, I experienced an overwhelming pang of loneliness. Then I remembered my tiny single bed currently sported ridiculous *Strawberry Shortcake* comforter. In case you're thinking I've gone completely screwy, I'll explain. Arnie peed on my lovely green grown-up comforter and Mum unearthed this bloody *Strawberry Shortcake* relic from God only knew where.

Maybe it wasn't such a bad thing, therefore, being doomed to spend another night alone but for Arnie's company. Because even if I did, by some miracle, manage to sneak Jason past Dad and into my room, my current boudoir décor was anything but conducive to seduction. If it weren't for those damn sedatives that even now were making it difficult to stifle a yawn, I'd be hinting to Jason to just keep driving on to his place, bruising or no bruising. But I knew it was not going to happen, not tonight, anyway.

Jason pulled up in front of Mum and Dad's and turned

off the engine.

"Do you think your mum and dad will let me take you out next weekend?" he asked, a trace of amusement in his voice.

I should have known Dad's embarrassing display of fatherly interference back there at the hospital would return to haunt me. I made a mental note to remind him in no uncertain terms that I was now twenty-six years old and *not* bloody six.

But, then again, two could play at this game.

"Well, that depends, doesn't it?" I teased, enjoying the easy intimacy that had sprung up so effortlessly between us.

"Depends? On what?"

"On where you are planning on taking me?"

Jason smiled. "What do you mean?"

"Because I can tell you now, if it's the club *or* that ratty tavern, they'll probably lock me in my room and refuse to let me out ever, and you will eventually die old and alone."

"Really!" replied Jason, raising an eyebrow. "Oh, well, in *that* case, where do you think they *might* let you go then?"

"I don't know. They *might* approve of that nice little Mexican restaurant that's just opened in town, TexMex, I think it's called," I responded, trying to keep a straight face.

A mischievous glint lit up Jason's eyes as he played along. "Oh, have a yearning for something hot, do you?"

I nodded coyly as a fierce wave of color crept up my cheeks. *Damn, am I that easy to read?*

"Well, if the lady wants spicy, I suppose I will just have to make sure she's satisfied, won't I?" he queried.

Then, going all serious on me, he continued, "Just so long as you're sure you can handle it. I wouldn't want you to get burned — again."

I got the impression we weren't talking about food anymore and my stomach began to dance about nervously.

"Are *you* sure?" I countered, feeling all flustered.

The atmosphere thickened between us and I was taken

aback by the sudden intensity in Jason's eyes.

"Need you ask? I've been sure since you stopped stomping all over my poor toes."

I winced with the shameful memory of my first ungainly attempts to master control over my clumsy feet.

"*They*, on the other hand," added Jason, glancing down and laughing, "begged me not to fall for you, fearing they'd be maimed for life, but I knew you were worth putting up with a little pain for."

I think that was by far the nicest thing anyone has ever said to me.

Chapter Twenty-Four

It was the first Friday I'd actually arrived early for my appointment with Margarita and I wasn't the only one surprised.

I wasn't so much eager to see her as mostly unemployed with a daunting amount of time on my hands. By rights, I should have been out looking for a job, of course, but at least for this week I was legitimately taking it easy, because that was what the good doctor suggested. As far as Mum was concerned, he might as well have stood beside a burning bush and carved his advice into a stone tablet. A doctor's word was as good as law and any orders were strictly adhered to for fear something dreadful would befall the poor hapless patient.

Mum had a reverence for doctors that hovered blasphemously close to religious fervor.

So, as you might well imagine, Mum had taken it upon herself to diligently enforce my 'week of rest' to the nth degree by not allowing me to so much as make myself a cup of tea. Subsequently, I was bored out of my slightly rattled brain and desperate to escape the house and her oppressive pampering now my week of rest was officially over.

Thank Christ the bruising had faded quite a bit in those few days. From the livid purple swelling I had woken up to on Saturday morning, the side of my face had gradually paled to a more acceptable dirty jaundiced yellow. Although it made me look as though I needed a good scrub with a washcloth, it was a vast improvement on the rainbow-hued mutant who had greeted me in the mirror that first morning.

Mutant or not, I had to admit I was secretly pleased with all the attention that had been bestowed on me. Ever since the scene outside the café and my brief hospitalization, Jason and Antonio had been busy vying for the position of chief worrywart for the better part of a week, Jason in person and Antonio by phone.

Jason had by now become a regular sight in our house, much to Mum's delight and Dad's growing resentment. This, I might add, was somewhat due to Dad being obliged to share his favorite shortbread biscuits with him after enjoying years of solitary gorging — Alex and I had developed a severe aversion after making ourselves sick on then one Christmas when we swiped a tin from under the tree and slunk away to the garage where we proceeded to stuff ourselves with the sugar-laden slabs.

Yep, it had certainly been a week full of conflicting emotions.

On one hand, I was floating on air as a result of Jason's declaration of love. I'll admit the painkillers were helping, too. Only in the odd moments when I let my guard down did I cast a brief mental glance over the truth of what Rachel had revealed that fateful night. Although the truth of their affair might have been out in the open now, I wasn't ready to examine it too closely. Instead, it was easier to push it to the back of my mind and bask in the warmth of Jason's affection.

With all that, it came as a surprise to find, despite all the trauma of the previous weekend, I'd passed the week nestled in a blissful cocoon of Jason-inspired euphoria. I felt as though I was fraudulently living someone else's fate. All week I'd been waiting for some miserable red-eyed girl to tap me on the shoulder and angrily demand I give her back her life, then slap me for having the effrontery to steal it from her in the first place.

I'd been so busy whiling away the hours of my convalescence dreaming of my first real date with Jason on Saturday night—watching telly with Mum and Dad only a whisper away didn't count—I'd given precious little thought to my upcoming session with Margarita.

When I greeted her with a Mona-Lisa-ish smile in place of my customary scowl, I could tell she was thrown. Her expression reflected her continuing confusion as I cheerfully flounced past her bulky frame into her office without the need of a cattle prod to guide me in the right direction.

"It's lovely to see you so bright this week," she said warily, shutting the door firmly behind her.

Once she made herself comfortable, Margarita stared across at me and gave me one of her 'now let's get down to business' looks.

"Fiona, before we begin today's session, I feel it only fair to tell you I have just spoken to your mother."

"What! *My* mother? Isn't that against the rules or something? Whatever happened to patient confidentiality?" I started angrily.

Oh, great!

My good mood began packing its bags, ready to stomp off out of the door.

"I can assure you *nothing* we discuss in the course of your therapy leaves this room. Your mother rang *me*, and I gained the impression she has been very worried about you."

Across from me Margarita's eyes widened in shock as she noticed for the first time the lingering remnants of last weekend's violence on my face. "My goodness," she said, clearly appalled. "I think I understand her concern now."

I quickly covered the offending side of my face with my palm and muttered something along the lines of, "Oh it's nothing."

Margarita's concern over the state of my face only briefly diverted my annoyance away from the fact my mother had actually taken it upon herself to ring up Margarita, as though she was my third-class teacher and I was having trouble with math.

I couldn't believe the effrontery of the woman.

"What did my mother want to talk to you about?" I asked, cheesed off.

It was a stupid question, anyway. I already had a fair idea. No wonder my ears had been burning on the way in here — Mum must have been on the phone the moment I left the house, eager to impart news of my latest arse-up!

"Your mother is very concerned for your well-being — both physically and emotionally," said Margarita as she continued staring at my face.

I didn't even think she was aware she was doing it.

I could have kicked myself then for not having the good sense to slap on some makeup before I left the house.

"*And*?" I prompted, growing more and more annoyed.

There had to be more to it than just that. I strongly suspected Margarita of holding something back.

"And she was simply looking for reassurance that both she and your father were doing all they could to help you through this stressful time."

There must be more than that. I just couldn't imagine Mum blithely ringing up Margarita, who, being a shrink, was only half a notch down from a doctor on Mum's exalted scale of respected professions, just to get a parental pat on the back.

"Well, anyway, I think this gives us a good starting point to today's session. How about you begin by going over the events leading up to this, um, incident?" she suggested, motioning toward my bruises.

Begrudgingly, I began my sorry tale. She'd get it out of me sooner or later so I may as well bypass our usual mental sparring and make it easier by cooperating, before she got out the thumbscrews. "I was meeting Jason for a coffee last Friday night and I have to admit, I was feeling a bit nervous."

"Jason, he's a friend of yours from dance class, is that right?"

I nodded.

Margarita wrote something down. "And why were you

nervous? Was it something to do with your friend Rachel — I seem to recall she's his girlfriend, isn't she?"

I winced. Hearing her name spoken out loud almost physically hurt. "Ex-girlfriend, actually."

And ex-ex-ex-friend, full stop!

"Go on," encouraged Margarita.

"I suppose I was nervous because, as I told you last week, not four hours before I'd had this huge fight with Kim and, well, they had no idea I was meeting Jason that night. They would have killed me had they known."

"That would certainly explain why you were so apprehensive."

"It wasn't *only* because of that," I admitted. "When I spoke to him a couple of nights before, he'd sounded a bit, oh, I don't know, strange, a bit on edge, I suppose. He wanted to talk to me about something. I presumed at the time it had something to do with Rachel and him, but still I couldn't shake the feeling he was about to tell me something awful."

"Like what?"

I hesitated for a second, "I don't know. Something like he was taking off. Going to, say, Bolivia to live."

Margarita pursed her lips and shot me a looked that said, 'Don't bullshit me, I can tell you're holding back.' She must have done her training with the CIA.

"And why would that create such a feeling of impending doom?"

"Well." I paused to figure out how was I going to word this without her thinking I was repeating the entire Antonio obsession — again. "I've come to realize during the last few weeks that I'd grown to really like Jason."

She stared back blankly.

"Really, *really* like him," I stressed.

Suddenly it twigged in her head, "Oh, I see. And did Jason reciprocate these feelings toward you?"

"The truth is at the time, I really didn't know. When he asked me to meet him, I thought he was going to confide in me as a *friend*, that he was in love with someone else."

"Why would you have thought that?"

"Because he apparently *told* Rachel he had met someone else."

Jeez, it's like trying to explain the theory of relativity to a bloody chimpanzee.

"Considering your feelings toward him, I can see how that must have felt very awkward for you."

I shrugged. "It was."

"You're saying he had no inkling that your feelings toward him had deepened?"

"I don't think he had any idea."

"Then what happened?"

"Well, we talked for a while, mostly about his breakup with Rachel and about me getting fired, then I asked him outright who his new girlfriend was. He hesitated a bit but said it was me he was falling for. I couldn't believe it. It was the last thing I expected to hear him say. That's when it all happened. Before I could say anything, Rachel suddenly appeared in the café and started hurling all sorts of abuse in our direction. Then she attacked me."

"For simply talking to Jason?"

"We were holding hands at the time."

"And that excuses her behavior?"

"Of course not. She just saw us, immediately put two and two together and went mental."

"But how did she know you were there?"

"We think she recognized Patrick outside the center where he was waiting to pick up Antonio after his dance class, and from there followed them to the café where they were supposed to be meeting us for a coffee."

Margarita looked confused, as well she might. "Who is Patrick?"

"Patrick was a stripper at this bachelorette night we went to ages ago, although he's really classically trained and shouldn't be wasting his talent like that."

This just added to her confusion. "*And* he's Antonio's boyfriend," I reluctantly confessed.

Just as I had feared, with the mention of Antonio's name, instant understanding wiped the look of confusion off her face, "Is this the same Antonio —"

"Yes!" I cut in impatiently. *Don't make me explain,* I silently implored.

Margarita immediately resumed writing.

Definitely not a good sign.

"Okay," she began, putting her pen down at last. "What happened next between you and Rachel?"

I breathed a sigh of relief.

"Well, Antonio and Patrick grabbed hold of her to stop her from attacking me again. Then it seemed like everyone in the café started yelling and screaming before the waitress threatened to ring the police. Not long afterward, they dragged Rachel outside. Kim and Janine were there and must have calmed her down a bit because she finally stopped shouting. Eventually I followed them outside while Jason got some ice to put on my face."

"And?"

"And I passed out or fainted or something. Probably from the shock. Someone called an ambulance and I woke up in the hospital a little while later. That was it. I'm fine now apart from a little bruising, and life goes on."

Sure, it was the abridged version, but I desperately wanted this little discussion over and done with, so I saw little point in dwelling on incidentals.

Margarita took a deep breath and leaned forward in her chair. "Is that all?"

"Yes."

She didn't look convinced. Taking off her glasses, she began rubbing her eyes before looking back at me with a hint of exasperation on her face.

"Fiona. I know how hard this must be for you. For the last few years, almost every aspect of your life has been the focus of an immense amount of stress. Your marriage and your work, for a start. Then you have had to deal with the unpredictable and, let's face it, quite volatile relationship you appear to have with your friends. I can only *imagine* how horrible it must have been for you to be the focal point of so much violence and hate, and from a girl who, for many years, you considered to be your friend, no less. So I must say it worries me somewhat that you haven't expressed even the slightest amount of anger or, for that matter, any emotion at all toward Rachel."

After a moment's silence, I replied somberly, "I don't want to even think about her at the moment."

Anyway, what Margarita had said wasn't quite true. Inside, I raged against the way Rachel had manipulated and used me — and probably Troy, as well, if I'm honest. And all for her own sick amusement. I felt totally defiled. Like someone had emotionally assaulted me. I was terrified to even consider what might happen if I did vent some of the anger I felt toward Rachel. The cold, hard reality was I couldn't deal with it. This amount of rage, combined with the shame I had been suppressing, was just too great. Just for a little while, I wanted to put all the unpleasantness aside and enjoy my life again — especially now Jason was a part of my future.

"I think that is the *very* reason why we should think about her, Fiona. The way she treated you was deplorable — criminal, in fact. You would have been perfectly entitled to press charges against her, considering the violence she inflicted on you. Why didn't you?"

"How do you know I didn't?" I retorted.

"Your mother told me you refused to file charges with the police, despite the urging of both her and your father."

Suddenly, I smelled the first whiffs of my approaching defeat.

I thought about it for a while before responding.

"I decided not to because I didn't see how it would solve anything. By getting the police involved, it would have just dragged out a horrible situation even more." My thoughts went back to the conversation I'd recently had with Stacey and I didn't want to think of Rachel as the scared child witnessing her father's brutality. "As far as Rachel's attitude toward me goes, I think having her charged with assault would be like trying to put out a fire with a flamethrower."

Margarita smiled.

"That's a very good analogy, Fiona. But if you take away the fuel a fire needs to burn, won't it burn itself out?"

Now *I* was confused.

"Okay, think about it this way. The way I see it, Rachel has been feeding her ego on a rich diet of your insecurities and misfortunes for years. I think just as you saw her friendship as a validation of your own self-worth, she, in turn, relied on you to boost her own ego as being that person she could look down on. Despite all her bravado, I think if you looked past her beauty and popularity, you'd find Rachel has very little self-esteem. She is probably just as scared of not fitting in as you were. But where you try to be everything to everyone, her way of dealing with her issues is by way of intimidation and if all else fails, violence. So how better to boost her own ego but to constantly put you down, and revel in your misery when things went wrong for you? You appear to think she leads some kind of charmed life because, like you have said yourself on many occasions, you consider her to be beautiful and consequently she is never short of male company. Well, let me say this. A constant stream of men in and out of her life probably does make her feel wanted in a temporary sense, but only a serious, committed relationship that grows out of mutual respect and trust will fill that void in her life."

Margarita's words had begun to light up a tunnel of enlightenment in my mind.

"Her attack on you only proves *she* is in fact threatened by *you*, especially considering your blossoming relationship with Jason. I imagine she sees your happiness as a threat to her, somehow, because if you get your act together and find true contentment in your life, it will highlight her own deep-seated insecurities and shortcomings."

Margarita paused for a moment. "Do you understand the

point I am trying to get across?"

It was a lot to take in and a part of me desperately wanted to believe her. But despite that, I still found it very difficult to believe Rachel could possibly feel threatened, and by me, of all people. Not the same Rachel who could probably intimidate Attila the Hun when in full screaming flight. But then again, certain things rang true, especially the bit about putting me down to make herself feel better.

"I think so. What you're saying is, while I keep acting like a victim, she will continue to heap shit on me and I should stand up for myself and take away the power she has over me."

"Kind of. I think you have allowed yourself to be treated badly not only by Rachel, but your other friends, and especially Troy."

"But…"

"I'm *not* saying you brought it all on yourself," she added quickly. "But nobody can make you a victim. That is a label you've given yourself. The way you have perceived yourself. Perhaps you have been using it as an excuse not to take control of your life and make your own decisions as an adult. I think you have let others control you to avoid making painful or difficult decisions."

"I have made decisions. Tough ones, too. I left Troy, and walking away from my marriage was the hardest decision I had ever had to make."

I knew I sounded defensive, but Margarita wasn't planting a flattering picture in my head and I felt obliged to at least try to make some attempt to stick up for myself.

Suddenly she smiled and a cold spike of apprehension tore through me. "Did *you* make that decision, or was it made for you?" she asked ominously.

"What do you mean?"

"Let me ask you this, then. If it wasn't for the fact your ex-husband infected you with a sexually transmitted disease, would you have left him?"

"I don't understand what you're getting at."

"It's a simple enough question," she responded, a little impatiently, I thought. "Can I tell you what I think?" she continued.

No, I wanted to shout, *you've said enough,* but somehow I knew it wouldn't make a scrap of difference.

"I think it was only when you were confronted with the undeniable proof of his infidelity you were forced to open your eyes and see your marriage for what it was. I think up until that point you were in denial concerning the rapidly deteriorating state of your relationship. From what you have revealed to me throughout our sessions, I suspect you knew from the very beginning your marriage was a big mistake, but still you clung on until the very last, as though it was some kind of a life raft, because you couldn't see yourself as a whole person without him. Or could it be he represented that part of you that wanted desperately to be accepted and envied by your friends?"

"No!" I cried painfully. "It was *nothing* like that."

Margarita's ruthlessness had completely taken me by surprise and my emotions were spinning dangerously out of control.

"Not only that," she continued, mercilessly ignoring my outburst, "I suspect you had some sort of an idea Troy was cheating on you — even before the doctor confirmed it with the test results. At your own admission, he was verbally abusive toward you. He ritually put you down and openly flirted with your friends with no thought to your feelings. He certainly showed you no respect as a woman or as his wife and he openly criticized and belittled you in front of others. If that is not a sign your marriage was in a state of crisis, I don't know what is."

Margarita's verbal onslaught had effectively wiped out my last reserves of strength, and a heavy feeling of impending doom besieged me.

"Now, I want to ask you again about Rachel. What happened outside the café that caused you to collapse?"

Gone was the placid, sympathetic expression Margarita

usually wore like a badge. In its place came a look of sheer determination that warned me playtime was over. She wasn't taking a backward step until she'd gotten what she wanted.

Suddenly, the events of the past week re-emerged for a mass assault on my emotionally scarred mind and I knew I hadn't the strength to fight the awful memories.

"Rachel, she said some terrible things," I mumbled through my tears.

"I gathered that. What kind of things did she say?" came the steely response.

I felt sick as that moment came racing back to me, that moment when the reality of her betrayal had been cruelly flung at me.

"She said…" I could hardly put it into words. "She told me she had been having an affair with Troy."

"And this came as a surprise?" Margarita queried without as much as a hint of shock in her voice.

"What!" I gasped as though I had been kicked in the chest. "Yes, of course, it did."

"For how long had it been going on?"

God, she sounded so clinical, so detached, so unsurprised, like she had known all along!

"Since before we were married, she told me."

"And still you had no idea?"

Words of denial were fighting to get out, but Margarita wouldn't let it rest yet. "It never seemed strange to you that Troy would openly flirt with her *or* you would come home from work to find she had been not only in your house, but in your bedroom, trying on your clothes when you were at work, which in itself was a gross invasion of privacy and showed what little respect she had for you?"

I couldn't believe I had let that slip.

"That only happened once. Or twice."

I didn't know why I was trying to defuse her words. With every word, every truth she spoke, another brick crumbled in the wall I had erected in my mind to block out the painful reality of my short-lived marriage.

"She not only introduced you to Troy, but she encouraged and approved of the relationship, when all the time she was sleeping with your husband, Fiona. And still nothing about this strikes you as being odd? I asked you before if you would have left Troy if you haven't been faced with undeniable proof of his infidelity. I suspect the proof was always there, lying just below the surface waiting for you to notice it, but the dream of a happy marriage – the kind of marriage your parents have – prompted you to turn a blind eye to a situation *you* didn't want to deal with."

Margarita's barrage had robbed me of the last reserves of resistance. The truth echoed in her words, cut a swathe through the last remaining threads of my battered defenses. Right at that moment I felt the overpowering need to run away. I felt completely emotionally exposed and it was terrifying. Knowing there was no way out of this just compounded my feelings of fear. I had built my life on an ideal that had proven to be not only a lie but now had turned on me in all its savagery.

"Are you ready to deal with it now, Fiona, or shall I continue?"

An image appeared in my head of Troy and Rachel, in each other's arms and laughing at me behind my back, knowing I would never find the courage to actually confront the awful truth of their duplicity. Every consoling word uttered by Rachel since the breakup of my marriage returned to taunt me afresh and, for the first time in my life, I saw myself as Rachel and others saw me. As a fool. A blind, pathetic fool, ever willing to let my so-called friends walk all over me, just so I could prove to myself I was popular and worthwhile as a person.

I nodded, miserably. "I'm ready."

Margarita smiled.

"That's good news."

For the remainder of the session we spoke more about Rachel and the destructive influence she'd had on my life, and examined the reasons I'd perhaps allowed her to bully me into being her emotional punching bag.

Then, to my absolute horror, Margarita brought out the dreaded anger release bag and my subjugation was complete.

Probably the most cringe-inducing moment of my entire life and one I never want to relive, *ever*. But, no, it got even worse. Staring at the stupid pillow, some kind of madness suddenly took hold of me and out of the harmless beige fabric came an image of Rachel's and Troy's faces.

Before I knew it, I began to beat the shit out of the cushion with a violence I never knew I possessed, until my tears mingled freely with the sweat dripping down my face and I could hardly lift my arm.

Once I had pounded and punched and slapped till I could pound and punch and slap no more, to my utter amazement I experienced a profound rush of calm throughout my entire body, bringing a soothing sense of, well, a sense of *release*. Funny, that. It was also then I realized how fortunate I really was to finally be free of Troy, Rachel and all those who had kept me from growing as a person these last few years.

Miraculously, I felt as though I was finally ready to accept my past and begin the painful process of growing up. I couldn't deny a scared thirteen-year-old girl with braces and puppy fat still lurked inside me, terrified of facing the harsh reality of an adult world, but Margarita had offered me a lifebelt to save myself and I determined to grasp hold of it. At last I felt free to begin living again, and love again.

And to think it was just a bloody handmade cushion, and a beige one at that.

Epilogue

One year later

As I walked out of Margarita's office, I paused for a moment to cast my eye over the drab beige walls and wilting pot plants one last time. With a smile, I fondly recalled the first time I'd grudgingly walked in through those doors to face my Beige Nemesis.

Weighed down with enough angst to satisfy an entire generation of tortured, histrionic teenagers, I remembered how desolate my life had seemed at the time. The memory of that awful period in my life brings with it not only a poignant sense of sadness for the pain I'd suffered, but also a sense of pride for the way I've managed to turn my life around since then.

Of course, it wasn't a case of simply waking up one morning to find the gods had decided to bless me with a perfect life. No, it had taken many months of painful soul-searching to wade through all the garbage that had been clogging up my emotions and blinding me to the truth behind the sad, insecure woman who'd cried her way through a mountain of tissues that first session.

Neither had I accomplished this feat of self-discovery on my own.

From my earlier contempt for not only Margarita, but also what I considered to be her Jungian psycho-crap, I'd eventually come to think of her as more of a friend than a therapist. Of course, I am not denying there had been times I could have gladly told her to fuck off. I think I did once or twice, but I now see that had she not pushed and provoked me into taking responsibility for my own part in the demise of my life, I would still be that self-effacing, pathetic excuse for a person, who for years had willingly allowed others to walk all over her.

Walking back out into the sunlight, even the air I breathed tasted better – the taste of freedom, I suppose. Not only had I irrevocably put to rest the demon of my disastrous marriage, but also at long last, I was ready to leave behind the cancerous taint of Rachel's influence and subsequent betrayal.

I couldn't bring myself to be bitter, though. I remembered something Stacey once said to me that went along the lines of 'give someone enough rope and they'll eventually hang themselves'.

Not that Stacey knew it at the time, but her words had proven to be prophetic, at least for some people.

For poor Kim, I suspect a noose would have been preferable to the situation she'd since found herself in. You see, about four months ago, Kim gave birth to a big healthy baby boy, whom she named Ivan. Much to Kim's abject horror, I believe, he has a lovely mop of curly red hair and is already displaying a peculiar fondness for Action Man figures – quite bizarre for a child so young. Also, from what Stacey has since told me, not only did Kim put on over forty pounds while pregnant, but she is living in a state of constant trepidation while she awaits the DNA results, praying for a miracle that they will prove Dangerous Dave is *not* the father of her red-headed little bundle of joy.

Unfortunately, it seems very unlikely. Dave is apparently going around acting every bit the proud daddy with a smile permanently plastered to his face and telling everyone who will listen of his baby-making prowess. And if Dave's constant presence is not enough to completely ruin Kim's chances of ever attracting another bloke, he is insisting on co-rearing their little Rambo-in-the-making.

Then, on top of that, came the shock announcement that after years of heartbreak and disappointment on the dating roundabout, Janine had finally found the love of her life. Yes, at last she has met someone who isn't intimidated by her grisly profession and blunt, down-to-earth nature.

Tamara, Janine's boss at the abattoir.

Her very female boss!

I suppose even I had to admit to being a little stunned at Janine's unexpected lifestyle metamorphosis.

I barely recognized Janine when I met up with her and Tamara a couple of months back for a drink at a particularly chic wine bar in the city. Gone was her subtle air of cool derision and disillusionment with the world in general that we'd grown used to over the years, and in its place was a certain serenity. But perhaps even more surprising was the absence of her long blonde hair. Had it not been for her familiar smile I would have walked straight past her, thinking her one of those sleek, lanky models that seem to grow in abundance in these trendy inner city venues.

Janine had always been good-looking in an athletic Iron Woman kind of way, but now she was nothing short of stunning. Her short-cropped hair was not the only part of her that had undergone a makeover. It was also the first time I had ever seen her wearing a *dress* — and a feminine one at that. And if that wasn't enough to shock me into the next century, she emanated a feeling of soft contentment and pure happiness as she sat shyly holding Tamara's hand while we chatted and caught up on recent happenings.

Unfortunately, Rachel and Kim hadn't been so understanding and open-minded about Janine's newfound sexuality and, from what Janine told me, relations between them had become frosty, to say the least. I couldn't say I was sorry to hear that, and neither was Janine. After a few drinks, she confided in me that she too had felt totally overwhelmed at times by the spitefulness Kim and Rachel appeared to thrive on, and had it not been for Tamara, she would never had found the courage to be herself and turn her back on a life that was gradually eroding her sense of identity.

Somebody else apparently having trouble finding himself is Troy — that is, he's having difficulty fighting his way from under a pile of nappies.

Who was to know twins ran in Troy's family? Certainly not Amanda, that was for sure.

Not that anyone has seen much of Troy lately, what with him all but under house arrest with two babies to look after while Amanda is back at work at the gym. And since she's gone back to teaching Tae Kwon Do, as well as her regular step classes, none of Troy's mates have been game to set foot in their house after Amanda threatened to kick them to within an inch of their lives if they did. According to Troy's father, he's well and truly met his match in Amanda, who, being a total fitness freak, has banned beer from the house and put Troy on a diet!

She doesn't want to be seen with an obese husband, apparently.

Yes, the wedding is only a month away now and from what Troy's dad told me, Amanda is making Troy's life Hell already.

While we're on that subject, I must tell you about Rachel. No, I haven't seen her since that last fateful night over a year ago now, but that hasn't stopped me from hearing all about her spiral into Loser Hell. This I've learned from my dear brother, Alex, who, since falling in love with Sharon, one of the skanks from the RSL, is now very rarely seen at home apart from when he needs his clothes washed or his belly filled with food. Sharon's devotion doesn't extend to cooking, apparently.

As it turns out, not long after my run-in with Rachel outside the café, she again attempted another coup to regain control of the sacred table. This time, without the support of Jason, who's since quit his night job as bouncer, things quickly degenerated into a massive brawl that saw Rachel not only banned from the RSL for life but, as a result of her blatant disregard for society's accepted boundaries of behavior, standing before a judge facing assault charges for the injuries she'd inflicted, not only on Sharon but poor Dave, as well. Dave, you see, having valiantly tried to break up the brawl, wound up in hospital with a broken nose and various lacerations. Battle wounds, he proudly refers to them as.

I must say the judge was certainly lenient, much to Mum's disgust. She's taken a shine to Sharon. Instead of placing Rachel in jail where, according to Mum, she belongs, the judge let her off with a twelve-month good behavior bond on the proviso she seeks counseling for her anger management problems. And the therapist assigned to her through the courts was, yes, you might have guessed, Margarita!

Life has certainly come full circle, not only for Rachel, but especially me.

Since my surprise bonding with the dreaded anger release bag, my life has continued to throw surprises at me — surprises of the nice variety, I'm pleased to report. First of all, I barely had time to enjoy the thrill of joining the unemployment line when I was offered a dream job in the city, by, of all people, Antonio!

His overseas interests had grown to the point he found it increasingly difficult to juggle his travels to Europe with the commitment to his thriving antiques business in the city. That was when he thought of me. At first, I didn't know if eight years of selling ladies' fashions at Wanker Brothers & Co qualified me to run a successful antiques business, but Antonio wouldn't be put off by my lack of confidence. Thus began my passion for antiques.

Which, of course, leads me onto my other passion. Jason. My soul mate, lover, confidante, therapist — sorry, Margarita — bodyguard, dancing partner, chef and all-round savior.

Ever since that fateful night when I met him at the café, braced for bad news, we've rarely been apart. Despite vowing to each other that we would take things slowly, from our first kiss there was no going back. I was in love and thrilled to have it reciprocated for once. From there our relationship grew and strengthened, and three months afterward, Jason moved out of his granny flat and we moved in together — taking Jason's granny with us! It's not as bad as it sounds. We found a place closer to the city with a lovely self-contained flat attached for his wonderful gran. It's ideal, really. She looks after Arnie when I'm at work and Jason and I are close by if she needs us — which isn't often.

Yes, life is good!

Exiting Margarita's, I immediately spied Antonio's midnight-blue Saab parked out front and smiled, for there in the driver's seat sat Jason.

"Come on, or we'll be late." He smiled.

"Late for what?" I teased.

"Late for the biggest day of your life?" he replied.

I couldn't help but smile back at the love shining from Jason's eyes.

"Oh, I had completely forgotten all about that," I continued, enjoying the moment.

"If you don't hurry up, they'll start without us."

I had to laugh. "I hardly think so. After all, we're the headlining act, aren't we?"

Jason rolled his eyes impatiently and reached across to open the door for me, and I climbed in.

Looking over into the back seat, I saw our bags lying neatly across it and a rush of excitement rose within me.

Somehow it didn't seem quite real. This was the day I'd been waiting for, for almost a year, but even now I struggled to contain the nerves crowding in on me.

"Are you sure this is going to be all right? We're not making a huge mistake, are we?"

"Of course it's going to be okay. Hasn't Antonio been telling you for the past two months you're ready?"

His reassurances weren't enough this time, though, to quell the butterflies in my stomach.

"Besides, he's waiting there for us now, Fi, so you can't back out."

My face in his hands, Jason drew my lips close to his and gently kissed me before whispering, "You will be fine. *We* will be fine, Fiona. I promise."

Instinctively, I looked down and for good luck touched the glittering diamond set into the antique engagement ring I wore proudly, and I knew he was right.

"Okay, let's get this over and done with, then."

I took a deep breath and Jason squeezed my knee as he pulled away from the curb and back out into the evening traffic.

It was only a short drive into the city, but despite my nerves, I couldn't wait to arrive at the impressive inner city venue. After all, Antonio and Patrick *were* waiting for us. And this was the moment I had only dared dream of, the moment when Jason and I would finally walk hand in hand onto the shiny parquetry floor and glide in perfect harmony, at one with the music and well as with each other, as we displayed our dancing skills on national television.

As we waited for our cue to walk out onto the set of *Strictly Dancing*, the rhythmic beat of Latin music rising to welcome us onto the dance floor, Jason squeezed my hand, reassuring me that we were ready. Looking down at the dazzling red dress Antonio had chosen for my dancing debut, I felt beautiful at last, worthy of all the love that surrounded me. Finally, it seemed, I had discarded the one remaining mental remnant of my previous existence. Looking up into Jason's eyes, I knew, at last, I was no longer a dance floor pariah.

More books from Totally Bound Publishing

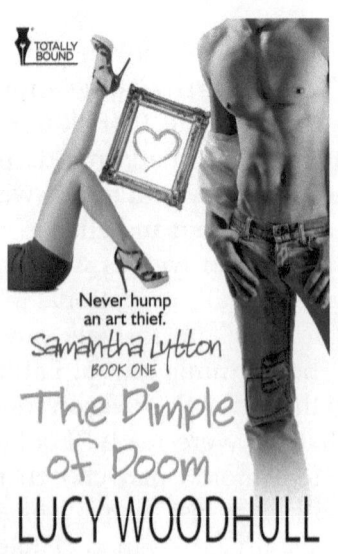

Book one in the Samantha Lytton series

Samantha Lytton is either going to end up in jail or famous. Maybe both.

JILL STEEPLES

She knows everything
there is to know
about love...
Doesn't she?

Molly Matthews
MEDDLES IN
Marriage

*Matchmaker extraordinaire Molly Matthews is an expert
in love, but her skills are put to the ultimate test when
international heartthrob Rory Campbell waltzes into her
office.*

If you must look back, only look at the best!

STACEY SOLOMON

BEST THINGS IN LIFE

Walk on By

Parties...check
Gay best friend...check
Happiness...?

Book one in the Best Things in Life series by Stacey
Solomon

*Ever since Charlotte Taylor was a little girl she's wanted
fame and fortune. She sings with the voice of an angel
and is soon plucked out of obscurity and launched into the
limelight as the overnight sensation 'Lola'.*

About the Author

Isla Dennes

Married, mother of one son and three daughters, Isla Dennes developed a love of writing while employed in her dream job as the owner of a bookshop in a seaside resort town in NSW, Australia. Not content to simply read every book in the store, she found herself compelled to create novels of her own.

Had she concentrated more on sales and less on writing, she might well have retired a wealthy woman, but writing won out in the end, with the result being a lifelong passion for creative writing across a number of genres, including a brief but regrettable sojourn into horribly sentimental New-Age poetry that's best forgotten...

Isla Dennes loves to hear from readers. You can find contact information, website details and an author profile page at https://www.totallybound.com/

Home of Erotic Romance